COLLECTOR'S EDITION

STAR WARS®

COLLECTOR'S EDITION

THE PHANTOM MENACE™
ATTACK OF THE CLONES™
REVENGE OF THE SITH™

SCHOLASTIC INC.
New York   Toronto   London   Auckland   Sydney
Mexico City   New Delhi   Hong Kong   Buenos Aires

www.starwars.com
www.scholastic.com

The Phantom Menace, ISBN 0-590-01089-1, Copyright © 1999 by Lucasfilm Ltd. & ™.
Attack of the Clones, ISBN 0-439-13928-7, Copyright © 2002 by Lucasfilm Ltd. & ™.
Revenge of the Sith, ISBN 0-439-13929-5, Copyright © 2005 by Lucasfilm Ltd. & ™.

12 11 10 9 8 7 6 5 4 3 2   6 7 8 9/0

Printed in the U.S.A.   23
ISBN 0-439-83533-X
First compilation printing, November 2005

Contents

EPISODE I

THE PHANTOM MENACE™

Patricia C. Wrede
Based on the screenplay and story
by George Lucas

CHAPTER ❶

The Galactic Republic's cruiser dropped out of hyperspace at last, giving Qui-Gon Jinn his first look at Naboo — or rather, at the menacing cloud of Trade Federation battleships that surrounded it. Like fat white maggots, they spread through space, blocking all access to the planet. Qui-Gon was not impressed. In the decades he had been a Jedi Knight, he had seen many battleships. The ships were unimportant; what mattered were the beings they carried.

The view screen lit. Leaning forward, Qui-Gon peered over the cruiser captain's shoulder. The screen showed a Neimoidian with grayish-tan skin and dull orange eyes, wearing a three-pronged headdress. *One of the Trade Federation's viceroys. Does he greet all incoming ships personally, or only ambassadors?* Qui-Gon wondered. "Captain," he said aloud. "Tell them we wish to board at once."

"Yes, sir." The captain looked back at her view

screen. "With all due respect for the Trade Federation, the ambassadors for the Supreme Chancellor wish to board immediately," she told the Neimoidian.

"Yes, yes, of course," the viceroy replied. "Ah, as you know, our blockade is legal, perfectly legal. We'll be happy to receive the ambassadors. . . ." The view screen went black.

The main Trade Federation battleship loomed ahead. Qui-Gon closed his eyes, carefully testing the feel of the Force. *The ship carries mainly Neimoidians. And they're nervous.* About what he had expected. And yet . . . something else hovered ominously on the edge of his perception, something he could not quite identify.

The impression faded as the cruiser settled to the floor of the battleship's docking bay. Qui-Gon opened his eyes. Whatever he had sensed, it was gone. Now he had more immediate duties to attend to.

Rising, Qui-Gon motioned to Obi-Wan. The younger Jedi's face was stern, as befitted an important mission, and Qui-Gon sighed. Not for the first time, he wondered what Master Yoda had been thinking all those years ago, when he brought Qui-Gon and Obi-Wan Kenobi together as Master and Padawan apprentice. Obi-Wan Kenobi had great skill, no question of that, but sometimes he was so . . . intense.

Qui-Gon smiled slightly. Master Yoda always saw farther than anyone else. Perhaps he had thought that an earnest young apprentice would be as good for Qui-Gon as Qui-Gon would be for the apprentice. It would be like Yoda to balance Obi-Wan's headstrong nature and by-the-book methods against Qui-Gon's patience and unconventional ways. He would have to ask Yoda about it, after Obi-Wan passed the trials and became a full Jedi Knight. *That will be soon*, Qui-Gon thought — though he hadn't said anything about it to Obi-Wan yet.

As he came down the exit ramp, Qui-Gon saw a protocol droid waiting below. Obi-Wan's eyebrows rose, and he gave Qui-Gon a quick, questioning look. Qui-Gon nodded in reassurance. Neimoidians were a nervous race, happiest doing business at a distance. They were probably still trying to get up the courage to face the ambassadors in person.

The droid led them to a large room equipped with a round conference table. One entire wall was made of windows, providing a spectacular view of the planet Naboo . . . and the fleet of battleships surrounding it. *Not the best background for peace talks*, Qui-Gon thought.

"I hope your honored sirs will be most comfortable here," the protocol droid said. "My master will be with you shortly." Bowing, it left.

Obi-Wan put back the hood of his cloak, revealing

short dark hair with a single thin braid dangling over one shoulder. He was shorter than Qui-Gon, and clean shaven. Qui-Gon wore his graying hair long, and sported a small, neat beard. Only their clothing was similar; both wore the dark, hooded cloaks and cream-colored tunics of the Jedi order.

Obi-Wan stared out the window at the battle fleet. "I have a bad feeling about this," he said finally.

"I don't sense anything," Qui-Gon said. The faint disturbance he had felt earlier had vanished completely. But though Obi-Wan was only twenty-five and not yet a full Jedi Knight, he had great sensitivity to the Force. Qui-Gon had learned to respect his apprentice's instincts. *Some new problem, then?*

"It's not about the mission, Master," Obi-Wan said quickly. "It's something elsewhere. Elusive . . ."

"Don't center on your anxiety, Obi-Wan," Qui-Gon warned. "Keep your concentration here and now, where it belongs."

"Master Yoda says I should be mindful of the future."

"But not at the expense of the moment," Qui-Gon said gently. "Be mindful of the living Force, my young Padawan."

Obi-Wan's preoccupied expression held a moment longer. Then he nodded. "Yes, Master."

The two men stood silent, looking out at the fleet. After a time, Obi-Wan said, "How do you think this trade viceroy will deal with the Chancellor's demands?"

"These Federation types are cowards," Qui-Gon said. "The negotiations will be short." But as he spoke, he wondered. The trade viceroy was taking a long time to arrive, even for a Neimoidian. He shook his head. Staring at the Trade Federation's fleet disturbed his thoughts. Deliberately, he turned away. Taking a seat at the table, he began to calm his mind.

After a moment, Obi-Wan joined him. "Is it in their nature to make us wait this long?" he asked, voicing Qui-Gon's own unease.

"No," Qui-Gon said. He paused, concentrating. "I sense an unusual amount of fear for something as trivial as this trade dispute."

Nute Gunray, the Trade Federation viceroy, had been nervous since the blockade began. He had been frightened ever since the Republic cruiser entered the Naboo star system. Now, standing on the bridge of his battleship and facing the communication hologram of Darth Sidious, he was quite frankly terrified.

Darth Sidious frightens everyone, thought Nute, but it was small comfort. The Sith Lord was a shadowy, evil figure. Even though the Trade Federation had followed him loyally, he always wore a hooded cloak that hid most of his face from his allies. *Mysterious . . . and powerful,* Nute reminded himself. Somehow the thought was not as reassuring as he had intended it to be.

Beside him, Daultay Dofine stammered objections and explanations to the Sith Lord's hologram. "The ambassadors are Jedi!" Dofine finished. "We dare not go against them."

The holographic image of Sidious shifted. "You seem more worried about these Jedi than you are about me, Dofine," came the soft, menacing voice. "I am amused."

Dofine seemed to shrink. Sidious turned. "Viceroy!"

Nute's skull ridges went cold, and he had to force himself to step forward. "Yes, my lord?"

"I don't want that stunted slime in my sight again," Sidious said. "Do you understand?"

"Yes, my lord," Nute said, and glared at Dofine until he ran off the bridge.

"This turn of events is unfortunate." Darth Sidious went on as if nothing had happened. "We must accelerate our plans. Begin landing your troops."

Nute stared, completely taken aback. Thousands of battle droids stood ready in the holds of his battleships, but he hadn't expected to actually have to *use* them. "Ahh, my lord . . . is that legal?" Nute asked tentatively.

"I will make it legal," the hooded figure said flatly.

Nute shivered. Sidious' tone left no room for doubts or questions. *If he can make an invasion legal, what else is he capable of?*

"And the Jedi?" Nute asked.

"The Chancellor should never have brought them into this," Sidious said. "Kill them immediately."

"Y-yes, my lord. As you wish," Nute stammered automatically. *Oh, no. Even he can't make that legal.* He stared at the dark figure in the hooded cloak and swallowed hard. *But if I refuse, he'll be angry. And facing Darth Sidious is terrible enough when he's pleased. . . .*

The figure chuckled, as if Sidious knew what Nute had been thinking. The hologram winked out. Nute took a deep breath of relief, then turned to the ship's interior controls. A touch of a button switched the main screen to a view of the docking bay where the Republic cruiser sat. Another button brought a gun to bear on the cruiser. Nute barely hesitated before he pushed the button down. The gun fired, and the Republic cruiser exploded.

"That was easy enough," Nute muttered to himself. "Now for the Jedi . . ."

Qui-Gon felt the deaths of the cruiser's crew at once. Immediately, he sprang to his feet, lightsaber in hand. He noted with approval that Obi-Wan also sensed the disturbance in the Force and reacted quickly. Together they scanned the room, weapons ready. No threat appeared, only the protocol droid dithering over its spilled drinks.

Qui-Gon nodded at Obi-Wan, and they turned off their lightsabers. The hum of the weapons died. In the quiet, Qui-Gon heard a faint hissing.

"Gas!" he called to Obi-Wan. He took a deep breath and held it. They would have to fight their way out quickly, or be overcome.

The holocam in the conference room showed only a thick green cloud. Nute Gunray studied the picture carefully. *The Jedi must be dead by now,* he thought. He switched to a view of the hallway outside the room, where a crowd of skeletal battle droids waited. "Go in and blast what's left of them," he ordered.

The droids readied their weapons. One of them opened the door, and the deadly gas billowed out. Nute tensed, seeing movement in the cloud, but it was only the protocol droid. *The Jedi are dead,* he thought with satisfaction. He reached to shut off the screen.

Two humming bars of light, one green and one blue, swept out of the fog. They passed through the nearest battle droids without pausing. The droids collapsed, cut in half. Alarms began to sound.

Nute leaned forward, trying to make sense of the

confused images. "What in blazes is going on down there?"

"Have you ever encountered a Jedi Knight before, sir?" asked his lieutenant, Rune Haako.

"Not exactly," Nute said. "But I don't —" A screen lit up, showing a string of corridors in red. *They're heading for the bridge!* "Seal the doors!" he shouted.

"That won't be enough, sir," Rune said almost sadly as the doors slammed shut. "That won't be nearly enough."

Qui-Gon's lightsaber sliced through a pair of battle droids. They collapsed in a shower of sparks. The door to the bridge was just ahead. As he parried a shot from another droid, he felt a surge in the Force. An instant later, a group of battle droids flew against the wall and collapsed in a tangle. Qui-Gon nodded approval. His apprentice was making good use of his skills.

He reached the bridge door and began to cut through it, trusting Obi-Wan to hold off any new battle droids. Almost at once, he felt a rush of fear from the room beyond. Then, with a loud rumble, a series of blast doors slammed, sealing the bridge even tighter.

Qui-Gon shook his head, almost amused. Blast doors could not keep out a Jedi. Shifting his grip on his lightsaber, he stabbed at the door. The laser melted the metal rapidly. It would not be long now.

Suddenly, he sensed a change close by. It took only a moment's concentration to find the source. "Destroyer droids!" he said to Obi-Wan, turning away from the blast door.

"Offhand, I'd say this mission is past the negotiation stage," Obi-Wan replied.

I suppose it's better to have a sense of humor that only shows up in the middle of a battle than to have no sense of humor at all, Qui-Gon thought.

The two men sprinted down the hall and took cover in a pair of service niches. An instant later, the destroyer droids appeared at the end of the hall. The droids marched past, firing steadily at the smoke-filled area in front of the bridge doors. As soon as they went by, Qui-Gon nodded at Obi-Wan. The two men stepped back into the hall, behind the droids.

One of the destroyer droids seemed to realize something was wrong. "Switch to bio," it commanded. "There they are!"

The droids began firing again, this time in the right direction. Qui-Gon and Obi-Wan used their lightsabers to send the shots back at the droids. But just before each shot struck, a bubble of energy appeared around its target, protecting the droids from damage.

"They have shield generators!" Obi-Wan said.

"It's a standoff," Qui-Gon replied. "Let's go." He and Obi-Wan had no hope of breaking into the bridge now, not with that kind of reinforcement. They'd have to find another way.

In the marble-walled throne room of the palace of Naboo, the Governing Council had assembled at last. Queen Amidala sat on the throne, watching them. The crisis with the Trade Federation had brought the governors from every city of Naboo here, to show their support for their newly elected Queen.

Amidala smiled and folded her fingers carefully together in her lap. She didn't want to touch the high collar that rose past her ears. *It's straight*, she told herself. *It must be straight. Eirtaé checked it before I came in.* The elaborate royal costumes and formal face paint were as much a part of her new position as the decisions she was called upon to make every day. And her appearance was especially important today, because she was about to speak with the Trade Federation. Their representatives, she knew, already thought that a fourteen-year-old girl was far too young to rule a planet. *That's probably why they picked Naboo for their blockade. Well, I'll show them that I'm capable.*

The large view screen lit up, showing the overbearing Trade Federation viceroy, Nute Gunray. "Again you come before me, Your Highness," he said. "The Federation is pleased."

Amidala stiffened. His words were civil, but his tone was . . . insolent. "You will not be so pleased when you hear what I have to say, Viceroy," she said in as cold a voice as she could manage. "Your blockade has ended."

The Neimoidian's mouth twitched into something very like a smirk. "I am not aware of such a failure."

"Enough of this pretense, Viceroy!" Queen Amidala said, allowing her anger to show. She felt a stir of approval from the councilors around her, and went on, "I know that the Chancellor's ambassadors are with you now —"

"I know nothing about any ambassadors," the viceroy said smoothly. "You must be mistaken."

Surprised, Amidala leaned forward and studied the screen closely. But she could not read the Neimoidian's expression. "Beware, Viceroy," she said at last. "The Federation is going too far this time." *He can't ignore representatives from the Supreme Chancellor! And the Senate will not put up with this blockade for much longer.*

"Your Highness, we would never do anything without the approval of the Senate," Nute said earnestly. "You assume too much."

Is he acting, or does he mean what he says? "We

will see," Amidala said, and signaled to end the transmission.

As the screen went black, a buzz of discussion rose from the councilors. Amidala tapped her fingers on the arm of her throne, thinking. After a moment, she turned to the Governor of Theed. "Governor Bibble! Contact Senator Palpatine at once." Palpatine represented Naboo in the Senate of the Galactic Republic. If things had changed on Coruscant, if the ambassadors had not been sent after all, Palpatine would surely know the reason.

But when they reached Senator Palpatine a few moments later, he seemed as bewildered by the viceroy's assertions as everyone else was.

"How could it be true?" he said. "I have assurances from Chancellor —" The communication hologram flickered, then steadied. "His ambassadors did arrive. It must be —" The hologram flickered again, and began to break up.

"Senator Palpatine!" Amidala said urgently. She needed his advice and his experience; he *had* to come through clearly.

"— get — negotiate —" The hologram sputtered and died completely.

Amidala turned to her dark-skinned head of security. "Panaka, what's happening?"

"A malfunction in the transmission generators?" Governor Bibble suggested doubtfully.

"You were right about one thing, Master," Obi-Wan said slyly. "The negotiations were short."

More battle humor. Qui-Gon snorted. Without replying, he slid out of the vent into the shadows around the edge of the hangar. A moment later, he felt Obi-Wan follow. Together, they stole silently toward the landing craft — and the waiting battle droids.

CHAPTER ❸ ━━━━━━━

The early morning mist was just beginning to thin as Jar Jar Binks waded through the Naboo swamp in search of breakfast. Like most Gungans, he preferred to catch his food fresh. The damp air felt good against the reddish ear-flaps that hung halfway down his back, and the murky water was pleasantly warm around his thick toes. All he needed now was —

A gleam of white caught his eye, half-hidden in the swamp ooze. *Oh, goody morning munchen!* Jar Jar thought happily. One wiry arm reached down and retrieved the clam. The shell snapped closed as Jar Jar's hand touched it. Jar Jar settled down to open his meal.

When the shell opened at last, Jar Jar scooped the clam out of the shell with his long tongue, enjoying its delicate flavor and smoothness. *Dissen the life*, he thought. *Goody munchen and no Captain Tarpals making fuss about little accidents.* He looked up, and froze.

A giant *thing* moved through the swamp, a thing like an enormous head without eyes. It was as big as the nightmarish monsters that rose out of the core rifts from time to time. Swamp creatures fled before it. Among the nuna and peko peko ran a tall, bearded Human, scarcely slowed by the water and rutiger tree roots. Even he could not stay ahead of it, though; the thing gained on him steadily. But Jar Jar could see that the monster was not chasing any of the creatures, not even the Human. It was headed straight for him, Jar Jar Binks.

"Noooo!" Jar Jar cried. Unfreezing, he dropped the clamshell and grabbed the Human running past. "Hep me! Hep me!"

"Let go!" the Human shouted, but Jar Jar clung tightly. The Human dragged him through the swamp, while the monster gained rapidly. Just before it reached them, the Human flung them both down in the mud. Jar Jar felt a hot wind against his back, and then the thing had passed by. As he pulled himself out of the mud, he saw the huge creature vanish into the mist.

"Oyi!" he said. In an ecstasy of relief, he hugged the Human who had saved him. "I luv yous!"

The Human left off wringing swamp water out of

his clothes to glare at Jar Jar. "Are you brainless?" he demanded. "You almost got us killed!"

"I spoke," Jar Jar said, taken aback. This Human had no right to be insulting, just because he had saved Jar Jar's life. And now that the creature was gone and Jar Jar was no longer so frightened, he could taste traces of fuel in the swamp air. The thing that had chased them had only been some sort of machine, and not a monster from the core after all.

"The ability to speak does not make you intelligent," the Human told him. "Now, get out of here!"

Jar Jar stared as the Human started off. "No, no," he said, following. "Mesa stay." What was that thing Humans said? Oh, yes — "Mesa yous humbule servaunt."

"That won't be necessary," the Human said absently, scanning the mist.

Jar Jar rolled his eyes. *Humans never understanding anything!* He told the man it was demanded by the gods, as a life debt.

The Human did not answer, but he didn't move off again, either. Encouraged, Jar Jar said, "Mesa called JaJa Binkss."

"I have no time for this now," the tall man muttered.

"Say what?" Jar Jar turned to see what he was looking at. Two strange flying machines broke out of the mist. Each carried a creature like a Gungan skeleton, tall and bone-white. They were chasing another Human. This one was younger and had no beard, but he wore the same sort of brown-and-tan robes as the man who had rescued Jar Jar.

"Oh, nooooo!" Jar Jar cried, his voice climbing higher and higher. "Wesa ganna —"

Something knocked him facedown in the mud, and he heard the bearded Human say, "Stay down!"

Jar Jar raised his head, spitting mud and water. "— die!" he finished, just as the flying machine fired two brilliant bolts of light. To Jar Jar's astonishment, a bar of green light appeared in the bearded Human's hand and bounced the shots back at the skeleton-creatures. The creatures and their machines blew up. Sparks and hot metal fell hissing into the swamp. Quiet returned, except for the panting of the Human the machines had been chasing.

"Sorry, Master," the newcomer said after a moment. "The water fried my weapon." He pulled a short, blackened tube from his belt and handed it to Jar Jar's rescuer.

The bearded man examined the tube, then gave the newcomer a severe look. "You forgot to turn your power off again, didn't you?"

The newcomer nodded sheepishly. Jar Jar cocked his head in sympathy as he picked himself up out of the mud. He understood how easy it was to forget things. He'd done it himself, far too often.

"It won't take long to recharge," the bearded man said, handing the tube back to the newcomer. "But I hope you've finally learned this lesson, my young Padawan."

"Yes, Master," the other man said in a subdued tone.

No more lecturings, Jar Jar thought. "Yousa sav-ed my again, hey?" he said, hoping to change the subject.

"What's this?" the newcomer said unenthusiastically.

"A local," the bearded man replied. "Let's go, before more of those droids show up."

The offhand dismissal annoyed Jar Jar briefly . . . and then the rest of the man's words sank in. "Mure? Mure, did you spake?" He did not want to see any more machines.

The two men began to run without replying. Jar Jar followed, thinking rapidly. None of his usual hiding places would be safe from the machines. But the machines had hovered above the swamp. They didn't look as if they'd work well underwater. And under the water was — "Ex-squeezee-me, but da moto grande safe place would be Otoh Gunga," he said as they ran. "Tis where I grew up. Tis safe city."

The men stopped running to look at him. "A city!" the bearded man said. "Can you take us there?"

Jar Jar hesitated. Otoh Gunga would be safe for

the Humans, but for him . . . "Ah, will, on second taut — no, not willy." Seeing their surprise, he looked down. "Iss embarrissing, boot — my afraid my've been banished. My forgotten der bosses would do terrible things to my, if my goen back dare."

In the distance, strange noises echoed through the swamp. "You hear that?" the bearded man said. "That's the sound of a thousand terrible things. Heading this way."

"And when they find us, they will crush us, grind us into little pieces, then blast us into oblivion," the second man added with unnecessary emphasis.

"Yousa point is well seen," Jar Jar said with as much dignity as he could manage. "Dis way. Hurry!"

The odd, froglike native led Qui-Gon and his apprentice to the shore of a lake. After warning them not to expect a warm welcome, he leaped high in the air and dove into the water. The two Jedi pulled breath masks from their belt packs and waded in after him.

Sunlight barely penetrated the murky lake water. Less than a meter below the surface, the light began to dim. Soon it was hard to see. As Jar Jar led the two Jedi deeper and deeper, Qui-Gon began to fear that they would lose him in the increasing darkness.

Suddenly Qui-Gon saw a gleam of light ahead.

In another moment, he could make out a string of amber bubbles, shining warm and bright through the dark water. Their rich yellow glow lit the water for meters around. The bubbles varied in size; the largest looked to be nearly seventy-five meters tall. A lacework of metal the color of old bronze topped each globe, helping the walls keep their shape and providing a place to link bubbles together.

As they drew nearer, Qui-Gon could make out buildings inside the bubbles. Gungans walked casually along the streets, while fish swam past a few meters away outside the bubble wall. They had almost reached the bubble city, and Qui-Gon began to look for a door or an air lock. But Jar Jar swam straight toward the side of the bubble — and passed right through it into the city inside. The bubble wall sealed seamlessly behind him. *Permeable hydrostatic membranes,* Qui-Gon thought. *They keep the seawater out, but let people through, so the city doesn't need an air lock. Impressive.* He followed Jar Jar, beginning to hope they would reach the Naboo palace in time after all.

But the bosses of Otoh Gunga were not willing to help. "Wesa no like the Naboo!" the head Gungan, Boss Nass, declared when the Jedi were brought before him. "Un dey no like uss-ens. Da Naboo tink day so smarty. Day tink day brains so big."

Obi-Wan tried to argue, but the bosses did not

want to listen. "Wesa no care-n about da Naboo," Boss Nass said flatly.

Talk was getting them nowhere. *And if we don't reach the capital soon, the Trade Federation's droids will have taken over.* Qui-Gon gestured, reaching out to touch the Gungan's mind. "Then speed us on our way," he said.

"Wesa ganna speed yousaway," the Gungan Boss said, responding readily to Qui-Gon's suggestion. "Wese give yousa una bongo. Da speedest way tooda Naboo tis goen through da core. Now go."

Qui-Gon thanked him and turned away. As they walked toward the exit, Obi-Wan whispered, "Master, what's a bongo?"

"A transport, I hope," Qui-Gon murmured. *Preferably a fast one . . .* He stopped. Jar Jar Binks stood between two guards, wearing handcuffs and plainly waiting for judgment.

Catching Qui-Gon's eye, Jar Jar said, "Ahh . . . any hep hair would be hot."

Obi-Wan frowned. "We are short of time, Master," he objected.

"We'll need a navigator," Qui-Gon said. "This Gungan may be of help." *Besides, we talked Jar Jar into coming here. If it weren't for us, he wouldn't be in trouble.* Qui-Gon turned back to the Gungan bosses. "What is to become of Jar Jar Binks here?"

"Hisen to be pune-ished," Boss Nass said. "Pounded unto death."

Jar Jar moaned. Obi-Wan looked startled, then worried. Plainly, he had not realized how serious Jar Jar's problem was. Qui-Gon studied the head Gungan. "I have saved Jar Jar Binks' life," he told the Boss. "He owes me what you call a life debt." He gestured, nudging the Gungan's mind once more. "Your gods demand that his life belongs to me now."

"Hisen live tis yos, outlaunder," Boss Nass said. "Begone wit him."

Jar Jar looked from one to the other, and shook his head. "Count mesa outta dis! Better dead here den deader in da core . . . Yee guds, whata mesa sayin?"

As the guards removed Jar Jar's handcuffs, Qui-Gon and Obi-Wan exchanged looks. *Traveling through the core doesn't sound much safer than facing the Trade Federation's battle droids,* Qui-Gon thought. *But at least this way, we have a chance of getting to the Naboo Queen before the droids do.*

If we survive the trip.

The hologram of Darth Sidious seemed to make the bridge of the battleship darker, just by being there. Nute glanced around to make sure Lieutenant Dofine was out of sight — there was no sense in annoying the Sith Lord by disobeying his direct order — and said, "The invasion is on schedule, my lord."

"Good. I have the Senate bogged down in procedures. By the time this incident comes up for a vote, they will have to accept your control of the system."

I wish I were that certain, Nute thought. "The Queen has great faith that the Senate will side with her," he told Sidious in a neutral tone.

"Queen Amidala is young and naive," Sidious said dismissively. "Controlling her will not be difficult. You have done well, Viceroy."

Nute sighed in relief as the hologram faded away. Dealing with Darth Sidious was almost as nerve-racking as that business with the Jedi had been.

As the last lines of the hologram vanished, Rune Haako turned toward Nute and said, "You didn't tell him about the missing Jedi."

"No need to report *that* to him until we have something to report," Nute said. And he hoped it was good news. He suspected that Darth Sidious wouldn't be nearly so pleased about the success of the invasion, once he learned that the Jedi were missing.

The bongo the Gungans had promised turned out to be a tiny, bat-winged submarine with three bubble canopies and a strange drive that looked like long, trailing tentacles. Obi-Wan eyed it dubiously, but it was better than walking. Or swimming. He slid into the pilot's chair.

"Dis is nutsen," Jar Jar muttered, taking the co-pilot's seat.

Obi-Wan glanced at him in irritation, then looked back at Qui-Gon, who was already sitting in the rear. "Master, why do you keep dragging these pathetic life-forms along with us?"

Qui-Gon only smiled.

The sub arched past tall coral pillars. Reefs stretched away in all directions, like forests made of lace. As the bongo started down into the dark waters below, Obi-Wan flicked a switch and the sub's lights came on. He could see Jar Jar becoming more and more uneasy as they went deeper. *Nervous guides make mistakes; best give him something else to think about.* "Why were you banished, Jar Jar?"

"Tis a longo tale," Jar Jar said. "Buta small part wowdabe, mesa . . . ooooh . . . aaaa . . . clumsy."

"They banished you because you're clumsy?" Obi-Wan asked skeptically. He had seen many different cultures during his years with Qui-Gon, but he had never seen or heard of one with laws against clumsiness.

"Mesa cause-ed mabee one or duey lettal bitty axadentes," Jar Jar said in an offhand tone, waving his arm expansively. "Yud-say boom da gasser, un crash Der Bosses heyblibber. Den —"

Something struck the bongo from behind, causing everyone to jerk forward in their chairs. Obi-Wan looked back and saw a glowing, fishlike creature behind them. It had grabbed the end of the bongo with its long, sticky tongue. The little sub shuddered as the creature began to pull them in.

Jar Jar shrieked. Obi-Wan wrestled with the controls, to no avail. The sea creature drew them closer and closer. Soon its jaws began grinding away at the rear of the sub.

Suddenly, they shot free. Hardly daring to believe their luck, Obi-Wan glanced over his shoulder. The fish that had tried to eat the sub was writhing in the teeth of an even larger sea monster!

"There's always a bigger fish," Qui-Gon commented as Obi-Wan turned back to the controls.

If it's bigger than that one, I don't want to meet it! Obi-Wan thought. *No wonder Jar Jar didn't want to come with us.*

As the sub dodged around a coral outcropping and into a tunnel, the lights flickered. Obi-Wan heard a sizzling noise. The giant fish had damaged the bongo. Water was dripping into the cabin, and the power lines were shorting. The sound of the drive lessened, and so did their speed. Obi-Wan pulled a multitool from his belt pack. *This is going to be tricky.* He couldn't shut the power off to work on the lines safely, so if he slipped, the energy would fry him.

Beside him, Jar Jar's voice climbed in panic, but Obi-Wan had no time to soothe the frightened Gungan. Then Qui-Gon's quiet voice said, "Stay calm. We're not in trouble yet."

"What yet?" Jar Jar yelled. "Monstairs out dare! Leak'n in here, all'n sink'n, and nooooo power! You nutsen. WHEN YOUSA TINK WESA IN TROUBLE?!"

Obi-Wan could see Jar Jar's point. He twisted the last wires, wondering whether he would ever attain his Master's unshakable serenity, or feel the Force as clearly and constantly as Qui-Gon. "Power's back," he said.

The lights flickered on as he spoke, revealing yet another enormous fish right in front of them.

"Monstair's back!" Jar Jar countered. "Wesa in trouble now?"

How many more of these things are there? Obi-Wan grabbed the controls and swung the ship around. The giant fish-creature darted after them. Obi-Wan increased their speed. The sub shot out of the tunnel — straight toward the huge, eel-like monster that had eaten the first fish!

Jar Jar shrieked again as the monster snapped at the bongo. Obi-Wan dodged, hoping his makeshift repairs would hold. The monster's teeth missed by inches. It snapped again, and its jaws closed around the fish-creature that had chased them through the tunnel. Taking advantage of the distraction, Obi-Wan sent the little sub zipping away.

For what seemed like hours, they wove and ducked and dodged past dozens of huge sea monsters, all of which had one thing in common: They were hungry. At last the water grew lighter, and the monsters fewer. Soon the sub was rising toward the surface.

In a cloud of bubbles, the bongo broke out into open air at last. The engine died, and the sub began drifting with the current. Obi-Wan switched off the bubble canopies, glad to be back in fresh air. He hadn't been entirely sure the sub's power supply would last long enough. They'd even come to the right place — the city of Theed, capital of Naboo, stretched along the shoreline.

Beside him, Jar Jar heaved a sigh of mingled relief and amazement. "Wesa safe now!"

But as they climbed onto shore, a mechanical voice behind them said, "Drop your weapons!"

As one, the Jedi turned. A skeletal Neimoidian battle droid stood threatening them with its lasers. "I said, drop your weapons," it repeated as Jar Jar joined them.

Qui-Gon lit his lightsaber and slashed the droid in half. Obi-Wan stared down at the sizzling wreckage. *They got here before us,* he thought. *This is going to be harder than we hoped.*

The elegant throne room of the Naboo palace was crowded with Trade Federation battle droids. The sight made Amidala want to weep. *I won't cry,* she thought. *I won't give them the satisfaction, even if the guards aren't paying attention to me.* Once she knew that the Trade Federation was really invading, she had switched places with one of her handmaidens. Now her friend and handmaiden Sabé wore the white face paint and the black feathered gown and headdress of the Queen, and Amidala was just . . . Padmé, who wore the same flame-colored robes as the rest of the Queen's handmaiden-bodyguards. "Padmé" did not exist . . . except when Amidala was in disguise. *I hope this works,* she thought. The use of a decoy was established by the rulers before her, but Amidala had never needed it until now.

As they worked their way through the palace, the battle droids brought their captives into the throne room. Amidala could see Governor Bibble and Captain Panaka, along with several of the palace guards. The smug Neimoidian viceroy examined his prisoners with barely concealed satisfaction. He didn't seem to have noticed anything odd about "Queen Amidala." Yet.

"How will you explain this invasion to the Senate?" Sio Bibble demanded when the viceroy looked at him.

"The Naboo and the Federation will sign a treaty," the viceroy said. "I have . . . assurances that the Senate will ratify it." He smiled at the "Queen."

"I will not cooperate," replied Sabé. *She's doing well,* Amidala thought. *She's got my tone of voice down perfectly.*

The viceroy did not seem suspicious. "Now, now, Your Highness," he said patronizingly to Sabé. "You are not going to like what we have in store for your people. In time, their suffering will persuade you to see our point of view."

Amidala ducked her head to hide her expression. *What is he going to do to my people?*

Turning to a nearby battle droid, the viceroy said, "Commander, process them."

"Yes, sir," the battle droid replied. It turned to a group of identical battle droids and said, "Take them to Camp Four."

Camps. They're herding my people into camps. And we can't stop them; they have more than enough droids to overwhelm our security forces. One of the battle droids shoved her toward the other handmaidens. Keeping her head lowered, Amidala joined them. *At least the switch worked; they don't know that's not really me. And they can't get a legal treaty without my signature. But . . . but what if the viceroy is right? Can I watch my people starve, and maybe die, and not give in?* Shivering, surrounded by battle droids, Amidala followed the other handmaidens and the "Queen" out of her palace.

CHAPTER 5

From a balcony just outside the Naboo palace, Qui-Gon studied the central plaza of Theed. Flowering vines climbed the golden stone walls. More flowers bloomed pink and red in wrought-iron boxes beneath nearly every window. *The people of Naboo must love living things,* he thought. The graceful arches and domes of the buildings demonstrated their love of elegance as well. The only jarring note, thought Qui-Gon, was the mob of tanks and battle droids assembled in the middle of the plaza.

A group of Humans, guarded by battle droids, came out of the arched entrance to the palace. Several wore the gray-and-red uniforms of the Naboo palace guards. From the pictures he had reviewed at the mission briefing, Qui-Gon identified one of the prisoners as Sio Bibble, Governor of Theed. In the center of the group stood a girl, dressed in an elaborately feathered black costume and wearing royal face paint. She had to be the young Queen of Naboo. Qui-Gon smiled as he signaled to Obi-Wan and Jar Jar.

As the prisoners rounded the corner, the two Jedi jumped down in front of them. "Are you Queen Amidala of the Naboo?" Qui-Gon asked, deliberately ignoring the battle droids.

"Who are you?" the black-clad girl demanded.

"Clear them away!" the commander of the battle droids said.

Qui-Gon watched calmly as four droids stepped forward. He heard the hum of Obi-Wan's lightsaber and ignited his own. An instant later, the droids were nothing but piles of twisted metal. The other battle droids closed in, but they were no match for the Jedi, either. In a few moments there were none left to guard the prisoners.

"Yousa guys bombad!" Jar Jar said admiringly, as the Naboo stared in astonishment.

Qui-Gon put his lightsaber away and bowed to the Queen. "Your Highness, we are the ambassadors for the Supreme Chancellor."

Sio Bibble sniffed and said, "Your negotiations seem to have failed, Ambassador."

"The negotiations never took place," Qui-Gon told him. "Your Highness, we must make contact with the Republic."

"They've knocked out all our communications," a guard wearing a captain's insignia said.

They'd have been fools not to. "Do you have transports?" Qui-Gon asked.

"In the main hangar," the captain replied. "This way." He led them down an alley and through the backstreets, to an unguarded service door behind the main hangar. They got inside with no trouble, and they met no droids in the hallways. When they reached the main hangar bay and peered cautiously inside, they found out why. The hangar was full of battle droids.

"There are too many of them," the captain said, shaking his head.

"They won't be a problem," Qui-Gon told him, and looked at the Queen. "Your Highness, under the circumstances I suggest you come to Coruscant with us."

The Queen shook her head. "Thank you, Ambassador, but my place is here."

Qui-Gon started to nod, then stopped as a premonition swept him. "They will kill you if you stay."

"They wouldn't dare!" Sio Bibble said, shocked.

The captain nodded agreement. "They need her to sign a treaty to make this invasion of theirs legal. They can't afford to kill her."

Qui-Gon shook his head. "The situation here is not what it seems, Your Highness. There is no logic to the Federation's move here." Naboo was a small, sparsely populated planet; the Trade Federation wouldn't risk losing their trade franchise by invading it unless there was something else behind their actions. "My feelings tell me they will destroy you," Qui-Gon finished.

Governor Bibble gave Qui-Gon a long, considering look. Then, wearing a thoughtful expression, he turned to the Queen. "Please, Your Highness, reconsider. Our only hope is for the Senate to side with us. Senator Palpatine will need your help."

"No," said the captain. "Getting past their blockade is impossible, Your Highness. The danger is too great."

As the Queen listened to the two men argue, Qui-Gon watched her closely. It was hard to read her expression through her face paint, but he could sense her indecision. Finally she turned to her handmaidens and said, "Either choice presents a great risk — to all of us."

One of the girls stepped forward and gave a tiny nod. "We are brave, Your Highness," she said firmly.

"If you are to leave, Your Highness, it must be now," Qui-Gon put in. He noted with interest that the handmaiden's words seemed to have ended the Queen's indecision.

"Then I will plead our case before the Senate," the Queen said.

Quickly, they sorted out who would come and who would stay behind. Qui-Gon was not surprised when the outspoken handmaiden was among those chosen to accompany the Queen. Several guards and the captain, whose name was Panaka, were also to come with the Queen's party. Two of the handmaidens joined Sio Bibble, who had volunteered to stay and do what he could for the people.

Finally everything was decided. Qui-Gon nodded to Obi-Wan, and they swung the door of the hangar open and strode through. The Queen, her handmaidens and guards, and Jar Jar followed.

The Naboo sense of beauty was evident even in the main hangar bay. The warm golden stone of the walls contrasted nicely with the dark metal of the fueling cables that ran up them. A row of sleek N-1 starfighters sat in their docks along one wall. The center of the hangar was occupied by a silver J-type long-range spacecraft . . . and by a large number of battle droids. More battle droids guarded a group of Naboo men and women in a far corner.

"We need to free those pilots," Captain Panaka said, nodding at the prisoners.

"I'll take care of that," Obi-Wan said. Without

breaking stride, he ducked under a hanging cable and vanished behind a fuel vat.

As Qui-Gon led the rest of the group toward the spaceship ramp, a battle droid stepped in front of him. "Where are *you* going?" it demanded.

Qui-Gon raised his eyebrows. "I'm ambassador for the Supreme Chancellor," he replied in a conversational tone, "and I'm taking these people to Coruscant."

"You're under arrest," the droid said. As it raised its blaster, Qui-Gon cut it down. The Queen and her handmaidens ran past him and up the boarding ramp. More battle droids converged on the ramp. Some of them fired as they came, so that Qui-Gon had to parry the shots in between chopping battle droids in half.

More shots sounded from the corner. Most of the pilots and ground crew ran for the exits; Obi-Wan and one of the pilots made for the royal spaceship. Belatedly, alarms rang through the hangar. As soon as he was certain that everyone was safe, Qui-Gon disposed of his last few opponents and leaped up the ramp.

The ship began to move. "We did it!" one of the guards shouted. "We got away!"

"We're not past the blockade yet," Captain Panaka replied gloomily.

Remembering the cloud of battleships around the

planet, Qui-Gon had to agree. They weren't safe yet, but he had done all he could. As the spaceship accelerated out of the planet's atmosphere, Qui-Gon and Panaka headed for the cockpit.

From here on, it was up to their pilot.

CHAPTER 6

The royal Naboo spacecraft was the most luxurious ship Obi-Wan had traveled on in a long time, but at the moment, he had no time to appreciate it. Having sent the rescued pilot, Ric Olié, to the cockpit to take off, Obi-Wan made sure that the Queen and her handmaidens were safely in their chamber. Then he stowed Jar Jar in a hold with the astromech droids, where the Gungan couldn't get into much trouble. As he hurried back up toward the cockpit, he felt the ship jolt. *We're already under fire from the blockade battleships!* His stride lengthened.

As he entered the control area, the ship jerked again, and alarms sounded. "We should abort, sir," Ric Olié said to Captain Panaka. "Our deflector shields can't withstand this."

"Stay on course!" Captain Panaka snapped.

The fat ball-within-a-circle battleships grew rapidly larger outside the cockpit windows. There seemed to be twice as many of them as Obi-Wan had seen when he arrived aboard the Republic cruiser. *Of course, it always looks as if there are more of them when they're firing at you.*

The ship rocked as yet another bolt from a Trade Federation battleship exploded against the shields. "Do you have a cloaking device?" Qui-Gon asked.

Panaka shook his head. "This is not a warship. We have no weapons. We're a nonviolent people."

Which probably has a lot to do with why the Trade Federation attacked them, Obi-Wan thought. *It's a lot safer to invade someone who isn't likely to fight back.*

Suddenly the ship rocked. *Something must have made it through the shields,* Obi-Wan thought as he straightened.

"Shield generator's been hit," Ric Olié confirmed.

A view screen lit up, showing astromech repair droids popping out of an air lock onto the damaged surface of the ship. "I hope they can fix it," the pilot muttered.

Two Trade Federation fighters swept by, firing at the repair droids. One astromech exploded, then another. Obi-Wan frowned and checked the readout. Every repair droid on the ship was out there; they had no spares left. "We're losing droids fast," he said.

"We won't make it," Olié said. "The shields are gone."

Another droid exploded. Now the view screen

showed only one left, a small, blue-domed unit. It worked steadily, reconnecting wires despite renewed shots from the fighter droids. Laser blasts whizzed around the little astromech. Several shots missed by barely a hair's breadth. Suddenly, Obi-Wan saw a spray of sparks. For one horrible moment, he thought they had lost the last droid. Then the dazzle cleared from the view screen, and he saw the blue unit heading back toward the air lock. Simultaneously, he heard a whoop of joy from the pilot.

"Power's back!" Olié shouted. "That little droid did it! Deflector shields up, at maximum."

And just in time, Obi-Wan thought. They were almost on top of the nearest battleship. For the next few minutes, the firing was intense, but no more shots penetrated the shields. "That's the worst of it," Obi-Wan said as the battleships shrank behind them.

"Maybe not," Olié responded. He pointed at the readouts in front of him. "The hyperdrive is leaking. There's not enough power to get us to Coruscant."

"Then we'll have to land somewhere to refuel and repair the ship," Qui-Gon said calmly. He brought up a star chart on a monitor and stared at it.

Obi-Wan leaned over and tapped the monitor. "Here, Master. Tatooine. The Trade Federation has no presence there."

"How can you be sure?" Captain Panaka asked.

"It's controlled by the Hutts," Qui-Gon replied in an absent tone as he studied the screen.

"The Hutts?" The captain sounded shocked. "You can't take Her Royal Highness there! If the Hutts discovered her —"

"— they'd treat her no differently than the Trade Federation would," Qui-Gon broke in. "Except that the Hutts aren't looking for her, which gives us an advantage."

The captain took a deep, frustrated breath. Obi-Wan suppressed a smile. He'd been on the receiving end of Qui-Gon's relentless logic often enough to sympathize, but this time they really had no choice. Not if they wanted to stay out of the hands of the Trade Federation long enough to get to Coruscant.

"Destroy all high-ranking officials, Viceroy," Darth Sidious commanded. "Slowly and quietly." He paused. "And Queen Amidala — has she signed the treaty?"

Nute Gunray had been dreading that question for hours. "She — she has disappeared, my lord. One Naboo cruiser got past the blockade."

"Find her!" Darth Sidious raged. "Viceroy, I want that treaty signed!"

Nute fought the urge to cringe. *It's only a hologram,*

he told himself. "My lord, it's impossible to locate the ship. It's out of range."

"Not for a Sith Lord," the hooded figure purred. Sidious gestured, and a second hologram appeared behind him — another mysterious cloaked and hooded being. Nute caught a glimpse of bright yellow eyes, and a face tattooed all over in red and black. And were those horns, poking up under his hood? Nute shivered. *I don't think I really want to know.*

"Viceroy, this is my apprentice, Lord Maul," Darth Sidious continued. "He will find your lost ship."

"Yes, my lord," Nute said. The hologram faded, and Nute shook his head. "This is getting out of hand. Now there are two of them!"

"We should not have made this bargain," Rune Haako said glumly. "What will happen when the Jedi learn of these Sith Lords?"

Nute shivered again. He had been wondering about that himself. *At least I don't have to find that ship. That's Lord Maul's job now.*

For some reason, that worried him almost as much as the missing ship.

As soon as the royal Naboo spacecraft was safely in hyperspace, Qui-Gon, Obi-Wan, and Captain Panaka were summoned to the Queen's chamber to bring her up to date. Panaka brought along the little blue-domed repair droid. When they arrived, Qui-Gon let Panaka describe the space battle and the droid's heroism. At the end of his report, the security captain presented the astromech droid to the Queen.

"Without a doubt," Panaka said, "this droid saved the ship. As well as our lives."

The Queen smiled at the little droid. "It is to be commended. What is its number?"

The droid beeped. The captain leaned over. Brushing dirt from the droid's side, he read aloud, "R2-D2, Your Highness."

"Thank you, Artoo-Detoo," the Queen said. "You have proven to be very loyal. Padmé!"

The Queen's favorite handmaiden came forward and bowed.

"Clean this droid up as best you can," the Queen told her. "It deserves our gratitude." She turned back to the captain. "Continue, Captain Panaka."

Panaka glanced toward Qui-Gon and hesitated. Taking advantage of the captain's uncertainty, Qui-Gon stepped forward and said, "Your Highness, we are heading for a remote planet called Tatooine. It's a system far beyond the reach of the Trade Federation. We'll make repairs there, then travel on to Coruscant."

"Your Highness," Captain Panaka put in, "Tatooine is very dangerous. It's controlled by an alliance of gangs called the Hutts. I do not agree with the Jedi on this."

It's not the first time someone's disagreed with my

plans, and I doubt it will be the last, Qui-Gon thought, amused. But all he said was, "You must trust my judgment, Your Highness."

The Queen exchanged a long look with Padmé. Then she nodded. *That handmaiden has too much influence on the Queen,* Qui-Gon thought. *It could mean trouble.*

Spaceship no goody place for Gungans, Jar Jar thought as he poked about in the storage cabinets. Every time he touched something, someone shouted at him to leave it alone. And when they didn't shout, whatever he touched spat springs or sparks or bits of metal, and *then* they shouted. And he had no job here — no clams to dig or subs to guide.

At the back of the cabinet, he found an oilcan. Maybe he could be useful to somebody after all. He picked it up and bounded into the central area of the ship, where the Queen's handmaiden was cleaning up Artoo-Detoo. "Hidoe!" he sang out as he came through the door.

The girl jumped and let out a scream. Artoo whistled reproachfully.

"Sorry," Jar Jar said, embarrassed. "No meanen to scare yousa."

"That's all right," the girl said kindly.

"I scovered oily back dare," Jar Jar said, holding out the oilcan. "Needen it?"

She smiled and took the can. "Thank you. This little guy is quite a mess."

"Mesa JaJa Binkssss," Jar Jar said.

"I'm Padmé," the girl told him. "I attend Her Highness." She looked at him curiously. "You're a Gungan, aren't you?"

Jar Jar nodded. Most Naboo didn't like Gungans any more than Gungans liked them, but this girl seemed nice. *And she not yelling over little mistakings, like everybody else.*

"How did you end up here with us?" Padmé asked.

"My no know," Jar Jar replied. He thought for a moment. "Mesa day starten pitty okeyday, witda brisky morning munchen. Den boom —" He pantomimed the giant, headlike troop transport. "Getten berry skeered, un grabben dat Jedi, and before mesa knowen it — pow! Mesa here." *With spaceships shooting and more dangerness than core monsters. And hyperdrive going bad, and maybe booming everybody before wesa getting to planet.* He shrugged, unable to put it all into words. "Getten berry berry skeered."

CHAPTER 7

The thing Qui-Gon hadn't expected about Tatooine was the light.

He had visited other desert planets, so he had expected the heat, and the air so dry that it was painful to breathe too rapidly. He had expected the endless yellow sand, the low hiss of the dawn wind, and the seedy atmosphere of the spaceports. But he had not expected the light.

The twin suns were just far enough apart to erase each other's shadows, except beneath the largest cliffs. At dawn and sunset, buildings and people cast long, double shades, but during the main part of the day, everything was drenched in light. It was ironic, Qui-Gon thought, that such a light-soaked planet should be home to so many criminals and outcasts.

Ric Olié had set the Naboo Queen's Royal Starship down on the outskirts of a small spaceport. Mos

Espa, the navigation system called it. After some quick consultation, they agreed that Obi-Wan would stay with the ship to guard the Queen, while Qui-Gon went in search of the parts they needed.

The hyperdrive generator had failed completely as they landed. *It's a good thing it didn't give out between star systems,* Qui-Gon thought, looking down at the mess Obi-Wan had just hauled out of the drive compartment. Perhaps that was what had made him so uneasy, these last few hours . . . but no, he could still feel disquiet in the Force.

He leaned closer, as if to inspect the drive. "Don't let them send any transmissions while we're gone," he said softly to Obi-Wan. "Be wary. I sense a disturbance in the Force."

"I feel it also, Master," Obi-Wan said.

Satisfied, Qui-Gon collected Artoo-Detoo and Jar Jar, and started for the city. They were only a few meters from the boarding ramp when someone shouted. Qui-Gon looked back. Captain Panaka and Padmé, the Queen's handmaiden, walked toward him. He noted with misgiving that Padmé wore rough-spun peasant clothes.

"Her Highness commands you to take her handmaiden with you," Captain Panaka said as he came up to Qui-Gon. "She wishes for her to observe —"

"No more commands from Her Highness today,

Captain," Qui-Gon interrupted, shaking his head. "This spaceport is not going to be pleasant."

"I've been trained in defense," Padmé said. "I can take care of myself."

Qui-Gon eyed her narrowly. This might be the Queen's command, but he sensed that the original idea had come from this girl. The last thing he needed was a spoiled handmaiden to watch out for, but . . . "I don't have time to argue," he said. "But this is *not* a good idea." He gave Padmé a stern look. "Stay close to me."

The girl nodded, and fell into line next to Artoo-Detoo. Artoo whistled happily at her, and Jar Jar smiled.

The twin suns beat down on the little group as they made their way into the city, but Amidala hardly noticed. Everything was so different from Naboo — the dry air, the endless yellow sand, the lumpy buildings of the spaceport — and the heat was only one more difference to wonder at. It had not been easy to convince Captain Panaka to risk letting her come, but she was already glad she had. *As long as everyone thinks I'm plain Padmé, I'm hardly in any more danger than I would be at the ship. And so far, nobody suspects.*

Walking on the loose desert sand was tiring. Even in the city, most of the streets were unpaved, though at least the constant traffic on the busier streets had packed the surface down. Artoo-Detoo didn't seem bothered, but Jar Jar complained bitterly.

Qui-Gon led them to a small open area surrounded by piles of worn-looking equipment and irregular, sand-colored shops. It looked very unpromising to Amidala, but Qui-Gon took a brief look around and nodded. "We'll try one of the smaller dealers," he said, and headed for a little shop with a stack of spaceship parts towering behind it.

As they entered, a pudgy blue-gray alien flew up to them, his wings beating so rapidly that all Amidala could see was a blur. He was only about half as tall as Qui-Gon, but he hovered so that his face was at the same level as the Jedi's.

"Hi chuba da nago?" he said to Qui-Gon.

"I need parts for a J-type 327 Nubian," Qui-Gon replied in Basic.

"Ah, yes," the alien said. When he spoke, his trunklike nose moved constantly. "Ah, yes, a Nubian. We have lots of that." He shouted something out the rear door of the shop, then turned back to Qui-Gon. "What kinds of parts?"

"My droid here has a readout of what I need," Qui-Gon said, waving at Artoo-Detoo.

A boy ran in through the rear door. He looked about nine years old, with light brown hair. His clothes were rough and ragged. The flying alien spoke to him briefly, then turned to Qui-Gon. "Sooo, let me take thee out back. You'll find what you need."

Qui-Gon and Artoo followed the junk dealer out the back door. Amidala wondered whether she should go with them — Qui-Gon *had* said to stay close. But Jar Jar clearly planned to stay inside, and somebody ought to keep an eye on him. It was all very well for Qui-Gon to say, "Don't touch anything," but Jar Jar was already studying the machines on the shelves with interest. *I'll stay here, for now*, she decided.

The boy seated himself on the counter and began to polish a piece of metal. As he worked, he stared at Amidala. His gaze made her uncomfortable; she caught herself wondering whether she had a smudge on her nose, or a leaf stuck in her hair. *This is ridiculous*, she thought. Forcing a smile, she turned away.

"Are you an angel?"

"What?" Amidala looked back at the boy, startled.

"An angel," the boy said seriously, his blue eyes fixed on her face. "They live on the moons of Iego, I think. They are the most beautiful creatures in the universe. They're good and kind, and so pretty they make even the most hardened space pirate cry."

Amidala was too astonished to answer. Finally, she said, "I've never heard of angels."

The boy studied her, no longer pretending to polish his bits of metal. "You must be one," he said as if it was the most obvious thing in the world. "Maybe you just don't know it."

At home, in the palace, she would have dismissed the remark as mere flattery. But this boy meant every word; somehow, she was sure of it. He felt like a friend she had known all her life — *but I just met him!* "You're a funny little boy," she said. "How do you know so much?"

"I listen to all the traders and pilots who come through here," the boy replied. He gave her a sidelong look. "I'm a pilot, you know. Someday I'm going to fly away from this place."

Amidala couldn't blame him for wanting to leave the heat and the dryness and the mean-looking creatures in the streets outside. But eyeing his ragged clothes, she wondered whether he had any real chance of achieving his dream. "Um, you're a pilot?" she asked.

"All my life," the boy said.

The mental image of a baby in the cockpit of a starfighter made Amidala smile. "Have you been here long?"

"Since I was very little," the boy replied. "Three, I think. My mom and I were sold to Gardulla the Hutt, but she lost us, betting on the Podraces with Watto. Watto's a lot better master than Gardulla, I think."

Sold? Master? Lost us? Amidala felt her smile slip. "You're . . . a slave?"

The boy's head came up, and he stuck out his chin. "I am a *person*. My name is Anakin."

"I'm sorry," Amidala said hastily. "I don't fully understand. This is a strange world to me."

A crash made them both jump. Amidala turned to see that Jar Jar had accidentally started up an odd little droid. The droid marched around at random, knocking things over, with Jar Jar clinging to it and shrieking. *Oh, and I was going to watch him!* Amidala thought.

"Hit the nose!" Anakin shouted. Jar Jar did, and the droid stopped and folded itself together. Amidala sighed in relief, then had to laugh at Jar Jar's sheepish expression.

Anakin laughed, too, but sobered quickly. He gave her another of his intent stares and said suddenly, "I'm going to marry you."

Amidala could not help laughing again. *A slave boy, marrying the Queen of Naboo?* But here she was only Padmé, she reminded herself.

At least Anakin did not seem put out by her involuntary laughter. "I mean it," he said seriously.

"You *are* an odd one," Amidala said. "Why do you say that?"

"I guess because it's true."

Something in the boy's manner made Amidala shiver. He seemed so *sure*. "Well, I'm afraid I can't marry you," Amidala told him. "You're just a little boy."

Anakin fixed her with his clear blue eyes. "I won't always be," he said simply.

A cold chill ran down Amidala's back, and she stared at him, unable to think of any response. *He sounds . . . older when he says that. And so positive. What does it mean?*

"Here it is!" the junk dealer cried, hovering in front of a pile of dusty parts. "A T-14 hyperdrive generator! Thee in luck. Saying of which, how's thee going to pay for all this?"

"I have 20,000 Republic dataries," Qui-Gon told him. Finding the parts so quickly meant that they could install the new hyperdrive and get off planet long before —

"Republic credits?" the junk dealer said indignantly. "Republic credits are no good out here. I need something more real."

There had to be a hitch, Qui-Gon thought. Luckily, this one was small, and easily dealt with. "I don't have anything else," he told the dealer. Waving his hand in the mind-altering gesture all Jedi learned, he nudged the alien's mind and added, "But credits will do fine."

"No, they won't," the dealer growled, wriggling his nose.

Surprised, Qui-Gon repeated the gesture and nudged harder. "Credits will do fine."

"No, they won't," the dealer said, more loudly than before. "What, you think you're some kind of Jedi, waving your hand around like that? I'm a Toydarian. Mind tricks don't work on me. Only money." He rubbed two clawed fingers together in the universal gesture for cash. "No money, no parts! And no one else has a T-14 hyperdrive, I promise you that!"

He was probably telling the truth. Dealers kept track of one another, and if anyone else had a hyperdrive to sell, this fellow might not have been so stubborn about the credits. Well, perhaps they could trade something from the ship for a new drive. Qui-Gon collected Padmé, Artoo, and Jar Jar, and they left the dealer's shop.

As soon as he found a quiet spot, Qui-Gon called the ship on his comlink. He explained the problem, then said, "You're sure there isn't anything of value left on board?"

Obi-Wan shook his head. "Not enough for you to barter with. Not in the amounts you're talking about."

"All right," Qui-Gon said. "Another solution will present itself. I'll check back." He put his comlink away, and started back out onto the main street.

"Noah gain," Jar Jar said, grabbing his arm. "Wesa be robbed un crunched."

"Not likely," Qui-Gon told him. "We have nothing of value." He sighed. "That's our problem." *And if we can't solve it, we'll be stuck here for a long, long time.*

CHAPTER 8

Anakin was still thinking about the strangers when he left Watto's junk shop and headed for home. They seemed different from the farmers and smugglers who usually did business with Watto. Especially Padmé. She was . . . even more different than the others. Anakin kicked at the sand. He felt as if he'd known her forever, even longer than all his life. *That's silly,* he thought . . . but it was still the way he felt. And she'd *apologized* to him for calling him a slave. Nobody had ever done that before. *For a while, she made it not matter that I'm a slave. I forgot all about it when I was talking to her.* And she'd been so interested in everything he said. Not even his best friends listened like that. Not even his mom.

Maybe they'd come back to Watto's shop before they left Tatooine. They hadn't bought anything, but Watto hadn't been as grouchy as he usually was when he lost a sale. Maybe it was because he knew nobody else had what they wanted. Maybe they'd *have* to come back before they left the planet.

As he turned onto the market street, Anakin saw one of the strangers ahead of him — the froglike nonhuman one. Sebulba was pushing him around. Anakin swallowed. Sebulba was a Dug, and the biggest bully in Mos Espa. He could use all four arms interchangeably, as long as he left himself one to stand on, so his opponents could never tell where the next blow was coming from. It gave him a big advantage in most fights.

A crowd had gathered to watch. Anakin crushed his fear down until it almost didn't exist, and shoved his way through the crowd. "Careful, Sebulba," he said in Huttese. "This one's very well connected." *If I can get Sebulba to believe that, he'll leave. Nobody messes with the Hutts.*

Sebulba stopped shoving the stranger with any of his hands and glowered at Anakin instead. "Connected? What do you mean, slave?"

"As in Hutt," Anakin said, crushing his anger at being called a slave, just as he had crushed his fear. "Big-time outlander, this one. I'd hate to see you diced before we race again."

"Next time we race, wermo, it will be the end of you," Sebulba snarled. "If you weren't a slave, I'd squash you right now."

"Yeah," Anakin muttered bitterly as Sebulba turned away. "It'd be a pity if you had to pay for me."

As the disappointed crowd started to break up, the rest of the strangers arrived. "Hi!" Anakin said to Padmé. "Your buddy here was about to be turned into orange goo. He picked a fight with a Dug."

"Nosir, nosir," said the alien that Anakin had rescued. "Mesa hate crunchen. Dat's da last ting mesa wanten."

"Nevertheless, the boy is right," the tall, bearded stranger said. "You were heading for trouble." He turned to Anakin. "Thank you, my young friend."

"Mesa doen nutten!" the alien insisted.

"Fear attracts the fearful," Anakin told him. "He was trying to overcome *his* fear by squashing you." The alien stared at him in astonishment. "Be less afraid," Anakin finished.

The tall man gave him a sharp look. Padmé smiled and said, "And that works for you?"

"To a point," Anakin said, returning her smile. His own fear had uncoiled and faded away now that the chance of a fight had passed . . . all but a hard little core. But *that* fear had been with him since the day he was old enough to understand what being a slave meant. He was used to it, and used to hiding it.

Padmé gave him an understanding smile, and for a moment Anakin wondered whether she had fears that had to be crushed sometimes. Then the tall man gestured, and the group continued down the street. They didn't seem to mind that Anakin had joined them.

A little farther along, they stopped at Jira's fruit stand. As he chatted with Jira, Anakin noticed Padmé eyeing the fruit. Struck by sudden inspiration, Anakin said, "I'll take four pallies today, Jira." Turning to Padmé, he added, "You'll like these." He dug in his pocket for the few coins he owned. *Two, three . . . I thought I had four truguts!* Hastily, he pulled the money out to check, and dropped one.

The tall man bent to retrieve it. As he did, his coat shifted, and Anakin glimpsed the handle of a laser sword stuck in his belt. *A lightsaber! He must be a Jedi!* Anakin shifted his gaze quickly. *He must not want people to know, or he'd wear it where everyone could see.*

The Jedi returned Anakin's coin. Anakin had to struggle to keep his voice normal as he said, "Ooops. I thought I had more. Make that three pallies, Jira. I'm not hungry."

The wind was rising, and shopkeepers were taking down their awnings and putting up shutters. "Gracious, my bones are aching," Jira said as she handed Anakin the pallies. "Storm's coming on, Annie. You'd better get home quick."

Anakin looked up at the tall stranger. "Do you have shelter?"

"We'll head back to our ship," he replied.

Anakin hesitated. Even a Jedi wouldn't survive long in a sandstorm. And he might not realize how fast storms came up, or how bad they could be. "Is it far?"

"On the outskirts," Padmé told him.

"You'll never reach the outskirts in time," Anakin said. "Sandstorms are very, very dangerous. Come with me. Hurry!" As soon as he was sure they were following, he headed rapidly for home.

Obi-Wan stood in front of the spaceship, staring across the desert. The wind whipped at his cloak, but he hardly felt it. The Force shook with the same elusive *wrongness* that had been disturbing him since the start of the mission — closer now, but no easier to sense. They needed to get off this planet soon, but there was still no sign of Qui-Gon.

He noticed Captain Panaka and the gathering sandstorm at the same time. "This looks pretty bad," the captain said. "We'd better seal the ship."

Reluctantly, Obi-Wan nodded. Not even Qui-Gon would try to make it to the ship in the middle of a sandstorm. As they turned toward the ramp, the captain's comlink beeped.

It was the pilot, Ric Olié. "We're receiving a message from home."

"We'll be right there," Panaka told him. Obi-Wan was already halfway up the ramp.

The Queen and her handmaiden were watching the transmission when he arrived. The hologram showed the governor, Sio Bibble, and though it faded in and out, the portions that came through clearly were disturbing. ". . . cut off all food supplies . . . death toll . . . catastrophic . . ." And the end was clear, too: "Please tell us what to do! If you can hear us, Your Highness, you must contact me. . . ."

"It's a trick," Obi-Wan said firmly, hoping he was right. "Send no reply." *If we transmit anything, the Trade Federation may trace it back to us. And if they find us, they'll catch us — without a hyperdrive, we're an easy target.*

Captain Panaka and the Queen looked at each other uncertainly. "Send no transmissions of any kind," Obi-Wan repeated, eyeing them until they both nodded.

In the middle of the room, the crackling message began to repeat itself.

Qui-Gon had seen smaller quarters than the slave hovels of Mos Espa, but not many. The shelters were little and stacked tightly; he had to duck to get through the doorway. Ahead of him, he heard the boy Anakin shouting, "Mom! Mom, I'm home!" He smiled slightly. The Force was strong in Anakin, amazingly strong — the boy practically glowed with it. But why had the Force brought Qui-Gon to him? For all his talent, Anakin was already much too old to be trained as a Jedi — Jedi teachers normally worked with very young children, whose emotions had not yet begun to shape their responses. Yet it was clear to Qui-Gon that encountering Anakin was no accident. Best to move slowly, and let things become clearer.

His thoughts were interrupted by the entrance of a dark-haired woman of around forty, presumably Anakin's mother. Her first words confirmed it: "Oh, my! Annie, what's this?"

"These are my friends, Mom," Anakin told her. "This is Padmé, and . . . oh, I don't know any of your names."

Qui-Gon could not help smiling. "I'm Qui-Gon Jinn, and this is Jar Jar Binks."

Beside him, Artoo beeped, and Padmé added, "And our droid, Artoo-Detoo."

"I'm building a droid," Anakin told her eagerly. "You want to see?"

"Anakin!" His mother's tone was sharper than necessary. "Why are these people here?"

"A sandstorm, Mom," Anakin said. "Listen." The howling of the wind had increased, even in the few minutes since they had come inside.

We made it just in time, Qui-Gon realized. "Your son was kind enough to offer us shelter," he told Anakin's mother. She still wore a wary, pinched expression, so while Anakin pulled Padmé and Artoo into the next room to see his droid, Qui-Gon dug in his belt pack for food capsules. Handing them to Anakin's mother, he said, "I have enough food for a meal."

"Oh, thank you!" the woman said. Her change in tone and manner told him just how worried she had been about feeding her unexpected visitors, and how little she had to spare. "I'm sorry if I was abrupt," she went on. "I'll never get used to Anakin's surprises."

"He's a very special boy," Qui-Gon said.

The woman gave him a look that was half-startled, half-wary. "Yes," she said softly. "I know." She turned away to begin preparing a meal.

Qui-Gon's comlink beeped. Staring thoughtfully after Anakin's mother, he answered it. It was Obi-Wan, who launched immediately into a description of a disturbing message the ship had just received from Sio Bibble on Naboo. "The Queen is upset," he finished, "but absolutely no reply was sent."

"It sounds like bait to establish a connection trace," Qui-Gon said.

Obi-Wan hesitated. "What if it is true, and the people are dying?"

"Either way, we're running out of time," Qui-Gon said, and cut the link. *If they're trying a connection trace, they must already know that we're on Tatooine. A planet is an awfully large area to search, but even so . . . we haven't much time. And I still have no idea how to get that hyperdrive generator.*

CHAPTER 9

Anakin's room had the same lumpy, sand-colored walls as every other building Amidala had seen in Mos Espa, and it was almost as full of odd bits and pieces as the junk shop. Anakin dragged her over to a workbench, where a partially completed android lay. Only one eye was finished, and none of its arms or legs had casings yet. "Isn't he great?" Anakin said proudly. Then, a little uncertainly, he added, "He's not finished yet."

"He's wonderful!" Amidala reassured him.

"You really like him?" Anakin said. "He's a protocol droid, to help Mom. Watch!"

He pushed a button, and the droid began to hum. It jerked several times, then stood up.

"How do you do," the droid said in a prim, precise voice. "I am See-Threepio, human-cyborg relations. How may I serve you?"

"He's perfect!" Amidala said, delighted. She had

met plenty of technicians in the palace at home, but she had never known anyone who put a droid together for fun. Anakin really was an amazing boy.

Artoo-Detoo was beeping and whistling at the protocol droid. "I beg your pardon," See-Threepio said to the astromech droid. "What do you mean, I'm naked? What's naked?"

Artoo beeped again, and the protocol droid looked down at himself. "My parts are showing? Oh, my goodness. How embarrassing!"

"Don't worry," Anakin told him. "I'll fix that soon." He turned back to Amidala. "I'm building a Podracer, too! When the storm is over, you can see it."

Amidala could not help smiling at his enthusiasm, though she wondered just what a Podracer was. It sounded a little . . . advanced. Anakin did not seem to notice her puzzlement. Happily, he showed her one incomprehensible gadget after another, until his mother called them to dinner.

Dinner got off to a good start. Anakin's mother — whose name turned out to be Shmi Skywalker — made excellent soup. But then the conversation turned to slavery. As tactfully as possible, Amidala asked why the slaves didn't try to escape.

"All slaves have transmitters placed inside their bodies somewhere," Shmi explained in a matter-of-fact tone.

"I've been working on a scanner to locate them," Anakin put in, "but no luck."

Shmi smiled at him and went on, "Any attempt to escape —"

"— and they blow you up . . . poof!" Anakin finished.

"How wude!" Jar Jar said, horrified.

Without thinking, Amidala said, "I can't believe there is still slavery in the galaxy. The Republic's antislavery laws —"

"The Republic doesn't exist out here," Shmi said sharply. "We must survive on our own."

Deeply embarrassed, Amidala ducked her head. This was all so different from Naboo. A disturbing thought occurred to her — *Is this what is in store for my planet if the Trade Federation's invasion succeeds?*

The silence stretched awkwardly, and then Anakin asked, "Have you ever seen a Podrace?"

Unwilling to chance another mistake, Amidala only shook her head. Beside her, Jar Jar's tongue shot out to snag a plum from a bowl at the far end of the table. Qui-Gon gave him a warning look, then said to Anakin, "They have Podracing on Malastare. Very fast, very dangerous."

"I'm the only human who can do it," Anakin said. His mother gave him a look, and he returned it indignantly. "Mom, what? I'm not bragging. It's true."

"You must have Jedi reflexes if you race Pods," Qui-Gon commented, then demonstrated his own by catching Jar Jar's long tongue as the Gungan attempted to snatch another plum. "Don't do that again," Qui-Gon said, and let the tongue snap back into Jar Jar's mouth.

Anakin stared at Qui-Gon for a moment, then said hesitantly, "I . . . I was wondering — you're a Jedi Knight, aren't you?"

"What makes you think that?" Qui-Gon asked.

"I saw your laser sword," Anakin replied. "Only Jedi carry that kind of weapon."

To Amidala's surprise, Qui-Gon did not seem disturbed by this. He leaned back, and with a slow smile said, "Perhaps I killed a Jedi and stole it from him."

"I don't think so," Anakin said in a positive tone. "No one can kill a Jedi Knight."

An expression of sadness crossed Qui-Gon's face, so quickly that Amidala wasn't even sure she had seen it. "I wish that were so," he murmured, half to himself.

"I had a dream that I was a Jedi," Anakin went on. "I came back here and freed all the slaves." He paused, studying Qui-Gon. "Have you come to free us?"

"No, I'm afraid not," said Qui-Gon.

"I think you have," Anakin said. "Why else would you be here?"

Oh, no, Amidala thought. *What can we tell him?* Somehow, she didn't want to lie to Anakin — but he was just a little boy, and they had only just met him. He could already get them in a lot of trouble, if he let the wrong people know that Qui-Gon was a Jedi. They shouldn't make things worse by telling Anakin the truth about why they were on Tatooine.

"I can see there's no fooling you," Qui-Gon said, and leaned forward. "You mustn't let anyone know about us. We're on our way to Coruscant on a very important mission, and it must be kept secret."

"Coruscant? Wow!" said Anakin. "How did you end up out here in the Outer Rim?"

"Our ship was damaged, and we're stranded here until we can repair it," Amidala put in quickly. Qui-Gon was behaving very oddly. There was no telling what else he might let these people know, if she didn't head him off.

"I can help!" Anakin said excitedly. "I can fix any-thing!"

"I believe you," Qui-Gon told him. "But our first job is to acquire the parts we need."

"Wit no-nutten mula to trade," Jar Jar added gloomily.

"These junk dealers *must* have a weakness of some kind," Amidala said.

"Gambling," Shmi said. "Everything here revolves around betting on those awful races."

"Podracing," Qui-Gon said in a thoughtful tone. "Greed can be a powerful ally, if it's used properly."

"I've built a racer!" Anakin said. "It's the fastest ever! There's a big race the day after tomorrow — you could enter my Pod. It's all but finished, and —"

"Anakin, settle down," Shmi said. "Watto won't let you —"

"Watto doesn't know I've built it," Anakin interrupted. He turned to Qui-Gon. "You could make him think it was yours, and you could get him to let me pilot for you."

Shmi's face went stiff. "I don't want you to race, Annie. It's awful."

The strength of Shmi's reaction startled Amidala slightly. Then she remembered what Qui-Gon had said earlier about Podracing. *Very fast, very dangerous.* She shivered, and looked at Anakin.

"But, Mom, I love it," Anakin protested. "And they're in trouble. The prize money would more than pay for the parts they need."

"Wesa ina pitty bad goo," Jar Jar agreed.

"Your mother's right," Qui-Gon said, and Amidala breathed a relieved sigh. The Jedi looked at Shmi. "Is there anyone friendly to the Republic who might be able to help us?"

Slowly, reluctantly, Shmi shook her head.

"We *have* to help them, Mom," Anakin insisted. "You said that the biggest problem in the universe is no one helps each other. You said —"

"Anakin, don't." Shmi's voice was faint.

Anakin broke off. For a moment everyone ate in silence. Finally Amidala could stand it no longer. "I'm sure Qui-Gon doesn't want to put your son in danger," she said to Shmi. "We will find another way."

Shmi sighed. "No, Annie's right. There is no other way." She paused, then went on with difficulty, "I may not like it, but he can help you." She gave Qui-Gon an odd, intent look. "He was meant to help you."

"Is that a yes?" Anakin demanded. "That is a yes!"

Amidala turned to Qui-Gon, expecting him to repeat his refusal, but he only nodded. *I'll have to talk to him later*, she thought. *He can't possibly be serious about this.*

The endless buildings of Coruscant made a twinkling background to Darth Sidious' hologram, but Darth Maul knew better than to be distracted by them. He kept his report brief and accurate, the way Darth Sidious liked them.

"Tatooine is sparsely populated," Darth Maul finished. "If the trace was correct, I will find them quickly, Master." He would have had them already, if they had responded to the message from Naboo. But they had not, and Darth Sidious was never interested in hearing about unsuccessful ploys.

"Move against the Jedi first," Sidious instructed

him. "You will then have no difficulty taking the Queen back to Naboo to sign the treaty."

Darth Maul felt a thrill of anticipation. "At last, we will reveal ourselves to the Jedi. At last, we will have revenge."

"You have been well trained, my young apprentice," Darth Sidious told him. "They will be no match for you." His expression was hidden by his hooded cloak, but his satisfaction was evident in his tone of voice. "It is too late for them to stop us now," he said, half to himself. "Everything is going as planned. The Republic will soon be in my control."

The following morning, Qui-Gon headed back toward Watto's junk shop. Padmé followed closely, and just as they reached the shop, she stopped him.

"Are you sure about this?" she asked. "Trusting our fate to a boy we hardly know?"

Qui-Gon looked at her without answering.

"The Queen will not approve," Padmé said, as if that settled the matter.

"The Queen does not need to know," Qui-Gon replied simply.

Padmé stared at him, then dropped onto a barrel just outside the shop door. "Well, *I* don't approve," she muttered in a sullen tone.

And so the little handmaiden discovers that her influence with the Queen has limits, Qui-Gon thought as he ducked through the doorway into the shop. Still, it was odd that she had been so *very* sure of herself. . . . He heard the sound of an argument, and put Padmé out of his mind.

Watto and Anakin looked up as he entered. "The boy tells me you want to sponsor him in the race," Watto said. "How can you do this? Not on Republic credits, I think!"

"My ship will be the entry fee." Qui-Gon pulled a small hologram projector from his belt pack and triggered it. A small, flickering image of the ship appeared above his hand.

"Not bad," Watto said, examining the projection closely. "Not bad."

"It's in good order, except for the parts we need," Qui-Gon said.

"But what would the boy ride?" Watto said. "He smashed up my Pod in the last race."

Anakin stepped forward quickly. "It wasn't my fault, really! Sebulba flashed me with his port vents. I actually *saved* the Pod. Mostly."

"That you did," Watto said, laughing. "The boy is good, no doubt there."

"I have . . . acquired a Pod in a game of chance," Qui-Gon said blandly. "The fastest ever built."

"I hope you didn't kill anyone I know to get it." Watto laughed again. "So, you supply the Pod and the entry fee; I supply the boy. We split the winnings fifty-fifty, I think."

"Fifty-fifty?" Qui-Gon scoffed. "If it's going to be fifty-fifty, I suggest *you* front the cash for the entry. No, if we win, you keep all the winnings, minus the parts I need. If we lose, you keep my ship." Watto hesitated, and Qui-Gon added persuasively, "Either way, you win."

"Deal!" Watto said at last.

The remaining details were settled quickly. Now that he was committed to the race, Watto was even willing to let Anakin spend the rest of the day getting "Qui-Gon's" Podracer ready. Soon they were all back at the slave quarters. Padmé, Artoo-Detoo, and Jar Jar helped Anakin and his friends work on the Podracer, while Qui-Gon called the ship to let Obi-Wan know of the new plan.

Obi-Wan was hardly more enthusiastic than Padmé had been, but at least he did not try to threaten Qui-Gon with the Queen's displeasure. *Of course, he's known me long enough to realize it would be a pointless thing to do*, Qui-Gon thought.

As he shut off the comlink, Shmi came out onto the porch that ran along the rear of the slave quarters. She watched the excited group around the Podracer for a moment, her expression grave.

Qui-Gon rose and joined her. "You should be proud of your son," he said gently. "He gives without any thought of reward."

"He knows nothing of greed," Shmi said. "He has —" She stopped short and gave Qui-Gon a sidelong look, as if she was not sure how much to say.

"He has special powers," Qui-Gon prompted.

"Yes." Shmi's voice was hardly more than a whisper.

"He can see things before they happen," Qui-Gon continued. "That's why he appears to have such quick reflexes. It is a Jedi trait."

"He deserves better than a slave's life."

"The Force is unusually strong with him, that much is clear," Qui-Gon murmured. He could feel that the Force was with this woman, too, though not nearly so strongly as with her son. Where had Anakin gotten such strength? "Who was his father?"

Shmi looked away. "There was no father, that I know of," she said in a low voice. "I carried him, I gave birth . . . I can't explain what happened." When Qui-Gon did not reply, she glanced back and said, "He was special from the very beginning. Can you help him?"

"I'm afraid not," Qui-Gon said, staring down at the Podracer. "Had he been born in the Republic, we would have identified him early, and he would have become a Jedi, no doubt. He has the way. But it's too late for him now. He's too old."

Even as he spoke, he wondered whether that were true.

The Council might make an exception for someone so talented. He was more and more certain that the Force had drawn him to Anakin for some specific purpose.

*   *   *

Anakin had never felt so happy. His Podracer *did* work — well, he'd always known it would, but it was different, actually having the engines ignite for real. He was entered in the Boonta Race, and Padmé would watch him. He would win this time, he knew it. *I have to win. For Padmé.* And he had a real Jedi Knight staying with him, even if it was only for a night or two. With a sigh of contentment, he leaned back to look at the stars.

"Sit still, Annie," said Qui-Gon from beside him. "Let me clean this cut."

The cut was nothing; he'd had hundreds of worse ones. But he couldn't contradict a Jedi. "There are so many stars!" he said instead. "Do they all have a system of planets?"

"Most of them," Qui-Gon replied.

"Has anyone been to them all?"

The Jedi laughed. "Not likely."

"I want to be the first one to see them all," Anakin said. To get away from Tatooine, to go to places where no one knew that he had ever been a slave, to see all the places Padmé must have seen, and more . . . Something pricked his arm. "Ow!"

"There," Qui-Gon said, wiping a patch of blood from Anakin's arm. "Good as new."

"Annie!" his mother shouted from inside. "Bedtime!"

Qui-Gon scraped some of the blood onto a small chip. Anakin stared. "What are you doing?"

"Checking your blood for infections," Qui-Gon said.

Anakin looked at him suspiciously. "I've never seen —"

"Annie!" His mother sounded almost cross. "I'm not going to tell you again!"

She would, though; he had at least one more "last time" call before she got really mad. And he still had a lot of questions . . . but Qui-Gon gestured him inside. "Go on," the Jedi said. "You have a big day tomorrow."

Anakin hesitated. "Good night," Qui-Gon said pointedly.

Grown-ups! Anakin rolled his eyes. But there was no getting out of it. He slid down from the porch railing and ran into the house.

Qui-Gon watched until the door closed behind Anakin, then inserted the blood-smeared chip into his comlink and called the ship. Obi-Wan answered at once. "Make an analysis of this blood sample I'm sending you," Qui-Gon told him.

"It'll take a minute," Obi-Wan said.

"I need a midi-chlorian count." The midi-chlorian symbionts channeled the Force to individuals. The more midi-chlorians were present in a person's cells, the more easily that person could sense the Force. Qui-Gon was sure that Anakin's blood would have a high number of midi-chlorians. *The question is how high. . . .*

"All right, I've got it," Obi-Wan said — but he did not continue.

"What are your readings?" Qui-Gon asked after a moment.

"Something must be wrong with the transmission." Obi-Wan sounded uncertain.

Qui-Gon pressed the test button on his comlink. "Here's a signal check."

"Strange," Obi-Wan said after a moment. "The transmission seems to be in good order, but the reading is off the chart — over twenty thousand."

"That's it then," Qui-Gon said with satisfaction. This was why the Force had brought him to Anakin. With a midi-chlorian count like that, the boy *needed* training, no matter how old he was.

"Even Master Yoda doesn't have a midi-chlorian count that high!" Obi-Wan continued.

"No Jedi has," Qui-Gon murmured. *Until now.* But the boy was a slave. How could they get him safely off Tatooine? They couldn't just buy him; they didn't even have enough money to buy hyperdrive parts.

"What does it mean?"

"I'm not sure," Qui-Gon said, and cut off the link. He would have to think about this. Leaning back, he looked out at the stars.

* * *

The long, sinister Sith spacecraft settled to the ground atop a rocky mesa in the Tatooine desert. Darth Maul checked the ship's readouts to make sure no one had detected the landing. There was not much more of Tatooine left to search, and he did not want to lose his prey at the last minute through care-lessness. He did not leave the ship until he was sat-isfied that no detectors were focused in his direction.

Outside, he studied the horizon briefly, then low-ered his electrobinoculars. Three more cities to check for the missing Jedi and their spaceship. Only three. *Soon, I will have them.* Two probes per city should be enough to do the job. He punched a code into the control pad on his wrist.

Six black globes floated out of the ship. As they started toward the distant city lights, they split up into pairs, two probe droids per city. Darth Maul watched until they vanished in the darkness. *Soon.*

The twin suns had just risen when Amidala, dressed once more in Padmé's clothes, came out into the yard to check on the Podracer. She thought she understood Shmi's worries a little better, now that she had gotten a good look at the thing. The Pod-racer resembled a chariot, pulled by two souped-up Radon-Ulzer Pod engines. Anakin's Pod was tiny, just large enough to hold him and all the controls. His engines, by contrast, were huge — narrow gold machines twice the length of the Podracer, and at least as big around, even with the foils closed.

Artoo-Detoo was still painting the Pod. "I hope you're about finished," Amidala said. Artoo gave a whistle that could only mean *yes*. As she turned away, Amidala saw Anakin's friend Kitster riding toward them on an eopie, leading a second animal behind him. *Time to go*, she thought.

She walked over to Anakin, who was still sleeping soundly beside the Podracer. He looked so young . . . and they were risking everything on him. *If Anakin doesn't win, we'll be stuck on Tatooine. What will become of my people then?* She sighed and touched Anakin's cheek.

Anakin stirred and looked up at her, blinking. "You were in my dream," he said hazily. "You were leading a huge army into battle."

"I hope not. I hate fighting." Amidala felt another little chill run down her spine. What *was* it about this boy that unnerved her so? "Your mother wants you to come in and clean up. We have to leave soon."

Nodding, Anakin stood up. He saw his friend and the eopies, and waved at the Podracer. "Hook them up, Kitster!" he called. Then he looked at Amidala. "I won't be long. Where's Qui-Gon?"

"He and Jar Jar left already," Amidala told him. Anakin nodded and ran inside.

I do not like this idea of Qui-Gon's, Amidala thought as she watched him leave. But it was too late for any more objections. They were committed.

Judging from the crowd in the Podracing hangar, the Boonta Race was a very important event. Qui-Gon could see natives of nearly every one of the Outer Rim worlds, from Malastare to Tund. Each of them had brought a custom-designed Podracer and a crew of droids and mechanics to work on them. The prize money for this race must be significant, to attract so many. Watto seemed to take it for granted; he flew alongside Qui-Gon without paying much attention to the racers or their crews.

"I want to see your spaceship the moment the race is over," Watto said as they made their way toward the area assigned to Anakin.

"Patience, my blue friend," Qui-Gon replied. "You'll have your winnings before the suns set, and we'll be far away from here." But with or without Anakin Skywalker? He still had no idea how to free the boy and his mother, though he had spent a considerable part of the night thinking about it. *An opportunity will arise.*

"Not if your ship belongs to me, I think," Watto said. "And I warn you — no funny business."

"You don't think Anakin will win?"

Watto laughed. "That boy is a credit to your race, but Sebulba there is going to win, I think. He always does. I'm betting heavily on Sebulba."

This is it. This is the chance I've been waiting for. "I'll take that bet," Qui-Gon said.

Abruptly, Watto stopped laughing. "What? What do you mean?"

"I'll wager my new racing Pod against . . . say . . . the boy and his mother."

"A Pod for slaves?" Watto considered. "Well, perhaps. But just one. The mother, maybe. The boy isn't for sale."

"The boy is small; he can't be worth much," Qui-Gon said persuasively. "For the fastest Pod ever built . . ."

Watto shook his head.

"Both, or no bet," Qui-Gon said. If he could free both of them . . .

Watto shook his head again. "No Pod's worth two slaves, not by a long shot. One slave or nothing."

"The boy, then," said Qui-Gon. Shmi wanted freedom for her son. She would understand. But would Anakin?

Watto pulled a red-and-blue chance cube from his pocket. "We'll let fate decide. Blue it's the boy, red his mother." As he tossed it down, Qui-Gon reached out with the Force and twitched the cube. It landed blue side up. Watto glared, first at the cube, then at Qui-Gon. "You won the small toss, outlander, but you won't win the race," he growled. "So it makes little difference." The thought seemed to cheer him, and he gave a gravelly laugh.

As Watto started toward the grandstand, Anakin's Podracer arrived in a parade of pieces. First came Anakin and Padmé, riding an eopie and dragging one engine behind them; then came Anakin's friend Kitster on a second eopie, dragging the other engine. Last of all, Artoo-Detoo pulled the Pod itself, with Shmi riding in it as if it were a landspeeder.

Watto stopped by Anakin's eopie. "Better stop your friend's betting," Qui-Gon heard him say in Huttese, "or I'll end up owning him, too." Still chuckling, he flew off.

"What did he mean by that?" Anakin asked with a scowl as he dismounted.

"I'll tell you later," Qui-Gon said. No need to put any more pressure on the boy. He had enough riding on his actions already, and he knew how important it was. Qui-Gon could sense the tension within him.

"This is so wizard!" said Kitster, pulling up with the second engine. "I'm sure you'll finish the race this time, Annie."

Padmé looked at Anakin. "You've never won a race? Not even *finished?*" She sounded horrified.

"I will this time!" Anakin said defiantly.

"Of course you will," Qui-Gon told him in a soothing tone. "Let's get this Podracer together." From the corner of his eye, he saw Padmé glaring at him, but the Queen's favorite could wait. Anakin was the one on whom their hopes depended.

As they checked the engines, Qui-Gon felt the dangerous tension within Anakin change slowly to normal excitement. The Jedi breathed a small sigh of relief. Though he did not doubt the power of the

Force, the Force could not act through a mind clouded by fear.

The signal came for the Podracers to take their positions. Anakin joined the row of pilots, while the rest of the group and the eopies hauled his Podracer out into the arena. The grandstand was huge and filled to overflowing. *There must be a hundred thousand beings here,* Qui-Gon thought.

Brightly colored canopies shaded the more expensive seats, and food vendors had set up stands in several places. The racecourse itself swung into the desert and out of sight. Most of the spectators had purchased small, specialized view screens so they could follow every minute of the Podrace. The excitement in the air was catching.

A two-headed Troig announcer began his commentary. Qui-Gon saw several of the sluglike Hutts ooze into a large box near the center of the grandstand. The pilots all bowed to them, while one of the Troig's heads announced, "His honor, our glorious host, Jabba the Hutt has entered the arena."

The Hutt in the center of the box waved to the crowd. As Kitster unhitched the eopies, Jabba began announcing the names and planets of the Podracers. Shmi bent and hugged Anakin tightly. "Be safe," she told him in a tone that was half-command, half-entreaty.

"I will, Mom," Anakin said. "I promise."

Unsteadily, Shmi walked toward the grandstand. Anakin was already double-checking the cables that held the engines to the Podracer.

". . . Anakin Skywalker tuta Tatooine . . ." boomed Jabba the Hutt's voice, and the crowd roared approval. Anakin waved, then returned to his work. *A good sign*, thought Qui-Gon. *He is not easily distracted.*

It was nearly time for them to go. Qui-Gon gestured for Jar Jar and Padmé to join Shmi in the stands. Jar Jar nodded and turned to Anakin. "Dis berry loony, Annie," he said. "May da guds be kind, mesa palo."

Anakin grinned at him. Padmé came up to him next, and Qui-Gon stiffened slightly. But all she did was kiss Anakin's cheek and say, "You carry all our hopes."

"I won't let you down," Anakin replied with determination.

As Padmé left to join Shmi, the Hutt finished his introductions. The crowd cheered. Qui-Gon helped Anakin into the Podracer and made sure that he was properly strapped in. "Are you all set, Annie?"

Anakin nodded.

Qui-Gon hesitated. "Remember, concentrate on the moment. Feel. Don't think. Trust your instincts." It was as near as he could safely come to telling Anakin to use the Force that flowed so strongly in him. Without training, more specific advice would only confuse the boy. Smiling, Qui-Gon added, "May the Force be with you."

As he walked to the stands to join the others, Qui-Gon heard the roar of dozens of Podracer engines starting.

It is up to Anakin now.

Anakin felt a familiar surge of excitement as his engines began to roar. Excitement, and fear — but Podracing fear was the only kind of fear that felt good. He could forget about Watto, and about being a slave. When he raced, *he* was in control of his fate. If he crashed, if he won, it was because of his own decisions, not his owner's. He had tried to explain to his mother once, but she was so worried about his racing that she didn't really listen.

The starting light flashed green, and Anakin forgot everything but the race. He shoved the control levers, hoping to establish a good position from the very beginning. The Podracer leaped forward . . . and the engines coughed and died.

No! They can't do this! Frantically, Anakin worked the controls as Podracer after Podracer swerved around him and vanished into the desert. Finally, he saw the problem — the fuel regulator had been manually adjusted to full open, and the engines had flooded. *How did that happen? Artoo checked it; Kitster checked it; I checked it. . . .* He lost more precious seconds waiting for the extra fuel to evaporate and the engines to start again. At last, they ignited.

Without waiting to see if the engines would keep running, Anakin sent his Podracer screaming after the pack. As he rounded the first turn, he glimpsed a smoking fireball smeared across the base of a rock formation. *Somebody swung too wide and crashed. Got to remember to watch that on the next lap.*

He sped easily through the series of stone arches; without other Podracers getting in his way, they were simple. The trailing Podracers came into view ahead of him. *I'm catching them!* Again, he worked the controls, feeding power first to one engine, then the other. The Podracer swept around the other stragglers, one after another. *If I can get out of this bunch, I can really catch up. . . .*

A Podracer just ahead of him slid sideways, blocking him. Anakin veered to the opposite side, but the other driver seemed to expect it, and cut him off again. And again. Anakin frowned in concentration. *There's a drop coming up — where I wiped out, two races ago.* He pulled back, leaving an extra length between his Podracer and the one that blocked him. Then, just as the other driver went over the drop, Anakin shoved both engine controls full open.

The Podracer surged forward. It flew off the edge of the cliff and over the blocking racer, barely missing the other driver's engines. The Pod came down with a jolt that rattled Anakin's teeth, but a quick check showed all the warning lights still shining green. *It worked! Too bad it happened way out here; I hope Padmé was watching a view screen.*

At the canyon dune turn, he saw another wreck ahead of him. Some instinct made him veer to one side, though he was nowhere close to the burning Podracer. An instant later, a shot bounced off the rear of his Pod.

Tusken Raiders! Good thing I dodged in time. He sped up unevenly, trying to make the Podracer a hard target to hit. He must have been successful; no more shots struck his Pod while he was still within range.

The next few racers were strung out along the course. Getting by them was easy, just a matter of speeding up on the turns. Soon he was past all of the stragglers. The grandstand flashed by as he came up on the central pack of racers. *Two laps to go. I can do this!*

It took him most of the second lap to work his way through the pack. Finally, he came within sight of the leading Podracers.

There were only five Podracers ahead of him now. Anakin sped up — and rounded the next corner, right into an enormous cloud of dust. *Somebody else crashed.* He swung wide, hoping to avoid hitting any of the pieces of the smashed racer. One of them hit the Podracer anyway, setting it swinging. Anakin barely compensated in time.

As he came out of the dust cloud, Anakin saw that he'd passed three others. The only racer left ahead of him was Sebulba's — there was no mistaking the odd shape of those engines. *Now I'll show you what a slave can do!* Anakin thought. Leaning forward, he gunned his engines. As the grandstand flashed by for the second time, he came up even with Sebulba. *One more lap. Just one.*

Engine to engine, they raced over the rocky course. A flap opened on the side of Sebulba's near engine, sending a stream of hot exhaust straight at Anakin's engine. *So that's why those other Podracers crashed! Sebulba melted holes in their engines!* Anakin pulled back just in time. Furious at Sebulba's maneuver, he whipped to the inside on the next tight corner and took the lead.

Keeping the lead was harder than taking it had been. Sebulba stayed on Anakin's tail, pushing him on every turn. Anakin clung grimly to his hard-won position. *It's the last lap. I only have to make it through a few more curves. . . .*

Something felt wrong — the left engine. The main inertial compensator was shaking loose. Rapidly,

Anakin adjusted the controls to use the backup system, but he wasn't quite fast enough. While he was changing over, Sebulba passed him.

I'm not going to lose now! But every move Anakin made, Sebulba blocked. And there were no more convenient drop-offs coming up; he wouldn't be able to play the same trick he'd used on that other driver, early in the race. *Something else, then . . .*

As they came around the final turn, Anakin pretended to dodge to the inside. It was the same maneuver he had used to pass Sebulba the first time — but when Sebulba dodged to block him, Anakin swung wide, trying to pass on the *outside*.

He did not quite make it all the way around Sebulba's Podracer. Side by side, they headed toward the finish line. Sebulba swerved, deliberately slamming his Pod into Anakin's. He swerved again, and his steering rods became tangled with Anakin's. Anakin fought for control. He could see Sebulba laughing as the finish line drew closer and closer. He tried to unlock the steering rods by pulling away from Sebulba's Podracer, but they were too tightly caught . . . and then Anakin's steering rod broke under the strain.

The Podracer began to spin. Grimly, Anakin hung on to the power controls. No steering, no stability — but he could still change the engines' speed. By instinct and feel, he kept the Podracer on course, heading for the finish line through the cloud of smoke and flame — *smoke and flame? Sebulba crashed?* Anakin crossed the finish line and brought the Podracer to a halt.

As the engines died, he heard cheers and saw Kitster running toward him from the crew pit. Looking back, he saw Sebulba hopping angrily about beside his wrecked Podracer. On the wrong side of the finish line. *Sebulba crashed! I won! I WON!*

Anakin unstrapped himself and stood up. *I never knew winning felt this good,* Anakin thought hazily. *I like this!* He had just time enough to hug Kitster, and then the cheering, chanting crowd swept him up and carried him off on their shoulders.

Watto was very unhappy about losing his bet. Qui-Gon had to threaten to take the matter to one of the Hutts before the blue alien agreed to provide the parts and release Anakin. While he waited for the junk dealer to deliver the hyperdrive generator, Qui-Gon arranged to borrow the two eopies to haul everything back to the ship. Though the race was over, he still felt uneasy. He wanted the Queen off planet and safely on her way to Coruscant as soon as possible. *The sooner we get the parts back to the ship, the sooner Obi-Wan can start the repairs.*

Obi-Wan was waiting at the ship to help unload, and the work went quickly. Padmé disappeared into the Queen's quarters, presumably to report on her experiences. She took Jar Jar with her.

"I'm going back," Qui-Gon told Obi-Wan as soon as everything was unloaded. "Some unfinished business. I won't be long."

"Why do I sense that we've picked up *another* pathetic life-form?" he asked disapprovingly as Qui-Gon mounted one of the eopies.

Trust Obi-Wan to pick that up right away. "It's the boy who's responsible for getting us those parts," Qui-Gon said in what he hoped was a firm, decisive tone.

Obi-Wan rolled his eyes. "Look," Qui-Gon told him, "just get that hyperdrive installed so we can get out of here."

"Yes, Master," Obi-Wan said. "It shouldn't take long."

Still harboring a vague sense of unease, Qui-Gon rode into Mos Espa, leading the second eopie behind him. He visited one of the junk dealers and sold the Podracer for a considerable sum. Then he returned the borrowed eopies and went looking for Anakin.

He found him rolling in the dust with a green-skinned, fishlike Rodian boy. Several other children of various species were watching, wide-eyed. "What's this?" Qui-Gon said.

The fighting stopped abruptly. With wary looks, the two boys climbed to their feet. "He said I cheated!" Anakin said.

"Well, Annie, you know the truth," Qui-Gon said. "You will have to tolerate his opinion. Fighting won't change it."

Anakin gave the Rodian a dark look, but nodded. Then he turned and walked away.

As they neared the slave quarters, Qui-Gon took out the money he had gotten for the Podracer. "These are yours," he said, handing the coins to Anakin. The boy stared, plainly not understanding. "We sold the Pod," Qui-Gon explained.

Anakin's face lit up, and he ran toward home, the fight forgotten. *But how will he feel when he learns that he is free — and his mother is not?* Slowly, Qui-Gon followed.

After all the excitement of the last day, cleaning up had a pleasantly familiar feel to Shmi. The Jedi and his friends would soon be gone, and the race — she tried not to think about the race. It had been wonderful to see Anakin win, but now Watto would want him to race more often. And she couldn't forget the flames rising from the wrecks. *It could have been Annie . . .*

The door banged open, and Anakin ran in. "Mom! Mom, he sold the Pod!" He pulled a fistful of coins from his pocket and shoved them into Shmi's hands. "Look at all the money we have!"

"Oh, my goodness!" Shmi said, staring at the coins. "That's wonderful!" As she hugged Annie, she saw the Jedi standing in the door behind him. She straightened, intending to thank him, and he said quietly, "And Anakin has been freed."

Shmi stared, her mind whirling. She heard at once what Qui-Gon *hadn't* said. Annie was free, but she was not. While Anakin leaped joyfully and hurled excited questions at the Jedi, she struggled to control her feelings. This was what she had asked Qui-Gon, after all — that he help Annie. Now her son had the chance she had always wanted for him. She would have to do her best to see that he took it.

"Now you can make your dreams come true, Annie," she said. "You're free!" Turning to Qui-Gon she asked, "Will you take him with you?" She caught her breath as a dazzling new possibility occurred to her. "Is he to become a Jedi?"

"Our meeting was not a coincidence," Qui-Gon said. "Nothing happens by accident." He looked at Annie. "You are strong with the Force, but you may not be accepted by the Council."

"A Jedi!" Anakin's eyes grew round. "Mighty blasters, you mean I get to go with you in your starship and everything?"

Qui-Gon knelt so that he could look directly into Anakin's eyes. "Anakin, training to be a Jedi will not be easy. And if you succeed, it will be a hard life."

"But it's what I want!" Anakin said. "It's what I've always dreamed about. Can I go, Mom?"

Shmi looked at Qui-Gon, unable to speak. He gave a slight nod of understanding and said to Anakin, "This path has been placed before you, Annie. The choice to take it is yours alone."

Anakin started to answer, then stopped, thinking. He looked at Shmi, then at Qui-Gon. Shmi held her breath. Finally, he said, "I want to go."

"Then pack your things," Qui-Gon said. "We haven't much time."

Elated, Anakin flung his arms around Shmi, then dashed for his room. Suddenly he stopped and looked back, his expression worried. "What about Mom?" he demanded. "Is she free, too? You're coming, aren't you, Mom?"

Qui-Gon looked at Shmi, then turned to Annie once more. "I tried to free your mother, Annie, but Watto wouldn't have it."

"But the money from selling —"

"It's not nearly enough," Qui-Gon said gently.

Annie looked stricken. Shmi sat down next to him and drew him close. "Son, my place is here. My future is here. It's time for you to let go of me. I cannot go with you."

"I want to stay with you," Anakin said in a small voice. "I don't want things to change."

"You can't stop change, any more than you can stop the suns from setting," Shmi said with a sigh. "Listen to your feelings, Annie. You know what's right."

Anakin bowed his head, and Shmi could feel him trembling. Finally, he looked up with tears in his eyes. "I'm going to miss you so much, Mom."

And I, you, every day and every hour. "I love you,

Annie," Shmi said, and hugged him tightly for a long moment. "Now hurry."

She watched him run into his room, storing up the sight against the empty days ahead. Then she turned to Qui-Gon. "Thank you."

"I will look after him," the Jedi said. "You have my word." He gazed at her with concern. "Will you be all right?"

Shmi gave a little half-nod and glanced back toward Annie's room. "He was in my life for such a short time," she whispered, almost to herself.

The first probe droid returned hours before Darth Maul expected it — an excellent sign. He checked its readouts with care, and grinned fiercely. *It's the Jedi, all right. On the far side of Mos Espa.* Signaling the droid to use maximum speed, Darth Maul climbed on his speeder and followed it back across the desert.

CHAPTER **14**

It didn't take Anakin long to pack. The only thing he really wanted to bring with him was See-Threepio, but the droid was far too large. He activated Threepio long enough to say farewell, then hurried out to meet Qui-Gon.

Kitster was waiting outside with Shmi, to say good-bye. "Thanks for every moment you've been here," he told Anakin. "You're my best friend."

"I won't forget," Anakin said, feeling hollow. *I have to go. I want to go. I've always wanted to get away from here, but . . . but . . .* He gave Kitster a quick hug and ran toward Qui-Gon, trying to outrun the hurt, to forget about what he was leaving behind. Not just Threepio and Kitster, but all his other friends as well — *they're not here; I won't even get to say good-bye to them.* And his mother . . . He slowed. Stopped. Looked back.

His mother was standing in the doorway, watching him with a sad smile that was more than he could bear. He ran to her, and with tears starting in his eyes, he said, "I can't do it, Mom. I just can't."

She knelt and wrapped her arms around him. He hugged her tightly, and for just a moment everything felt safe and right and ordinary again. Then she sat back and stroked his hair. "Annie, this is one of those times when you have to do something you don't think you *can* do. I know how strong you are, Annie. I know you can do this."

Anakin nodded, not really believing it. "Will I ever see you again?"

"What does your heart tell you?"

"I hope so," Anakin said. Usually, he was certain, the way he had been certain when he told Padmé he would marry her, but this — he wanted this so badly that he couldn't *tell.* "Yes. I guess."

His mother squeezed his arms. "Then we will see each other again."

Anakin swallowed hard. "I . . . I *will* become a Jedi. And I will come back and free you, Mom. I promise."

"No matter where you are, my love will be with you," his mother said. "Now be brave . . . and don't look back." She gave him a little shake, and repeated, "Don't look back."

He gave her one final hug, then turned and marched grimly toward Qui-Gon. *I won't look back,*

Mom. Watch me. I'm not looking back. I'll make you proud, Mom. I won't look back.

Silently, Qui-Gon fell into step beside him. The Jedi did not speak until the slave quarters were out of sight behind a building. Then he gestured Anakin to the left. "We have to stop at Watto's shop."

Startled, Anakin looked up. "Why?"

"To get your slave transmitter neutralized."

The process didn't take long, but it left Anakin feeling odd, as if he had suddenly become an entirely new and different person. *I never thought not being a slave would feel so strange*, he thought as he trudged along beside Qui-Gon.

Suddenly, the Jedi spun. His lightsaber hummed out of nowhere. Anakin heard a loud crack, and saw a round, black droid drop in fizzing pieces to the sand. "What is it?" he asked.

"Probe droid," Qui-Gon replied in a grim tone. Bending, he examined the droid more closely. "Very unusual — it's not like anything I've seen before." He stood up and scanned the street, then looked down at Anakin. "Come on." He started running.

Qui-Gon's long legs made it hard for Anakin to keep up, but he did the best he could. He was only a little way behind when the spaceship came into sight. It looked peaceful and normal, but Qui-Gon didn't slow down. "Qui-Gon, sir, wait!" Anakin called.

Qui-Gon turned. His eyes widened and he shouted, "Anakin, drop!"

Without hesitation, Anakin threw himself face-down on the hot sand. He heard a high whine and felt a rush of wind on his back. When he raised his head a moment later, he was just in time to see a man in a black, hooded cloak leap at Qui-Gon from a speeder bike. Swinging a red lightsaber.

Another Jedi? But a Jedi wouldn't attack Qui-Gon! Anakin climbed to his feet, watching in confusion as the two men slashed at each other.

"Annie!" Qui-Gon shouted. "Get to the ship! Tell them to take off! Go, go!"

Anakin ran for the ship, hoping he would reach it in time.

"Everything checks out," Ric Olié said as he removed the last test wires. "We can leave as soon as Qui-Gon gets back."

"Good." Obi-Wan wondered why he did not feel more relieved. *Something is very wrong.*

Captain Panaka burst through the cockpit doorway, followed by Padmé and an unfamiliar brown-haired boy. "Qui-Gon is in trouble," the captain said. "He says to take off!"

Olié flung himself at the pilot's chair before Panaka finished speaking. The ship was airborne in moments, without even waiting to close the entry ramp. "I don't see anything," he said as he circled above the desert.

Peering anxiously through the cockpit windows, Obi-Wan spotted a small cloud of dust in the distance. At its center, he felt a great disturbance in the Force — and Qui-Gon. "Over there!" he told Olié. "Fly low!"

The pilot obeyed. The ship skimmed across the surface of the desert, barely a meter above the tops of the dunes. As they came closer, Obi-Wan caught a glimpse of lightsabers flashing amid the dust — *two lightsabers? No wonder Panaka said Qui-Gon was in trouble!* He swallowed hard, hoping that Qui-Gon would see the open entry ramp as the ship passed. He didn't dare use the Force to let his Master know they were coming. In a fight as fierce as that one, even a small distraction could be fatal. *He'll see it. He has to see it.*

As the ship passed over the battle, Obi-Wan felt a surge in the Force. In sudden relief, he let out the breath he hadn't realized he was holding. *He made it!* "Qui-Gon's on board," he told Olié as the ramp closed. "Get us out of here!"

Without waiting to see whether the pilot obeyed, Obi-Wan started for the main hall. The young boy followed him. They found Qui-Gon in a dusty heap just inside the entry, covered with sweat and breathing hard. *I've never seen him in such bad shape after a fight! If we hadn't gotten to him when we did . . .*

"Are you all right?" the boy demanded, voicing part of Obi-Wan's worry.

"I think so," Qui-Gon panted. He sat up, and slowly began to breathe more normally. "That was a surprise I won't soon forget."

"What was it?" Obi-Wan asked.

"I don't know," Qui-Gon replied. "But he was well trained in the Jedi arts."

Obi-Wan blinked. *A renegade Jedi? Impossible!* He caught a look from Qui-Gon that meant "we'll discuss it later," and smothered his questions.

"My guess is that he was after the Queen," Qui-Gon continued.

"Do you think he'll follow us?" the boy asked. He sounded more curious than worried, now that he knew Qui-Gon was not injured.

"We'll be safe enough once we're in hyperspace," Qui-Gon told him. "But I have no doubt that he knows our destination."

"What are we going to do about it?" the boy demanded.

Obi-Wan could not help frowning at the boy. He shouldn't be bothering Qui-Gon like that, especially now. But Qui-Gon did not seem disturbed by the boy's insistent questions. "We will be patient," he said firmly. Then, as if he knew what Obi-Wan had been thinking, he added, "Anakin Skywalker, meet Obi-Wan Kenobi."

"Pleased to meet you," the boy said politely. As he turned to shake hands, he looked straight at Obi-Wan for the first time. His eyes widened. "Wow! You're a Jedi, too?"

The boy's enthusiasm was hard to resist. *But what is Qui-Gon thinking, to get a child mixed up in the middle of a mission? And what will he do with the boy once we get to Coruscant?* Obi-Wan studied Anakin doubtfully. *I don't know about this. I just don't know.*

CHAPTER 15

*T*his spaceship is freezing, Anakin thought. And the coldest part of it was the sleeping quarters. Nobody else seemed to mind; they were all snoring their heads off. But after shivering under the thin blanket for an hour without falling asleep, Anakin gave up. The main area was a little warmer. Surely no one would mind if he curled up in a corner there.

When he got to the main room, he found to his relief that he wasn't the only one who'd thought of sleeping there. Jar Jar was stretched out in a chair, head back, murmuring quietly in his sleep. Artoo-Detoo rested in standby mode next to the wall. Anakin found a corner and sat down.

It was still too cold. No matter how tightly he curled, he didn't feel warm. *This is too different,* he thought miserably. Qui-Gon and Padmé were too busy to talk, and no one else on board cared about him. Well, maybe Jar Jar and Artoo-Detoo. *I shouldn't have come. I should have stayed with Mom. I want to go home!*

A soft sound in the passageway caught his attention. A moment later, Padmé entered the room. She looked tired, and the sadness on her face made Anakin feel even worse than he already did. He shrank back into the corner, hoping she wouldn't see him.

At first, she didn't. She crossed to one of the monitors and switched on a crackly recording of a hologram message. The sound was too low for Anakin to hear clearly, but whatever it was saying made Padmé look sadder than ever. He clenched his teeth to keep them from chattering.

Suddenly, Padmé looked up and saw him. She came over and looked at him with concern. "Are you all right?"

"It's very cold," Anakin admitted, trying to control his shivering.

Padmé *tsk*ed and stripped off her red silk overjacket. "You're from a warm planet, Annie," she said as she tucked it around him. "Too warm for my taste. But space is cold."

Encouraged by her kindness, Anakin said, "You seem sad."

"The Queen is worried," Padmé said softly. "Her people are suffering . . . dying. She *must* convince the Senate to intervene, or . . ." She shook her head. "I'm not sure what will happen."

How can I help with that? Anakin thought. *I don't know anything about queens. I guess I'll have to learn.* Suddenly, he felt very lonely. Padmé was the Queen's handmaiden, part of a whole world he knew nothing about. When they reached Coruscant, she would go with the Queen, and he would go . . . wherever people went to be trained as Jedi. But Qui-Gon had said the Council might not accept him. If they didn't —

"I'm — I'm not sure what's going to happen to me," Anakin said in a low voice. "I don't know if I'll ever see you again." He squirmed to get a hand into his pocket, and pulled out the pendant he had been working on. "I made this for you," he said, not daring to look directly at Padmé. "So you'd remember me. I carved it out of a japor snippet." He held it out to her. "It will bring you good fortune."

Padmé took it. After a moment, she said, "It's beautiful, but I don't need this to remember you." Anakin looked up, and she smiled at him. As she hung the pendant around her neck, her expression changed. "Many things will change when we reach the capital, Annie," she said soberly. "But my caring for you will always remain."

"I care for you, too," Anakin told her. "Only — only I miss —" He stopped, blinking back tears.

"You miss your mother." Padmé's voice was soft and gentle and understanding. She leaned forward

It is good to be Queen Amidala again, thought Amidala, but it was also hard. She had not realized how much the responsibility weighed on her mind until she had let go of a tiny fraction of it to become Padmé. Now she knew — but she was still the elected Queen of Naboo, and her people were depending on her. *Why else did I come to Coruscant?* She had taken back her proper role as the ship entered Coruscant's atmosphere; now she sat with Senator Palpatine, planning their presentation to the Galactic Senate.

Senator Palpatine had put more than half his living quarters at his Queen's disposal. The rooms were as lavish as the royal palace on Naboo — and a great relief after the cramped quarters on the Royal Starship. Too much of a relief, perhaps; Amidala found it difficult to concentrate on what Palpatine was telling her.

"The Republic is not what it once was," Palpatine said as he paced the floor before her. "There is no interest in the common good — no civility, only politics. It's disgusting." He paused and said in a heavy tone, "I must be frank, Your Majesty. There is little chance the Senate will act on the invasion."

Amidala frowned, startled. "Chancellor Valorum seems to think there is hope."

"If I may say so, Your Majesty, the Chancellor has little real power," Palpatine said. "The bureaucrats are in charge now."

If that is true, then this whole trip has been wasted effort. Amidala pressed her lips together. *I will not let it be wasted.*

"What options do we have?" she asked.

"Our best choice would be to push for the election of a stronger Supreme Chancellor," Palpatine said. "You could call for a vote of no confidence in Chancellor Valorum."

"But he has been our strongest supporter." To force him out of office would feel like betraying him. She couldn't do it . . . but to save her people? Her planet? "Is there any other way?"

"We could submit a plea to the courts."

"There's no time for that," Amidala said. The courts took even longer to decide things than the Senate. Remembering Governor Bibble's message, she went on, "Our people are *dying*, Senator. We must do something quickly to stop the Federation."

Palpatine shook his head. "To be realistic, Your Highness, I'd say we are going to have to accept Federation control. For the time being."

Amidala stared at him. How could he speak of it so calmly? Perhaps he had been on Coruscant too long; perhaps he had forgotten too much about the ordinary people he represented in the Senate. "That is something I cannot do," she told him. *I will find a way to stop this invasion. Even if I have to face down every bureaucrat on Coruscant to do it.*

* * *

The Jedi Council chambers were located at the peak of the Jedi Temple, just below its crowning spire. The glass walls of the circular room looked out over Coruscant in all directions, interrupted only by the great pillars that supported the spire above. Qui-Gon had been there often over the years, to report on his various missions. Now he and Obi-Wan stood once more before the Jedi Council — twelve Jedi from different planets and different species who guided the whole Jedi order. This time, Qui-Gon's report to them was different. He touched only briefly on the events on Naboo and the Podrace, but he described the fight on the Tatooine dunes in great detail. Then he finished, "My only conclusion can be that it was a Sith Lord."

There was an instant silence. Qui-Gon could feel the Council's shocked surprise. Then Mace Windu, a senior Jedi on the Council, leaned forward, his dark face grim. "A Sith Lord?"

"Impossible!" said Ki-Adi-Mundi, raising his bushy eyebrows almost to his skull ridge. "The Sith have been extinct for a millennium."

On the other side of Mace Windu, Master Yoda's long ears twitched. "The very Republic is threatened, if involved the Sith are."

"I do not believe they could have returned without us knowing," Mace said.

"Hard to see, the dark side is," Yoda responded. Around the Council circle, heads nodded. "Discover who this assassin is, we must."

"I sense he will reveal himself again," Ki-Adi-Mundi said slowly.

"This attack was with purpose, that is clear," Mace Windu said. "And I agree that the Queen is his target."

Yoda turned toward Qui-Gon. "With this Naboo Queen you must stay, Qui-Gon. Protect her."

"We will use all our resources here to unravel this mystery and discover the identity of your attacker," Mace added. "May the Force be with you."

The other Jedi Councilors echoed him, plainly expecting Qui-Gon to leave. Qui-Gon stayed where he was. After a moment, Yoda said in a dry tone, "Master Qui-Gon, more to say have you?"

"With your permission, my Master," Qui-Gon said respectfully. Yoda nodded, and Qui-Gon continued, "I have encountered a vergence in the Force."

The Council stirred. Yoda eyed Qui-Gon narrowly. "A vergence, you say?"

"Located around a person?" Mace Windu asked.

Qui-Gon nodded. "A boy. His cells have the highest concentration of midi-chlorians I have seen in a life-form. It is possible that he was conceived by the midi-chlorians."

Mace Windu sat back. "You refer to the prophecy of the one who will bring balance back to the Force." He gave Qui-Gon a long, skeptical look. "You believe it's this . . . boy?"

"I don't presume —" Qui-Gon began.

"But you do!" Yoda broke in. "Revealed, your opinion is."

"I request the boy be tested," Qui-Gon said stiffly. Whatever they thought of his opinions, he had the right to request that much.

The Council members exchanged looks. Then Yoda said, "Trained as a Jedi, you request for him?"

"Finding him was the will of the Force," Qui-Gon replied firmly. "I have no doubt of that. There is too much happening here. . . ."

"Bring him before us, then," Mace said.

"Tested, he will be," Yoda added in an ominous tone.

Qui-Gon nodded. Bowing, he turned and left the Council chamber.

CHAPTER 16

The Galactic Senate chambers reminded Amidala just a little of the Tatooine Podracing arena. But instead of a semicircle of viewing stands, ranks of floating platforms hugged the curving walls of the Senate chambers. Each carried representatives and their aides from one of the member planets or organizations; most displayed the symbols or banners of their homeworlds. Sternly, Amidala repressed the urge to gawk. She wasn't here to stare at the Senators, but to persuade them to help Naboo.

Beside her, Senator Palpatine urged her yet again to force a change in the Senate leadership. *He knows more of Coruscant than I do,* Amidala thought. *But Chancellor Valorum has done so much for us. . . . Surely it won't be necessary to force him out of his position.*

From the central pillar, the Chancellor announced that Naboo would address the Senate. The Naboo platform dipped smoothly to take up a position next to the Chancellor's pillar. Amidala's stomach lurched. She was eager to speak.

Senator Palpatine stood and described the history of the dispute between Naboo and the Trade Federation. The Senators from the Trade Federation tried to interrupt, but the Chancellor quashed them. Palpatine finished his remarks and said, "I present Queen Amidala of Naboo, to speak on our behalf."

As Amidala rose to address the Senate, she heard a smattering of applause. "Honorable representatives of the Republic," she began, "I come to you under the gravest of circumstances. The Naboo system has been invaded by force. Invaded — against all the laws of the Republic — by the droid armies of the Trade Fed —"

"I object!" the Trade Federation delegate interrupted loudly. "There is no proof."

Proof? I was there! Amidala thought. She opened her mouth to reply, but the Trade Federation Senator went on, "We recommend a commission be sent to Naboo to ascertain the truth."

A commission? My people are dying! Surely, the Chancellor won't take this proposal seriously! But other delegates were speaking in favor of the delay, and talking about procedures. And Chancellor Valorum was listening. *Was Palpatine right, after all? If Valorum does not support us . . .*

At last the Chancellor turned back to the assembly. "The point is conceded," he said heavily. "Queen Amidala of Naboo, will you defer your motion in order to allow a commission to explore the truth of your accusations?"

They didn't even let me finish speaking! "I will *not* defer," Amidala said angrily. "I have come before you to resolve this attack on our sovereignty *now.*" She took a deep breath. "I move for a vote of no confidence in Chancellor Valorum's leadership."

"What?" Valorum said, horrified. "No!"

Around the hall, the delegates murmured in surprise, then began to cheer. In a few moments, the motion had been seconded. The Trade Federation tried to send this motion, too, to a committee, but the rest of the Senate would not cooperate. In unison, the delegates began chanting, "Vote now! Vote now!"

Palpatine leaned toward Amidala. "You see, Your Majesty? The time is with us. Valorum will be voted out, and they will elect a new Chancellor, a strong Chancellor, one who will not let our tragedy continue."

Amidala stared at him. He sounded so certain and so . . . complacent. As if it did not matter that she had been forced to bring down one of Naboo's oldest and strongest supporters. Almost as if he were *pleased* about it.

The vote was set to begin the following day. As the

final arrangements were made, Valorum turned toward the Naboo box. "Palpatine, I thought you were my ally — my *friend*," he said. "How could you do this?"

Palpatine bowed his head almost sadly, but Amidala thought she saw the ghost of a smile cross his face. *He's only pleased because we now have a chance to make the Senate stop the invasion,* she reassured herself. *And we didn't have any other choice. I couldn't let them spend months studying the situation while my people die. I had to call for the vote.* But looking at former Chancellor Valorum, she knew his expression of betrayal would haunt her dreams for a long, long time.

The setting sun washed the balcony outside the Jedi Council chambers with soft color, and tinted the forest of buildings below to match. The view of Coruscant was unequalled. But, Obi-Wan noticed, Qui-Gon was not watching the view. His eyes kept straying toward the Council chambers, where Anakin Skywalker was being tested by the Jedi Council. Obi-Wan sighed.

"The boy will not pass the Council's tests, Master, and you know it," he said. "He is far too old."

"Anakin will become a Jedi," Qui-Gon said with renewed calm. "I promise you."

Did his confidence come from one of the rare

glimpses of the future that sometimes came to Jedi Masters? Or did Qui-Gon plan to train Anakin whether the Council approved or not? Obi-Wan frowned. "Don't defy the Council, Master," he said, half-warning, half-pleading. "Not again."

"I will do what I must."

He is planning to defy them, Obi-Wan thought with a sinking feeling. "Master, you could be sitting on the Council by now — if you would just follow the Code."

Qui-Gon said nothing. Obi-Wan sighed again. *Qui-Gon can be so stubborn. . . .* "They will not go along with you this time," he warned. *And I don't want to have to watch what will happen then.*

Much to Obi-Wan's surprise, Qui-Gon smiled. "You still have much to learn, my young apprentice," he said quietly.

Uneasily, Obi-Wan turned back toward the city.

The Jedi tests were nothing like what Anakin had expected. Not that he'd actually thought much about what they would be like. *Maybe they're just confusing because I'm older,* he thought. The Jedi Master named Mace Windu had a view screen in front of him, which Anakin couldn't see. As images flashed on the screen, Anakin had to see if he could sense what they were. It was an exhausting challenge — Anakin had no idea how he was doing. Finally, the screen clicked off, and he relaxed a little.

"Good, good, young one," said Master Yoda. "How feel you?"

"Cold, sir," Anakin replied without thinking. He had been cold ever since he left Tatooine, it seemed.

"Afraid, are you?" Master Yoda said.

"No, sir," Anakin said, startled. That wasn't the kind of cold he'd been thinking of at all.

Beside Master Yoda, Mace Windu stirred. "Afraid to give up your life?"

Oh, that's what they meant. Anakin hesitated. "I don't think so."

"Be mindful of your feelings," Mace Windu said.

"Your thoughts dwell on your mother," the alien Ki-Adi-Mundi added.

"I miss her," Anakin admitted.

"Afraid to lose her, I think," Master Yoda said almost gleefully.

"What's that got to do with anything?" *Aren't Jedi allowed to have mothers?*

"Everything." Master Yoda's scratchy voice was emphatic. "Fear is the path to the dark side. Fear leads to anger; anger leads to hate; hate . . . leads to suffering."

"I am not afraid!" Anakin said angrily. Did they *want* him to fail?

Master Yoda thrust his head forward, studying Anakin. "A Jedi must have the deepest commitment, the most serious mind. I sense much fear in you."

Anakin took a deep breath. As he had done

before, on Tatooine, he crushed his fear down inside him until it almost did not exist. Almost. Hoping that would be good enough, he raised his chin and said quietly, "I am not afraid."

There was a long pause. Finally, Master Yoda half-closed his eyes and said, "Then continue, we will."

But as Mace Windu picked up the view screen, Anakin could not help wondering whether he had just passed another one of the Jedi tests . . . or failed it.

As the sky darkened, the lights of Coruscant shimmered on. They made the city look beautiful, Amidala thought, but it was still a cold and artificial place. She had been standing at the window of Palpatine's quarters for half an hour, and she hadn't found a single patch of green. *Coruscant is made of glass and metal. No wonder the Senate is more interested in playing political games than in helping my people.*

Jar Jar Binks joined her by the window, but he seemed more interested in studying her face than in watching the city. "Yousa tinken yousa people ganna die?" he asked.

"I don't know," Amidala answered, feeling hollow. *Only Jar Jar would be so blunt. But . . . I have done all I can do through negotiation and diplomacy. And it hasn't been enough. My people will die if the Republic doesn't send help soon.*

"Gungans ganna get pasted too, eh?" Jar Jar said.

"I hope not." But she sounded unconvincing, even to herself.

Jar Jar must have heard the desperation in her voice, because he said reassuringly, "Gungans no die'n without a fight. Wesa warriors! Wesa gotta grande army." He gave Amidala a sidelong look and added, "Dat why you no liken us, metinks."

Before she could reply, the far door flew open. Captain Panaka and Senator Palpatine hurried in and bowed. "Your Highness," Captain Panaka said, "Senator Palpatine has been nominated to succeed Valorum as Supreme Chancellor of the Galactic Senate!"

"A surprise, to be sure," Palpatine said. "But a welcome one. I promise, Your Majesty, if I am elected, I will bring democracy back to the Republic. I will put an end to corruption."

Why should I care about democracy and corruption in the Republic, when my people are dying? But she couldn't say that. "Senator, I fear that by the time you have control of the bureaucrats, there will be nothing left of our cities, our people, our way of life."

Palpatine looked grave. "I understand your concern. But the law is in their favor."

Amidala turned away. "There is nothing more I can do here," she said, half to herself. Coruscant was the Senator's arena. *I am Queen Amidala of*

Naboo; my place is with my people. It was time to return home.

"Captain Panaka!" she called. "Ready my ship."

"Please, Your Majesty, stay here, where it is safe," Palpatine said.

"No place is safe, if the Senate doesn't condemn this invasion," Amidala replied somberly, and Palpatine did not contradict her.

The members of the Jedi Council watched with grave expressions as Obi-Wan and Qui-Gon joined Anakin in the center of the chamber. Obi-Wan wondered briefly whether they looked so solemn because Anakin had passed, or because he had failed; then Master Yoda raised his chin and said, "Correct you were, Qui-Gon."

"The boy's cells contain a very high concentration of midi-chlorians," Mace Windu said.

Ki-Adi-Mundi nodded. "The Force is strong with him."

"He's to be trained, then," Qui-Gon said with considerable satisfaction.

The Council members exchanged glances. "No," said Master Windu. "He will not be trained. He is too old; there is already too much anger in him."

I knew it, Obi-Wan thought. *And if the Council will not train Anakin, there is nothing more Master Qui-Gon can do.*

"He *is* the chosen one," Qui-Gon insisted, resting his hands comfortingly on Anakin's shoulders. "You must see it."

Master Yoda shook his head. "Clouded, this boy's future is. Masked by his youth."

Qui-Gon took a deep breath. "I will train him then. I take Anakin as my Padawan learner."

Stunned, Obi-Wan jerked his head to face Qui-Gon. *Is this what he had in mind all along?*

Master Yoda frowned. "An apprentice, you have, Qui-Gon. Impossible, to take on a second."

"We forbid it," Mace Windu said flatly.

"Obi-Wan is ready —" Qui-Gon turned to look at Obi-Wan.

He expects me to help him do this! Obi-Wan realized. He glared back at Qui-Gon. *Well, if he'd rather be Anakin's Master, let him!* "I am ready to face the trials," he said to the Council.

"Ready so early, are you?" Master Yoda said sarcastically. "What know you of ready?"

"He is headstrong," Qui-Gon said. "And he has much to learn about the living Force, but he is capable. There is little more he will learn from me."

He means it, Obi-Wan thought. *He really thinks I'm ready; it's not just because of Anakin. But then why didn't he warn me he was going to do this?*

"Our own counsel will we keep on who is ready," Master Yoda replied. "More to learn, he has."

"Now is not the time for this," Mace Windu broke in. "The Senate is voting for a new Supreme Chancellor, and Queen Amidala has decided to return home. That will put pressure on the Trade Federation."

"And could draw out the Queen's attacker," Master Yoda added.

"Go with the Queen to Naboo and discover the identity of this dark warrior," Mace Windu commanded. "That is the clue we need to unravel this mystery of the Sith."

Master Yoda nodded. "Young Skywalker's fate will be decided later."

Despite himself, Obi-Wan let out a breath of relief. *Later* wasn't a decision that might make Qui-Gon defy the Council. Then he tensed again as Qui-Gon said, "I brought Anakin here. He must stay in my charge. He has nowhere else to go."

"He is your ward, Qui-Gon," Mace answered. "We will not dispute that."

"Train him not," Master Yoda said emphatically. "Take him with you, but train him not!"

"Protect the Queen, but do not intercede if it comes to war," Mace Windu continued. "And may the Force be with you."

Still numb from the decision of the Jedi Council, Anakin waited on the landing platform outside the

Naboo royal starship. He had been so sure that he would be a Jedi . . . now what would he do? Tagging along after Qui-Gon would only remind him of everything he couldn't have. *At least I didn't fail the tests*, he thought. *It's only that I'm too old.* But it was small comfort. And on top of everything, Obi-Wan and Qui-Gon were arguing — about him.

"The boy is dangerous," Obi-Wan told Qui-Gon as they came onto the landing platform. "They all sense it. Why can't you?"

"His fate is uncertain, not dangerous," Qui-Gon replied with a touch of irritation. "The Council will decide Anakin's future. That should be enough for you. Now, get on board."

Reluctantly, Obi-Wan headed up the landing ramp. Anakin looked up as Qui-Gon came over to him. "Master Qui-Gon, sir, I don't wish to be a problem."

"You won't be, Annie," Qui-Gon assured him.

But I am already, Anakin thought sadly. *That's why you and Obi-Wan were arguing.*

As if he sensed Anakin's mood, Qui-Gon looked seriously down at him. "I'm not allowed to train you, so I want you to watch me and be mindful," he said. "Always remember: Your focus determines your reality. Stay close to me, and you will be safe."

Anakin nodded, thinking hard. Master Qui-Gon was not allowed to train him, but perhaps he was allowed to answer questions. "Master . . . Sir, I've been wondering," Anakin said. "What are midi-chlorians?"

"Midi-chlorians are a microscopic life-form that resides within all living cells and communicates with the Force," Qui-Gon answered readily.

"They live inside of me?"

"In your cells," Qui-Gon said, smiling. "We are symbionts with the midi-chlorians."

The unfamiliar word made Anakin frown. "Symbionts?"

"Life-forms living together for mutual advantage," Qui-Gon explained. "Without the midi-chlorians, life could not exist, and we would have no knowledge of the Force. They continually speak to you, telling you the will of the Force."

"They do?"

"When you learn to quiet your mind, you will hear them," Qui-Gon told him.

Anakin shook his head. "I don't understand."

Qui-Gon smiled. "With time and training, Annie . . . you will."

But I'm not allowed to have any training, Anakin thought as he followed Qui-Gon into the spaceship. *At least maybe I'll see Padmé again. And maybe I can learn some more, if I can figure out the right questions to ask Qui-Gon.* It wasn't as good as being trained to be a Jedi, but it was something.

* * *

Outside the Naboo palace, night hid the droids that occupied the city of Theed, making everything look almost as usual. Inside the palace, the cool lights of the throne room made the marble floor gleam . . . except where the communications hologram stood. Nute Gunray looked at the hooded image and shivered. *I'm just a little cold*, he told himself.

"The Queen is on her way to you," Darth Sidious said in his soft, precise voice. "I regret she is of no further use to us. When she gets there, destroy her."

"Yes, my lord," Nute said. Beside him, Rune Haako shifted uneasily. *As soon as we're done, he'll probably lecture me again about how dangerous Darth Sidious is.* But it was too late now to break with the Sith Lord. Far too late.

"Is the planet secure?" Sidious went on.

"Yes, my lord," Nute answered, relieved to have good news. "We have taken over the last pockets of primitive life-forms. We are in complete control now."

"Good," Darth Sidious said. "I will see to it that things in the Senate stay as they are. I am sending Darth Maul to join you. He will deal with the Jedi."

"Yes, my lord," Nute repeated, swallowing hard. The temperature in the throne room really was much too cold; he'd have to have one of the repair droids look at the control system.

The hologram faded. When it was completely

gone, Rune turned to stare at Nute. "A Sith Lord, here? With us?" he said in horror.

"The Naboo Queen is coming back," Nute reminded him. "And the Jedi. Do you want to face them yourself?"

"Of course not! But —"

"The Sith Lord will take care of the Jedi," Nute said. "All we have to do is capture the Queen.

"And destroy her."

CHAPTER 18

After consulting with Captain Panaka and her handmaiden-bodyguards, Amidala decided that she would become Padmé the handmaiden again as soon as the ship came within reach of the Trade Federation. Until then, she would keep her royal clothes and face paint. She spent most of the voyage back to Naboo in her chambers, thinking about her people, her planet, and the invasion.

None of her advisors believed that returning home was a good idea. Even Qui-Gon Jinn seemed puzzled by her decision. Yet it felt right, as deeply right as defying the Trade Federation in the first place — even though she did not know what she would do when they arrived. Merely sharing her people's fate no longer seemed enough. But how could she fight the vast armies of droids that the Trade Federation possessed?

Armies . . . Jar Jar had spoken of armies. He

seemed sure that his people would fight. Perhaps if the Humans of Naboo had cooperated more with the Gungans, the Trade Federation's invasion would not have succeeded so quickly and easily. Perhaps even now, if they all cooperated . . . But that would mean starting a real war. *The Trade Federation invaded us. Talking and diplomacy haven't helped. Sometimes . . . sometimes you just have to fight back.*

Gradually, an idea took shape in her mind. It would be risky, but Tatooine and the Podrace had taught her something about taking risks. As they neared Naboo, she called her advisors together to tell them her plan.

Captain Panaka had clearly been worrying. "I still don't understand why you insisted on making this trip," he complained. "The moment we land, the Federation will arrest you and force you to sign the treaty."

"I agree," Qui-Gon said. He looked at Amidala. "I'm not sure what you hope to accomplish."

Amidala took a deep breath. "I'm going to take back what's ours."

"There are only twelve of us, Your Highness," Captain Panaka said gently. "We have no army."

Qui-Gon smiled slightly, then shook his head. "And I cannot fight a war for you, Your Highness. I can only protect you."

"I know," Amidala said. She looked over his shoulder, to where Jar Jar stood. "Jar Jar Binks!"

The Gungan looked around, as if he expected someone else to answer. "Mesa, Your Highness?"

"Yes," said Amidala firmly. This was the part she had not dared mention to anyone else until now. The Gungans and the Humans had disliked and misunderstood each other for so long — but if she could persuade Jar Jar, then perhaps she could persuade the rest of his people as well. "I need your help," she told him, and waited with bated breath for his reply.

Anakin spent most of the trip to Naboo in the cockpit with Ric Olié and Obi-Wan, asking questions about the controls. *If I can't be a Jedi, maybe I can be a pilot*, he thought. Olié told him he was a natural, and even Obi-Wan seemed to approve. They actually let him take the copilot's seat once, though there wasn't much piloting to do while the ship was in hyperspace.

Everyone grew tense as they neared Naboo, but when they came out of hyperspace at last, no Trade Federation ships hung between them and the planet. "The blockade is gone!" Captain Panaka said in surprise.

"The war's over," Obi-Wan said. "No need for it now."

"I have one battleship on my scope," Ric Olié said.

Obi-Wan glanced over and nodded. "The Droid Control Ship."

"They've probably spotted us," Captain Panaka said, and his expression grew more worried.

"We haven't much time," Obi-Wan agreed, and the next thing Anakin knew, everyone was preparing to leave the ship. As they gathered in the main hold, waiting for the spacecraft to land, Anakin saw Padmé among the Queen's handmaidens.

"Padmé!" he called joyfully, running over. *I haven't seen her since we got to Coruscant!* "Where have you been?"

"Annie!" Padmé said in surprise. "What are you doing here?"

"I'm with Qui-Gon," Anakin said, and looked down. "But . . . they're not going to let me be a Jedi. I'm too old."

"This is going to be dangerous, Annie," Padmé told him.

"Is it?" Anakin said. "I can help! Where are we going?"

"To war, I'm afraid," Padmé said with a sigh. "The Queen has had to make the most difficult decision of her life. She doesn't believe in fighting, Annie." Her voice became pensive, and she added, almost to herself, "We are a peaceful people. . . ."

"I *want* to help," Anakin assured her. He smiled. "I'm glad you're back."

The smile Padmé gave him in return was just a little

preoccupied, but Anakin was so glad to see her that he didn't care.

Ric Olié brought the Naboo Queen's Royal Starship to a smooth landing in the Gungan swamp. As soon as they were down, Obi-Wan went looking for Qui-Gon. During the voyage, there had been some coldness between them because of the argument on Coruscant. Very likely they would soon be in the middle of a war. Obi-Wan wanted to talk to Qui-Gon while he had the chance.

He found Qui-Gon staring out over the Gungan lake, as if he were waiting for the Gungan bosses to emerge from the water at any moment. "Jar Jar is on his way to the Gungan city, Master," Obi-Wan told him a little uncertainly.

Qui-Gon nodded absently. "Good."

"Do you think the Queen's idea will work?"

"The Gungans will not be easily swayed," Qui-Gon answered. "And we cannot use our power to help her." He looked sternly at Obi-Wan.

Obi-Wan hesitated. He had many things he wanted to say: That he had come to know Anakin better during the voyage, that he had begun to see the boy's potential, that he had been wrong to fear that Qui-Gon wanted to dismiss him. "I — I'm sorry for my behavior, Master," he began. "It is not my place to disagree with you about the boy. And . . . I am grateful that you think I am ready for the trials."

For a long moment, Qui-Gon looked at him. Then he smiled. "You have been a good apprentice," he said warmly. "You are much wiser than I am, Obi-Wan. I foresee you will become a great Jedi Knight."

"If I do, it will be because of what you have taught me," Obi-Wan replied.

The surface of the lake bubbled briefly. Jar Jar emerged and came to join them; by the time he arrived, everyone else had gathered, too.

"Dare-sa nobody dare," Jar Jar said. "All gone. Some kinda fight, I tink."

"Do you think they have been taken to camps?" Captain Panaka asked.

"More likely they were wiped out," Obi-Wan said. The Gungans' primitive electropoles would be little help against the blasters of the Trade Federation's droids.

"No," Jar Jar said. "Mesa no tink so. Gungans hiden. When in trouble, go to sacred place. Mackineeks no find them dare."

"Do you know where they are?" Qui-Gon asked.

Jar Jar nodded, and started off into the swamp. Obi-Wan glanced at Qui-Gon, who shrugged and followed. *I hope it's not far,* Obi-Wan thought. *We haven't much time before the Trade Federation droids come looking for us.*

CHAPTER 19

So this is Padmé's planet, Anakin thought as he sloshed through the swamp after Jar Jar. *It's very wet.* The patches of open water were even stranger than the grass-covered hillocks and the tall trees all around. He'd never seen so much water in all his life. Even the air was thick with damp. It felt like breathing soup. Cold soup.

Jar Jar stopped at last under a stand of trees that looked, to Anakin, like every other stand of trees they had passed. "Dissen it," he said, and made an odd chattering noise.

Gungan guards materialized out of the mist, riding creatures like giant, wingless birds. They took the group farther into the swamp, to the ruins of a huge building. Massive heads, carved of stone, stood among the ruins. Everything was half-buried in weeds and muck; some of the heads had sunk up to their eyes in the swamp.

More Gungans appeared all around. Several of them stood on top of one of the heads; from the way they dressed, Anakin could tell they were important. One stepped forward and looked down at the group. "Jar Jar," he said, "yousa paying dis time. Who's da uss-en others?"

The Naboo Queen stepped forward. Padmé, Captain Panaka, and the two Jedi took up positions behind her. Since Anakin had been told to stay near Qui-Gon, he stepped up beside them. *This is great,* he thought. *I can see everything!*

"I am Queen Amidala of the Naboo," the Queen said to the Gungans. "I come before you in peace."

The head Gungan snorted. "Naboo biggen. Yousa bringen da Mackineeks. Day busten uss-en omm. Yousa all bombad. Yousa all die'n, mesa tink."

Captain Panaka looked around nervously as the Gungan guards lowered their electropoles. Qui-Gon and Obi-Wan were still relaxed, though. If they weren't worried, Anakin wasn't, either. *They must have a plan.*

The Queen seemed as uneasy as Captain Panaka, but she continued, "We wish to form an alliance —"

"Your Honor!"

Anakin's head whipped around. *That was Padmé! Why is she interrupting the Queen?*

The head Gungan seemed just as puzzled as

Anakin. "Whosa dis?" he demanded as Padmé came forward to stand next to the Queen.

"I am Queen Amidala," Padmé said with dignity. She pointed at the royally dressed girl beside her and went on, "This is my decoy, my protection . . . my loyal bodyguard."

Anakin stared, openmouthed. *Padmé is the Queen? She can't be the Queen!*

"I am sorry for my deception," Padmé continued, "but under the circumstances, it has become necessary to protect myself." She paused and looked up at the Gungans. "The Trade Federation has destroyed all that we have worked so hard to build. You are in hiding; my people are in camps. I ask you to help us." She hesitated. "No, I beg you to help us."

Padmé dropped to her knees in front of the Gungans. Captain Panaka and his troops gasped, but she ignored them. "We are your humble servants," Padmé told the Gungan Council. "Our fate is in your hands."

Slowly, Captain Panaka and his men also knelt. Qui-Gon and Obi-Wan exchanged glances, then went down on one knee. Anakin joined them, still feeling stunned. *Padmé is the Queen of Naboo?*

After a moment, the head Gungan began to laugh. "Yousa no tinken yousa greater den da Gungans!" he said. "Mesa like dis. Maybe wesa bein friends."

Padmé and her troops rose to their feet, smiling. Automatically, Anakin imitated them, but he was hardly aware of what he was doing. His eyes were fixed on Padmé — *Queen Amidala. She's Queen Amidala, not Padmé. She won't have time to talk to me anymore.* He felt hollow, the way he had when he left his mother on Tatooine. Even Qui-Gon's comforting hand on his shoulder didn't help. *She's a Queen, and I'm not even going to be a Jedi. I should never have left home.*

After a brief talk with the Gungan leaders, Amidala sent Captain Panaka out to discover what had been happening on Naboo. Meanwhile, she consulted the Gungan generals. By the time Panaka returned, they had come up with a plan.

"What is the situation?" Amidala asked Captain Panaka as he joined the group.

"Almost everyone is in camps," Panaka replied. "A few hundred police and guards have formed an underground movement. I brought as many of the leaders as I could. The Federation's army is much larger than we thought. And much stronger." He hesitated. "Your Highness, this is a battle I do not think we can win."

Amidala smiled. "The battle is a diversion. The

Gungans will draw the droid army away from the cities. We can enter the city using the secret passages on the waterfall side. Once we get to the main entrance, Captain Panaka will create a diversion so that we can enter the palace and capture the viceroy. Without him, they will be lost and confused."

She turned to Qui-Gon and Obi-Wan, who had stayed silently with her ever since she had revealed her true identity. "What do you think, Master Jedi?"

"The viceroy will be well guarded," Qui-Gon pointed out.

"The difficulty is getting into the throne room," Captain Panaka said. "Once we're inside, we shouldn't have a problem."

"Many Gungans may be killed," Qui-Gon said, looking at Boss Nass.

The Gungan leader shrugged. "Wesa ready to do are-sa part."

"We will send what pilots we have to knock out the Droid Control Ship that is orbiting the planet," Amidala assured him. "If we can get past their ray shields, we can sever their communications, and the droids will be helpless." *It was my idea to bring Gungans into this; the least I can do is keep them all from dying,* she thought.

"A well-conceived plan," Qui-Gon said, nodding. "However, there's great risk. The weapons on your fighters may not penetrate the shields on the Control Ship."

"And if the viceroy escapes, Your Highness, he will return with another droid army," Obi-Wan added.

Amidala put her chin up. "That is why we must not fail to get the viceroy," she told them. "Everything depends on it."

The Trade Federation viceroy does not look happy, thought Darth Maul. But then, reporting bad news to Darth Sidious was enough to make anyone unhappy. At least his master did not seem disturbed by the news that the Queen had returned to gather an army.

"She is more foolish than I thought," was all that Darth Sidious said when Nute Gunray finished his report.

"We are sending all available troops to meet this army of hers," Gunray said. "It appears to be made up of primitives. We do not expect much resistance."

Darth Maul stirred. "I feel there is more to this, my master," he said, ignoring the dark look Nute Gunray gave him. "The two Jedi may be using the Queen for their own purposes."

"The Jedi cannot become involved," Sidious said dismissively. "They can only protect the Queen. Even Qui-Gon Jinn will not break that covenant." He paused, considering. "This will work to our advantage."

"I have your approval to proceed then, my lord?" Nute Gunray asked nervously.

"Proceed," said Darth Sidious. His mouth curled into a small smile below his dark hood. "Wipe them out. All of them."

door. As they took up their positions, Amidala saw Qui-Gon lean toward Anakin.

"Once we get inside, Annie, you find a safe place to hide," the Jedi ordered. "And stay there."

"Sure," Anakin said, a little too casually.

Qui-Gon gave him a stern look. "And *stay* there!"

Amidala hoped the boy would listen. She would never forgive herself if anything happened to Anakin. . . . Something moved in the shadows on the far side of the plaza, behind the Trade Federation tanks. Captain Panaka was in position. Raising a small laser light, she signaled to him. A moment later, his troops opened fire on the tanks.

Battle droids and tanks headed for the far side of the plaza, leaving the door to the main hangar clear. Amidala and her forces ran into the hangar and began firing at the battle droids inside. True to their orders, Obi-Wan and Qui-Gon did not attack the droids directly. They used their lightsabers only to deflect laser bolts that were aimed at Queen Amidala. But, Amidala noticed, every shot they deflected bounced back and hit a battle droid. The two Jedi were destroying more droids than all the rest of her people put together.

"Get to your ships!" Amidala commanded, and the pilots and their repair droids ran for the starfighters. *Anakin! Where's Anakin?* She blasted another battle droid into fragments of bone-white metal. *I*

The Gungan army began its march before dawn. Amidala left shortly afterward with the little group of Naboo guards, fighter pilots, and repair droids that Captain Panaka had assembled. Qui-Gon and Obi-Wan came with her, and so did Anakin Skywalker. She had abandoned her Padmé disguise completely and wore the burgundy battle uniform of the Naboo rulers.

She led her troops through the passages behind the waterfall and into the city. The streets were silent and empty. Looking at them, Amidala's lips tightened angrily. *This city belongs to my people, and the Trade Federation has taken it away from them. I was right to come back.*

Near the main hangar, the little group split up. Captain Panaka took most of the guards and slipped around to the far side of the plaza, while Amidala, the Jedi, and the pilots slipped closer to the hangar *hope he found somewhere safe, the way Qui-Gon told him to.*

As soon as the hangar door opened, Anakin ducked sideways underneath one of the fighters. It made a good hiding place for the first few minutes, but then the pilots swung up into their ships, and the ships began to take off. Anakin looked around for a better spot to hide, and Artoo-Detoo whistled at him from the rear of a nearby starfighter. Quickly, Anakin glanced around. All the pilots had ships already; this one wouldn't be going anywhere. He ran over and climbed into the cockpit.

After a moment the firing lessened. Cautiously, Anakin peeked over the edge of the cockpit. Qui-Gon, Obi-Wan, and Padmé — *Queen Amidala. She's Queen Amidala* — were heading for the exit with the rest of the Naboo guards. "Hey!" Anakin called. "Wait for me!"

"No, Annie, you stay there," Qui-Gon said as Anakin started to climb out of the fighter. "Stay right where you are."

"But I —"

"Stay in that cockpit," Qui-Gon commanded, and turned back to join the troops.

The hangar door opened. Standing in the doorway was a dark, hooded figure. The Queen's troops scattered. Obi-Wan and Qui-Gon stepped forward, tossing their cloaks aside. "We'll handle this," Qui-Gon said.

The menacing figure in the doorway also threw his cloak aside. Anakin gasped. The man's face was completely covered by a red-and-black tattoo, and instead of hair, short horns protruded from his head. As the Jedi lit their lightsabers, the newcomer pulled out one of his own. When he lit it, red bars of light appeared at both ends. *A two-sided lightsaber.* Anakin stared. The tattooed man grinned fiercely and attacked the Jedi.

Behind Anakin, Artoo whistled urgently. Anakin looked around. Six wheel droids had rolled into the far side of the hangar. As he watched, they rose into their battle positions and began firing at Pad — Queen Amidala. "Oh, no!" Anakin said. "We have to do something, Artoo!"

Artoo whistled, and the ship's systems came on. "Great idea!" Anakin said. "Let's see . . ." He turned the ship to point toward the droids and studied the controls. They were different from the ones Ric Olié had shown him on the Royal Starship, but only a little different. *Where's the trigger?* He pressed a button, and the ship shook. *Ooops, wrong one. Maybe this one?* He tried again, and this time the lasers fired. The explosion wiped out two of the destroyer droids. "Yeah, all right! Droid blaster!"

Anakin looked back over his shoulder. The Jedi

and the man with the double lightsaber were engaged in a fierce battle in the middle of the hangar. They paid no attention to the Queen and her troops, who ran quickly out a door on the far side. *She's safe!*

With Amidala gone, the wheel droids fired at Anakin. *Shields up! Shields up!* Frantically, Anakin thumbed switches, trying to remember Ric Olié's instructions. *Always on the right — shields are always on the right . . .*

Suddenly, the ship began moving. Rapidly. Artoo beeped.

"I *know* we're moving!" Anakin shouted back. "I'll shut the energy drive down." *If I can figure out which switch it is . . . that one there, that's the last one I pushed.* He pressed the button again, hoping it would shut the engine off. Instead, the fighter picked up speed. It headed out of the hangar as if it had a mind of its own. Artoo beeped worriedly.

"I'm not doing anything!" Anakin cried as the ship left the city behind and arrowed toward space.

The Gungan army made a grand sight. Hundreds of armored warriors carrying electropoles rode wingless, birdlike kaadu. Hundreds more marched along on foot. Behind them, heavy, reptilian fambaas trudged steadily forward, carrying the Gungan shield generators. Ammunition wagons carried energy balls that glowed blue through their plasma skins. Now that they were out of the swamp, the long lines of warriors and equipment were easy to see as they crossed the rolling plains.

Jar Jar was not enjoying any of it. He had fallen off his kaadu several times already, and nearly poked one of the other Gungans with his electropole. And his armor was very uncomfortable. *Mesa not goody warrior, mesa think.* But Boss Nass had decided to make him one of the Gungan generals. Now Jar Jar was stuck in the forefront of the Gungan army with General Ceel and the other Gungan leaders. *Mesa not liking this.*

Someone shouted. Jar Jar looked up and saw a row of enormous tanks drawn up on a low ridge in front of the army. *Oie boie. Now wesa starting.*

"Energize the shields!" called General Ceel.

The fambaas plodded forward, each carrying a large generator. Red rays shot out of the generators toward a large dishlike amplifier carried by another fambaa. The amplifier spread the rays out into a protective umbrella, completely covering the Gungan army.

It was just in time. The Trade Federation tanks opened fire just as the energy shield was completed. Jar Jar and the Gungans around him cheered as the shield absorbed the blasts.

The tanks stopped firing and moved aside. Giant

transports moved forward. Their doors opened, and racks of battle droids unfolded. The Gungan army went silent, watching the thousands of droids assemble and march toward them.

At General Ceel's command, the line of Gungans threw their electropoles like spears, knocking over some droids and shorting out others. Jar Jar didn't see whether his actually hit anything, but he hoped it had. With their poles gone, some of the Gungans used slingshots to throw balls of energy at the droids. Others loaded larger gobs of energy goo into mortars that fired into the center of the mob of battle droids.

Jar Jar charged forward as the battle droids reached the energy shield. The next few minutes were very confused, with droids firing and Gungans firing back. Somehow, Jar Jar found himself tangled in the remains of a half-destroyed battle droid. Its blaster was still firing, so Jar Jar tried to keep it pointed at the other droids while he worked himself free; he was a general, after all, so he'd better not shoot any of his own troops.

When he got untangled at last, he looked up and saw wheel droids rolling out of the transports toward the battle. Hundreds of wheel droids. *Thissen very, very bad*, he thought.

Then the wheel droids attacked.

* * *

Obi-Wan had never been in such a lightsaber battle before. *So this is a Sith Lord,* he thought fleetingly as he dodged and leaped. It was taking every skill he knew just to stay alive. The Sith Lord seemed to cloud Obi-Wan's use of the Force, making it hard to sense his opponent's moves and counter them in time.

Slowly, the Sith Lord forced Qui-Gon and Obi-Wan back. Out of the hangar and down a long hall they fought, then on into the Theed power generator plant. The Sith Lord leaped from one service catwalk to another, and the two Jedi followed. Qui-Gon was in the lead now, taking the brunt of the attacks. The narrow bridge gave them little room to maneuver. Obi-Wan tried to close in on their opponent, but the Sith Lord twisted and kicked him off the catwalk.

The bridge just below was out of reach. Obi-Wan fell several levels before he landed on another ramp. He looked up, searching for the quickest way to get back to the fight. His Master and the Sith Lord had moved farther along the catwalk. As he watched, Qui-Gon knocked the Sith off the bridge.

The Sith Lord landed heavily two levels down. Qui-Gon leaped after him, but the Sith picked himself up and backed through a small doorway. Obi-Wan ran forward as Qui-Gon darted after their opponent. As he reached the door, a series of laser walls went up all along the hallway on the other side — deadly force fields designed to keep unauthorized people and droids out of the area. Obi-Wan peered down the corridor. There were four laser walls between him and Qui-Gon, and five between Obi-Wan and the Sith Lord.

Through the sheets of laser fire, Obi-Wan saw Qui-Gon calmly sit and begin to meditate. He tried not to think about just how badly his Master might need that rest. After the fight on Tatooine, Qui-Gon had been nearly exhausted. Impatiently, Obi-Wan paced along the edge of the laser wall. It would go down again in a minute or two, and the fight would begin again. *The Sith Lord can't get much farther; there shouldn't be anything at the end of this hall except a melting pit. I'll be able to catch up as soon as the laser walls go down.*

He refused to consider what might happen if he didn't.

CHAPTER 21

The palace was full of battle droids. Amidala and her troops blasted several groups of them, but there always seemed to be more. "We don't have time for this!" she cried in frustration as they came around a corner to find more battle droids.

"Let's try outside," Captain Panaka said. Turning, he shot out one of the windows. Amidala, Panaka, and about half the troops climbed through; the others, and the Queen's handmaidens, stayed in the hall to hold off the battle droids.

The Trade Federation didn't seem to be watching the outside of the palace. Amidala and her forces fired cables from their ascension guns and hauled themselves up. It was a little tricky, but much easier than fighting off hordes of battle droids. In a few minutes, they had reached the level of the throne room. Panaka shot out another window, and Amidala and the others climbed through into a hallway. The door to the throne room was at the far end. *We've almost made it. . . .*

Suddenly, two destroyer droids appeared on either side of the throne room door. Amidala turned and saw two more at the opposite end of the hall. They were trapped. *Battle droids we can fight, but these — our weapons will get through their shields eventually, but by then, they'll have shot most of us.* Amidala dropped her laser pistol. "Throw down your weapons," she said to Captain Panaka. "They win this round."

"But we can't —"

"Captain, I said throw down your weapons." Amidala stared at him until he and his troops dropped their pistols. The destroyer droids moved forward to escort them into the throne room.

The wheel droids rolled through the Gungan army's energy shield, reshaped themselves into their battle configuration, and began blasting. One of them hit a shield generator. The generator exploded, killing the fambaa that had been carrying it, along with several Gungans.

Uh-oh, Jar Jar thought, looking up. The protective shield wavered and began to fall apart.

"Retreat!" shouted General Ceel.

Jar Jar was only too happy to comply. With the rest of the Gungans, he turned and ran. Glancing back, he saw tanks moving up behind the destroyer droids. The Trade Federation droid general had lost no time in taking advantage of the weakened shield. In another moment, the tanks were in among the Gungans, firing steadily.

One of the explosions lifted Jar Jar off the kaadu he was riding. He shrieked as he flew through the air . . . and landed on top of one of the tanks. The tank swung its gun around, trying to knock Jar Jar off, but he clung to the barrel. *At least thisen not shooting Gungans righty now,* he thought. *Oie boie, what mesa thinking? Mesa getting killed here!*

A Gungan warrior rode his kaadu up beside the tank and signaled. Gratefully, Jar Jar jumped down behind him. *Maybe mesa not dying yet, hey?* Another tank shot exploded close by, and Jar Jar flinched. But there were explosions everywhere now.

That Queen saying her pilots stopping the droids, Jar Jar thought. *Mesa hoping they hurry. Or wesa losing bombad.*

The starfighter, with Anakin inside, continued to rise. Artoo beeped worriedly.

"The autopilot is *what?*" Anakin replied. He studied the controls. "There *is* no manual override, Artoo! You'll have to rewire it or something."

Artoo beeped that he was trying. Anakin looked up. Ahead, he could see the sharp golden Naboo starfighters buzzing like wasps around a large, circular battleship. *That must be the Trade Federation's Droid Control Ship.* Clouds of droid starfighters had emerged from the Trade Federation ship and were attacking the Naboo craft. And the autopilot was taking them straight into the battle.

"Artoo!" Anakin screamed. "Get us off autopilot!"

Artoo screeched an answer. Hoping it was positive, Anakin flipped a switch and tried the controls. This time, the ship responded. "Yes! I've got control. You did it, Artoo!" Frantically, he pulled on the controls, dodging shots and enemy fighters. *As long as I'm up here, maybe I can get one of them. That'd be something to tell Pad — Queen Amidala!*

But figuring out the strange controls in the middle of a battle was not easy. As much by luck as skill, Anakin dodged and ducked and avoided the Trade Federation droid ships. *Or maybe the Force is with me — maybe that's . . . whoops!* A shot whizzed by, narrowly missing him. Artoo shrieked.

"I *know* this isn't Podracing, Artoo!" Anakin said, just as another shot connected with his ship, sending it into a spin. Anakin struggled to regain control as the ship headed straight for the Trade Federation space station.

Desperately, he hauled on the steering. The ship responded sluggishly. *I'm going to smash into the Droid Control Ship! Wait — there's an opening.*

Anakin aimed for it, trying to kill his momentum. It wouldn't do any good to dodge into the opening if he smashed into a wall on the inside.

The opening was some sort of ship hangar. Anakin had to dodge droids and transports. At last he found the right switch, and the reverse thrusters fired. The crippled starfighter skidded to a stop just short of the rear wall. Anakin heaved a sigh of relief and bent to examine the control panel. "Everything's overheated, Artoo. All the lights are red."

Artoo's answering beep sounded frantic. Cautiously, Anakin peered over the edge of the cockpit. *Battle droids! Lots of battle droids. This is not good.* He ducked back down, wondering how long it would take Artoo to fix the ship.

The deadly laser walls cycled off, and Obi-Wan sprinted down the hall. Ahead, he could see Qui-Gon, already battling the Sith Lord. The two fighters circled the melting pit, aiming terrible blows at each other. *I will make it in time. . . .*

Something flickered at the edge of his vision; the laser walls behind him were closing. Obi-Wan flung himself forward — but not quite far enough. The last laser wall flickered into being just in front of him, so close that he nearly ran straight into the deadly rays. *No!* he thought, but it was too late. He was trapped again, just short of the battle, unable to help Qui-Gon.

Obi-Wan stared through the laser wall. For just an instant, Qui-Gon's opponent seemed to be wearing a black helmet, and Obi-Wan felt a cold chill. *This is wrong, this is all wrong. I'm supposed to be the one fighting the Dark Lord.* Obi-Wan shook his head, trying to clear it. The Sith Lord wasn't wearing a helmet; it was only the light of the laser walls on the black of his tattoo. And Qui-Gon was fighting more fiercely than Obi-Wan had ever seen him fight before. Yet the feeling persisted: *That should be me out there, not Qui-Gon.* Obi-Wan shook his head again. *Won't these laser walls ever come down again?*

Qui-Gon blocked one awful stroke and parried another, then struck back. The Sith Lord blocked — and then slammed the wide handle of his lightsaber into Qui-Gon's chin. Qui-Gon staggered backward, half-dazed from the force of the unexpected blow. The Sith Lord grinned in triumph. Reversing his lightsaber, he struck Qui-Gon through.

Qui-Gon crumpled to the floor.

"NO!" Obi-Wan screamed. The sound echoed strangely, almost as if some other voice had joined his in crying out the same desperate denial. But the laser wall was down at last, and Obi-Wan had no more time for thinking. He leaped forward to face the Sith Lord.

Alone.

CHAPTER 22

The Neimoidian viceroy was waiting inside the throne room with more battle droids. Amidala looked at him with dislike, and he smiled.

"Your little insurrection is at an end, Your Highness," he said smugly. "Time for you to sign the treaty —"

The door opened again. Sabé appeared, dressed in a uniform identical to Amidala's and wearing royal makeup. Behind her, Amidala could see the ruins of several destroyer droids, and she felt a surge of new hope.

The Neimoidian looked uncertainly from Amidala to her double. Sabé called, "I will not be signing any treaty, Viceroy! You've lost!" Turning, she vanished down the hall.

"After her!" the viceroy shouted. "This one's a decoy!"

As most of the droids rushed out of the room, Amidala crossed slowly to her throne. The viceroy turned back to her. "Your Queen will not get away with this!" he said.

Amidala sank down on the throne as if overcome . . . and pressed the security button. The hidden panel in her desk slid open — and the laser pistols were still inside! She tossed two to Captain Panaka and another officer, then snatched a third for herself and blasted the last of the battle droids.

One of her officers ran toward the open door — *no, toward the door control panel. Good idea.* Amidala hit the switch on her desk that closed the door, and the officer jammed the controls. For the moment, they were safe. "Viceroy, this is the end of your occupation," she said fiercely.

"Don't be absurd," the viceroy said, though he was plainly frightened. "There are too few of you. It won't be long before hundreds of destroyer droids break in here to rescue us."

Not if my pilots blow up your Control Ship, Amidala thought. But they hadn't succeeded yet, or the destroyer droids wouldn't be active. *What's keeping them?*

The lights on Anakin's control panel were still red. "The system's still overheated, Artoo," he said softly, hoping the astromech droid would hear . . . and the battle droids surrounding his starfighter wouldn't.

"Where's your pilot?" a mechanical voice outside the ship demanded.

They haven't seen me! Anakin thought as Artoo whistled a reply.

"*You're* the pilot?" the battle droid said skeptically. "Let me see your identification!"

The lights on the control panel blinked green. "Yes!" Anakin cried, and started the engine.

"You!" the battle droid called. "Come out of there or we'll blast you!"

"Not if I can help it!" Anakin retorted, flipping the switch to raise his shields.

More battle droids were arriving through the open door at the end of the hangar. *This should stop them!* Anakin fired, first his lasers, then the ship's torpedoes. The lasers hit, but the torpedoes flew over the heads of the droids and through the wide-open doors behind them.

"Darn it, I missed," Anakin muttered. A moment later, he heard an explosion as the torpedoes went off somewhere inside the Droid Control Ship. Through the doors, he caught a glimpse of a large, unidentifiable object beginning to come apart. *At least I did some damage!* "Come on, Artoo. Let's get out of here!"

Swinging the ship around, Anakin gunned the engines. The starfighter roared through the hangar and back out into space, just ahead of a sheet of flame. "Now, this is Podracing!" Anakin shouted. "Whoopee!"

Behind him, the Droid Control Ship began to shake. Fire burst from its ports and windows as it slowly exploded from the inside out. Anakin grinned. *I wish Padmé had seen that!*

Trade Federation battle droids had rounded up the Gungan army. The officers were the first to be captured. "Disa bad," Jar Jar said to General Ceel as they watched. "Berry bombad."

"Mesa hopen dissa working for da Queen," the general replied.

Abruptly, all of the droids paused. Some began to shake. Others ran in circles. A few of the flying machines crashed. Then, suddenly, they all stopped moving completely.

The Gungans stared in frozen surprise. When the droids stayed motionless, the Gungans came slowly forward. Jar Jar pushed one of the battle droids. Like a wobbly statue, it fell over.

"Weirding," Jar Jar said. *The Queen be keeping her promise*, he thought. *Looks like wesa winning after all.*

The Sith Lord attacked Obi-Wan relentlessly, backing him around the melting pit. All Obi-Wan's efforts could not break through his guard. And Obi-Wan was tiring, while his opponent seemed as fresh as ever.

Halfway around the melting pit, Obi-Wan dodged a vicious swing. The Sith Lord was on him before he could recover his balance. With a mighty stroke, the Sith knocked the young Jedi into the melting pit.

Time seemed to slow. Obi-Wan could hear the voices of his teachers in his memory: Qui-Gon saying over and over, *Trust the living Force, my young Padawan*, and Master Yoda, long ago, commanding, *Do, or do not. There is no try.* And now, for this moment, he understood. As he twisted to grab one of the input nozzles on the side of the pit, he thought dreamily, *That's what I have been doing wrong. I've been trying.*

On the walkway, the Sith Lord looked down at him, grinning evilly. With deliberate malice, he kicked Obi-Wan's lightsaber into the melting pit and watched it fall. Then he raised his lightsaber for the kill.

At the last minute, Obi-Wan flipped himself back up onto the walkway. Using the Force, he called Qui-Gon's lightsaber to him. The weapon slapped into his hand as he landed. The unexpected move caught the Sith Lord off guard. Smoothly, without trying, resting in the living Force, Obi-Wan swung his Master's lightsaber. The Sith Lord tried to parry, but he could not get his weapon around in time. He screamed and fell into the melting pit. Obi-Wan felt the tremor in the Force as he died.

Turning off the lightsaber, Obi-Wan ran back to Qui-Gon. "Master!"

"It is too late," Qui-Gon said in a voice filled with pain. "It's —"

"No!"

"Obi-Wan, promise —" Qui-Gon fought to get the words out. Obi-Wan could feel the effort he was making not to give in to the call of the Force. "Promise me you'll train the boy."

"Yes, Master."

Qui-Gon's face had a gray undertone, and his voice was growing fainter. Someone outside was cheering, and Obi-Wan had to lean closer to hear what his Master was saying. "He is the chosen one," Qui-Gon said. "He will . . . bring balance . . ." He gasped. "Train him!"

As the distant sounds of celebration grew louder, Obi-Wan felt the last breath leave Qui-Gon's body. He wanted to deny it, to refuse to believe, so that he could pretend to have even one more moment with the man who had been the only father he had ever known, but he could not. Weeping quietly, Obi-Wan knelt beside his dead Master, while outside the citizens of Naboo rejoiced in their sudden victory.

CHAPTER ㉓

The following day, word came that the new Supreme Chancellor of the Galactic Republic would be arriving soon. *Better late than never,* Queen Amidala thought, although she had to admit that she would have been glad indeed to see him if her plans had failed.

The cruiser landed in the courtyard in front of the main hangar. Amidala had her troops bring the two Neimoidians, Nute Gunray and Rune Haako, to meet the ship. As they waited for the entrance ramp to be lowered, she turned to Gunray and said, "Now, Viceroy, you are going to have to go back to the Senate and explain all this."

"I think you can kiss your trade franchise goodbye," Captain Panaka added with considerable satisfaction.

The ramp opened at last. Obi-Wan and Panaka led the Neimoidians toward the ship as the new arrivals disembarked. First came Supreme Chancellor Palpatine, followed by several Republic guards. After them, a number of beings in Jedi robes came down the ramp. Obi-Wan stopped to talk to them.

Amidala moved forward to greet Palpatine. "Congratulations on your election, Chancellor," she said warmly. "It is so good to see you again."

"It is good to be home," Chancellor Palpatine said, smiling. "But it is you who should be congratulated. Your boldness has saved our people."

But many died, Amidala thought sadly. *Many of my people, and many Gungans. And Qui-Gon Jinn.* That news had hurt more than she would have believed possible.

"Tomorrow, we will celebrate our victory," she told the Chancellor. "Tonight . . . tonight we will grieve for those who are no longer here to celebrate."

The afternoon was a busy one. Obi-Wan spoke with Yoda and the other Jedi Masters, describing the battle with the Sith Lord in detail. When he finished, Mace Windu frowned. "There is no doubt. The mysterious warrior was a Sith."

"Always two there are," Master Yoda said pensively. "No more, no less. A master and an apprentice."

Master Windu nodded. "But which one was destroyed — the master, or the apprentice?"

No one had an answer. *But either way, there's still one of them out there,* Obi-Wan thought. *And if that was an apprentice, I hope I never have to face the master.*

When the discussion ended at last, Obi-Wan made his request — that once he passed the trials and became a full-fledged Jedi Knight, he be allowed to take Qui-Gon's place as Anakin Skywalker's Master. *I can never take his place, not really. But I can train Anakin.* The Masters looked thoughtful, and went off to confer in private. Late in the day, they summoned him again.

To Obi-Wan's surprise, only Master Yoda waited in the many-windowed room. He knelt and waited for the Jedi Master to speak. Master Yoda paced back and forth several times before turning to say abruptly, "Confer on you the level of Jedi Knight, the Council does." He frowned. "But agree with your taking this boy as your Padawan learner, I do not!"

"Qui-Gon believed in him," Obi-Wan said steadily. "I believe in Qui-Gon."

Yoda resumed his pacing. "The chosen one, the boy may be. Nevertheless, grave danger I fear in his training."

A shiver ran down Obi-Wan's spine, but he raised his head. "Master Yoda, I gave Qui-Gon my word. I *will* train Anakin. Without the approval of the Council, if I must."

"Qui-Gon's defiance I sense in you," Yoda said. "Need that, you do not!" He sighed. "Agree, the Council does. Your apprentice, young Skywalker will be."

Anakin stood staring at the funeral pyre. Everyone was here — Queen Amidala, Captain Panaka and his troops, Jar Jar and the Gungan leaders, Chancellor Palpatine, and the entire Jedi Council. Anakin looked around at them all, once, and then his eyes came back to the pyre where Qui-Gon's body burned. *He told me that if I stayed near him, I would be safe.* He sniffed, and rubbed the back of his hand against his nose. *I've lost everybody — Mom, Padmé, all my friends at home, and now Qui-Gon.*

Hands touched his shoulders, and he looked up. Obi-Wan looked gravely down at him. "He is one with the Force, Anakin," the Jedi said. "You must let go."

"What will happen to me now?" Anakin asked. Even to himself, he sounded forlorn.

"I am your Master now," Obi-Wan said solemnly.

Anakin looked up, startled. *Master? Not just guardian?* He felt hope rising. *I get to be a Jedi after all?*

As if he could read Anakin's thoughts, Obi-Wan smiled and nodded. "You will become a Jedi. I promise."

Comforted, Anakin stared into the flames. *I'll work hard to become a great Jedi,* he swore silently to Qui-Gon as the sparks of the funeral pyre rose into the night sky. *I'll make you proud of me.*

I'll make you both proud.

EPISODE II

ATTACK OF THE CLONES™

Patricia C. Wrede
Based on the story by George Lucas and the screenplay
by George Lucas and Jonathan Hales

A *long time ago in a galaxy far, far away . . .*
   For generations, the Jedi Knights had kept peace
among the many worlds of the Galactic Republic.
They did not make the laws — that was the task of
the Galactic Senate. The Jedi merely enforced them.
Sometimes they negotiated; sometimes they used their
awesome fighting skills; sometimes they used the mysterious power of the Force. Their methods had been
extremely effective. For a thousand generations, there
had been no major war in the galaxy. Only a few
planets had experienced severe conflicts.
   One of these planets was the small, watery world
of Naboo. During an argument over taxing trade
routes, the powerful Trade Federation landed a huge
droid army on Naboo. The recently elected Queen
of Naboo, young Padmé Amidala, refused to surrender. Her heroism and the efforts of the Jedi
brought a quick end to the conflict, but many of the
Naboo people had been hurt or killed.

The experience left a strong impression on Padmé. When she finished her two terms of office as Queen, she did not retire from politics. Instead, at the urging of the new Queen, she ran for the office of Galactic Senator, and became Naboo's representative. In the Senate, she was a strong voice for peace.

Such a voice was much needed. The Senate had become large and choked with bureaucracy. Many people were frustrated; some even talked of leaving the Republic and forming their own government. These Separatists were not a serious threat until Count Dooku, a former Jedi Knight, brought them together under his leadership.

The Separatist movement made it difficult for the limited number of Jedi Knights to continue to maintain peace. As the Jedi's task grew harder, more and more star systems joined the Separatists. Many in the Senate feared that if the Separatists refused to see reason, there would be war — and everyone knew that there were too few Jedi to keep the peace. For the first time in a thousand generations the Senate had to vote on whether to create an army.

Tension rose as those who feared the chaos caused by the Separatists clashed with those who feared that creating an army would destroy all hope for peace. Senator Padmé Amidala was one of the leaders fighting to prevent the creation of an army. Her passion and her commitment to peace, strengthened during the brief invasion of Naboo ten years earlier, made her arguments very convincing when she spoke to the Senate. More than one of the Senators who favored creating an army would have been glad to see Padmé disappear for good.

Padmé knew the danger, but her sense of duty was strong, and her love of peace was stronger. As the time for the final decision drew near, she headed for Coruscant to cast her vote against the Military Creation Act.

CHAPTER ①

Senator Padmé Amidala stared out the main window of her spacecraft at the approaching planet. *Even from space, Coruscant looks different from other worlds,* she thought. Most worlds showed colors on their daylight side — the greens of the forest worlds, the blues of watery planets, the glittering white of ice worlds, the sandy yellow of desert planets like Tatooine. On their night side, most planets were dark, with an occasional twinkle of light marking the largest cities.

Coruscant's day side was a dull, metallic gray, the color of the millions of buildings and platforms that covered its entire surface. Its night side glowed amber from the lights of those same buildings, like the stars of the galaxy in miniature. *Only on Coruscant is night more attractive than day,* Padmé thought.

The royal Naboo cruiser and its three fighter escorts curved around Coruscant toward their assigned landing platform. Padmé hadn't wanted the escorts, but her security officer had insisted that she was in danger. Captain Typho was good at his job, so she had reluctantly agreed. Since the trip had been uneventful, she already regretted giving in.

The three lobes of the landing platform came in sight. The royal cruiser landed on the center leaf. The three fighters took the other leaves, two to one side and one to the other. Captain Typho, who had been piloting one of the fighters, swung out of his cockpit and removed his helmet.

"We made it," he said. "I guess I was wrong; there was no danger at all."

Padmé hardly heard him. On the platform, she could see Dormé, one of her handmaiden-bodyguards, waiting among the landing crew. Dormé looked tired and tense. *She's just worried*, Padmé thought. *She can't know how easy the trip was.*

The cruiser's ramp lowered. Padmé's guards came down first, then the rest of the Senatorial party. As they reached the foot of the ramp, the ground crew watched their arrival.

In the next instant, something knocked Padmé flat. Through the roaring in her ears, she heard cries of terror. She choked and blinked to clear the dark afterimage from her eyes — the image of the royal cruiser exploding. *Captain Typho was right after all*, she thought, and then, *Cordé! Is Cordé all right?*

She was still a little breathless from her fall, but she could not wait. She shoved herself to her feet and ran toward the wreckage. At the foot of the ramp lay several crumpled figures; one was Cordé, the decoy double who had been pretending to be Senator Amidala . . . pretending much too successfully for her own good.

Padmé ripped off her pilot's helmet and gathered Cordé in her arms. "Cordé . . ."

Cordé's eyes opened. She stared blankly at Padmé for an instant, then seemed to recognize her. "I'm sorry, M'lady," she gasped weakly. "I'm . . . not sure I . . . I've failed you, Senator."

Failed? No! But before she could speak the words, Padmé felt the life leave Cordé. She gathered her decoy's body close, as if she could call her back by sheer force of will. "No," she whispered. "No!" *Not now, not here, not when we were safe on Coruscant.*

But Coruscant was not safe. Captain Typho had thought that any attack would come during the trip, when an assassin would have all of space in which to flee. That was why he had insisted that Padmé pilot one of the fighters instead of relying solely on her double. "A decoy is no help if you're standing right next to it," he'd told her. "As long as you're on board, anyone who attacks the cruiser will attack you, even if Cordé is playing the Senator. You have to be somewhere else." So she had been, and now Cordé had died, just when they should all have been able to stop worrying at last.

As if in echo of her thoughts, Padmé heard Captain Typho's voice beside her saying urgently, "M'lady . . . you are still in danger here."

Gently, Padmé lowered Cordé — Cordé's body — to the ground. She looked up and saw other motionless bodies: two of her guards, another handmaiden. She swallowed hard and forced her eyes to move onto the twisted wreckage of the starship. *The cruiser's pilot was still on board, and others . . . how many others?* Tears stung her eyes. "I shouldn't have come back," she murmured, half to herself.

"This vote is very important," Typho reminded her. "You did your duty — and Cordé did hers. Now come."

Padmé hesitated, blinking the tears away. The least she could do was to see these people clearly, these people who had given their lives for her. *I will not let their sacrifice be in vain,* she promised silently. *There WILL be peace.*

"Senator Amidala, please!"

Captain Typho's voice sounded desperate as well as urgent. He was right again; she should go. Padmé took a last look around, printing the picture of the wreckage on her memory. Then she turned and fell into step beside him. Behind her, she heard a small whimpering noise from her faithful droid, R2-D2, but she did not turn. She had work to do.

It took longer than Padmé had expected to change and get to the Senate chamber. By the time she and her escorts arrived, most of the flying platforms that covered the walls of the vast arena were occupied and the session had started. Padmé heard one of the Senators shouting as she entered her platform.

". . . needs more security now! Before it comes to war."

Padmé craned her neck. The speaker was Orn Free Taa, the fat, blue-skinned Twi'leck Senator who was one of the biggest supporters of the Military Creation Act.

"Must I remind the Senator that negotiations are continuing with the Separatists?" Chancellor Palpatine said firmly. Padmé found it hard to understand how he could remain so calm in the face of such constant provocation, but somehow Palpatine always seemed unaffected by the angry shouting around him. "Peace is our objective here," the Chancellor went on, "not war."

As the Senators shouted responses to the Chancellor's comments, Padmé flicked the controls of her platform, setting it in motion. Deftly, she maneuvered around the other platforms already hovering near the center of the arena. As she passed them, she noted the occupants of the other pods — Ask Aak of Malastare, Darsana of Glee Anselm, and, of course, Orn Free Taa, all supporters of the bill. It was a good thing she had arrived when she did.

"My noble colleagues, I concur with the Supreme Chancellor!" Padmé said as soon as she reached the speaking area. "At all costs, we do not want war!"

To Padmé's surprise, a stunned silence fell over the entire Senate. A moment later, cheers and applause sounded from every platform. Even Orn Free Taa and Ask Aak joined in, though with less enthusiasm.

"It is with great surprise and joy that the chair recognizes the Senator from Naboo, Padmé Amidala," said Chancellor Palpatine. The unusual emotion in his voice told Padmé what had happened.

They must have heard about the explosion, Padmé thought. Well, perhaps she could use the attack to show them just how important this bill was. "Less than an hour ago, an assassination attempt was made against my life," she began. "One of my bodyguards and six others were ruthlessly and senselessly murdered." Her voice wavered as she remembered Cordé, but she forced herself on. She *must* show them how important it was to avoid war.

"I was the target," Padmé continued, "but more important I believe this security measure before you was the target. I have led the opposition to build an army . . . but there is someone in this body who will stop at nothing to assure its passage."

Some of the Senators booed. Padmé kept her face calm with the skill of long practice, but inwardly she was dismayed to see how many of her colleagues were slipping toward supporting the army bill. "I warn you," she said, "if you vote to create this army, war will follow. I have experienced the misery of war firsthand; I do not wish to do it again.

"Wake up, Senators!" Padmé cried over the rising shouts from other platforms. "You must wake up! If we offer the Separatists violence, they can only show us violence in return!" With growing passion, she pleaded with the Senators to reject the "security measure," but the response was a chorus of groans and boos.

Orn Free Taa moved his platform next to hers and addressed the Chancellor. "My motion to defer the vote must be dealt with first. That is the rule of law."

Padmé glared at him. From the central podium, Chancellor Palpatine gave her a sympathetic look, but his voice was as firm as it had been when he rebuked Ask Aak earlier. "Due to the lateness of the hour and the seriousness of this motion we will take up these matters tomorrow. Until then, the Senate stands adjourned."

What is he doing? Padmé thought as she maneuvered her platform back toward its docking place. *Is he so sure that we will lose the vote?*

A small viewscreen on the platform pinged, announcing a message. Padmé looked down. The

Chancellor was asking her to a private meeting in his office. Perhaps she would get some answers there.

Chancellor Palpatine's office, high in a skyscraper overlooking the Senate building, was vast but comfortable. The deep-cushioned blue sofa that faced the Chancellor's desk was wide enough and low enough to accommodate almost any life-form in the Republic with ease. Thick rugs covered the floor; tall windows let in light from every direction. The two royal guards, flanking the door in their new red robes and helmets, stood out against the soothing background, a reminder of both the power and the danger of the Chancellor's position.

Yoda approved of the windows, but the rest failed to impress him. Earned it, the Chancellor certainly had — no one could say he had not worked hard for the Republic and for peace. But Jedi preferred simpler surroundings, though none of the senior members of the Jedi Council who had come to discuss the situation with Chancellor Palpatine would ever have said so. The luxury made Yoda's ears twitch.

"I don't know how much longer I can hold off the vote, my friends," the Chancellor told the four Jedi facing him. His soft voice sounded tired. "More and more star systems are joining the Separatists."

And the Senators grew more afraid, and the more fearful they grew, the worse the situation became. *Fear feeds the dark side*, Yoda thought sadly. The clearest example of the spreading chaos was the explosion of Senator Amidala's space cruiser. *Seen it, we should have — seen it and prevented it.* But the Jedi had not seen, and now many lives had been lost and the fear among the Senators grew as the Separatists threatened to break away and perhaps start a civil war.

"If they do break away —" Mace Windu began reluctantly.

"I will not let this Republic that has stood for a thousand years be split in two!" Palpatine interrupted. "My negotiations will not fail!"

Afraid, the Chancellor is not, Yoda thought. He could sense the fearful emotions of the Senators, reflected in the Force, even at a distance. But from Palpatine he felt nothing but determination and confidence. Yet everyone knew that the Chancellor's best efforts had only delayed the Military Creation Act, not stopped it.

Mace Windu looked at Palpatine with a grave expression, and continued where he had left off. "But *if* they do, you must realize there aren't enough Jedi to protect the Republic. We are keepers of the peace, not soldiers." Beside him, Ki-Adi-Mundi nodded agreement.

Palpatine stared at them for a moment, then turned. "Master Yoda, do you think it will really come to war?"

Yoda closed his eyes and folded his long, flexible

ears down, the better to feel the future shifting of the Force. The dark side hung like a thick fog over everything, hiding even the near events that usually were so clear, and growing more dense the further ahead he tried to look. Lightsabers flashed blue and green in the fog, but few, too few, and he caught more and more glimpses of a glowing red that no Jedi would ever wield. "Worse than war, I fear," he murmured. "Much worse."

"What?" Palpatine demanded.

"What do you sense, Master?" Mace Windu asked almost simultaneously.

"The dark side clouds everything," Yoda said, shaking his head. "Impossible to see, the future is. But this I am sure of —" He opened his eyes. "Do their duty, the Jedi will."

The other Jedi looked at him, considering, while Palpatine turned to answer a buzzer on his desk. Yoda looked back, unsmiling. He had seen the Republic weather many crises during his near nine hundred years as a Jedi, but this one — this one was different. Never had the dark side felt so strong.

The office door opened. Even before the delegation of loyalist Senators entered, Yoda felt a familiar presence. Smiling a little sadly, he rose and moved forward to greet Senator Padmé Amidala. It was like her to insist on returning to work at once, despite the attempt on her life and the deaths among her crew.

Though her face was calm, Yoda could sense her grief. He spoke directly to it. "Padmé, your tragedy on the landing platform, terrible."

Padmé gave a tiny nod, as if she could not bear to speak.

"With you, the Force is strong, young Senator," Yoda went on, tapping her lightly with his cane. "To see you alive brings warm feelings to my heart."

"Thank you, Master Yoda," Padmé replied softly. She looked up at the other Jedi and asked, "Do you have any idea who was behind this attack?"

"Our intelligence points to disgruntled spice miners on the moons of Naboo," Mace Windu told her.

Padmé frowned. "I don't wish to disagree, but I think that Count Dooku was behind it."

Even Padmé's security officer looked startled by this announcement; apparently the young Senator had not told him of her theory. The other Senators murmured among themselves, except for Bail Organa, who studied Padmé thoughtfully. Mace Windu and Ki-Adi-Mundi exchanged glances. Then Mace said gently, "You know, M'lady, Count Dooku was once a Jedi. He wouldn't assassinate anyone. It's not in his character."

"In dark times, nothing is what it appears to be," Yoda put in before the young Senator could say anything rash. He looked at his colleagues and twitched his ears reprovingly. They should know better than to make assumptions, and in any case, this was no time to start an argument about the character of a former Jedi. Besides, they were drifting from the most important point. "The fact remains for certain, Senator: in grave danger you are."

Padmé's frown deepened. Chancellor Palpatine studied her for a moment, then rose and went to the window. Looking out over the city, he said, "Master Jedi, may I suggest that the Senator be placed under the protection of your graces?"

"Do you think that is a wise decision during these stressful times?" Bail Organa asked, glancing at Padmé.

"Chancellor," Padmé said, sounding slightly put out, "if I may comment, I do not believe the situation —"

" — is that serious." Chancellor Palpatine picked up the sentence and finished it for her. "No, but I do, Senator."

"Chancellor, please!" Padmé looked appalled. "I don't want any more guards!"

The Chancellor gave her a mildly reproving glance. "I realize all too well that additional security might be disruptive for you, but perhaps someone you are familiar with . . ." He paused for a moment, his expression thoughtful. Then he smiled. "An old friend, like . . . Master Kenobi?" He nodded inquiringly at Mace Windu.

"That's possible," Mace replied slowly. "He has just returned from a border dispute on Ansion."

"You must remember him, M'lady," Palpatine said, turning back to Padmé. "He watched over you during the blockade conflict."

"This is not necessary, Chancellor!" Padmé insisted.

"Do it for me, M'lady, please," Palpatine almost begged. "I will rest easier. We had a big scare today. The thought of losing you is unbearable."

Padmé sighed and nodded.

"I will have Obi-Wan report to you immediately, M'lady," Mace Windu said gravely. He and Ki-Adi-Mundi rose to leave.

Yoda paused before following them. Something more was needed. He studied Padmé, who was biting her lip in evident frustration, then leaned in close to her ear. "Too little about yourself you worry, Senator, and too much about politics."

Padmé looked at him, startled. Yoda smiled slightly. "Be mindful of your danger, Padmé. Accept our help."

As they left the Chancellor's office, Yoda was pleased to see Padmé looking thoughtful instead of annoyed. Her heart was good, but too often did she act on impulse. Better she would do if she stopped to think, and let wisdom guide her passion.

The hydrolift door slid open, letting in a wash of cool, damp air. *Of course*, thought Anakin. *Padmé has set the climate to feel like Naboo.* In the past ten years, he had grown accustomed to worlds that were too cold and too damp — after growing up on Tatooine, nearly everywhere else felt too cold and too damp to him. But *this* damp cold was different. It reminded him of his first spaceship flight, aboard the royal Naboo cruiser, when Padmé had found him shivering in the main room in the middle of the night. She had covered him with her overjacket . . . he could still remember the faint scent on the red silk. He shook himself and followed Master Obi-Wan out of the lift.

Anakin had been hoping that Padmé would be there to greet them, but the only person in sight was Jar Jar Binks. The Gungan's long orange earflaps hung down over his robes, but Jar Jar's enthusiastic — and slightly awkward — greeting made it clear that his years in Galactic politics had not changed him much from the clumsy, confused Gungan Anakin remembered.

"It's good to see you, too, Jar Jar," Obi-Wan said, smiling in spite of himself.

"And dis is yousa apprentice," Jar Jar said, with an attempt at dignity. Then he peered more closely at Anakin. "Noooo! Annie? Noooo! Little bitty Annie? Yousa so biggen!"

"Hi, Jar Jar," Anakin said, grinning. He hoped the Gungan wasn't going to remind everyone of his childhood. Still, Jar Jar's happiness was irresistible, and he let himself be pulled into an enormous hug.

"Shesa expecting yousa," Jar Jar went on, and

Anakin's heart leaped. Jar Jar looked at him again, shook his head, and said, "Annie . . . mesa no believen!"

When Jar Jar finished exclaiming over them, he led the way into a room off the main corridor. Anakin had a vague impression of light and understated elegance, but his attention was caught immediately by the sight of Padmé and one of her handmaidens conferring with a man wearing an eye patch and a Naboo captain's uniform.

Anakin stopped short. Light gleamed on the coils of Padmé's dark hair, and a long blue velvet vest clung to her slender figure. She was even more beautiful now than she had been at fourteen, even more beautiful than the rosy memory he had treasured for ten years. The thought that someone wanted to hurt her made his heart ache. He hardly heard Jar Jar say, "Lookie, lookie, Senator! Desa Jedi arriven."

Padmé and the others turned. When she saw Obi-Wan, Padmé smiled in recognition and rose to greet him. *She hardly even saw me,* Anakin thought.

"It's a pleasure to see you again, M'lady," Obi-Wan said.

Padmé smiled and took his hand. "It has been far too long, Master Kenobi. I'm so glad our paths have crossed again." She hesitated. "But I must warn you that I think your presence here is unnecessary."

Obi-Wan said only, "I'm sure the Jedi Council has their reasons."

Releasing Obi-Wan's hand, Padmé moved in front of Anakin. He looked down at her as she stared up doubtfully at him. Surely she remembered! Finally, she said hesitantly, "Annie??"

Anakin nodded. Padmé stared for another moment, then said weakly, "My goodness, you've grown."

"So have you," Anakin replied. *What a stupid thing to say, when I'm looking down at her!* "Grown more beautiful, I mean. And much shorter —" *Why did I have to say that? But it's so odd, when I remember her as so much taller than me.* "— for a Senator, I mean." *She's going to think I'm an idiot.*

Obi-Wan clearly thought so; the disapproving look he gave Anakin was all too familiar. But to his relief, Padmé only laughed and shook her head. Then she said, "Oh, Annie, you'll always be that little boy I knew on Tatooine."

Discomfited, Anakin looked down. *I'm not a little boy anymore!* He was almost glad when Obi-Wan distracted her, saying, "Our presence will be invisible, M'lady, I assure you."

"I'm very grateful you're here, Master Kenobi," the Naboo captain said. "The situation is more dangerous than the Senator will admit."

"I don't need more security," Padmé said firmly. "I need answers. I want to know who is trying to kill me."

"We're here to protect you, Senator, not to start an investigation," Obi-Wan said, frowning.

Anakin couldn't stand the look on her face. "We will find out who's trying to kill you, Padmé, I promise you!" he burst out.

Obi-Wan gave him another, even more disapproving look, and said sternly, "We are not going to exceed our mandate, my young Padawan learner."

"I meant in the interest of protecting her, Master, of course," Anakin replied. How could they keep her safe if they didn't know who was behind the assassination attempt? Surely Obi-Wan could see the need. If only he weren't always so determined to follow the rules. . . .

As if he had heard Anakin's thoughts, Obi-Wan shook his head. "We are not going through this exercise again, Anakin. And you will pay attention to my lead."

"Why?" Anakin persisted. He knew he was on dangerous ground, but this concerned Padmé.

"What??!!"

"Why else do you think we were assigned to her, if not to find the killer?" Anakin explained hastily. "Protection is a job for local security, not Jedi. It's overkill, Master. Investigation is implied in our mandate." At least this time Obi-Wan was listening.

"We will do as the Council has instructed," Obi-Wan said. "And you will learn your place, young one."

Anakin nodded, but he noticed that Obi-Wan had not repeated his statement that they were only supposed to act as guards. That was enough, for now. He could push more for the investigation later on. He would *make* Obi-Wan see.

"Perhaps with merely your presence, the mysteries surrounding this threat will be revealed," Padmé said, and Anakin was not sure whether she intended to be sarcastic or not. "Now, if you will excuse me, I will retire."

Anakin stared gloomily after Padmé and her handmaiden as Obi-Wan and the Naboo captain discussed security arrangements. The captain departed, leaving only Jar Jar, who was still burbling about how happy he was to see them. *Jar Jar isn't the one I wanted to feel happy*, Anakin thought, and immediately felt guilty. Jar Jar had a good heart. But . . .

"She didn't even recognize me, Jar Jar." The words slipped out before he realized. "I've thought about her every day since we parted, and she's forgotten me completely."

Jar Jar blinked at him, then said with surprising gentleness, "Shesa happy. Happier den mesa see-en her in longo time."

"Anakin, you're focusing on the negative again," Obi-Wan put in. "Be mindful of your thoughts. She was glad to see us. Now, let's check the security here."

It was something to do, and it would serve Padmé. Even if she didn't care whether or not he served her. "Yes, Master," said Anakin.

*   *   *

Zam Wesell pulled her speeder up to the side of the skyscraper and set the controls to hover. Her contact was already waiting for her, fully armed and armored. She snorted softly. Why Jango Fett made such a thing out of wearing that Mandoralian battle armor all the time, she couldn't understand. *I'm surprised he doesn't wear it when he's not on a job.*

She considered morphing into another form, just to annoy him. Changelings could pass for whatever race they chose; the ability was part of what made her such a successful bounty hunter. Fett could use the reminder, after the way his last little plan had gone wrong. She smiled behind the veil that hid the lower half of her face. She'd agreed to work with Fett on this, but she didn't have to keep him happy. On the other hand, they *did* have to work together. She decided not to waste the energy.

If Jango was having any similar thoughts about her, his helmet hid them. "We'll have to try something more subtle this time, Zam," he said without preamble as soon as she was close enough. "My client is getting impatient."

I'll bet, Zam thought, but she only nodded.

"There can be no mistakes this time," the other bounty hunter went on. "Take these. Be careful. They're very poisonous."

He reached out, offering her a short, fat tube. Through the clear sides, she saw several kouhuns —

foot-long creatures that looked like giant worms with hundreds of legs. She took the tube, her mind racing. Poisonous — she'd have to be sure the Senator was alone, and unlikely to notice their approach. Giving Jango an absentminded nod, she tucked her new assassination weapon under her arm and walked back to her airspeeder, lost in contemplation of the job ahead.

The wide hallway near the center of the Jedi Temple was lit only by the light that seeped through the doorways at either end. Yoda had always liked the play of light against dark, but tonight, walking down the hallway with Mace Windu, it saddened him. Too much of the growing dark side, it reminded him.

Mace Windu broke the silence. "Why couldn't we see this attack on the Senator?" His deep voice was full of concern.

"Masking the future, is this disturbance in the Force," Yoda replied calmly.

"The prophecy is coming true," Windu said, frowning. "The dark side is growing."

Yoda nodded. "And only those who have turned to the dark side can sense the possibilities of the future." He could feel Mace's unquiet at his words, and he understood it well. A good part of the Jedi's remarkable success came from their ability to anticipate the future. The young ones had always relied on it — perhaps a little too much. Eight hundred years gave one a different perspective. The loss of their ability to see the future didn't worry Yoda nearly as much as the growing strength of the dark side that had caused the loss.

After a short silence, Mace said, "It's been ten years, and the Sith still have not shown themselves."

"Out there, they are," Yoda said, but he nodded in approval. Learned well the ways of the Force, Mace Windu had. He saw past his own concern to the heart of the real problem. "A certainty, that is."

Mace nodded, and they continued their walk toward the light in silence.

An eddy in the Force roused Anakin from his meditation. Someone was coming. Anakin's lightsaber leaped into his hands almost before his eyes opened; then, as he felt the presence more clearly, he smiled and replaced the weapon at his belt. It was only Obi-Wan, returning from his security check.

The door of Padmé's apartment slid open. "Captain Typho has more than enough guards downstairs," Obi-Wan said as he entered. "No assassin will try that way. Any activity up here?"

"Quiet as a tomb," Anakin replied without thinking, then shivered slightly at the phrase. He caught Obi-Wan's look, and answered the question his

Master had not asked aloud. "I don't like just waiting here for something to happen to her."

Obi-Wan nodded understandingly, and pulled a pocket viewscreen from his belt pack. A moment later, he frowned and held it up. The screen showed R2-D2, powered down, in a corner near the door of Padmé's bedroom, but there was no image of the bed, or of Padmé herself. "What's going on?" Obi-Wan asked.

Anakin shrugged. "She covered that camera. I don't think she liked me watching her."

"What is she thinking?" Obi-Wan said, shaking his head.

"She programmed Artoo to warn us if there's an intruder."

"It's not an intruder I'm worried about," Obi-Wan replied. "There are many other ways to kill a Senator."

"I know, but we also want to catch this assassin," Anakin said. "Don't we, Master?"

Obi-Wan's eyes widened. "You're using her as *bait*?"

"It was her idea," Anakin said defensively. She'd insisted, in fact. "Don't worry, no harm will come to her. I can sense everything going on in that room." Where Padmé was concerned, his normal sense of the Force was heightened; he could sense her breathing, if he tried. But he couldn't explain that to Obi-Wan. "Trust me."

"It's too risky," Obi-Wan said, frowning. "And your senses aren't that attuned, young apprentice."

Yes, they are! But Anakin had heard the faint extra emphasis on "*your* senses"; maybe Obi-Wan would let this go on, after all. "And yours are?"

"Possibly," said Obi-Wan. He made no move to wake Padmé, and Anakin suppressed a grin of satisfaction. They *would* get the assassin this way. After a moment, Obi-Wan said, "You look tired."

"I don't sleep well anymore," Anakin admitted.

"Because of your mother?" Obi-Wan asked gently.

"I don't know why I keep dreaming about her now," Anakin said. *Especially such awful dreams.* His mother was strong and gentle; his memories of her did not include menacing omens or threats. But his dreams did. He hunched his shoulders. "I haven't seen her since I was little."

"Dreams pass in time."

These hadn't. If anything, they were growing more frequent. But he didn't want to discuss it with Obi-Wan right now. Obi-Wan had never met Shmi Skywalker; he couldn't really understand. "I'd rather dream of Padmé," he said slyly, knowing it would distract his Master. "Just being around her again is . . . intoxicating."

"Be mindful of your thoughts, Anakin," Obi-Wan said sharply. "They betray you. You've made a commitment to the Jedi Order — a commitment not easily broken. And don't forget, she's a politician. They're not to be trusted."

"She's not like the others in the Senate, Master," Anakin said, stung by the unexpected criticism.

Obi-Wan shrugged. "It's been my experience that Senators are focused only on pleasing those who fund their campaigns — and they are more than willing to forget the niceties of democracy to get those funds."

"Not another lecture, Master," Anakin groaned. He found both politics and economics boring, and Obi-Wan would go on for hours once he got started. "Besides, you're generalizing. The Chancellor doesn't appear to be corrupt."

"Palpatine is a politician," Obi-Wan replied. "He's very clever at following the passions and prejudices of the Senators."

"I think he is a good man," Anakin said firmly. "My instincts are very positive about —" He broke off, stunned by a sudden feeling of menace radiating from Padmé's room. He glanced at his Master.

"I sense it, too," Obi-Wan said, and together they charged for the bedroom door.

Padmé! Anakin threw himself over the bed, his lightsaber humming through the air. Behind him, he heard the crash of breaking glass, but all his attention was concentrated on two kouhuns hissing on Padmé's pillow and flicking their stinger tongues. His swing passed a hair's breadth from Padmé's frozen face and sliced the deadly worms in half. *How did they get in here?*

Lightsaber still ready, Anakin turned. There was no sign of Obi-Wan, only the shattered bedroom window and the nighttime lights of buildings and flyers outside. Then Anakin saw a Probe Droid flying out into the city traffic, with his Master clinging grimly to two of its projections. His first thought was, *So that's how the kouhuns got in;* his second was, *But we're more than a hundred stories up! If he loses his grip . . .*

Anakin whirled. Padmé was sitting up in bed, her horrified eyes also fixed on the rapidly departing Assassin Droid. He could feel Captain Typho and his guards approaching; they could handle things here for the time being. He had to follow Obi-Wan. "Stay here!" he barked at Padmé, and ran out past Captain Typho and the guards, heading for the express elevator.

This was not the best idea I have ever had, Obi-Wan thought as he swung from the droid. But he hadn't expected it to take off the way it had. He certainly hadn't expected it to dodge into the heart of the speeder traffic, or to swing in and out in an attempt to get rid of him. Somebody had done a good job programming it.

The droid sent out an electric shock, and Obi-Wan almost lost his grip. Even the Force couldn't save him if he fell hundreds of stories. He grabbed at a wire on the back of the droid, and it came loose. The droid's power failed, and the electric shocks stopped . . . but so did the droid's antigravity. They dropped nearly thirty stories before Obi-Wan got the wire connected again. *Definitely not one of my best ideas.*

The wild ride continued. The droid knocked against walls, trying to scrape Obi-Wan off; swooped low over a roof; pulled into the hot exhaust stream of a speeder. Obi-Wan hung on. If he didn't capture the droid, they would have no clue to the assassin — and he didn't want to think about what Padmé and Anakin might come up with next time, if using her as bait failed!

The droid dropped toward an alcove in the side of a building, still high above the ground. Peering over its top, Obi-Wan saw a beat-up yellow airspeeder and a muffled figure in brown waiting in the alcove. The figure saw the approaching droid and pulled out a laser rifle. "I have a bad feeling about this," Obi-Wan muttered. A moment later, explosions burst all around the him. *If I could just use my lightsaber . . .* But he couldn't reach his weapon without letting go of the droid, and the minute he did that, the droid would find a way to throw him off. All he could do was hope that the assassin had very bad aim.

The assassin didn't. A shot hit the droid dead on. The explosion threw Obi-Wan up in the air — *Oh, great,* he thought hazily, *now I have farther to fall* — and away from the building, with nothing between him and the ground far below.

Half stunned, Obi-Wan saw a speeder approaching as he fell. He grabbed for it and barely caught the back end. As he hauled himself up to relative safety, he realized that the pilot was his apprentice. "That was wacky!" Anakin said cheerfully as Obi-Wan reached the passenger seat and collapsed into it. "I almost lost you in the traffic."

Obi-Wan could sense the depth of the relief that Anakin wouldn't speak aloud. "What took you so long?" he said, knowing that Anakin would understand his unspoken thank-you in the same way.

"Oh, you know, Master, I couldn't find a speeder I really liked," Anakin said. "With an open cockpit, and the right speed capabilities . . . and then you know I had to get a really gonzo color . . ." As he spoke, he pulled the speeder into a steep climb, following the scruffy flyer who had been firing at Obi-Wan.

"If you'd spend as much time working on your saber skills as you do on your wit, young Padawan, you would rival Master Yoda as a swordsman," Obi-Wan told him.

"I thought I already did," Anakin said, grinning.

"Only in your mind, my very young apprentice . . . Careful!" Obi-Wan clutched at the side of the speeder as Anakin dodged rapidly in and out of the traffic. Shots flew past; the assassin was firing at them. "Hey, easy!"

"Sorry," Anakin said, whipping past a large commuter vehicle with almost no room to spare. "I forgot you don't like flying, Master."

"I don't mind flying," Obi-Wan said, "but what you're doing is suicide."

"I've been flying since before I could walk," Anakin said confidently, skimming by a commuter train almost close enough to scrape paint off the side of the speeder. "I'm very good at this."

It only takes one mistake. "Just slow down!"

Anakin paid no attention. The assassin tried to lose them in a convoy of huge freight vehicles, then zipped through several sharp turns into impossibly narrow spaces between buildings. Anakin followed every move.

"There he goes!" Obi-Wan said, pointing as the yellow speeder dove out of the traffic lane and around a corner. Then, as Anakin followed, Obi-Wan realized where the assassin was heading — straight into a tram tunnel. "Wait! Don't go in there!"

"Don't *worry*, Master," Anakin said soothingly . . . and sent the speeder into the tunnel right after the assassin.

He sounds as if he's humoring me, Obi-Wan thought. *But this is — oh, no!* The light just ahead wasn't the end of the tunnel; it was one of the giant passenger trams heading straight for them.

Barely in time, Anakin and the assassin whipped their speeders around and headed back the way they had come. They made it out of the tunnel just ahead of the high-speed tram. Obi-Wan let out a breath he had not realized he had been holding. "You know I don't like it when you do that," he commented.

"Sorry, Master," Anakin said unrepentantly. "Don't worry. This guy's going to kill himself any minute now."

Someone is going to get killed, Obi-Wan thought as the wild ride continued. *I hope it isn't us. . . .*

They rounded a corner, past a row of banners waving in the wind, and the near wing clipped one of the flags. The speeder lurched as the flag draped over its front end. "That was too close," Obi-Wan said.

"Clear that!" Anakin snapped.

"What?" For a moment, Obi-Wan did not understand; then he realized that the flag was blocking one of the air scoops. Without air, their engine was strangling. He leaned out of the speeder, but the flag was too far away to reach.

"Clear the flag!" Anakin struggled with the controls, scowling fiercely. "We're losing power! Hurry!"

There was only one thing to do. Obi-Wan crawled out onto the engine until he could reach the flag. He pulled it free — and the speeder lurched forward, regaining all the speed it had lost. The jerk almost made Obi-Wan lose his grip; he slid backward more than a meter before he caught himself.

"I don't like it when you do that," he complained as he crawled back into his seat.

"So sorry, Master," Anakin said, and this time Obi-Wan thought he really did mean it, at least a little. *But only a little.*

The incident with the flag had cost them time — the assassin's speeder was well ahead of them now. Anakin played his controls like a musician, narrowing the gap once more. *He was flying Podracers when he was barely a boy,* Obi-Wan thought, and shook his head. He reminded himself of that every time they got into one of these chases, and it never made him feel any better . . . because it also reminded him that Anakin had crashed every Podracer he had flown, except the last. *It's a wonder he survived. . . . What? Wait a minute!*

The assassin was heading straight for a power refinery. "It's dangerous near those power couplings!" Obi-Wan warned. "Don't go through there!"

But Anakin dove after the other speeder. The presence of the two vehicles triggered giant electric arcs; Obi-Wan's skin tingled with the nearness of their passage. "What are you *doing?*"

"Sorry, Master!"

Anakin sounded a little harried. Obi-Wan clamped his mouth shut over any further comments until they were out of the refinery. Then he said sarcastically, "Oh, that was good!"

"That was crazy," Anakin said flatly. His eyes were still fixed on the speeder ahead of them.

"I'm glad you agree" was on the tip of Obi-Wan's tongue. Then the other speeder twisted sideways and stopped in the mouth of an alley, firing at them point-blank.

"Stop!" Obi-Wan yelled. If they kept on this course, they would crash right into the other speeder — no, maybe not. There was an impossibly small gap just under the assassin's vehicle, and Anakin was aiming for it.

"We can make it," Anakin said, and the next minute they were under the assassin's ship. They made it through the gap, but hit a pipe on the other side and spun wildly. Anakin struggled to regain control. Obi-Wan saw a construction crane swing by, and a pair of supporting struts. He felt a jolt as the speeder brushed against something, and a giant gas ball enveloped them. The speeder spun, bumped against a building, and stalled.

Why do I always let him drive? "I'm crazy," Obi-Wan muttered, dropping his head onto his hands. "I'm crazy."

"I got us through that one all right," Anakin said in a satisfied tone.

Obi-Wan raised his head angrily. "No, you didn't! We've stalled. And you almost got us killed!"

"Oh, I think we're still alive," Anakin said absently as he fiddled with the controls. The engine coughed, then roared back to life, and he smiled.

The smile made Obi-Wan furious. Anakin wasn't even listening. "*It was stupid!*" he said.

His tone finally seemed to get through to his apprentice. Anakin blinked, then hung his head. "I *could* have caught him. . . ."

"But you didn't!" Obi-Wan glared at Anakin. "And now we've lost him for good!"

Suddenly an explosion rocked the speeder. Obi-Wan ducked, hearing the unmistakable *pzing* of laser bolts striking nearby.

"No, we haven't," Anakin said, and Obi-Wan felt the speeder lean sideways as Anakin tried to get them out of the ambush.

Through the smoke and flames, Anakin saw their quarry take off into the night traffic. He sent the speeder roaring after it, but with less enthusiasm than before. This chase was getting them nowhere. The yellow speeder pulled down and left, and disappeared between two buildings. Anakin smiled and pulled away to the right. He had an idea. *Now, if he just goes where I think . . .*

"Where are you going?" Obi-Wan demanded. "He went down there, the other way."

His Master was still angry about the stall. Anakin sighed. "Master, if we keep this chase going, that creep is going to end up deep-fried. Personally, I'd very much like to find out who he is and who he's working for. This is a shortcut." He paused, then added honestly, "I think."

"What do you mean, you *think*?" Obi-Wan paused, waiting. When Anakin didn't react to his sarcasm, he repeated, "Well, you lost him."

Anakin brought the speeder to a halt, hovering halfway up between two giant buildings. "I'm deeply sorry, Master," he said absently. Trying to explain now would just mean more argument; there wasn't time. Obi-Wan would understand when . . . He saw the movement he had been waiting for, and began counting to himself.

"Some shortcut," Obi-Wan muttered. "He went completely the other way. Anakin —"

"Excuse me for a moment," Anakin interrupted, and jumped out of the speeder and into the air.

He had timed it perfectly; their scruffy quarry was several stories below, and Anakin landed on the roof of the yellow speeder. Before he could find a hand-hold, the pilot gunned the engines and Anakin nearly slid off. Then, as he clawed his way forward, the assassin brought the vehicle to an abrupt stop. Anakin flew forward. He grabbed one of the front forks of the speeder just in time. The assassin started firing at him.

Anakin dodged the first few bolts, then found a position that shielded him from the attack. The assassin took off again. A quick glance upward told Anakin that Obi-Wan had taken over the controls of the other speeder and was gaining on them. *Good; this guy has two things to worry about now.*

Slowly, Anakin worked his way back to the roof of the speeder. Pulling out his lightsaber, he began melting his way inside. A shot from inside the speeder knocked the lightsaber out of his hand. *I bet I hear about that from Master Obi-Wan,* Anakin thought gloomily, ducking another shot as the lightsaber fell away below them. *But first I have to get that blaster away from this guy.* The hole he'd started melting in the roof wasn't large enough to climb through, but there was plenty of room for his arm. He shoved his hand into the cockpit and snatched at the pistol, using the Force to help.

The assassin jerked, startled, and looked up. For just an instant, a woman's eyes stared at Anakin. *Hey, that guy isn't a guy! They sent a woman to assassinate Padmé!* Anakin reached out with the Force to confirm his observation, and felt an unusual quiver. *She's female, but she's not as human as she looks. A shape-changer?* Sure enough, the assassin changed again into Clawdite. Distracted, Anakin's grip on the blaster slipped. The pistol went off, blowing a hole in the floor of the speeder.

The speeder dove toward the street, out of control. All Anakin could do was hang on. At the last minute, the assassin pulled the nose up just enough to slide the speeder to a hard landing. Sparks showered everywhere, and people dodged out of the way. Anakin flew over the front of the speeder and landed in the street.

That woman is nearly as good a pilot as I am, Anakin thought. He picked himself up in time to see the assassin jump out of the wrecked speeder and run up the street. He followed, shoving through a rapidly growing crowd of seedy-looking aliens and scruffy droids. *Reminds me of Tatooine . . .*

Anakin was gaining steadily on the assassin now, but suddenly she ducked through the door of a nightclub, the Outlander. Panting slightly, Anakin reached the nightclub door just as another speeder came in for a much less spectacular landing. Obi-Wan climbed out, holding Anakin's lightsaber. *Uh-oh. I knew I was going to hear about that.*

"Anakin!" said Obi-Wan.

"She went into that club, Master," Anakin said, trying to distract him.

"Patience," Obi-Wan told him. "Use the Force, Anakin. Think."

"Sorry, Master," Anakin said automatically. Think? He thought the assassin was getting away. Surely Obi-Wan could see —

Obi-Wan sighed. "He went in there to hide, not run."

Oh. "Yes, Master," Anakin said.

Obi-Wan held out the lightsaber. "Here. Next time, try not to lose it."

That wasn't so bad. Anakin nodded and reached for the weapon.

Obi-Wan pulled it back. "A Jedi's saber is his most precious possession."

"Yes, Master." He wasn't going to escape the lecture after all. He reached for the sword again, and Obi-Wan pulled it away once more.

"He must keep it with him at all times," Obi-Wan said.

"I *know*, Master," Anakin said.

"This weapon is your life."

Anakin barely kept from rolling his eyes. "I've heard this lesson before."

"But you haven't learned anything, Anakin." Obi-Wan held the lightsaber out at last, and Anakin grabbed it before he could change his mind.

"I try, Master."

Obi-Wan sighed and turned toward the nightclub. "Why do I think you are going to be the death of me?" he said almost absently.

A chill ran down Anakin's spine. "Don't say that, Master!" he burst out, careless of the crowd who might overhear. Obi-Wan looked at him and lifted his eyebrows in a combination of question and reproof. Anakin swallowed and continued in a lower tone, "You're the closest thing I have to a father. I love you. I don't want to cause you pain." *I don't want to lose you, the way I've lost my mother.* Remembering his dreams, Anakin shivered. Would he start having nightmares about Obi-Wan, too?

But Obi-Wan only looked at him and said mildly, "Then why don't you listen to me?"

"I *am* trying."

Obi-Wan nodded. He glanced out over the crowded room and said in the same, almost-lecturing tone, "Do you see him?"

"I think he's a she," Anakin said. Rapidly, he scanned the crowd, but he did not see anyone who looked like their quarry. Remembering the strangeness he had sensed, he added, "And I think she's a changeling."

"Then be extra careful," Obi-Wan said. Anakin blinked in surprise, and his Master nodded gently toward the room. "Go and find her."

"But — but where are you going, Master?" Anakin said as Obi-Wan moved off into the crowd.

"To get a drink," Obi-Wan said over his shoulder.

Anakin blinked again, then began working his way around the edge of the room. Beings of all sorts stared at him, then looked away; most were too large or too small, or had too many appendages, to be the assassin. *Obi-Wan must be really worried,* he thought with the corner of his mind that wasn't hunting for the assassin. It wasn't like his Master to leave Anakin to do the work, but perhaps . . . Anakin glanced back toward the bar and saw the assassin at last — standing right behind Obi-Wan with a blaster in one hand.

Before Anakin could shout a warning, Obi-Wan whirled. His lightsaber hummed across the sudden silence, slicing through the assassin's arm. Anakin headed toward the bar. He could sense the assassin's pain and the growing anger of the beings around him, but his Master felt calm and centered, as always. *He expected this to happen*, Anakin thought indignantly. *He set himself up as bait!* Then he was at Obi-Wan's side. The assassin lay in a heap at Obi-Wan's feet. The assassin's arm — and blaster — lay in a pool of blood a little to one side.

"Easy," Anakin told the crowd. "Official business. Go back to your drinks."

Slowly, the bar patrons complied; apparently two lightsabers were more than any of them cared to face, especially with one person already in pieces. Obi-Wan snapped off his lightsaber; a moment later, Anakin did the same. Together, they carried the injured assassin outside.

"Do you know who it was you were trying to kill?" Obi-Wan asked as he tended her shoulder.

"The Senator from Naboo," the assassin replied readily.

"Who hired you?"

The woman glared at Obi-Wan, and Anakin thought that she was not going to tell them anything more. Then she said, "It was just a job. And the next one won't make the same mistake I did."

"Tell us!" Anakin demanded, pushing at her with the Force. "*Tell us now!*"

"It was a bounty hunter called —" The woman twitched, gave one surprised blink, and died. Anakin heard a *whoosh* and looked up in time to see an armored figure wearing a jetpack fly up and around a building. *A bounty hunter! Probably the one who had hired her. And there's no way we can catch him; the speeder is out front, and he'll be gone long before we could get to it.*

Obi-Wan leaned forward. His fingers brushed the assassin's neck; then he held out a small, fat dart about as long as his finger for Anakin's inspection.

"Toxic dart," he said unnecessarily.

And we still don't know who's trying to kill Padmé, Anakin thought. *This is not good.*

CHAPTER 4

Obi-Wan hated making incomplete reports to the Jedi Council, but it was plainly necessary now. First thing next morning, they returned to the Jedi Temple to tell their story to the assembled Council members.

The Jedi Council sat in a circle, to emphasize the equality of the members; nevertheless, everyone knew that Master Yoda and Master Windu were the first among them. When Obi-Wan finished speaking, there was a moment of silence; then everyone looked at Yoda. Yoda studied his fellow Council members briefly, as if he were collecting their votes without speaking. Then he said, "Track down this bounty hunter, you must, Obi-Wan."

"Most importantly, find out who he's working for," Mace Windu added.

Beside him, Obi-Wan felt some of the tension leave Anakin. He appreciated Anakin's confidence in his ability to find the assassin, but Anakin should have learned by this time that receiving an assignment didn't necessarily mean completing it successfully. And there was still Padmé to consider. "What about Senator Amidala?" he asked. "She will still need protection."

"Handle that, your Padawan will," Yoda said.

Obi-Wan looked at Yoda in consternation. Anakin, alone, guarding Padmé . . . *He's too young, and too interested in her. They should assign someone else.* But he couldn't say that to the Jedi Council in front of Anakin, not without a strong reason. All he had was an uncomfortable feeling. He stayed silent.

"Anakin," Mace Windu said, "escort the Senator back to her home planet. She'll be safer there. And don't use registered transport. Travel as refugees."

"It will be very difficult to get Senator Amidala to leave the capital," Anakin said.

At least he's thinking. Obi-Wan began to feel less worried. As long as Anakin thought about what he was doing, instead of charging ahead on impulse, he would be fine.

Master Yoda's ears turned down firmly. "Until caught this killer is, our judgment she must respect."

Anakin still looked doubtful — with reason, Obi-Wan thought. *Senator Amidala isn't going to like taking orders from someone she remembers as a little boy.* Mace Windu looked thoughtfully at the two of them, then said, "Anakin, go to the Senate and ask Chancellor Palpatine to speak with her."

The other Council members nodded. It was a

good idea, Obi-Wan had to admit. If anyone could persuade Padmé to follow the Jedi's advice, Palpatine could. So why did he have such a bad feeling about all this?

Anakin hurried past the Senate and into the huge office building beside it. He had only been to the Chancellor's office a few times before, usually with his Master, but there was no way to go wrong. Palpatine's office occupied the very top of the skyscraper.

When he heard the problem, Chancellor Palpatine nodded in understanding. "I will talk to her," he told Anakin. "Senator Amidala will not refuse an executive order. I know her well enough to assure you of that."

"Thank you, Your Excellency." Anakin replied. He took a last glance out the window — the Chancellor's office had a matchless view of the endless city below, and Anakin had always found it compelling.

Before Anakin could say farewell, Palpatine smiled warmly. "So, my young Padawan, they have finally given you an assignment," he said, and Anakin could sense his interest and approval. "Your patience has paid off."

"Your guidance, more than my patience," Anakin said, but he couldn't help being gratified, as always, by Palpatine's interest. When they had first met on Naboo just after the war, Anakin had only been nine. He hadn't really expected so important a person as the Chancellor to remember him. But Chancellor Palpatine had said then that he would follow Anakin's career with interest, and he had done just that. The Chancellor kep his promises; Anakin couldn't understand why Obi-Wan insisted on doubting him just because he was a politician.

"You don't need guidance, Anakin," the Chancellor said seriously. "In time, you will learn to trust your feelings. Then you will be invincible." He turned to walk to the door with Anakin. "I have said it many times: You are the most gifted Jedi I have ever met."

Anakin felt a shiver of pleasure at the compliment. It meant even more, coming from the Chancellor. *He's not even a Jedi, and he can see I have talent!* "Thank you, your Excellency," he said.

Palpatine smiled, as if he knew how good his praise made Anakin feel. "I see you becoming the greatest of all the Jedi, Anakin. Even more powerful than Master Yoda."

Slightly dazzled by such an impressive vision of his future, Anakin could only mutter his thanks and appreciation once more. But as he left the building, he felt as if he were floating on air.

As soon as the Jedi Council adjourned, Obi-Wan went in search of Master Yoda. He couldn't hurt Anakin by expressing his doubts about the mission in public, but he could certainly ask Yoda for advice privately.

He found Yoda making the circuit of the Jedi Temple halls in a floating chair. He was deep in discussion with Master Windu, who walked beside him. The two looked at Obi-Wan encouragingly. Obi-Wan hesitated only a moment when he saw them both. He'd only planned to talk to Master Yoda, but another point of view might be very useful, and Master Windu was certainly as understanding as Master Yoda.

"I am concerned for my Padawan," Obi-Wan told them. "He is not ready to be given this assignment on his own yet."

Yoda tilted his head, looking up at him slantwise. "The Council is confident in this decision, Obi-Wan."

"The boy has exceptional skills," Master Windu added.

"But he still has much to learn, Master," Obi-wan said. "And his abilities have made him . . . well, arrogant."

To his surprise, Yoda nodded emphatically. "Yes, yes," the little Jedi Master said. "It is a flaw more and more common among Jedi. Too sure of themselves they are. Even the older, more experienced ones."

And Master Yoda is worried about it, Obi-Wan thought. *Or he wouldn't be so emphatic, or call it a common flaw.* He thought back to his first encounters with Anakin. The boy had been much older than normal to begin Jedi training — too old, some had said. But if Anakin had been too old to begin training, Obi-Wan had certainly been very young to take on a Padawan apprentice. *Perhaps there was arrogance on more than one side.* Was it really Anakin he doubted, or was it his own abilities as a teacher?

"Remember, Obi-Wan," Master Windu said. "If the prophecy is true, your apprentice is the only one who can bring the Force back into balance."

"If he follows the right path," Obi-Wan said without thinking. Then he did think, and shivered. Prophecies were tricky things, and the dark side of the Force was growing stronger. Anakin would never choose that path, of course, but —

But what would happen if he did?

Padmé dropped a silk jacket into her carry bag and tucked it into place with exaggerated care. She hated to be driven away from Coruscant after all she had gone through to get back in time for the vote. *Be honest; you just hate running away, period.* But Chancellor Palpatine had been very firm.

She saw Dormé give her a wary, sidelong look, and sighed. She shouldn't be taking her temper out on people who had nothing to do with the problem.

She put a skirt into the bag and glared at the doorway, where Anakin stood talking to Jar Jar Binks, just as if this were normal. *There* was the problem — that overgrown apprentice Jedi who'd talked Chancellor Palpatine into making her leave Coruscant.

Jar Jar caught her glare and looked at her uncertainly. Padmé sighed again. This wasn't his fault, either. From Jar Jar's expression, it was clear that Anakin hadn't fully explained. Well, he couldn't; *he* wasn't the Senator, after all. Forcing a smile, she said to Jar Jar, "I am taking an extended leave of absence. It will be your responsibility to take my place in the Senate. Representative Binks, I know I can count on you."

"Mesa honored to be taken on dissa heavy burden," Jar Jar replied, a little pompously. "Mesa accept this with muy muy humility and da —"

Padmé walked over and gave him a hug, which completely derailed his speech. "You are a good friend, Jar Jar," she said. "But I don't wish to hold you up. I'm sure you have a great deal to do."

"Of course, M'lady," Jar Jar said. As he left, he nodded to Anakin, which only made Padmé feel more cross.

As soon as Jar Jar was gone, Padmé turned to Anakin. "I *do not like* this idea of hiding," she complained.

Anakin raised his hands placatingly. "Don't worry," he told her. "Now that the Council has ordered an investigation, it won't take Master Kenobi long to find that bounty hunter."

As if that was the main problem! Padmé frowned at him. "I haven't worked for an entire year to defeat the Military Creation Act in order not to be here when its fate is decided!"

"Sometimes we have to let go of our pride and do what is requested of us."

He sounds as if he's lecturing a small child! Just because he's gotten so tall . . . "Pride?" She drew herself up in all her Senatorial formality and dignity. "Annie, you're young, and you don't have a very firm grip on politics. I suggest you reserve your opinions for some other time."

She saw the flash of hurt in his expression before he, too, sought refuge in formality. "Sorry, *M'lady*," he said. As he turned away, she heard him murmur, "I was only trying to . . ."

To what? To help? Annie had always tried to help. But now she could feel him withdrawing from her, and somehow she knew that he was doing so only because he thought it was what she wanted. "Annie!" she protested. "No!"

His head came up, and he looked at her for a long moment. He seemed almost more hurt than before. Then he said softly, "Please don't call me that."

"What?" She hadn't insulted him; she had only called him —

"Annie."

Bewildered, Padmé stared at him, her anger forgotten. "But I've always called you that. It's your name, isn't it?"

"My name is Anakin," he said, and she heard an echo in his voice of the nine-year-old boy telling her firmly, *My name is Anakin, and I'm a person.* "When you say Annie it's like I'm still a little boy. And I'm not."

"I'm sorry, Anakin," she said sincerely. Then she grinned and let her gaze travel slowly from his feet up — and up — until her head tilted back so that she could see his face. "It's impossible to deny that you've grown up."

Anakin reddened, and his eyes fell. "Master Obi-Wan manages not to see it," he muttered.

"Mentors have a way of seeing more of our faults than we would like," Padmé said, thinking of her own teachers on Naboo. "It's the only way we grow."

"Don't get me wrong," Anakin said, looking up. "Obi-Wan is a great mentor, as wise as Master Yoda and as powerful as Master Windu. I am truly thankful to be his apprentice. Only . . ." He hesitated, as if he weren't sure he should say what he really wanted to.

Padmé nodded reassuringly, and after a moment Anakin went on, "Although I'm a Padawan learner, in some ways — a lot of ways — I'm ahead of him. I'm ready for the trials, I know I am! He knows it, too.

234

But he feels I'm too unpredictable." He was almost talking to himself now; the words had the sound of something he'd said inside his head many times. "Other Jedi my age have gone through the trials and made it. I know I started my training late, but he won't let me move on."

"That must be frustrating," Padmé said, trying hard to keep from smiling.

"It's worse," Anakin burst out. "He's overly critical. He never listens! He just doesn't understand. It's not fair!"

Despite herself, Padmé laughed. Anakin looked at her in surprise, and she shook her head. "I'm sorry, but you sounded exactly like that little boy I once knew . . . when he didn't get his way."

"I'm not whining," Anakin insisted. "I'm not!"

Still smiling, Padmé shook her head again. "I didn't say it to hurt you."

"I know," Anakin said softly, and she knew that he did.

"Anakin," she said after a moment's silence, "don't try to grow up too fast."

"I am grown up," he replied. "You said it yourself." He looked down into her eyes.

The intensity of his gaze was disturbing. She couldn't remember the last time someone had looked at her like that — not at Senator Amidala or Queen Amidala or the earnest young legislator, but just at

Padmé. *And he has the deepest eyes* . . . She shook herself. "Please don't look at me like that," she said.

Anakin blinked. "Why not?"

"Because I can see what you're thinking." She hadn't meant to say that, straight out.

"Ahh," Anakin nodded, laughing. "So you have Jedi powers, too?"

Padmé turned away. This ex-slave boy had no business laughing at her. "It makes me feel uncomfortable," she said stiffly.

"Sorry, M'lady." Anakin sounded sincere, but Padmé couldn't shake the feeling that he was still laughing at her. Her lips tightened, and she walked firmly away to finish packing.

Obi-Wan, Captain Typho, and Dormé all went along with Anakin and Padmé to the spaceport freighter docks. Privately, Obi-Wan felt that even that was too many people, but Captain Typho was Padmé's official security head, and Padmé was worried about her handmaiden, who would be taking her place as "Senator Amidala" in hopes of fooling the assassins, so he hadn't tried very hard to talk them out of coming. He had, however, insisted that no one but Padmé and Anakin would get off the little transport that carried them to the docks. A Jedi, a Naboo officer in uniform, and "Senator Amidala" would attract far too much attention, and the whole point of sending Padmé by ordinary freighter was to get her away from Coruscant unnoticed.

Anakin and Padmé wore loose peasant clothes of gray and brown. Anakin had bundled his Padawan braid into a knot at the back of his head to make it less obvious. A Jedi Padawan accompanying a young woman on a refugee transport would be unusual enough to cause considerable comment. For the hundredth time, Obi-Wan studied them, and decided again that their disguises would do.

The transport pulled up at the docks at last. While Padmé and Dormé began a rather tearful good-bye, Obi-Wan pulled Anakin aside. Ignoring Anakin's frown, he repeated the mission instructions, with a little added emphasis. "Anakin, you stay on Naboo. Don't do anything without first consulting either myself or the Council."

"Yes, Master," Anakin said in the tones of someone who'd heard this too many times already.

Obi-Wan sighed, wishing he could believe it. Not that he thought Anakin was lying; he was quite sure his apprentice *meant* to follow instructions. Anakin always meant well. But Anakin was impulsive, and too sure of himself and his abilities. If he thought there was a need, he might easily forget his promise and jeopardize everything. *This is the only way to be sure of Padmé's safety*, Obi-Wan told himself. That last assassin had come too close. Still, he could not shake his feeling of unease.

Padmé finished saying farewell to her handmaiden, and joined them. Her expression was grave. Obi-Wan nodded and said, "I will get to the bottom of this plot quickly, M'lady. You'll be back here in no time."

"I will be most grateful for your speed, Master Jedi," Padmé replied formally.

She's still angry about leaving Coruscant, Obi-Wan thought. He was almost ready to call the trip off, to look for some other alternative, but Anakin picked up their battered travel cases and said, "Time to go."

Padmé gave Dormé one last hug, and she and Anakin went to the door of the transport, where R2-D2 waited to accompany them.

"May the Force be with you," Obi-Wan said to Anakin.

"May the Force be with you, Master," Anakin replied.

Why do I feel as if we're saying good-bye to each other for the last time? Obi-Wan shook himself. He was doing just what he always scolded Anakin for — focusing on the negative. But as he watched Anakin and Padmé and R2 disappear into the spaceport, he could not help murmuring to Captain Typho, "I hope he doesn't try anything foolish."

Captain Typho glanced at Obi-Wan and shook his head. "I'd be more concerned about her doing something than him."

Well, you don't know Anakin. On the other hand, some of the things Padmé had done during the Naboo war had been just as risky as anything his apprentice had come up with. Perhaps that was the source of his unease.

239

They waited in silence until the freighter took off. Obi-Wan even stretched his Jedi abilities to make sure that Anakin and Padmé were on board — he'd almost been afraid that Padmé would talk Anakin into letting her stay at the last minute.

As soon as he knew that everything had gone smoothly, Obi-Wan sent the transport back toward the diplomatic section of Coruscant. He let Captain Typho and Dormé off at the Senator's apartment to continue their dangerous masquerade, and went on to the Jedi Temple. He had promised Padmé he'd finish this investigation quickly, and he wanted to get to work.

The analysis cubicles at the Temple were busy, but he found an empty one. Pulling out the toxic dart that had killed the attempted assassin, he put it on the sensor tray. "I need to know where this came from and who made it," he told the Analysis Droid.

"One moment, please," said the droid. It retracted the tray and began its work.

Obi-Wan waited, watching diagrams and data scroll rapidly past on the droid's display. Then, to his surprise, the screen went blank.

"Markings cannot be identified," the droid announced. "As you can see on your screen, subject weapon does not exist in any known culture. Probably self-made by a warrior not associated with any known society. Stand away from the sensor tray, please." The tray slid out, waiting for him to take back the dart.

"Excuse me," Obi-Wan said. "Could you try again, please?"

"Master Jedi, our records are very thorough," the droid said. If it were human, Obi-Wan thought it would have sounded miffed at the suggestion that it hadn't checked everything the first time. "If I can't tell you where it came from, nobody can."

Obi-Wan looked at the dart. *Nobody can? Hmm. I wonder . . .* "Thank you for your assistance," he told the droid as he pocketed the dart. He turned away and said, half to himself, "I know who can identify this."

He could have sworn he heard an incredulous sniff from behind him as he left the analysis cubicle.

At first glance, Dex's Diner looked like every other low-level eatery in this tough part of town. Shiny maroon booths lined the walls, slick tile covered the floor, and the counter along the wall was edged in shiny chrome. Dex's was, however, much cleaner and smelled far better than most of the other such places Obi-Wan had been in.

The Waitress Droid cleaning the booths was initially unhelpful when he asked to see Dexter. "He's not in trouble," Obi-Wan told her. "It's personal."

The droid gave him a long, evaluating look. Then

she called through the open serving hatch, "Someone to see you, honey." Lowering her voice slightly, she added, "A Jedi, by the looks of him."

A cloud of steam and a huge head poked out of the serving hatch. "Obi-Wan!" Dexter called cheerfully. "Take a seat! I'll be right with you!"

Smiling slightly, Obi-Wan chose an empty booth. The Waitress Droid, reassured at last, brought over two mugs of steaming ardees. A moment later, Dexter emerged from the back room. He hadn't changed much since the last time Obi-Wan had seen him — he was a little older, a little balder, and perhaps a little heavier, though with his bulk a few more pounds made almost no difference. Beaming, he squeezed his bulk and his four arms into the seat across from Obi-Wan.

"So, my friend, what can I do for you?" he asked, gesturing with all four arms.

"You can tell me what this is," Obi-Wan said, sliding the dart across the table.

Dexter's eyes widened. "Well, whaddya know," he said softly. With a delicacy surprising in one so large, he picked up the dart and turned it over. "I ain't seen one of these since I was prospecting on Subterrel, beyond the Outer Rim."

"Do you know where it came from?" Obi-Wan asked, leaning forward.

Dexter grinned. "This baby belongs to them cloners. What you got here is a Kamino Saberdart."

Anakin gave her a penetrating look. Padmé looked away and saw R2-D2 rolling up, carrying two chunks of bread. As she blinked in mild surprise, the little droid extended a tube and filled two bowls with mush. *I thought this ship didn't serve droids. Well, I always knew R2 was resourceful.* "Are you hungry?" she asked Anakin.

He nodded, and she passed him one of the bowls. "Thanks," he said.

"We went to lightspeed a while ago," Padmé said neutrally. If he didn't want to talk about his nightmare, she wouldn't force him to.

"I look forward to seeing Naboo again. I've thought about it every day since I left. It's by far the most beautiful place I've ever seen." He gave her an intense look as he spoke, as if willing her to understand some secret meaning in his words.

Padmé shifted uncomfortably. She didn't want him to mean more than what he said. She certainly didn't want him idealizing Naboo and . . . and its people. He would surely be disappointed. "It may not be as you remember it," she said. "Time changes perception."

"Sometimes it does," Anakin said, still with that same intense gaze. "Sometimes for the better."

More uncomfortable than ever, Padmé looked down and took a mouthful of mush. *Time to change the subject,* she thought. "It must be difficult having sworn your life to the Jedi," she said. "Not being able to visit the places you like, or do the things you like . . ." Too late, she remembered that Anakin had been a slave when they met, even less in control of his life than a Jedi apprentice. To him, being a Jedi must mean more freedom in his life, not less.

But Anakin was nodding. "Or be with the people I love," he said.

"Are you allowed to love?" Padmé asked. "I thought it was forbidden for a Jedi."

"Attachment is forbidden," Anakin said slowly. "Possession is forbidden. But compassion, which I would define as unconditional love, is central to a Jedi's life. So you might say we're encouraged to love."

Was this thoughtful, serious young man the same Anakin as the little boy she remembered? "You have changed so much," she said without thinking.

"You haven't changed a bit," Anakin told her. "You're exactly the way I remember you in my dreams. I doubt if Naboo has changed much, either."

He dreams about me? She wasn't sure whether that pleased her or frightened her. "It hasn't," she admitted, and then firmly turned the subject. "You were dreaming about your mother earlier, weren't you?"

Anakin looked away. "Yes. I left Tatooine so long ago, my memory of her is fading. I don't want to lose it. And lately I've been seeing her in my dreams —

vivid dreams. Scary dreams." His voice became lower and softer. "I worry about her."

No wonder he would rather dream about me . . . and Naboo, of course. Padmé looked at him in sudden sympathy. He ducked his head to continue eating. *He's more worried than he wants to admit. And he's a Jedi; they just know things sometimes.* A shiver of apprehension ran through her as she remembered the strong, gentle woman she had met so long ago on Tatooine. She wanted to believe that nothing awful could have happened to her, but Shmi Skywalker had been a slave, like her son, and Tatooine had so many dangers. . . .

CHAPTER 6

The Jedi archives had always been one of Obi-Wan's favorite places in the Jedi Temple, at once peaceful and busy. The silent banks of computer panels held more information than any other data center in the galaxy, and no matter what the time of day or night, three or four consoles were always occupied by Jedi studying trends or searching for some key piece of knowledge that would aid them on their missions. Today, not only were several consoles occupied, but four or five Jedi sat scattered around various tables in the center of the room, studying printed materials from the archives. Even with all the information the Storage Droids had put into the computers, some things still needed to be looked at in their original forms.

It should have been simple to get the coordinates for Kamino from the computers, but to Obi-Wan's surprise, there were no records of the place. After spending half an hour fruitlessly searching the information banks, Obi-Wan pressed a button that would summon one of the archivists to help him. Then he stood up, stretched, and began to pace, careful not to disturb his fellow Jedi at their work.

Near the doorway, Obi-Wan stopped by a row of bronze busts. He realized after a moment that the bust directly in front of him was Count Dooku, and he studied it with interest. There was nothing in the long, chiseled face and stern expression to hint at the path he had chosen. Leader of the Separatists, who might well plunge the Republic into civil war — how could a Jedi, even one who had left the order, come to that? And why *had* he left? It had happened shortly after the Naboo war. Obi-Wan had been off-planet and busy with his new responsibilities as a full-fledged Jedi Knight; by the time he came back to Coruscant, the Count was gone. He had never found out what happened.

He heard a small sound, and turned to find the Jedi archivist, Jocasta Nu, standing next to him. With her neat gray hair and thin face, she looked deceptively frail in her Jedi robes; most people would never guess that she was more than a desk-bound librarian. Obi-Wan knew better. Jocasta had been a formidable Jedi warrior in her youth, and though she now spent most of her time organizing and searching the archives for her fellow Jedi, she still went out on missions from time to time. "Did you call for assistance?" she asked pointedly.

"Yes," Obi-Wan said, tearing his eyes away from the bust. "Yes, I did."

Jocasta smiled in understanding. "He has a powerful face, doesn't he? He was one of the most brilliant Jedi I have had the privilege of knowing."

"I never understood why he quit," Obi-Wan said. Jocasta Nu was also a Jedi; surely she had wondered the same things he did. "Only twenty Jedi have ever left the Order."

"The Lost Twenty," the archivist said with a sigh. "And Count Dooku was the most recent — and the most painful." She paused. "No one likes to talk about it. His leaving was a great loss."

If nobody wanted to talk about it, there was only one way to find out. "What happened?" Obi-Wan asked bluntly.

Jocasta smiled slightly, but answered readily enough. "Well, Count Dooku was always a bit out of step with the decisions of the Council." She gave Obi-Wan a look that he could not decipher. "Much like your old Master, Qui-Gon Jinn."

"Really?" The idea was surprising . . . and disturbing. *But Master Qui-Gon would never have left the Order. Never.*

"Oh, yes," the elder Jedi said. "They were alike in many ways. Very individual thinkers. Idealists . . ."

She looked at the bust and went on, half to herself, "He was always striving to become a more powerful Jedi. He wanted to be the best. With a lightsaber, in the old style of fencing, he had no match. His knowledge of the Force was . . . unique."

He sounds a little like Anakin, Obi-Wan thought, and frowned.

Jocasta sighed and turned her head, as if she could not bear to look at the bust any longer. "In the end, I think he left because he lost faith in the Republic. He always had very high expectations of government. He disappeared for nine or ten years, then just showed up recently as the head of the Separatist movement."

Obi-Wan waited, but she didn't seem inclined to say any more. "Interesting," he said at last. "I'm still not sure I understand completely."

"Well, I'm sure you didn't call me over here for a history lesson," the archivist said. "Are you having a problem, Master Kenobi?"

Obi-Wan gestured at the screen he had been using. "Yes, I'm trying to find a planet system called Kamino. It doesn't seem to show up on any of the archive charts."

"Kamino?" Jocasta repeated. "It's not a system I'm familiar with. Let me see." She studied the screen for a moment. "Are you sure you have the right coordinates?"

"According to my information, it should be in this quadrant somewhere — just south of the Rishi Maze."

"No coordinates?" The archivist frowned. "It sounds like the sort of directions you'd get from a street tout — some old miner or Furbog trader."

"All three, actually," Obi-Wan said with a smile, thinking of Dex.

Jocasta gave him a skeptical look. "Are you sure it exists?"

"Absolutely."

She looked at him a moment longer, then nodded. "Let me do a gravitational scan." Her fingers flew over the controls, and the screen display changed. She studied it for a moment, and pointed. "There are some inconsistencies here. Maybe the planet you're seeking was destroyed."

That was possible, but — "Wouldn't that be on record?"

"It ought to be," the archivist admitted. "Unless it was very recent." She looked at him and shook her head. "I hate to say it, but it looks like the system you're searching for doesn't exist."

Obi-Wan thought of the toxic dart in his pocket. "That's impossible. Perhaps the archives are incomplete."

Jocasta stiffened, as if he had insulted her personally. "The archives are comprehensive and totally secure, my young Jedi," she snapped. "One thing you may be absolutely sure of — if an item does not appear in our records, it does not exist!"

This was starting to sound familiar — *If I can't tell you where it came from, nobody can . . . If it isn't in our records, it does not exist . . .* Obi-Wan stared at the map screen and frowned suddenly. Gravitational anomalies . . . *something* had been where Dexter said the Kamino system was, records or not.

Obi-Wan shook his head. None of this made sense. According to the Jedi records, Padmé's attempted assassin had been killed by an unidentified dart from a nonexistent world. He didn't know which was more disturbing — reaching a dead end in his investigation or finding such obvious gaps in the Jedi information systems. And he had run out of other sources.

He thanked the archivist for her help, and copied the map to a portable display reader, to think about later. He must know *someone* who could think of another place to try.

Naboo looked and sounded and smelled even better than Anakin's memories of it. The rose-gold domes of the city, the flowers that scented the air, the distant music of the waterfalls — nothing had changed. Well, this time there were no armies of Trade Federation Battle Droids trying to kill them, but that could only be counted a plus. Except for the cold, it was perfect.

Padmé seemed to enjoy being back on Naboo as much as he did. She insisted that they go straight from the spaceport to the palace, so that she could report to the Queen, but once that was settled, she seemed to shed some of her fierce, determined Senatorial persona. She seemed more like the Padmé Anakin had known on Tatooine when he was small. The thought made Anakin wonder about Padmé's girlhood, and he asked, "Tell me, did you dream of power and politics when you were a little girl?"

Padmé laughed, startled, and turned to look at him. "No, that was the last thing I thought of." Her face took on a thoughtful, remembering look. "I was elected for the most part because of my conviction that reform was possible. I wasn't the youngest Queen ever elected, but now that I think back on it, I'm not sure I was old enough." She glanced back toward the palace, and her eyes lingered on a section of the polished surface that was newer than the rest, shaped like a blaster scar that had been repaired. "I'm not sure I was ready," she murmured.

"The people you served thought you did a good job," Anakin pointed out, hoping to cheer her up. "I heard they tried to amend the Constitution so you could stay in office."

"Popular rule is not democracy, Annie," Padmé said. "It gives the people what they want, not what they need. Truthfully, I was relieved when my two terms were up — but when the Queen asked me to serve as Senator, I couldn't refuse her."

"I think the Republic needs you," Anakin said firmly as they reached the palace steps. "I'm glad you chose to serve."

Padmé smiled at him, and they went inside. An aide conducted them up the stairs to the marble-lined throne room. It was odd to see Queen Jamillia on the throne, wearing the royal face paint, when in Anakin's memory it was Padmé who belonged there. But the handmaidens in their flame-red robes were the same, and so were some of the Queen's advisors. Anakin even recognized one of them, Sio Bibble, who had stayed on Naboo during the war.

The Queen greeted Padmé like an old friend. "We've been worried about you," she said, taking Padmé's hand. "I'm so glad you are safe."

"Thank you, Your Highness," Padmé replied. "I only wish I could have served you better by staying on Coruscant for the vote."

"Given the circumstances, Senator, it was the only decision Her Highness could have made," Sio Bibble said sternly.

"How many systems have joined Count Dooku and the Separatists?" the Queen asked.

"Thousands," Padmé said. "And more are leaving the Republic every day. If the Senate votes to create an army, I'm sure it's going to push us into a civil war."

Anakin let his attention drift as the two women discussed the possibility of war, the reactions of the bureaucrats, and the position the Trade Federation would take in any conflict. He never had understood what Padmé found so interesting about politics. His attention came back to the conversation with a snap when he heard Padmé say, "There are rumors, Your Highness, that the Trade Federation Army was not reduced as they were ordered."

The Queen looked startled and skeptical. Anakin didn't blame her; after what they had done on Naboo, it was unthinkable for the Trade Federation to keep their huge armies of Battle Droids. But Anakin suspected that Padmé was right, and he wondered why the Jedi had not investigated the rumors. He remembered the Naboo war all too well, and it galled him to think that the Trade Federation had weaseled out of its well-deserved punishment.

"We must keep our faith in the Republic," Queen Jamillia said firmly. "The day we stop believing democracy can work is the day we lose it."

"Let us pray that day never comes," Padmé murmured.

"In the meantime, we must consider your own safety," the Queen went on. Anakin stiffened, wondering whether she intended to discuss arrangements in front of all her attendants, but Sio Bibble nodded and the rest of the court melted away. When only he and the Queen were left, he looked at Anakin and said, "What is your suggestion, Master Jedi?"

Anakin opened his mouth but Padmé was there before him. "Anakin's not a Jedi yet, Counselor. He's still a Padawan learner. I was thinking —"

"Hey, hold on a minute," Anakin said, thinking, *A Padawan is still a member of the Order, and this is my assignment!* Besides, she hadn't had to make a point of it. His Padawan braid was clearly visible; Sio Bibble must have seen it and known what it meant.

"Excuse me!" Padmé said stiffly over her shoulder. Turning back to the Queen, she went on, "I was thinking I would stay in the Lake Country. There are some places up there that are very isolated."

She has no business dismissing me like that! Anakin thought angrily. "Excuse *me*," he said coldly. "I am in charge of security here, M'lady."

Padmé turned and said deliberately, "Annie, my life is at risk, and this is my home. I know it very well; that is why we're here. I think it would be wise for you to take advantage of my knowledge in this instance."

That's not the problem, and you know it! Anakin almost blurted out the words, but he saw the Queen and Sio Bibble exchange amused glances, and restrained himself. Padmé was trying to annoy him; she had called him Annie again, the little-boy name he was growing to hate. But he couldn't take chances with her safety just because he was annoyed with her. Taking a deep breath, he muttered, "Sorry, M'lady."

"Perfect," the Queen said. "It's settled, then." She rose, and looked at Padmé. "I had an audience with your father yesterday. He hopes you will visit your mother before you leave. Your family is very worried."

That was unexpected, but it didn't sound like a security problem. And Padmé's family — Anakin had never thought about what sort of family she must have. He looked at her, and was surprised to see a faintly apprehensive look on her face. What was she worried about? Maybe she was afraid they'd tell him about her childhood pranks. He grinned suddenly. It would be nice to have some ammunition to use the next time Padmé started calling him Annie. Still grinning, he followed her out of the throne room.

Yoda looked out over the training floor, watching the class of four-year-olds at their practice. The Force was bright and strong in these children of all species, and it was a pleasure to teach them. Each child held a miniature, low-powered lightsaber and wore a training helmet that could block out sight, so that they had to depend on the Force in order to strike the small droids that danced around them. The intense focus of so many young minds made Yoda almost forget his own centuries of age.

"Don't think," he said, sensing a faltering in one small figure. "Feel. Be as one with the Force. Help you, it will."

The child relaxed, and her next swing connected with the training remote. Yoda smiled. Then he saw a different movement on the far side of the room. Obi-Wan Kenobi came through the door, and though he smiled at the practicing children, Yoda sensed that his mind was elsewhere. "Younglings, enough," Yoda called. "A visitor we have. Welcome him."

As the children powered down their lightsabers, Yoda moved slowly forward. "Master Obi-Wan Kenobi, meet the mighty Bear Clan," he said, nodding at the children.

"Welcome, Master Obi-Wan!" the children chorused.

Obi-Wan nodded a greeting, but turned at once to Yoda. "I am sorry to disturb you, Master," he said.

"What help to you can I be?" Yoda answered.

"I'm looking for a planet described to me by an old friend. I trust him. But the system doesn't show up on the archive maps."

The implications were obvious, and serious, but there was no reason to upset the children. And this would make an excellent training problem. Yoda twitched his ears up and said calmly, "Lost a planet, Master Obi-Wan has. How embarrassing." One of the children smothered a giggle; he pretended not to notice. "Liam, the shades. An interesting puzzle." He stumped over to Obi-Wan and waved his cane at his class. "Gather, younglings, around the map reader. Clear your minds, and find Obi-Wan's wayward planet, we will try. Bobby, the lights, please."

Obediently, the children clustered around the shaft of the map reader as the lights dimmed. This class had not seen it in use before, and there were exclamations of surprise when Obi-Wan brought out a small glass ball — the portable map record — and placed it in the hollow top of the reader shaft. The surprise turned to delighted laughs when a three-dimensional hologram of the galaxy sprang up, occupying a large part of the room. Stars of varying brightness seemed to float in the classroom air, and a few of the children tried to catch them.

Obi-Wan walked into the hologram and stopped. "This is where it ought to be — but it isn't. Gravity is pulling all the stars in this area inward to this spot. There should be a star here . . . but there isn't."

"Most interesting," Yoda said. "Gravity's silhouette remains, but the star and all of its planets have disappeared. How can this be?" Again, he turned to his class. "Now, younglings, in your mind, what is the first thing you see? An answer? A thought? Anyone?"

There was a moment of silence. Then a boy raised his hand. Yoda nodded, and the child said, "Master? Because someone erased it from the archive memory."

"Yes!" called the other children happily. "That's what happened. Someone erased it!"

Obi-Wan was staring at the children. A small, serious girl looked at him and explained, "If the planet blew up, the gravity would go away."

Yoda chuckled, as much at the expression on Obi-Wan's face as out of pleasure at the performance of his students. "Truly wonderful, the mind of a child is. The Padawan is right. Go to the center of gravity's pull, and find your planet you will."

Still looking a little stunned, Obi-Wan retrieved his map. "But Master Yoda," he asked as he turned to go, "who could have erased information from the archives? That's impossible. Isn't it?"

Strong is the Force with this one. He sees past his own troubles. Yoda frowned, but he could not refuse an answer to one who had asked the proper question. "Dangerous and disturbing this puzzle is," he admitted. "Only a Jedi could have erased those files." He felt Obi-Wan's startled concern, and nodded. "Who, and why, harder to answer are. Meditate on this, I will. May the Force be with you."

Obi-Wan repeated the wish with more sincerity in his voice than was usual, even among Jedi. As he walked back to his class, Yoda found himself nodding. *May the Force be with us all.*

CHAPTER 7

Obi-Wan gave his starfighter a last inspection. The R4 droid swiveled in its socket in the wing of the small red-and-white spacecraft, and everything seemed to be in order.

Beside him, Master Windu watched, his dark face solemn. "Be wary," he said as Obi-Wan finished. "This disturbance in the Force is growing stronger."

Obi-Wan nodded. Every Jedi could feel it now, and he'd heard that even some of the students could sense it.

More than ever, it made him worry about Anakin and Padmé. *I don't care how sure the Council is; we should not have been given this assignment. He's drawn to her too strongly.* Master Windu looked at him, as if asking what was wrong. Obi-Wan sighed. "I'm afraid Anakin won't be able to protect the Senator," he said.

Mace Windu considered. "Why?" he asked calmly.

"He has a — an emotional connection with her," Obi-Wan said. "It's been there since he was a boy. Now he is confused, distracted —"

"Obi-Wan, you must have faith that he will take the right path," Master Windu interrupted.

Obi-Wan nodded. Yet he could not help wondering whether Master Windu really understood what he was trying to say. Perhaps he should leave a message for Master Yoda. No, Master Windu would surely tell him, and in any case, there was nothing any of them could do about it now. *Anakin will have to manage on his own.* He climbed into the starfighter and punched the button to close the canopy.

"May the Force be with you," Mace Windu said as the protective cover slid closed.

The planet Kamino was exactly where it ought to have been. Obi-Wan frowned and muttered to R4 as he brought his starfighter in toward the planet. In spite of Master Yoda's words, he hadn't wanted to admit to himself that someone had tampered with the Jedi archives, but plainly, someone had. *Who? And what else have they erased?* He shook his head and put the questions out of his mind. That was Master Yoda's problem now. His job was to track down the mysterious bounty hunter in the silver armor and jetpack.

His request for landing instructions was answered

by a Kaminoan who introduced herself as Taun We. "You'll want to land at Tipoca City," she told him. "There's an open landing platform on the south side; I'll transmit the coordinates."

Obi-Wan took his time about landing. Kamino's sun was a hot star, and most of its surface was water; the combination meant that clouds and rain wrapped the planet almost continuously. *Good weather here probably means a day when there's no lightning and the wind isn't blowing the rain sideways,* Obi-Wan thought as he wrestled with his controls. When the ship was down at last, he donned his cloak and ran through the dark, driving rain toward the tower at the far side of the landing platform. As he neared, a door slid open. Gratefully, he went inside.

The sounds of the storm outside cut off abruptly as the door slid shut behind him. The inner walls of the tower glowed bright white, lighting the hall with cool, shadowless brilliance. The sudden light made Obi-Wan squint, unable to see clearly for a moment.

"Master Jedi, so good to see you," said a soft voice.

Obi-Wan pushed back his soaking hood, wiped the rain from his face, and saw Taun We waiting for him. Their brief discussion over the viewscreen had shown him her huge almond-shaped eyes and paper-white skin, but he had not realized how tall and thin she was. More surprising was the genuine pleasure he sensed in her as she went on, "The Prime Minister expects you."

"I'm expected?" Had someone warned these people about him? Why?

"Of course!" she replied cheerfully. "He is anxious to see you. After all these years, we were beginning to think you weren't coming. Now please, this way!"

This is extremely odd, Obi-Wan thought as they made their way through the corridors of the city. But he sensed no fear or dismay, not from his guide and not from any of the other beings they passed. The Kaminoan took him through a maze of corridors directly to a large office. The room had no windows, but it hardly needed any; its walls glowed with the same cool, bright light as the corridors. As they entered, another Kaminoan rose politely from his seat behind a wide glass-and-metal desk. Taun We introduced him as Lama Su, the Prime Minister.

"I trust you are going to enjoy your stay," Lama Su told him once the courtesies were out of the way. "We are most happy you have arrived at the best part of the season."

They call this good weather? But remembering Dexter's comment about manners, Obi-Wan smiled and nodded. "You make me feel most welcome."

"You will be delighted to hear that we are on schedule," Lama Su continued. "Two hundred thousand units are ready, with another million well on the way."

Two hundred thousand . . . units? Of what? "That is . . . good news," Obi-Wan said cautiously.

"Please tell your Master Sifo-Dyas that we have every confidence his order will be met on time and in full. He is well, I hope?"

Obi-Wan blinked. "I'm sorry — Master . . . ?"

"Jedi Master Sifo-Dyas." Lama Su tilted his head forward. "He's still a leading member of the Jedi Council, is he not?"

"I'm afraid Master Sifo-Dyas was killed almost ten years ago," Obi-Wan said slowly. *More like eleven or twelve years, I think — but I could have the times mixed up. I'll have to check with Master Yoda later.*

"I'm sorry to hear that." Lama Su sounded sincere, and Obi-Wan sensed no falsehood in his statement. "But I'm sure he would have been proud of the army we've built for him."

An army? Dexter had said the Kaminoans were cloners. *A million units,* Obi-Wan thought numbly. *An army of a million troops. That's enough to conquer the Republic.* He swallowed hard, then hesitated, trying to think how best to phrase his next question. "Tell me, Prime Minister," he said at last, "when my Master first contacted you about the army, did he say who it was for?"

"Of course he did," Lama Su said in a reassuring tone. "This army is for the Republic."

For the Republic? Obi-Wan struggled to make sense of what he was being told. Sifo-Dyas had ordered this army ten years ago — that must have been just after the Naboo war. He had been a powerful Jedi. Had he forseen the need, even then?

Lama Su rose and went on, "You must be anxious to inspect the units for yourself."

He has no idea how true that is, Obi-Wan thought. Aloud, he said, "That's why I'm here."

After a brief visit with Padmé's family, Anakin escorted her up to the Lake Country. The lodge Padmé had chosen for them to stay at was beautiful, like everything else on Naboo, and just as isolated as she had promised. The island it stood on was one of several that glowed a rich green in the middle of a shimmering blue lake at the foot of a mountain range. The caretaker drove them out to the lodge in a water speeder, which gave Anakin plenty of time to study it. It only took a few seconds to see that anyone approaching the lodge would be easy to spot long before they arrived, so Anakin relaxed and enjoyed the view.

The lodge itself seemed large to Anakin, though it was small compared to the palaces that lined the streets of the capital. He paused on a terrace just outside, leaning on a carved marble balustrade that separated the terrace from the flower garden just below. Padmé joined him, and it was no effort at all to turn his attention from the distant mountains to the girl beside him.

"I love the water," Padmé said dreamily.

"I do, too," Anakin said, looking down at her. "I guess it comes from growing up on a desert planet."

Padmé gave him a sidelong look, then dropped her eyes to the lake once more. "We used to lie on the sand and let the sun dry us, and try to guess the names of the birds singing."

"I don't like sand. It's coarse and rough and irritating, and it gets everywhere. Not like here. Here everything is soft . . . and smooth." Without thinking, he touched her arm.

Padmé gave him another nervous glance and waved at the lake, pulling her arm away as if by accident. "There was a very old man who lived on the island," she said. "He used to make glass out of sand. And vases and necklaces out of the glass." She smiled, and looked up at him as if to share her memories. "They were magical."

"Everything here is magical," Anakin said, staring down into her eyes. She had the most beautiful brown eyes. . . .

"You could look into the glass and see the water. The way it ripples and moves," Padmé went on. She lowered her eyes. "It looked so real . . . but it wasn't."

"Sometimes, when you believe something to be real, it becomes real."

"I used to think that if you looked too deeply into the glass you would lose yourself," Padmé said softly.

But she didn't seem to be talking about the glass anymore.

"I think it's true," Anakin said. He felt warm, and he couldn't look away from Padmé. He didn't *want* to look away. He wanted to be here, with her, forever. He bent forward and kissed her.

At first, she didn't resist; then suddenly she pulled away. The abrupt movement brought Anakin back to his senses as well, and he let her go.

"No. I shouldn't have done that," Padmé said.

"I'm sorry," Anakin replied. Well, he wasn't sorry that he had kissed her; his lips still tingled from the pressure of hers. But he was sorry that she was distressed. "When I'm around you, my mind is no longer my own."

"It's the situation," Padmé said, carefully not looking at him. "The stress —"

"The view," Anakin put in softly, his eyes lingering on the soft curve of her neck. But Padmé's head was still turned away, and she didn't see.

Lama Su and Taun We began Obi-Wan's tour with the replication area where racks of embryos were growing in fluid-filled glass balls. "Very impressive," Obi-Wan said.

"I'd hoped you would be pleased," Lama Su said, smiling. "Clones *can* think creatively. You'll find that they are immensely superior to droids."

You may be manufacturing them, but they're people,

not droids. Obi-Wan could feel the living Force in each of the clones, just as it existed in every other living thing. But he kept his face calm as they went on to an ordinary classroom filled with boys about ten years old. Except that these boys had identical faces below the exact same black, curly hair.

"You mentioned growth acceleration," Obi-Wan said in a neutral tone.

"Oh, yes," Lama Su said earnestly. "It's essential. Otherwise, a mature clone would take a lifetime to grow. Now we can do it in half the time."

Obi-Wan stared at the boys. "These?"

"Were started about five years ago," Lama Su replied, obviously pleased by Obi-Wan's surprise.

Their next stop was an eating area. Hundreds of identical young men sat at long tables. Again, Obi-Wan saw the same dark hair, the same strong features. Even their expressions were the same.

"You'll find they are totally obedient, taking any order without question," Lama Su said. "We modified their genetic structure to make them less independent than the original host."

"Who *was* the original host?" Obi-Wan asked, hoping the question sounded casual.

"A bounty hunter called Jango Fett," Lama Su answered readily. "We felt a Jedi would be the perfect choice, but Sifo-Dyas handpicked Jango Fett himself."

A bounty hunter! Obi-Wan kept his expression neutral. "Where is this bounty hunter now?"

"He lives here, but he's free to come and go as he pleases," Lama Su replied. He waved Obi-Wan through into the sleeping quarters, and continued, "Apart from his pay, which is considerable, Fett demanded only one thing — an unaltered clone for himself. Pure genetic replication. No tampering with the structure to make it more docile, and no growth acceleration. Curious isn't it?"

"I would like to meet this Jango Fett," Obi-Wan said. *I would like it very, very much.*

"I would be most happy to arrange it for you," Taun We told him.

Their last stop, Lama Su said, would be the training ground. Obi-Wan followed him out onto a balcony. Thousands of men in identical white body armor were drilling in the courtyard below. *He said it was an army*, Obi-Wan thought numbly.

"Magnificent, aren't they?" Lama Su said proudly.

Slowly, Obi-Wan nodded, feeling very cold. *The only thing you can do with an army is fight a war.* But Jedi didn't fight wars; they worked to keep the peace and the laws of the Republic without fighting. Obi-Wan stared down at the endless lines of clones marching past, wishing Sifo-Dyas were still alive to explain.

CHAPTER 8

True to her promise, Taun We arranged for Obi-Wan to meet Jango Fett as soon as the tour of the clone factories was over. She escorted him there herself. Obi-Wan took careful note of their route through the corridors, and even more careful note of the locking mechanism on Fett's apartment door once they arrived.

A boy of about ten answered the door, and Obi-Wan blinked, surprised in spite of himself. The boy had the same dark, curly hair and strong features as the young clones he had seen in the training school, but his expression was sharper somehow, more aware. *This must be Jango Fett's unmodified clone*, Obi-Wan thought.

"Boba, is your father here?" Taun We asked. The boy studied them for a moment, then nodded warily. "May we see him?"

"Sure," Boba said, not moving. When he finally

stepped aside and let them in, Obi-Wan felt as if he had barely managed to pass some hidden test.

They stepped into a modest apartment that impressed Obi-Wan mainly by how ordinary it seemed. Looking more closely, he realized that the room was well organized as well as neat. Though Jango Fett must have lived here for at least ten years, Obi-Wan saw few personal items. *He's a bounty hunter; he never knows who might come after him, or when he might have to leave in a hurry.*

"Dad!" Boba called. "Taun We's here."

A man entered from the next room. Though he was instantly recognizable as related to the clones, he looked older than the oldest of them — somewhere in his thirties, Obi-Wan guessed — and he moved with an assurance that the clones could not match. A scar ran down one side of his face, but even without it, he would have looked hard and tough. He nodded at Taun We and eyed Obi-Wan suspiciously.

"Welcome back, Jango," Taun We said. "Was your trip productive?"

"Fairly," Jango said without taking his eyes from Obi-Wan.

"This is Jedi Master Obi-Wan Kenobi," Taun We went on. "He's come to check on our progress."

"That right?" Jango's expression was skeptical and his tone was cold.

Obi-Wan smiled disarmingly. "Your clones are very impressive. You must be very proud."

"I'm just a simple man, trying to make my way in the universe, Master Jedi," Jango replied.

"Aren't we all?" Obi-Wan asked.

Through the partially open door behind Jango, Obi-Wan noticed some body armor lying on the floor of the next room. Before he could get a good look at it, Jango moved slightly, blocking his view. "Ever make your way as far as Coruscant?" Obi-Wan asked. He moved slightly to one side, hoping to get a better look.

Jango moved again, hiding the door. "Once or twice."

"Recently?"

"Possibly."

"Then you must know Master Sifo-Dyas," Obi-Wan said.

"Boba, close the door," Jango said to the boy. He smiled stiffly at Obi-Wan as the boy complied. Then he asked Obi-Wan, "Master who?"

"Sifo-Dyas," Obi-Wan repeated. "Isn't he the Jedi who hired you for this job?"

"Never heard of him," Jango declared. "I was recruited by a man called Tyranus on one of the moons of Bogden."

"Sifo-Dyas told us to expect him," Taun We put in. "And he showed up just when your Jedi Master said he would. We have kept the Jedi's involvement a secret until your arrival, just as your Master requested."

Curious, Obi-Wan thought.

"Do you like your army?" Jango asked, the spite clear in his voice.

"I look forward to seeing them in action," Obi-Wan replied carefully.

Now the bounty hunter grinned nastily. "They'll do their job well," he said. "I'll guarantee it."

And just what do you think their job will be? But asking that might make the bounty hunter more wary than he already was, so Obi-Wan merely nodded. "Thanks for your time, Jango," he said cordially.

"Always a pleasure to meet a Jedi," Jango replied.

Wondering if he had imagined the sarcasm in the bounty hunter's voice, Obi-Wan left with Taun We. He made his farewells to Lama Su and let the Kaminoans lead him back to the platform where he had left his starfighter. The rain and wind outside were even worse than he'd remembered, but he pulled his cloak close about himself and pretended to fiddle with something until he sensed that those inside had left. When he was certain no one was watching, he signaled R4. He had to send a message to Master Yoda and Master Windu at once. They needed to know what he had discovered, and he needed their direction. The situation was much too complex to risk making a false step now.

*   *   *

In spite of Padmé's determination to forget about Anakin's kiss, she couldn't. The memory kept returning at odd moments during the day when Anakin looked at her — and sometimes, when he didn't look at her. She should, she thought, have been annoyed.

But she couldn't be annoyed when Anakin was in such an exuberantly cheerful mood. He teased her and made fun of her until she stopped talking about politics. He juggled fruit, adding piece after piece until there were too many and they all fell on his head. He made her laugh, over and over, and he laughed with her.

It felt good to have someone to laugh with. But by evening, as she and Anakin sat before a huge fire in the open hearth at the lodge, Padmé was wondering whether coming to the lake lodge had been such a good idea after all. *This was a good choice*, she told herself for the hundredth time. Remote, isolated, easy to see in all directions — everything she had said to Anakin was true. The lodge was perfect for security purposes.

Unfortunately, it was perfect for other things, as well. She couldn't pretend not to see it anymore: Anakin *did* care for her. And the more time she spent with him, especially here, where some of her happiest childhood memories were, the more she cared —

Stop that, she told herself firmly. *You have important work to do. You don't have time to fall in love.* But being firm didn't stop the empty feeling in her stomach, or keep her from feeling . . . happy when she saw him come around a corner unexpectedly. And it didn't erase the memory of that kiss —

She heard a rustle of movement and looked up as Anakin bent toward her. *He's going to kiss me again*, she thought, and even as she turned her head away, she knew she wanted him to. "Anakin, no," she said, and the words came out sad instead of firm and decisive.

Anakin looked at her. After a moment, he began to speak — softly, without the confidence she had become used to seeing in him.

"From the moment I met you, all those years ago, a day hasn't gone by when I haven't thought of you," he told her. "Now that I'm with you again, I'm in agony. The closer I get to you, the worse it gets. The thought of not being with you makes my stomach turn over — my mouth go dry. I feel dizzy. I can't breathe. I'm haunted by the kiss you should never have given me. My heart is beating, hoping that kiss will not become a scar. You are in my very soul, tormenting me. What can I do? I will do anything you ask."

Anything? Would you forget that kiss? Would you stop looking at me all the time, the way you do — let

277

both of us get back to our jobs? Padmé knew she should say the words, but she couldn't force them out.

After a moment, Anakin went on, "If you are suffering as much as I am, tell me."

Padmé turned her head away. "I . . . I can't. We can't. It's just not possible."

"Anything's possible," Anakin said. The confidence was returning to his voice. "Padmé, please listen —"

"*You* listen," Padmé snapped. Why did she have to be wise for both of them? "We live in a real world. Come back to it. You're studying to become a Jedi Knight. I'm a Senator. If you follow your thoughts through to conclusion, they will take us to a place we cannot go — regardless of the way we feel about each other."

"Then you *do* feel something!" Anakin said exultantly.

Hadn't he heard anything else she'd said? "Jedi aren't allowed to marry," Padmé said slowly and clearly, as if she were speaking to the little boy she remembered, instead of to this handsome young man she — "You'd be expelled from the Order. I will not let you give up your future for me."

"You're asking me to be rational," Anakin said after a moment. "That is something I know I cannot do. Believe me, I wish I could wish my feelings away, but I can't."

"I am *not* going to give in to this," Padmé said, half to herself. "I have more important things to do than fall in love." But the words rang hollowly in her ears.

"It wouldn't have to be that way," Anakin said. "We . . . we could keep it a secret."

"Then we'd be living a lie," Padmé told him gently. "And one we couldn't keep up even if we wanted to. I couldn't do that. Could you, Anakin?" She stared at him, willing him to understand, to accept. "Could you live like that?"

There was a long silence, and she began to be afraid that he would not answer. Finally he said, "You're right." He looked into the flames, and added almost under his breath, "It would destroy us."

Padmé shivered. There was a frightening conviction in Anakin's last words. She should be satisfied, she told herself. But she could not shake the feeling that they hadn't settled anything.

The more of Obi-Wan's report Yoda heard, the more disturbing he found it. He sensed the same concern in Mace Windu. But they both waited patiently for Obi-Wan to finish — the hologram signal was weak, and neither of them wanted to risk missing a crucial detail.

"Do you think these cloners are involved in the plot to assassinate Senator Amidala?" Mace asked when Obi-Wan finished.

279

"No, Master," Obi-Wan said. "There appears to be no motive."

"Do not assume anything, Obi-Wan," Yoda said reprovingly. "Clear, your mind must be if you are to discover the real villain behind this plot."

"Yes, Master," Obi-Wan replied. "They say a Sifo-Dyas placed the order for the clones almost ten years ago. I was under the impression he was killed before that. Did the Council ever authorize the creation of a clone army?"

"No," Mace Windu said decisively. "Whoever placed that order did not have the authorization of the Jedi Council."

Important, this clone army was, certainly; but also a distraction. Yoda frowned. How to reconcile the two? "Into custody, take this Jango Fett," he told Obi-Wan at last. "Bring him here. Question him, we will."

"Yes, Master," Obi-Wan said. "I will report back when I have him."

The hologram faded. Mace Windu reached out and turned the receiver off. *Move carefully, we must,* Yoda thought. *Lose our way, we might, in this maze of possibilities and deception.*

Padmé did not sleep well that night. Toward morning, she heard muffled cries from Anakin's room, but they stopped before she had to decide whether to go in or not. Another nightmare, she supposed.

She woke early and decided to sit on the balcony for a while before breakfast. Fresh air was just what she needed to clear her head. As she started out onto the balcony, she realized that Anakin was there before her. She hadn't noticed him at first because he was cross-legged on the floor, meditating. Quietly, she turned to leave.

"Don't go."

Padmé glanced back. Anakin's eyes were still closed, and he did not appear to have moved at all. "I don't want to disturb you," she said uncertainly.

"Your presence is soothing," Anakin assured her.

That's nice, Padmé thought. *But I don't think I can just stand here and be soothing for very long.* "You had a nightmare again last night," she said after a moment.

"Jedi don't have nightmares," Anakin said bitterly.

"I heard you."

Anakin opened his eyes and looked at her, and she could see in them all the torment he was feeling. "I saw my mother. I saw her as clearly as I see you now." He swallowed hard. "She's suffering, Padmé. They're killing her! She is in pain. . . ."

Stunned by the conviction in his voice, Padmé said nothing as Anakin rose to his feet. He closed his eyes again for a moment, as if he could not quite bear to look at her. Then he opened them and said miserably, "I know I'm disobeying my mandate to protect you, Senator. I know I will be punished, and possibly thrown out of the Jedi Order. But I have to go. I have to help her." He looked down. "I'm sorry, Padmé," he finished barely above a whisper. "I don't have a choice."

There has to be another choice, Padmé thought. She couldn't stand seeing him so wretched . . . and then she had it. "I'll go with you."

Anakin looked at her as if he could not make sense of what she had just said. Padmé held his eyes and continued, "That way, you can continue to protect me, and you won't be disobeying your mandate."

She still wasn't completely sure he had understood, until he took a deep breath and said, "What about Master Obi-Wan?"

Padmé sighed in relief; it was so good to see hope and determination take the place of his misery. A tiny part of her was frightened by the idea of having so much power over someone — a word or two was all it had taken to restore Anakin's confidence and good humor. Only a word or two, from her. She brushed the thought aside and smiled. Taking Anakin's hand, she said, "I guess we won't tell him, will we?"

Obi-Wan shut down his transmitter. *Take Jango Fett into custody. Right.* He looked out at the torrents of rain pouring down just outside the protective canopy of his ship, and sighed. Then he pulled up his hood and opened the ship. Quietly, he slipped back into Tipoca City.

The Force let him sense and avoid the various people in the corridors, and he reached Jango Fett's apartment without incident. To his surprise, the door slid open at his touch, and he knew at once what he would find inside. The rooms were no longer neat and well organized. Empty drawers hung open, and the few personal items had vanished. *I knew he was ready to leave fast, but I didn't realize he could leave* this *fast!*

They couldn't have been gone long; it hadn't *been* that long since Obi-Wan had left them. He checked the wall computer and quickly tracked down the

landing platform where Fett kept his ship. *Slave I —
what an appropriate name for a bounty hunter's
ship*, he thought when he read the platform listings.
The ship was still there. Obi-Wan took just enough
time to call up a map and find the shortest route to
the platform. Then he left the apartment at a run.

The two Fetts were still loading their ship when he
arrived. Jango was handing crates up to Boba. In
his silver-gold body armor and jetpack, he was
clearly the same man who had killed the assassin
outside the nightclub. He had his back to the door,
and Obi-Wan charged forward into the rain, hoping
to surprise him. But the boy saw him coming and
shouted, "Dad!"

Jango Fett drew his blaster as he turned. Obi-Wan
pulled out his lightsaber just in time to deflect the
blast. By then, he was almost on top of Fett, and he
swung the lightsaber.

"Boba, get on board!" Jango shouted, and triggered his rockets. He shot up into the air, avoiding
Obi-Wan's blow.

Obi-Wan spun as Jango flew over his head and
landed behind him. The bounty hunter circled, firing
toxic darts. Obi-Wan deflected them with the lightsaber. Though he aimed them back at Jango, the
bounty hunter avoided most of them, and the rest
bounced harmlessly off his armor.

Suddenly, the bounty hunter shot into the air again

and hovered out of reach. An instant later, a laser shell whizzed past Obi-Wan and blew a chunk out of the landing tower. The explosion threw Obi-Wan to the ground, knocking his lightsaber out of his hand. *The boy in the ship — he's firing at me!* So was Jango Fett, but Obi-Wan could deflect those shots with his lightsaber. That is, he could deflect them if he *had* his lightsaber.

Jango Fett landed just in front of him. Obi-Wan charged forward and grabbed him. *As long as we're close together, Boba can't fire without hitting his father.* But Jango used his rockets again, then kicked Obi-Wan loose in midair. Obi-Wan fell heavily and skidded across the smooth, wet surface, grabbing desperately for a handhold.

Just when he thought he had one, something flashed down and wrapped his wrists. *Clingwire!* Obi-Wan thought, and then he was being dragged rapidly toward a support column. Jango clearly meant to smash him against it, but Obi-Wan rolled sideways in time. He used his momentum to pull himself to his feet, then suddenly threw all of his weight against the wire.

The clingwire dug painfully into his wrists, but the sudden jerk brought Jango down. The bounty hunter lost his jetpack and slid off the flat landing area, down the slope toward the edge of the platform, pulling Obi-Wan with him. Faster and faster they went. Just as Jango Fett was about to slide off the edge, Obi-Wan saw claws extend from his armor to anchor him in place. Then, as he slid past Jango and over the edge, he sensed a flare of satisfaction from his opponent . . . and the wire around his wrists went slack.

Automatically, Obi-Wan grabbed hold of the loosened wire as he fell into the wind-whipped rain, feeling with the Force for the other end that Jango must have just released. For an eternal instant, he could not find it. Then he had it, and the Force sent it sideways among the great columns that supported the landing platform, to wrap around a cross beam. The wire cut into his hands again as he came to the end of it, but it was better than falling into the angry waves and being smashed against the support columns. He held on and swung under the landing platform.

Below him and a little ahead, he saw a small shelf — probably some sort of service platform — just above the waves. Thankfully, he let go of the wire and dropped onto it. Sure enough, there was a service door. Obi-Wan waved it open and charged up the stairs inside.

He arrived at the landing platform just as Fett's ship lifted to hover a few meters above the ground — the first step in takeoff. He barely had time to snatch a small magnetic tracker from his belt pouch and hurl it at the ship. Then *Slave I* took off, racing for the sky — but even through the pelting rain, Obi-Wan had heard the *clank* of the device attaching firmly to the ship's hull. With a relieved sigh, he picked up his lightsaber. All he had to do now was follow.

Tatooine hadn't changed. It was hot and dry — Anakin was surprised to find that he felt a little *too* hot; apparently, he was more used to cooler worlds now than he had realized. But the same motley collection of shady-looking beings made their way between the same blocky, sand-colored buildings, along the same packed-sand streets. He could have walked to Watto's junk shop blindfolded.

Yet he didn't feel . . . comfortable. Perhaps the problem was that he could see now how shoddy and backward this world was. He remembered how shocked Padmé had been to discover that he was Watto's slave; now he understood why.

Watto hadn't changed, either. The fat little Toydarian's first reaction to seeing a Jedi Padawan was "Whatever it is, I didn't do it!" But he seemed pleased to see Anakin, once he recognized him, and he was willing to help.

"Shmi's not mine no more," he told Anakin. "I sold her to a moisture farmer named Lars. I heard he freed her and *married* her. Can you beat that?"

Watto's trunklike nose wrinkled in evident amazement that anyone would pay good money for a slave in order to turn around and free her, no matter how he felt. "Long way from here — someplace over on the other side of Mos Eisley."

So Anakin and Padmé took the little Naboo starship they had borrowed and flew to Mos Eisley. The directions Watto had given them were easy enough to follow, and by late afternoon they were landing near a small homestead outside the city.

They left R2-D2 with the ship and started toward the buildings. A human-shaped droid straightened up from a condenser as they approached. "How may I be of service? I am See —"

"Threepio?" Anakin said, grinning and noticing that the Protocol Droid he had created now had coverings.

"Oh, my," said C-3PO, cocking his head to one side. "Oh, my maker! Master Anakin! I knew you would return."

"I've come to see my mother," Anakin told him.

C-3PO froze, as if his power had been suddenly disconnected. Anakin felt a sudden lump of fear in his throat. *Something is very wrong. I knew it.* C-3PO twitched and said, "I think — I think — Perhaps we'd better go indoors."

Anakin followed, torn between wanting to know what had happened and being afraid to hear what it was. C-3PO led them down to the sunken court-yard and introduced Anakin to Owen Lars and his girlfriend, Beru. Owen was a stocky young man who already had the quiet, solid look of a farmer; Beru had a practical air that was enhanced by the neat blonde braids that wrapped her head.

"I guess I'm your stepbrother," Owen said. "I had a feeling you might show up someday."

"Is my mother here?" Anakin burst out, unable to bear wasting more time being polite.

"No, she's not," said a grim voice.

Anakin turned. A small floating chair moved out of the main house. In it was a large older man who re-sembled Owen. One of his legs was wrapped in new bandages. The other leg was missing entirely.

"Cliegg Lars," the man said by way of introduc-tion, extending one hand awkwardly. "Shmi is my wife. Come on inside. We have a lot to talk about."

Just tell me where Mom is! Anakin thought angrily, but he couldn't shout at a man in a float chair. So he followed Cliegg into the house, to the underground dining area. Beru served steaming cups of ardees while Cliegg began his story.

"It was just before dawn," he said, his voice hoarse with emotion. "They came out of nowhere. A hunting party of Tusken Raiders —"

Anakin's mind shut off. Tatooine was controlled by the Hutt criminal organization; it was a haven for smugglers, thieves, and other lowlifes. But even on Tatooine, the Tusken Raiders were considered vicious. They tortured people for fun, and they had his mother? He felt cold. *No, Mom, no . . .*

Cliegg was still talking. Anakin heard only snatches. "Thirty of us went out after her . . . I couldn't ride anymore . . . This isn't the way . . . been gone a month." Anakin forced his attention back to the present, just as Cliegg finished heavily, "There's little hope she's lasted this long."

You don't have my nightmares, Anakin thought. He stared around the table, seeing the shocked sympathy on Padmé's face, the hopeless grief on Cliegg's, the wary hope on Owen's. They all seemed far away, almost unreal, separated from him by the icy fear that had settled around his heart. Abruptly, he stood up.

"Where are you going?" Owen asked.

"To find my mother." He hardly heard Padmé's protest, or Cliegg's objections. "I can feel her pain, and I *will* find her."

They stared at him for a moment, then Owen said, "Take my speeder bike," and Anakin felt a distant warmth. Owen, at least, understood.

"I know she's alive," he said to that small, faraway understanding. Then he turned and went out. He'd seen a swoop bike near the stairs as they came down; that must be the one Owen meant.

As he reached the top of the steps, Padmé came running out. Before she could say anything, before she could ask him to let her come with him or, worse yet, ask him not to go, he said, "You are going to have to stay here. These are good people, Padmé. You'll be safe." She had to be safe. He needed to have something to come back to if . . . after he found his mother.

Padmé looked at him for a moment, and he was afraid she would argue, but she only said his name and hugged him. It almost cracked the ice that had settled around his heart. He wanted to smile at her, but he couldn't. "I won't be long," he said as he swung onto the swoop bike.

He started off across the desert. The noise of the speeder bike drowned out other sounds and the dusty wake behind it hid Padmé and the Lars homestead from sight almost immediately.

Hang on, Mom. I'm coming.

CHAPTER ⑩

Although the tracking device was working fine, Obi-Wan pushed his Delta-7 starfighter to top speed as he followed *Slave I*. He didn't want Jango Fett to get out of range. He had almost caught up when they reached a planetary system — the ship's databanks said it was called Geonosis — and the tracking signal vanished.

They seem to have discovered the tracker. Cautiously, Obi-Wan scanned the area. Fett had hidden in an asteroid belt. As soon as he realized Obi-Wan had found him again, he started releasing sonic charges. The two ships dodged and wove through the asteroids, firing at each other and trying to avoid a crash. *This is why I hate flying,* Obi-Wan thought, and then Fett connected and he was too busy struggling with the controls to think.

Fett's ship was larger and more heavily armed than Obi-Wan's; the next missile was a guided torpedo. Following Fett openly into the asteroid field had been a mistake, Obi-Wan decided as he swerved in and out among the asteroids in a vain attempt to lose the torpedo. It was time to try something tricky.

He picked out a large asteroid and headed straight into it at top speed. The torpedo followed mindlessly. "Arfour, prepare to jettison the spare parts canisters," Obi-Wan said as they approached. The little droid beeped acknowledgment. Obi-Wan relaxed into the Force, sensing for the exact right moment. "Release them now!" he commanded, and whipped the starfighter up and sideways.

The torpedo struck the asteroid behind him in a huge explosion that flung rock and the spare parts back into space. Obi-Wan ducked into one of the craters on the far side of the asteroid and shut down his power systems. With luck, Fett would be sure that the Jedi's ship had crashed and exploded, but Obi-Wan wasn't going to take chances. The bounty hunter might be clever enough to do a scan for power systems, just to make sure Obi-Wan's starfighter had really been destroyed.

He waited for what seemed like hours, then cautiously brought the power systems back up and took off. There was no sign of Jango Fett. With a relieved sigh, Obi-Wan sent his starfighter along Fett's last known route, down toward the planet of Geonosis.

Geonosis was a bare, rocky world. Dusty red

mesas baked by day and froze by night. R4's projection of Jango Fett's course took them to the night side. Obi-Wan saw no sign of cities, only huge stone spires that looked like stalagmites. *But stalagmites can only be built up inside, in caves*, Obi-Wan thought. *And it looks as if Fett was heading right for that one. Hmmm.*

At the edge of a small mesa near the stone spire, Obi-Wan found a rock ledge that stuck out far enough to hide his starfighter. Carefully, he maneuvered his ship into the gap underneath and landed. He double-checked his bearings, then started walking.

At the top of the trail, Obi-Wan paused. Pulling out a pair of electronic binoculars, he studied the plain around the strange spire. *Definitely not natural*, he thought, *and . . . what's that?* He brought the view back and saw a number of Trade Federation Core Ships parked in neat rows beside the spire. As he watched, a gap opened in the ground at one side as a lift platform dropped; a moment later, it returned, carrying row upon row of skeletal Battle Droids. *There must be a factory underground. I need to get a closer look.*

Sneaking into the spires was much easier than he had expected. The Core Ships and Battle Droids clustered around one side, probably the front; all Obi-Wan had to do was to climb up the back and slip in through a window. The interior was like a hive, full of narrow corridors that opened suddenly into huge spaces. Several times, he sensed someone coming barely in time to duck behind a pillar or into a doorway.

He reached a vast open area, high and wide and apparently deserted. As he was about to cross, he heard voices and darted behind a pillar.

A mixed group emerged from one of the corridors and started across the square. There were several tall, insectlike Geonosians and a number of off-worlders. Obi-Wan blinked in surprise as he recognized two of them: Nute Gunray, the Trade Federation Viceroy who had led the attack on Naboo ten years before, and the former Jedi, Count Dooku! He leaned forward to catch what they were saying.

"— persuade the Commerce Guild and the Corporate Alliance to sign the treaty," Count Dooku intoned.

"What about the Senator from Naboo?" Nute Gunray said, his wide mouth twisting. "Is she dead yet? I'm not signing your treaty until I have her head on my desk."

"I am a man of my word, Viceroy," Dooku replied.

Nute Gunray and Count Dooku are behind the assassination attempts! Padmé was right. Obi-Wan slipped through the shadows to the next pillar, hoping to get close enough to hear more, but one of the Geonosians began talking about the Battle Droids and then they passed through an arched doorway and out of earshot.

I need to find out what they're up to. Obi-Wan checked quickly to see if anyone else was coming, then crossed to a stairway next to the door. He was in luck; the stairs led to a long gallery overlooking the room below. Dooku seemed to be having a major conference; in addition to Nute Gunray and the Geonosians, Obi-Wan recognized several of the Senators who supported the Separatist movement, as well as representatives from the Commerce Guild and the Intergalactic Bank Clan.

As he listened to their conversation, Obi-Wan frowned. The Corporate Alliance and the Trade Federation — and their huge droid armies — were joining the Separatists. It looked as if Dooku really did mean to start a civil war. *Master Yoda must know about this at once,* Obi-Wan thought. He snuck back down the stairs and headed toward his ship.

It was after midnight when Anakin finally parked the speeder bike at the edge of a cliff overlooking the Tusken camp. He knew it was the right place. He had felt himself drawing nearer all night, just as he could feel his mother now in one of the hide-covered huts below. *Her pain* — he forced himself to stop trembling. *I'm almost there, Mom.*

Pulling his hood over his head, he crept down and into the camp. The Tusken Raiders had posted two guards at the front of the hut, but Anakin had never intended to walk in through the door. Carefully, he made his way through the shadows to the back of the hut. After checking to make sure no one was near, he lit his lightsaber.

The hide wall gave way quickly, and in a few moments he was inside. Moonlight fell through the smoke-hole in the roof, making it just possible to see the spent candles that littered the floor, the wooden frame in the center of the hut . . . and the figure of a woman hanging from the frame.

Without conscious thought, Anakin swung his lightsaber, and the ropes that held her parted. Dropping the weapon, he caught her as she fell. Even in the moonlight, he could see bruises on her face and arms; her eyes were swollen almost shut, and there was blood — he couldn't look at the blood, he wouldn't see it. "Mom," he said desperately. "Mom!"

His mother's eyes opened. "Annie?" she said in a faint, hoarse voice. "Is it you?"

Anakin choked, feeling the pain of her injuries even more clearly now that he was holding her. *She's . . . she's . . . I have to get her home!* "I'm here, Mom," he said urgently. "You're safe. Hang on." *Please, please hang on!* "I'm going to get you out of here."

But Shmi didn't seem to hear his words. Her eyes had finally focused on his face, and her battered features relaxed in an expression of tenderness. "Annie?

You look so handsome. My son . . . my grown-up son." She gasped and went on with evident difficulty. "I'm so proud of you, Annie. So proud." Her voice grew fainter; Anakin had to strain to hear the words. "I missed you so much. Now I am complete."

"Just stay with me, Mom," Anakin begged. The icy fear was closing around his heart again. "I'm going to make you well again. Everything's going to be fine." He reached for the Force as he spoke; surely he could do something that would help, that would ease the terrible pain he felt in her, that would give strength back to the life he could feel fading away between his arms. Something that would give her more time. The Force was there, but he didn't know how to use it for this.

Shmi tried to smile at him. She whispered, "I love . . ." and went horribly, finally still.

Anakin stared at her numbly. After a moment, he reached over and closed her eyes. *The Tusken Raiders did this. Animals, Cliegg called them — they're worse than animals. They're . . . they're . . . vicious, mindless, murdering things. I'll show them! I'll get them all!*

Oh, Mom. Mom . . .

After worrying through most of the night, Padmé heard Beru shouting outside. "He's back! He's back!" She ran outside in time to see Anakin land the swoop bike. *He's all right!* she thought, and then she saw his face as he lifted his mother's body from the bike, and wondered if he would ever be all right again.

Anakin said nothing to anyone; he took Shmi's body inside the homestead and then went out to the workroom alone. *He is in pain,* Padmé thought. She frowned in worry at the closed workroom door for a long time. Then she went to the kitchen and set up a tray of food. If Anakin wouldn't come out, she'd go in after him.

When she carried the tray into the workroom, Anakin was fiddling with a welder and some parts. He didn't look up.

"I brought you something," Padmé said.

Anakin stayed bent over the workbench. "The

shifter broke," he said in a tense voice that she hardly recognized. "Life seems so much simpler when you're fixing things." His face tightened. "I'm *good* at fixing things. But I couldn't —" He slammed the parts down on the bench and looked up, and Padmé saw tears in his eyes. "Why did she have to die?" he demanded. "Why couldn't I save her? I know I could have!"

"Sometimes there are things no one can fix," Padmé said gently. "You're not all-powerful, Annie."

"I should be!" Anakin said, suddenly angry. "Someday I *will* be! I will be the most powerful Jedi ever! I will even learn to stop people from dying."

Padmé could feel the emotions swirling around him: hurt, frustration, anger, grief . . . and fear. It frightened her, but she didn't know what to do about it. Uncertainly, she said, "Anakin —"

"It's all Obi-Wan's fault!" Anakin shouted. "He's jealous! He knows I'm already more powerful than he is. He's holding me back!" He hurled his wrench across the room, and Padmé stared, shocked. His hands were trembling; he looked at them as if they belonged to someone else.

This isn't just about his mother. There's something else going on. Padmé took a deep breath. "Annie, what's wrong?"

"I — I killed them," Anakin whispered, and Padmé went cold. "I killed them all. They're dead, every single one of them. Not just the men. The women and the children, too." He looked up at last, his face working, and Padmé had to force herself not to back away from the look in his eyes. "They're like animals," he spat, "and I slaughtered them like animals. I hate them!" Then the angry mask crumbled away, and he broke into sobs.

Without thinking, Padmé stepped forward and cradled him in her arms. Part of her was still shocked and horrified — *Women and children? My Anakin killed them all?* — and she knew she ought to tell him so. But she couldn't bear to add to his grief.

"Why do I hate them?" Anakin stammered between sobs. "I didn't — I couldn't — I couldn't control myself. I don't want to hate them . . . but I just can't forgive them."

"To be angry is to be human," Padmé said.

"To control your anger is to be a Jedi." Anakin sounded lost, and she could feel him shaking. *That's it — he's afraid they'll tell him he can't be a Jedi,* she thought. *But Jedi aren't superhuman. He knows he shouldn't have done this. They'll understand.*

"Shhh," she told him, rocking him gently.

"No," Anakin argued, "I'm a Jedi. I know I'm better than this. I'm sorry — I'm so sorry."

"You're human. You're like everyone else. Shhhh."

She stayed with him for a long time, then made him eat something. He seemed to her so brittle that a harsh word would break him, and she did not want to leave him alone. Near noon, Beru came to tell them that Owen and the homestead's droids had finished digging Shmi's grave, and they went out to the simple burial.

The ceremony did not take much time. Cliegg made a short speech, and Owen and C-3PO lowered Shmi's body into the grave. Cliegg looked down, tears running across his face. "You were the most loving partner a man could ever have," he said. "Goodbye, my dearest wife, and thank you."

Anakin stepped forward and knelt for a moment at the side of the grave. In a low voice, he said, "I wasn't strong enough to save you, Mom, but I promise I won't fail again." Then, in a whisper that only Padmé was near enough to hear, he added, "I miss you so much."

The silence that followed was broken by a string of beeps and whistles. Padmé turned angrily and saw R2-D2 rolling toward them. "Artoo, what are you doing here?"

C-3PO stepped forward. "It seems that he is carrying a message from someone called Obi-Wan Kenobi," the Protocol Droid translated. "Does that mean anything to you, Master Anakin?"

Padmé looked at Anakin uncertainly, but he only nodded and rose to his feet. They made a hasty farewell to the Lars homestead, and Owen told

Anakin to take C-3PO with him. Then they all hurried back to Padmé's starship to play Obi-Wan's message.

The recording started calmly enough, with a request to retransmit the message to Coruscant. Padmé made the proper connections and they settled back to watch.

The news was grim. Obi-Wan had found the assassin, but he had also stumbled across a secret alliance between Count Dooku and the Commerce Guilds. "They have both pledged their armies to Count Dooku," the little image of Obi-Wan said, "and are forming an — Wait! What!"

Padmé jerked upright in her seat as the recording showed Obi-Wan being attacked by droidekas, the Trade Federation's rolling Security Droids. Anakin jumped out of his chair and began pushing buttons, but no matter how he tried, he could not make contact with Obi-Wan again. Then he tried Coruscant. He got through quickly, but the response was not reassuring.

"We will deal with Count Dooku," Jedi Master Mace Windu told them. "The most important thing for you, Anakin, is to stay where you are." He frowned sternly. "Protect the Senator at all costs. That is your first priority."

"Understood, Master," Anakin replied in a dull tone.

"They'll never get there in time," Padmé burst out as the hologram shut off. "They have to come halfway across the galaxy. Look, Geonosis is less than a parsec away."

"You heard Master Windu," Anakin said in the same dead voice. "He gave me strict orders to stay here."

You told me before that Obi-Wan was like a father to you — and you just lost your mother. You can't just let him die. Padmé pressed her lips together to keep from speaking the hurtful words. *And Obi-Wan is my friend, too.* She reached out and flicked the flight preparation switches on the starship's cockpit. "He gave you strict orders to protect me," she said, "and I'm going to save Obi-Wan. So if you plan to protect me, you will have to come along."

For a moment, Anakin stared at her uncertainly. Then he gave her a wobbly grin and took the controls.

I hope we're in time, Padmé thought as the starfighter rose from Tatooine. *We have to be in time.*

The Geonosian prison cell was not particularly uncomfortable; it was just that the energy field in which Obi-Wan was suspended did not allow him any movement. There was a crackle, and a sharp, tingly pain shot through his arm. *Oh, yes, and the electric restraints are definitely unpleasant.*

He must have gotten careless on his way back to

the starfighter, he thought. If the Geonosians or any-one else had spotted him while he was eavesdrop-ping on the meeting, they'd have stopped him before he got his message off. He hoped Anakin had retransmitted it without doing anything hare-brained. Anything *else* harebrained, he amended; what *was* the boy doing on Tatooine? If Obi-Wan hadn't thought to widen the signal when he couldn't raise Anakin on Naboo, he would never have gotten his message through. . . .

The door of the cell opened, and Count Dooku walked in. If he could have moved, Obi-Wan would have stiffened.

"Hello, my friend," the Count said. "This is a mis-take, a terrible mistake. They've gone too far. This is madness."

"I thought you were their leader, Dooku," Obi-Wan said, trying not to wince as the electric re-straints crackled again.

"This had nothing to do with me, I assure you," Dooku said in a sincere-sounding tone. "I promise you, I will petition immediately to have you set free."

He can't *know what I saw,* Obi-Wan thought. In what he hoped was a casual tone, he said, "Well, I hope it doesn't take too long. I have work to do."

"It's a great pity that our paths have never crossed before, Obi-Wan," Dooku went on. "Qui-Gon always spoke very highly of you. I wish he were still alive."

So do I. Obi-Wan suppressed the pang of grief he

still felt when he thought of his Master, killed by a Sith Lord during the Naboo war ten years before.

"I could use his help right now," Dooku continued, watching Obi-Wan narrowly.

Despite himself, Obi-Wan stiffened. "Qui-Gon Jinn would *never* join you."

"Don't be so sure, my young Jedi," Dooku said gently. "He was once my apprentice, just as you were once his. He knew all about the corruption in the Senate, but we would never have gone along with it if he had known the truth as I have."

"The truth?" What truth could justify starting a civil war?

"What if I told you that the Republic was now under the control of the Dark Lords of the Sith?"

"No," Obi-Wan said. "That's not possible. The Jedi would be aware of it." *But a Sith Lord killed Qui-Gon . . . and Master Yoda said there are always two. Where has the other one been these ten years?*

"The dark side of the Force has clouded their vision, my friend," Dooku said sadly. "Hundreds of Senators are now under the influence of a Sith Lord called Darth Sidious."

Obi-Wan tried to reach out with the Force to sense the truth of what Dooku was saying, but the electric restraints crackled again and he could not maintain his concentration. "I don't believe you," he told Dooku.

"The Viceroy of the Trade Federation was once in

league with this Darth Sidious, but he was betrayed. He came to me for help. The Jedi Council would not believe him. I've tried many times to warn them, but they wouldn't listen to me." Dooku leaned forward, almost touching the force field. "You must join me, Obi-Wan, and together we will destroy the Sith."

Obi-Wan stared. Dooku's claims about the Senate and the Sith Lord were deeply disturbing — but the fact remained that Dooku had plotted with that same Trade Federation Viceroy to assassinate Senator Amidala, and he was preparing to start a civil war that could tear the galaxy apart. *I am a Jedi. I will not be a party to such things.* "I will never join you, Dooku."

Dooku studied him for a moment, then shook his head. As he turned to leave, he said casually, "It may be difficult to secure your release." Then he was gone.

The message was clear: *Join me, or you stay here.* Hung up in a force field with electric restraints, with no chance to escape and report what he had learned — Obi-Wan tried to shake his head, but the energy field kept it from moving. Maybe he should pretend to join Dooku; then as soon as they let him out, he could . . . but no, that wouldn't work. Dooku had been a Jedi. He would sense Obi-Wan's true purpose.

And what if Dooku had told the truth? If the Senate

was under the control of the Sith, if the Jedi Council had ignored his warnings . . . But surely Master Yoda would not do such a thing.

Obi-Wan stared at the closed door, feeling very much alone.

As Obi-Wan's message finished playing, Yoda frowned. He could sense the shock in the other members of the Jedi Council as Obi-Wan spoke of the treachery of the Trade Federation. *But incomplete was Obi-Wan's report,* Yoda thought. He looked at Mace Windu. "More happening on Geonosis, I feel, than has been revealed," he said.

"I agree," Mace said.

Their first step was to contact Chancellor Palpatine, for the threat to the Republic was plainly greater than anyone had thought. They met in the Chancellor's office, along with the loyalist Senators who supported Palpatine.

Everyone listened carefully to Mace Windu's summary; then Bail Organa shook his head. "The Commerce Guilds are preparing for war — there can be no doubt of that."

Yoda's ears twitched. Listen, these Senators did not. They feared, and reacted. They did not *think*.

"Now we *need* that clone army!" Senator Ask Aak burst out.

But everyone knew the Senate would never give its approval for that — not until it was too late. And there were not enough Jedi to hold off an army of droids.

"Through negotiation, the Jedi maintains peace," Yoda said pointedly. "To start a war, we do not intend." There might, even yet, be time to talk a way out of the conflict . . . but he sensed no patience in the room, only fear and urgency as the Senators discussed what to do.

"The Senate must vote the Chancellor emergency powers," Mas Amedda suggested at last. "Then he could approve the use of the clones."

War, you mean, Yoda thought sadly. What other use was there for an army? Not in centuries had Yoda so wanted to comment, to interfere in the politics playing out before him, but he had already said what was needed, and the Senators had not grasped his meaning. He held his peace. *Jedi serve. Make laws, we do not.*

The Senators looked at one another. Plainly, they thought the idea was a good one, but none of them wanted to be the one to propose such a huge change in the way the government ran. Finally, Jar Jar Binks stepped forward.

"Mesa proud to proposing the motion to give

yousa honor emergency powers," he said to Palpatine, and the matter was quickly settled. Jar Jar would bring the motion up, and the other Senators would support it. When it passed, Chancellor Palpatine would approve the emergency use of the clone army.

Barely an hour later, Yoda sat beside Mace Windu, looking down from the visitors' balcony as the Senate seethed. The news had leaked out; he could feel the fear hanging over the chamber like dense fog. *Fear is the path to the dark side*, he thought, but the Senate would not understand even if there were some way he could tell them.

With almost indecent haste, the motion to give Chancellor Palpatine full emergency powers was proposed and passed. The Senate cheered Jar Jar's courage, and Palpatine rose to speak.

"It is with great reluctance that I have agreed to this," the Chancellor said. "The power you give me, I will lay down when this crisis has abated. And as my first act with this new authority, I will create a grand army of the Republic to counter the increasing threats of the Separatists."

Yoda shook his head sadly. Beside him, Mace Windu stirred. "It is done, then," he said heavily. He looked at Yoda. "I will take what Jedi we have left and go to Geonosis to help Obi-Wan."

That left the other task to him. Yoda nodded, accepting it. "Visit I will the cloners on Kamino, and see what it is they are creating." *And to see whether there still is some way this war to avoid.*

Piloting the Naboo starship to Geonosis was easy. Too easy; Anakin still felt shaken and unsure, and he wanted a job that would keep him too busy to think. Fear coiled around his heart: fear that he would lose control again; fear that Obi-Wan was already dead; fear that Obi-Wan was alive and would despise him when he learned what Anakin had done. It was no good telling himself that Obi-Wan was a Jedi and Jedi didn't hate. *I'm a Jedi, and I hate those Tusken Raiders.*

The thought made his stomach clench, and brought back the bloody scene at the camp. He fought back tears, unable to say whether they were tears of re-morse or hatred. To distract himself, he leaned over the instrument panel. Perhaps there was some way to get to Geonosis faster . . .

Dragging every possible bit of speed out of the starship kept Anakin's mind occupied for the rest of the trip. When they reached the planet at last, R2-D2 pinpointed the area where Obi-Wan's transmission had originated, and they headed for it. Anakin kept the ship close to the ground, partly to keep from being detected and partly because dodging the many rock formations kept his mind fully occupied. Padmé looked for a place to hide the starship.

"See those columns of steam straight ahead?"

Padmé said suddenly, pointing. "They're exhaust vents of some type."

"That'll do," Anakin said, and sent the starship down one of them. He landed at the bottom. As he shut the engines down, Padmé turned toward him.

"Look, whatever happens out there, follow my lead," she told him. "I'm not interested in getting into a war here. Maybe I can find a diplomatic solution to this mess."

"Don't worry," Anakin said, forcing a grin. "I've given up trying to argue with you." But he couldn't help wondering whether she thought he *needed* the warning, after what he'd done on Tatooine.

R2 whistled plaintively as Anakin and Padmé left the ship. Preoccupied, Anakin nodded at the droids; most of his mind was concentrated on sensing the Force, searching for life-forms that they should avoid.

The tall underground corridors seemed empty, but Anakin felt uncomfortable. His unease grew as they went farther into the city. Finally, he stopped. "Wait," he called to Padmé, and concentrated. There was something . . . behind; behind and *above* . . .

Anakin's lightsaber leaped into his hands, and he whirled just as a large, insectlike creature swooped down on him. He cut it down, but more were coming. Padmé dashed through a door at the end of the corridor. Anakin cut down three more of the creatures and followed.

They found themselves on a narrow walkway

above some sort of factory, full of droids and conveyer belts and noisy machinery. The door slid shut behind them, and the walkway began to retract. A moment later, more of the winged creatures poured into the area.

Anakin readied his lightsaber while Padmé tried to open the door, but there was no switch on their side. The ledge they stood on grew narrower. Padmé looked at Anakin, then at the retreating walkway — and then, to his horror, she jumped off.

"Padmé!" Anakin cried, and leaped after her. She had landed on one of the conveyor belts, and was already well ahead of him. He started toward her, but the winged creatures attacked and he had to stop to fight them off.

One of the flying things attacked Padmé. Frantic to get to her, Anakin slashed at the creatures surrounding him, but more and more of them kept coming, blocking him. From the corner of his eye, he saw her fall into a huge empty vat, one of a line moving along another conveyor belt. *At least these things can't get at her in there,* Anakin thought, cutting several more creatures in half. And then he saw where the vat was headed — toward a huge cauldron to be filled with molten iron.

Padmé! The vat was too deep and smooth for her to climb out. *She'll be killed — no, Padmé, please, no . . .* As he struggled to reach her through the clouds of flying attackers, he saw a squat, cylindrical shape fly past on rocket jets. A tiny part of his mind wondered what R2-D2 was doing there, but he was too busy fighting to do more than notice the little droid. *Padmé* . . .

His foot slipped. Anakin fell sideways and landed on a molding device. He slid, and his arm caught in the machine. Slowly, it pulled him toward an enormous cutter. He struggled, but to no avail. *No! I have to get to Padmé!*

A triumphant whistle pierced the din. *That sounded like R2.* Anakin craned his neck, and saw one of the vats tip over just before it reached the filling station. Padmé rolled out of it onto a walkway. *R2 must have reprogrammed the controlling computer*, he thought, and then the cutter came down just ahead of him. He had to reserve all his attention for his own plight.

He twisted, trying to get himself out of the way of the cutter. His lightsaber was in the hand that was caught; he switched it on, hoping to be able to turn it enough to free himself in time.

The cutting blade came down again, smashing the lightsaber. The next strike would take off his arm . . . and then the machines froze.

Anakin looked up. He was surrounded by droidekas. Farther down, he saw Padmé, also surrounded. An armored figure dropped from the ceiling on a jetpack — *that's the bounty hunter we were looking for!* — and pointed a blaster at him.

"Don't move, Jedi!" the bounty hunter said.

So much for rescuing Obi-Wan, Anakin thought bitterly. *I couldn't save my mom, either, and now I've brought Padmé right to the people who've been trying to kill her. I've failed at everything.*

When the Geonosians did not kill them at once, Padmé's mind began working rapidly. By the time the guards led her and Anakin into a large conference room, she was calm and ready. As they entered, she saw Count Dooku sitting at a large table. The bounty hunter stood behind him, and there were Geonosian guards everywhere, even though the first thing their captors had done was to confiscate their weapons. *They certainly aren't taking any chances,* she thought.

Before anyone else could speak, Padmé stepped forward. "You are holding a Jedi Knight, Obi-Wan Kenobi," she said in her best Senatorial voice. "I am formally requesting that you turn him over to me. Now."

Count Dooku studied her calmly. "He has been convicted of espionage, Senator," he said. "And he will be executed. In just a few hours, I believe." He smiled gently, as if the thought pleased him.

"He is an officer of the Republic!" Padmé said, outraged. "You can't do that!"

"We don't recognize the Republic here, Senator," the Count replied, and smiled again. "But . . . if Naboo were to join our Alliance —"

So that was his game. She was Naboo's official representative in galactic matters; in some ways, she had as much power as the Queen. If she committed Naboo to the Separatists, her planet and her Queen would be bound by her decision. She listened with half an ear to the Count's smooth arguments, thinking, *I can't betray my planet and my principles, not even for Obi-Wan, not even for Anakin.* She couldn't see Anakin; he was standing behind her, and she was almost glad. She wasn't sure she could bear to look at him right now. *Oh, Anakin, I'm sorry I got you into this.*

Finally, she looked at the Count and said clearly, "I will not forsake all I have honored and worked for. I will not betray the Republic."

The Count sighed. "Then you will betray your Jedi friends? Without your cooperation, I can do nothing to stop their execution."

"And what about me?" Padmé asked, raising her chin.

"There are individuals who have a strong interest in your demise, M'lady," the Count said. "It has nothing to do with politics; it's purely personal."

Nute Gunray of the Trade Federation, Padmé thought. *Obi-Wan's message said he was behind the assassination attempts. He hates me because I led the successful counterattack when he invaded Naboo ten years ago.*

"I'm sure they will push hard to have you included

in the executions," the Count continued. "Without your cooperation, I've done all I can for you."

The Count sat back in his chair, and the bounty hunter waved to the guards. "Take them away," he said in a harsh voice.

The Geonosian guards took them to separate holding cells, and Padmé had time to think. The more she thought, the more certain she became that they were going to die. The Jedi knew Obi-Wan was on Geonosis, but they couldn't move without authorization from the Senate, and she had served in the Senate long enough to know that it would take days of debate before the Senators would agree to such a ticklish rescue mission. She didn't think the Geonosians would wait that long.

She was right. A few hours later, she and Anakin were brought to a large courtroom. The Archduke of Geonosis and his aide stood in the judge's box; to one side, Padmé saw Count Dooku, along with several Senators who she knew supported the Separatists. Beside them stood representatives from most of the Commerce Guilds, the Trade Federation, and the Intergalactic Bank Clan.

The Geonosians got right to the point. "You have been charged and found guilty of espionage," said one, and before they could respond, the Archduke asked, "Do you have anything to say before your sentence is carried out?"

"You are committing an act of war, Archduke," Padmé said. "I hope you are prepared for the consequences."

The Archduke laughed. "We build weapons, Senator; that is our business! Of course we're prepared." He waved at the guards. "Take them to the arena!"

Padmé's faint hope vanished. The guards dragged them out of the room and down to a dimly lit tunnel, where they were tied to the sides of a small, open cart. Miserably, Padmé looked across at Anakin. *This is all my fault. I insisted on coming, and now I've gotten us both killed.*

"Don't be afraid," Anakin said earnestly. He seemed more worried about her than about himself.

"I'm not afraid to die," Padmé told him. She looked down. If ever there was a time for truth, this was it. She couldn't lie to herself anymore, and she certainly couldn't lie to Anakin, not even by keeping silent. "I've been dying a little bit each day since you came back into my life."

Anakin's eyes widened, and he went very still. "What are you talking about?" he asked, as if he wasn't quite sure of what he had just heard.

Well, she would make it clear. "I love you," she said.

"You love me?" Anakin sounded as if he didn't know whether to be outraged or elated. "I thought we decided not to fall in love. That we would be forced to live a lie. That it would destroy our lives —"

Yes, we said all those things. But this turns out to be something that I can't just decide rationally. "I think our lives are about to be destroyed anyway," she said. Groping for the right words, she went on slowly, "My love for you is a puzzle, Annie, for which I have no answers. I can't control it — and now I don't care." She looked directly into his eyes, wishing she could touch him once more. But they were tied to opposite sides of the cart, and she couldn't reach him. "I truly, deeply love you, and before we die I want you to know."

Anakin's lips trembled. Slowly, hesitantly, he leaned forward. Padmé stretched toward him, and for the second time their lips met.

And then the cart jerked forward, throwing them both off balance. As Padmé regained her feet, she heard the roar of a crowd, growing louder and nearer. A moment later, they came out of the tunnel into the execution arena.

Obi-Wan leaned against the execution post in the center of the Geonosian arena and once more tested the chains that held his arms over his head. What were the Geonosians waiting for? They'd had him out here for half an hour already, and the crowd was getting restless. Not that Obi-Wan was in any particular hurry . . .

The crowd roared, and Obi-Wan looked up. A small cart was pulling into the arena, and when he saw its passengers, Obi-Wan sighed and closed his eyes momentarily. *I knew Anakin was going to do something else harebrained, I just knew it.*

But there was no point in scolding Anakin now, and from the look on his face, there was no need to. Obi-Wan waited while the Geonosians chained Anakin to the post next to him. From the corner of his eye, he saw Padmé slip something small into her mouth behind the guards' backs just before they turned and chained her to the post beside Anakin.

"I was beginning to wonder if you'd gotten my message," Obi-Wan said as the guards started out of the arena.

"I retransmitted it just as you requested, Master," Anakin said earnestly. His neck muscles twitched, as if he was trying not to look at Padmé. "Then we decided to come and rescue you."

Obi-Wan glanced up at his chained hands. "Good job!"

In the stands, he saw Nute Gunray and the other trade and commercial delegates crowding into a large luxury box with the Geonosian Archduke. Count Dooku was near the front, along with his bounty hunter bodyguard. As soon as the cart left the arena, the Archduke made a formal announcement that Obi-Wan, Anakin, and Padmé were to be killed — as if anyone in the arena hadn't known that — and then declared loudly, "Let the executions begin!"

The crowd roared again, even more loudly than before, and three large gates opened on the far side of the arena. From the first gate came an enormous, broad-shouldered beast with great horns. *A reek*, Obi-Wan thought. *Powerful, but stupid.* Through the second gate came a gigantic catlike creature with long fangs — a nexu — and the third gate disgorged an acklay, which was a starfighter-sized lizard equipped with pincers large enough to chop a man in half. Behind each of the monsters came a horde of

Geonosian picadors riding smaller beasts and carrying long spears.

The picadors prodded the three monsters toward the center of the arena. "I've got a bad feeling about this," Anakin said.

"Take the one on the right," Obi-wan said, nodding at the reek. "I'll take the one on the left."

"What about Padmé?" Anakin asked.

Obi-Wan looked past Anakin and smiled slightly. Padmé had picked the lock on one of her restraints — *So that's what she was hiding from the guards! A lock pick!* — and used the chain as a rope to climb to the top of her post. She was balanced there, alternately fiddling with the remaining handcuff and pulling at the chain to loosen it from the pillar. "She seems to be on top of things," Obi-Wan said dryly.

Startled, Anakin glanced toward Padmé. Then he gave Obi-Wan a grin that held only a trace of the cockiness Obi-Wan remembered in his apprentice.

What happened *to him?* Obi-Wan thought, and then the monsters charged.

The acklay headed straight for Obi-Wan, its pincers open wide. *Those things are nearsighted,* Obi-Wan thought. *If I time this right . . .* Just before the acklay reached him, he dodged behind the post.

The acklay continued its charge. Its pincer closed around the execution post, right where the Jedi should have been, and the post splintered. Obi-Wan yanked the restraining chain free and glanced quickly around.

Anakin had jumped on the reek's back and looped the chain that held him around one of the reek's horns. The reek was shaking its head and straining against the chain; it wouldn't take much longer to pull the restraints free. The nexu was trying to climb the pole to get at Padmé. As Obi-Wan watched, she swung down on the chain and struck it with both feet, knocking it back. *Padmé can take care of herself — for a while.*

The acklay finished reducing the pole to splinters. Shaking its head, it peered around as if hunting for the tasty tidbit that it knew should have been in there somewhere. It saw Obi-Wan and started forward again.

Obi-Wan ran for the edge of the arena, where the picadors with their long spears were grouped. Startled, one of the riding beasts reared. While the picador was busy trying to deal with his mount, Obi-Wan grabbed the end of his spear and jerked it out of his hands. Planting the far end, he let his momentum and the long spear carry him up and over the picador.

Close behind him, the acklay slammed into the riding beast, knocking the picador off. The Geonosian screamed once before the acklay's pincer closed around him. The other picadors scattered before the acklay's charge, but they would be back soon enough. *One thing at a time,* Obi-Wan thought. The picador's spear wasn't much of a weapon, but it might be enough if he could hit the beast in the right place. He aimed and threw.

The spear caught the acklay in the side of its neck. The acklay screeched, dropped the picador's body, and charged. *Well, that didn't help much,* Obi-Wan thought, ducking behind the dead picador's riding beast.

The acklay followed him, but more slowly than it had before. Obi-Wan kept ahead of it, but he couldn't widen the gap between them. Then he saw the reek coming toward him — with Anakin and Padmé on its back, and the nexu bounding angrily after it. Anakin seemed to have found a way to steer the creature with the aid of the Force. Obi-Wan leaped up.

He landed behind Padmé. Glancing over his shoulder, he saw the nexu attack the wounded acklay. *That's two of them out of the way, for a while. If we can —*

Gates opened all around the arena, and droidekas rolled out. They circled the reek and uncoiled, activating their shields and bringing their powerful blasters to bear. The reek snorted and shook its head, turning in circles to avoid the Security Droids, but the droidekas were everywhere. *We're dead. Why haven't they started firing?*

A sudden silence fell. Obi-Wan looked up at the

crowd and his eyes widened. All over the arena, blue and green lightsabers flared. *There must be at least a hundred Jedi up there!* He glanced toward the archducal box and his jaw dropped. At this distance, he couldn't make out the features of the man in the Jedi robes standing next to Count Dooku — but he didn't have to. Only one Jedi carried a purple lightsaber. *Master Windu!*

As the reek carrying Anakin, Padmé, and Obi-Wan bounded past the archducal box, Count Dooku suppressed a smile. They were certainly an inventive group, but their tricks would make no difference in the long run.

Beside him, Viceroy Nute Gunray turned angrily. "This isn't how it's supposed to be! Jango, finish her off!"

Dooku motioned for Fett to stay where he was. Really, the Neimoidian was almost as entertaining as the Jedi. "Patience, Viceroy," Dooku said to Nute with a slight smile. "She will die."

The Viceroy snorted and turned back to the arena. Amusing as it was to watch his frustration, it was time to end things. Dooku signaled surreptitiously, and his hidden droidekas poured from gates all around the arena. The crowd cheered and Nute Gunray sat back in satisfaction, but Dooku sensed only a feeling of chagrin from behind them where

Jango Fett was standing. He turned to see what his bodyguard had noticed.

Mace Windu stood next to Jango, his lightsaber glowing a clear purple. *The noise of the crowd must have covered the sound when he ignited it,* Dooku thought. He hid his surprise with an elegant nod of welcome. "Master Windu, how pleasant of you to join us. You're just in time for the moment of truth." He gestured at the arena. "I think these two new boys of yours could use a little more training."

Master Windu's grim expression did not change. "Sorry to disappoint you, Dooku," he said in a low, hard voice. "This party is over." He gestured, and all around the arena, lightsabers blazed to life.

Dooku curled his lips in a combination of amusement and pleasure. *This is going even better than I had hoped. There are over a hundred Jedi out there, plus Master Windu; we will kill them all.* "Brave, but foolish, my old Jedi friend," he said gently to Mace. "You're impossibly outnumbered."

"I don't think so," Master Windu snapped. "The Geonosians aren't warriors. One Jedi has to be worth a hundred Geonosians."

"It wasn't the Geonosians I was thinking about," Dooku said, allowing his smile to grow. "How well do you think one Jedi will hold up against a *thousand* Battle Droids?"

Even as he spoke, the first of the new Super Battle Droids appeared in the corridor behind Mace Windu.

They began firing immediately. Master Windu de-flected the blasts easily, but to do so, he had to take his attention from the others in the archducal box. Im-mediately, Jango Fett raised his flamethrower and fired.

Master Windu dodged, but the flames caught the edge of his robe and set it on fire. As more Battle Droids flooded into the arena, he jumped over the wall to the sand below. Count Dooku shook his head at such stubborn foolishness and settled back to en-joy the mayhem. *Yes, this will be very interesting in-deed.*

For a moment, seeing Master Windu, Obi-Wan felt relieved; then Battle Droids began pouring into the arena from all directions. The Geonosians fled as en-ergy bolts began to fly. *So many droids! Can we —*

The reek bucked, and Obi-Wan went flying. He landed rolling and dodged an energy bolt. The droidekas were firing. He couldn't dodge all of them for very long. He needed a lightsaber.

As if in answer to his thoughts, a lightsaber came flying toward him. He caught it and activated it in one smooth movement, saluted the Jedi who'd tossed it to him, and deflected four energy bolts back toward Battle Droids. Anakin had a lightsaber now, too, he saw, and Padmé had found a blaster somewhere.

The fight was the worst Obi-Wan had ever been through. It was far worse than Naboo had been. The

Battle Droids kept coming and coming, endlessly. No matter how many they destroyed, there were always more. At one point, he found himself back-to-back with Mace Windu. They seemed to be making progress — and then Jango Fett rocketed down to join the fight. Mace went after the bounty hunter, and Obi-Wan was on his own again.

There are too many of them! Obi-Wan lost count of the droids he had destroyed. He could feel Jedi dying around him, overwhelmed by sheer numbers. The sand of the arena was soaked with blood and littered with droid parts, and more Battle Droids were still coming. The three execution-monsters were dead — Obi-Wan vaguely remembered killing the acklay himself — but that hardly seemed to matter.

Suddenly the droids stopped firing. Obi-Wan lowered his tired arms and looked around. Mace Windu, Padmé, Anakin, and about twenty Jedi stood in the center of the arena, surrounded by Battle Droids. *Only twenty!* he thought in shock. There must have been at least a hundred lightsabers shining in the arena when he'd first looked up and seen them. The other Jedi must all be dead.

"Master Windu!" Count Dooku's voice rang through the arena. "You have fought gallantly. You are worthy of recognition in the history archives of the Jedi Order. Now it is finished." He paused, then went on. "Surrender — and your lives will be spared."

"We will not be hostages for you to barter with,

Dooku." Mace Windu's deep voice was firm, though he had to know what Dooku's reaction would be.

"Then I'm sorry, old friend," Count Dooku said. "You will have to be destroyed." He raised his hand, and the Battle Droids raised their weapons.

"Look!" Padmé shouted. Obi-Wan glanced quickly around, confused; he saw nothing but Battle Droids. Then he realized that Padmé was pointing upward. He tilted his head back and saw six gunships drop through the open air above the arena.

The gunships landed in a ring between the tiny circle of Jedi and the Geonosian Battle Droids. The arena filled with harsh white light as the thousands of Battle Droids and Super Battle Droids fired their lasers — and the bolts bounced off the shields of the gunships. Obi-Wan stared in disbelief and wonder. *Who are they? Where did they come from?*

And then troops in white body armor came pouring out of the ships, and he knew. *The clone army! But how . . . ?* The clone troopers poured rapid, deadly fire on the droids, forcing them back.

Master Yoda appeared in the doorway of one of the gunships and motioned to the stunned Jedi. "Hurry!" he called.

Everyone raced to the gunships. As he boarded the nearest ship, Obi-Wan glanced up at the archducal box. It was empty. He looked down and saw the clone boy, Jango Fett's son, near one wall.

The boy was kneeling beside the battered helmet his father had worn. *So Master Windu disposed of the bounty hunter,* Obi-Wan thought. He felt sorry for the boy and wondered what would become of him, but there was nothing he could do now.

We're not finished with this yet, he thought as the gunships rose out of the arena. *There are still all those Trade Federation Core Ships in the landing area.*

And then there's Count Dooku to deal with.

CHAPTER ⑭

Anakin knew the fight was not over, but he was glad to have a minute to rest. Padmé was safely aboard, and there were no Battle Droids within reach of his lightsaber. The white-armored troopers inside the gunship fired one last time at the few Battle Droids still standing in the arena. Then the gunship lifted, and they were outside at last.

Outside — but not out of the fight. In spite of himself, Anakin's hand clenched his borrowed lightsaber. A mass of Trade Federation Core Ships and droids covered the ground around the arena. *No wonder they kept coming like that!* Anakin thought dazedly. He had no idea there were so many of them.

But the Trade Federation ships were themselves attacked. Thousands of men in white battle armor were firing into the rows of ships; beyond, Anakin could see Republic Assault Ships landing and more men heading for the battle.

"Look!" Obi-Wan called from the other side of the gunship. "Over there!"

Anakin peered out the open side of the gunship. A Geonosian speeder was heading rapidly away from the battle. In the open cockpit was the black-clad figure of Count Dooku.

"It's Dooku!" Anakin turned to the gunship's pilot. "Go after him!"

The pilot nodded and the gunship began to turn. Suddenly something exploded below the ship. The vessel lurched sideways. Caught by surprise, Padmé fell toward the edge of the ship. Anakin grabbed for her, but he was off balance and too far away, and she tumbled out.

"Padmé!" he cried in horror, then called frantically to the pilot. "Put the ship down! Down!"

Obi-Wan ran foward. "Don't let your personal feelings get in the way," he told Anakin sternly. Turning to the pilot, he waved toward the fleeing Count Dooku and commanded, "Follow that speeder."

Anakin glared at Obi-Wan. "Lower the ship," he told the pilot.

The pilot's helmet swiveled from Anakin to Obi-Wan in confusion.

Obi-Wan didn't seem to notice; his eyes were fixed on Anakin. "Anakin, I can't take Dooku alone," he said. "I need you. And if we catch him, we can end this war right now. We have a job to do."

"I don't care," Anakin said. After all they'd been through, to lose Padmé now would be unbearable. "Put the ship *down*."

"You'll be expelled from the Jedi Order," Obi-Wan warned.

Anakin swallowed hard and looked back. Padmé had rolled to the bottom of a dune. The sand was soft; she might be all right. *She must be all right.* But he couldn't tell, and there were still Trade Federation Battle Droids nearby. "I can't leave her," he said softly.

"Come to your senses," Obi-Wan said sharply.

Anakin looked up, startled, and a little angered by his Master's tone. Then he saw Obi-Wan's eyes — full of compassion and understanding, but still unyielding. "What so you think the Senator would do if she were in your position?" Obi-Wan asked softly.

Anakin fought to deny the answer, but he could not. "She would do her duty," he said heavily. He turned away as Obi-Wan ordered the pilot back on course. He kept his eyes on the unmoving Padmé until she was completely out of sight.

They followed Dooku to a hangar tower. The gunship landed just long enough for Obi-Wan and Anakin to jump off, then it started back toward the main battle while the two Jedi headed inside. They found Dooku at a hangar control panel. A small, fast Solar Sailer ship sat in front of the hangar doors, ready for takeoff.

He's running away, Anakin thought. Anger filled

him. "You're going to pay for all the Jedi you killed today, Dooku!" he said as the Count looked up from the controls.

Obi-Wan drew his lightsaber. "We move in together," he said. "You, slowly on the —"

"No," Anakin said. The anger that filled him was changing, becoming like the hate-filled rage he had felt on Tatooine, in the Tusken Raider camp. If he waited, if he went slowly, he would lose control again. *I am a Jedi! I can't feel like this!* "I'm taking him now!"

"Anakin, no!" Obi-Wan shouted as Anakin started forward. Anakin almost hesitated. But Obi-Wan didn't know about Tatooine and the Tusken Raiders. Obi-Wan must never know. And the only way to keep him from seeing Anakin in the same mindless rage was for Anakin to charge *now*, while he still had control of himself.

Count Dooku smiled faintly as Anakin approached. Anakin raised his lightsaber — and felt a surge in the Force. Dooku thrust out his arm and Anakin was thrown violently into the air. He had a moment to realize bitterly that he had failed *again*, and then he slammed hard into the far wall of the hangar and lost consciousness.

As Anakin slumped to the ground at the foot of the wall, Obi-Wan reached out to the Force. To his relief, he sensed that Anakin was not seriously hurt. But he could not wait for his apprentice to recover; Count Dooku was already moving toward him.

"As you can see, my Jedi powers are far beyond yours," Dooku said conversationally.

"I don't think so," Obi-Wan replied. Alone, he knew he had little chance of winning against Dooku. Not only was Dooku a master swordsman, he was rested and fresh, while Obi-Wan was already weary from the fight at the arena. *But I have to try,* Obi-Wan thought. He raised his lightsaber.

Dooku smiled and parried the first cut easily. He barely needed to move to parry the second and third strokes as well. "Master Kenobi, you disappoint me," he said. "Yoda holds you in such high esteem."

He's trying to distract me. Grimly, Obi-Wan fought on. His exhaustion was starting to tell; his breath came in harsh gasps. He backed off, hoping for a respite.

"Come, come, Master Kenobi," Count Dooku taunted. "Put me out of my misery."

Taking a deep breath, Obi-Wan shifted his grip and dove into the battle once more. Dooku gave ground, surprised by the ferocity of the attack, and for a moment Obi-Wan hoped that he might defeat the Count after all. But even drawing on the Force for strength, he was too tired to keep up the pace for long. The Count began to drive him back.

As Obi-Wan gave ground, Dooku quickened the

pace. His every move was economical and elegant; his lightsaber seemed to be everywhere. Obi-Wan remembered Jocasta Nu telling him, *With a lightsaber, in the old style of fencing, he had no match.* Now he could see what she meant. Unfortunately.

Obi-Wan missed a parry, and Dooku's lightsaber flashed into his shoulder. The pain was incredible. His lightsaber slowed a fatal fraction, and the Count's weapon hummed out and sliced his thigh.

The leg gave, and Obi-Wan stumbled back against the wall. His lightsaber dropped from his hand and went sliding away across the floor. He saw the Count raise his arm for the final blow, and he braced himself.

Count Dooku brought his weapon down — against a brilliant bar of blue light. Anakin stood over Obi-Wan, his face a mask of grim determination, his lightsaber forcing Dooku's back, away from his Master.

"That's brave of you, boy," Dooku said calmly. "But foolish. I would have thought you'd learned your lesson."

"I'm a slow learner," Anakin said, and charged.

To Obi-Wan's surprise, Anakin's attack caught the Count off balance and forced him back. The Count looked just as surprised as Obi-Wan, but he recovered quickly.

"You have unusual powers, young Padawan,"

Dooku said to Anakin. "But not enough to save you this time."

"Don't bet on it!" Anakin said.

But Dooku is right, Obi-Wan thought through the haze of pain and exhaustion. *Anakin is no match for him . . . unless Anakin does something unexpected.* Using all his remaining strength, he reached out with the Force. "Anakin!" he called, and flung his lightsaber to his apprentice.

Anakin caught the weapon in his free hand and attacked again. But even with two lightsabers, he could not hold back Count Dooku for long. The Count smiled and began to toy with him, knocking the extra lightsaber out of Anakin's hand.

Retreat, Obi-Wan thought. *Stall him.* But Anakin was not retreating; he was being driven back. The combat had almost come full circle, back to where Obi-Wan lay. The Count smiled slightly — Obi-Wan was not sure at whom — and his blade flicked out almost too fast to see. Anakin screamed as his right arm dropped to the floor, cut off at the elbow. He fell beside Obi-Wan, curling up in agony. Dooku looked down at the two Jedi and moved in for the kill.

Yoda pressed the switch to open the hangar doors. The battle with the Trade Federation droids was nearly finished; they no longer needed him there. Here, he sensed, was where he should be.

The doors slid open reluctantly, and Yoda walked

inside. *Yes, needed here, I am,* he thought as he saw Count Dooku standing over the fallen figures of Obi-Wan and Anakin. He stopped just inside the hangar, waiting.

Count Dooku saw him and stepped away from Anakin and Obi-Wan. Yoda bent his head in acknowledgment and regret. "Count Dooku."

"Master Yoda." The Count's tone was almost scornful, but Yoda sensed an eagerness in him — eagerness, and something darker. Dooku face hardened as he went on, "You've interfered with our plans for the last time."

Plans of conquest, Yoda thought sadly. *But a Jedi seeks not power.* Truly, Dooku had left the path of the Jedi Order. He felt Dooku gathering power, and he bowed his head in shock and sorrow as he sensed the true source of the Count's increased ability. An instant later, Dooku raised his hands and sent a stream of deadly Force lightning toward him.

Yoda blocked the lightning automatically, grieved by this final evidence of Dooku's change in allegiance. Only those who turned to the dark side of the Force misused their abilities so. This he had feared ever since Count Dooku left the Jedi Order, but only now was he certain. His old student had not just left the path of the Jedi; he had betrayed everything he had once stood for. He had joined the dark side. "Much to learn you still have," Yoda told him.

A startled expression crossed Dooku's face at the

utter failure of his attack. Then his eyes narrowed. He lowered his hands and replied, "It is obvious that this contest will not be decided by our knowledge of the Force, but by our skills with the lightsaber." As he spoke, he reignited his weapon and whirled it in the formal salute that Yoda remembered teaching him some fifty years before.

Yoda drew his lightsaber and answered the salute. In contests, he had no interest, but in stopping Count Dooku, he had a great deal of interest indeed. And Dooku had left him no other choice.

Count Dooku charged forward. Yoda sighed. *Nothing has he learned. Nothing has he remembered.* He closed his eyes, bowed his head, and felt the Force that bound all things, even himself and the Count. His lightsaber moved effortlessly, flowing with the Force to find the balance point between them and block Dooku's every stroke. He did not even have to step back.

The Count's attack grew more desperate, to no avail. Breathing hard, he backed away, but Yoda did not pursue him. To stop Dooku was all that was necessary, and he could not pass Yoda to reach his Solar Sailer.

The Count slowed once more, then stopped, his blade braced against Yoda's. Yoda could feel him drawing on the dark side in an attempt to press Yoda's weapon back, but the dark side was only an easier path, not a stronger one. Backed by the full power of the true Force, Yoda's lightsaber was un-movable.

"Fought well, you have, my old Padawan," Yoda said gently, giving him the truth, though he knew that the Count would not want to hear it. Count Dooku had never been happy to merely fight *well*; the *best* he must be, always. But not this time.

"This is just the beginning," the Count snarled.

Yoda felt a great surge in the Force as Count Dooku pulled one of the service cranes off balance. The mass of metal and wire plummeted directly toward Obi-Wan and Anakin. Yoda could feel the two exhausted, injured Jedi reaching for the Force to keep the crane from falling, but they did not have enough strength left. The falling crane slowed but did not stop; it would surely crush them when it landed.

No decision was necessary. *Too many Jedi have we lost today.* Yoda bent his mind toward the crane, concentrating. The crane stopped abruptly in midair as if it had landed on some invisible table. Slowly, Yoda moved the crane away from Obi-Wan and Anakin, to an empty part of the hangar where it could settle safely to the ground.

Behind him, he sensed the engines of the Solar Sailer start, then felt them fade into the distance. The Count had escaped. But Anakin and Obi-Wan were still alive.

For now, that was enough.

CHAPTER 15

Cautiously, Count Dooku's Solar Sailer approached Coruscant. The Count was in no hurry. The important thing was to avoid detection, and he'd had plenty of practice at that. He was sure he wouldn't be late for his meeting. He had allowed himself plenty of time.

The ship slid through Coruscant's warning systems without triggering them, and glided down toward the surface of the planet. The Count steered toward a burned-out section that had been abandoned eight years before. It was still deserted, and it made a perfect place for him to slip in and out of Coruscant unnoticed.

Dooku flew toward one of the buildings and landed inside, out of sight. As he lowered the ramp, he saw a hooded figure waiting in the shadows. *He always knows,* the Count thought. *But then, he should. That is why he is the Master.*

Leaving his ship, Dooku crossed to the waiting figure. He bowed low. "The Force is with us, Master Sidious."

His Master lowered his head briefly in acknowledgment. "Welcome home, Lord Tyranus," Darth Sidious said in his precise, whispery voice. "You have done well."

"I bring you good news, my Lord," Dooku said. Though he knew that everyone on Coruscant must already have heard, his instructions had been to return here with the news — and Darth Sidious had a short and unpleasant way with anyone who disobeyed even the smallest part of his orders. "The war has begun."

"Excellent." Sidious's dry voice sounded almost enthusiastic, and his lips — the only part of him visible beneath the deep hood — curved in a slight smile. "Everything is going as planned."

Count Dooku returned the smile. *Darth Sidious plans well, and carefully. Soon we two will rule the galaxy. Soon.*

Obi-Wan stood beside Mace Windu, staring out the window at the great plaza below the Jedi Temple. Yoda sat nearby in his Council chair. It was good to be home, Obi-Wan thought, but Coruscant felt different now. Clone troopers in their smooth white body armor were everywhere. The Senate thought that their presence made people feel safe, but to

Obi-Wan they were only a reminder of the vicious battle on Geonosis and all the Jedi who had not returned from it.

Bacta treatments had mended both his wounds and Anakin's, though even that powerful healing agent could not regrow Anakin's arm. Anakin would have to make do with a mechanical replacement. He wouldn't be the first Jedi to have to do so. *And he probably won't be the last,* Obi-Wan thought somberly. Count Dooku had gotten clean away; he would undoubtedly make more trouble.

The thought brought to mind some of the things the Count had told him, and he turned to Master Windu. "Do you believe what Count Dooku said about Sidious controlling the Senate?" he asked. "It doesn't feel right."

"Become unreliable, Dooku has," Yoda said before Mace could reply. His voice dropped. "Joined the dark side. Lies, deceit, creating mistrust are his ways now."

Master Windu held up a hand. "Nevertheless, I feel we should keep a closer eye on the Senate."

Yoda nodded. "I agree."

Mace Windu turned back to Obi-Wan. "Where is your apprentice?"

"On his way to Naboo," Obi-Wan said. "He is escorting Senator Amidala home." Anakin had told him of Shmi's death; that was why he and Padmé had gone to Tatooine, he said. Obi-Wan had talked to Padmé later, and she had explained that Shmi had been kidnapped and killed by Tusken Raiders.

Neither of them had been willing to go into much detail, and from what Obi-Wan knew of the Tusken Raiders, he didn't blame them. It was no wonder Anakin seemed shaken, if his mother had been tortured and killed. One day, perhaps, Anakin would be willing to tell him the whole story. In the meantime, Padmé's presence seemed to cheer Anakin up, and it would be good for Anakin to spend a little time on a beautiful planet like Naboo. It might take his mind off the horror of his mother's death, and of the battle on Geonosis.

They had lost so many Jedi. Two hundred had gone to Geonosis; barely twenty had returned. Still, they had won. "I have to admit, without the clones it would not have been a victory," Obi-Wan said.

"Victory?" Yoda sat indignantly upright in his chair. "Victory, you say?"

Obi-Wan turned. Yoda looked around the almost-empty Council chamber, and his ears drooped sadly. "Master Obi-Wan, not victory," he said softly. "Only begun, this Clone War has."

The words rang in Obi-Wan's head. He closed his eyes, remembering the endless lines of clone troopers on Kamino. They were on Coruscant now — tens of thousands of clones, boarding Republic Assault

Ships that would take them to fight on the Separatist worlds. There were many times as many troopers as there were Jedi, and the Kaminoans had a million more on the way. *It takes more beings to fight a war than it does to keep the peace,* Obi-Wan thought gloomily, and realized that Yoda was right. The war had only begun.

If Padmé had ever thought about her wedding, she had pictured a formal ceremony with her family and friends as witnesses. She had never, in her wildest dreams, expected to be married secretly on an isolated island with only a pair of droids to watch the Holy Man's blessing. But she was here, and she could imagine no more perfect place to marry Anakin than the balcony of this lake lodge where she had begun to discover her love for him. The roses in the garden below were past their prime, shedding petals at the slightest breeze. The fading flowers drenched the air with their perfume.

Anakin seemed serious, almost sad, as they exchanged their vows, and for a moment Padmé wondered if they were doing the right thing. But it was too late to change her mind now; the vows were spoken.

The Holy Man blessed them, and Anakin turned to smile down at her. Padmé smiled back, trying to set her misgivings aside. He raised his hand to her shoulder — his right hand, the one that was now only a clever mechanical imitation of a real arm. Was it only her imagination, or were the wires and metal too cool against her neck?

Anakin's blue eyes darkened and his smile faded slightly. Did he sense the doubts she had tried to hide, or was it his own uncertainty she saw in his eyes? *It would destroy us*, he had said, and he had sounded so sure, as if he knew. But he had lost so much; surely he didn't have to lose this, too. *Not doing this would destroy us, too*, Padmé thought. *We'll make it work. Somehow.*

Then Anakin bent and kissed her, and she had no more doubts. There was only Anakin, and the scent of the dying roses in the garden below.

EPISODE III

REVENGE OF THE SITH™

Patricia C. Wrede
Based on the story and screenplay
by George Lucas

A long time ago, in a galaxy far, far away. . . .

The Republic was at war. For two thousand years, the Jedi Knights had kept the peace, but even their formidable skills could not prevent the strife this time. Led by the former Jedi, Count Dooku, the Separatist coalition broke away from the Galactic Republic. War erupted during a rescue mission on Geonosis, and many Jedi died. Jedi Master Yoda arrived unexpectedly with clone troops, in time for the Republic to win that first battle — but too late to stop the war.

At first, many in the Republic were sure that their clone troopers would end the war quickly. But the Trade Federation, with its enormous army of droids, supported the Separatists. Even with the forced-growth techniques of the clone masters, it took longer to grow a clone trooper than to produce a battle droid. The Clone Wars raged on, and spread to many systems.

Only the Jedi were not surprised. For on Geonosis, Obi-Wan Kenobi and his Padawan apprentice, Anakin Skywalker, had learned that Count Dooku had turned to the dark side of the Force — and the power of the dark side had been growing for years. The Jedi knew that defeating the Separatists would be neither quick nor easy with a Dark Lord of the Sith aiding them.

As soon as they recovered from the injuries they had received during their battle with Count Dooku, Anakin Skywalker and Obi-Wan Kenobi rejoined the war. Together they became heroes of the Republic, sometimes leading clone troopers in pitched battles, sometimes making daring raids in secret. For their work, Anakin was made a full Jedi Knight, and Obi-Wan was given a seat on the Jedi Council and the title of Master.

No one, not even the Jedi, knew that one of the things driving Anakin was his desire to be back on Coruscant, the home of the Galactic Senate. In defiance of the Jedi Order, he had secretly married Senator Padmé Amidala, who spent most of her time working there. As the fighting spread into the Outer Rim Worlds, the moments Anakin could steal to be with his wife became fewer.

Then the Separatists struck a paralyzing blow, straight at the heart of the Republic. A fleet of ships commanded by the dreaded Separatist General

Grievous slipped through the outer line of defenses to attack Coruscant itself. In the confusion the Separatists kidnapped Supreme Chancellor Palpatine, the elected leader of the Republic.

But Coruscant was not only the heart of the government and the location of the Galactic Senate. It was also the home of the Jedi Temple. As the Separatist attack began, a message was beamed to the Outer Rim, summoning the Jedi's greatest warriors home. Before the Separatist fleet could leave the Coruscant star system with the Chancellor, they found themselves under attack. Waves of clone starfighters, led by Obi-Wan and Anakin, stormed around their ships. . . .

CHAPTER 1

Laser beams flashed around Obi-Wan's Jedi Interceptor as his fingers danced across the controls. The small starfighter danced in response, avoiding the beams. *Space is* supposed *to be empty,* Obi-Wan thought as he wove through the swarm of droid trifighters.

Not that the space around Coruscant had ever been empty. The capital planet of the Galactic Republic attracted thousands of ships every day, carrying diplomats and Senators, tourists and refugees, food and goods from strange and distant star systems. The ships that filled the sky now, however, were fighters and cruisers and battleships, not freighters and transports.

At least a lot of them are ours, Obi-Wan thought. His ship rocked as a droid fighter exploded a little too close by. Anakin had scored a hit. Obi-Wan grimaced. He didn't enjoy this sort of flying, not the way his former apprentice did. "Flying is for droids," he muttered.

As the fireball cleared, Obi-Wan saw movement against the stars. "Look out," he said into his comm. "Four droids, inbound."

He swerved as he spoke to avoid the oncoming tri-fighters. Off to one side, Anakin's Interceptor made the same move in perfect unison. They swept around one side of the droid formation, then swooped unexpectedly close to the two nearest ships. One droid saw them and followed, but the ship behind it kept to its original course, and the two fighters collided.

Two down, two to go. But the remaining droids wouldn't fall for the same trick. "We've got to split them up!" he said into the comm.

"Break left," Anakin's voice said in his ear. "Fly through the guns on that tower."

"Easy for you to say," Obi-Wan grumbled as he sent his fighter hurtling toward the gun towers of the nearest cruiser. "Why am I always the bait?"

"Don't worry," Anakin said soothingly. "I'm coming around behind you."

Obi-Wan would have snorted, but he was too busy with the controls. Flying this close to a large starship was tricky, even with the Force to help. The droids weren't having much trouble, though. Both of them had stuck with him, and they were gaining.

Laser fire flashed, barely missing the Jedi fighter.

"Anakin, they're all over me!" Obi-Wan complained.

"Dead ahead!" Anakin's voice said happily. "Move to the right so I can get a clear shot at them. Closing . . . Lock onto him, Artoo!"

Obi-Wan heard a faint beep in the background from Anakin's astrodroid, R2-D2. A moment later, one of the tri-fighters behind him exploded. Obi-Wan would have been better pleased if the second fighter hadn't kept on firing. Its aim was improving, too. That was the trouble with droids; you couldn't distract them. "I'm running out of tricks here," Obi-Wan said to Anakin.

The cruiser dropped away behind them. Out in open space, he was a sitting duck. He needed something else to dodge behind. A Separatist battleship loomed — not the best idea, perhaps, but the only one available at the moment. "I'm going down on the deck," he told Anakin. He swung his fighter, narrowly avoiding another barrage of laser fire.

"Good idea." Anakin sounded cheerful. "I need some room to maneuver."

What, space isn't big enough? But once again Obi-Wan was too busy skimming the surface of a battleship to speak. And this one was firing at him, right along with the droid fighter on his tail. *This may not have been such a good idea*, he thought as he dodged blasts coming from all directions.

"Cut right!" Anakin said, and for the first time his voice sounded a little strained. "Do you hear me? Cut right! Don't let him get a handle on you." The comm crackled, but did not cut off. "Come on, Artoo, lock on!" Anakin said. "Lock on!"

"Hurry up," Obi-Wan said. "I don't like this." A laser blast struck one of his wings. The ship bucked and twisted. Obi-Wan's hands flickered from one control to another. Behind him, his astrodroid beeped emphatically. "Don't even try to fix it, Arfour," Obi-Wan told it. "I've shut it down." So dodging the droids would be even harder. If Anakin didn't hurry . . .

As if he could hear Obi-Wan's thoughts, Anakin said, "We're locked on. We've got him," and an instant later, the droid tri-fighter exploded. "Good going, Artoo!"

Obi-Wan blew out a quiet sigh of relief. "Next time, *you're* the bait," he told Anakin. He could picture his former Padawan's answering grin, and added firmly, "Now, let's find the command ship and get on with it."

"Straight ahead," Anakin responded. "The one crawling with vulture droids."

"I see them." They were hard to miss; dozens of the broad, half-flattened shapes crouched ominously behind the blue force field that shielded the open hangar. "Oh, *this* should be easy," Obi-Wan said sarcastically.

"Come on, Master," Anakin said. "This is where the fun begins!"

Obi-Wan shook his head, though Anakin couldn't see him. They'd taken on similar odds before, and won ... barely. If this had been an ordinary battle, Obi-Wan might have joined Anakin. *Though I wouldn't have been happy about it.* But a mistake now might cost the Chancellor's life. "Not this time," Obi-Wan said. "There's too much at stake. We need help." He changed the comm's settings and called in the nearest squad of clone fighters.

A moment later, he was glad he had. The droids lifted off, rising from the hangar in a dark cloud. They headed straight for Anakin and Obi-Wan.

The clone squad of ARC-170 starfighters swung into formation behind them. Obi-Wan just had time to acknowledge their arrival before the Separatist droids were on them. He blasted one, then swung to back up Anakin. More droid fighters appeared from behind the cruiser.

Obi-Wan fired at one droid, dodged a series of laser blasts from two others, and called a warning. "Anakin, you have four on your tail!"

"I know, I know."

"And four more closing from your left."

"I know, I know!" Anakin's ship swung wildly from side to side, dodging laser fire. "I'm going to pull them through the needle."

Obi-Wan stared at the Trade Federation battleship. At the end of a long trench, a conning tower stood on two metal struts like legs, with only a narrow slit between them. Anakin was right; the droid fighters would never make it through that. Even a Jedi could easily crash. "Too dangerous," he warned. "First Jedi rule: Survive."

Another burst of laser fire erupted around Anakin's ship. "Sorry, no choice," Anakin said. His fighter dodged and shuddered. "Come down here and thin them out a little."

Obi-Wan shook his head again, but he plunged toward the eight vulture droids as Anakin's fighter shot down the trench toward the impossibly narrow slit ahead.

The laser fire was nearly continuous. *Where is Obi-Wan?* Anakin thought as he made his ship jump and dodge. He felt a larger explosion somewhere behind him and glanced at his rear viewscreen. Several of the vulture droids had vanished in a large fireball. *Good. Now if the rest of them will just keep following me. . . .*

The "needle" was getting close. R2-D2 beeped nervously. "Easy, Artoo," Anakin said. "We've done this before."

"Use the Force," Obi-Wan's voice said over his

comm unit. "Feel yourself through; the ship will follow."

As if I didn't know that already. It annoyed Anakin when his former Master treated him as though he were still a Padawan learner, instead of a full Jedi Knight, just as good as Obi-Wan was. *Or better.* But there wasn't time now to be annoyed with Obi-Wan, not with the conning tower almost on top of him.

R2-D2 squealed in panic as Anakin tilted the ship sideways just in time to skim through the gap. "I'm through!" he broadcast to Obi-Wan.

He pulled out, away from the battleship, and saw Obi-Wan's fighter driving the last of the vulture droids into a fireball clinging to the legs of the conning tower. *Tried to follow me and missed,* Anakin thought with satisfaction.

Obi-Wan pulled up long before he was close to the tower, and the two Jedi Interceptors flew side by side. Around them, the clone starfighters dodged and wove and fired in a deadly dance with a huge cloud of vulture droids. The clones were badly outnumbered.

"I'm going to help them out!" Anakin said, and started to turn his fighter.

"No," Obi-Wan told him firmly. "They're doing their job so we can do ours. Head for the command ship!"

Anakin complied, feeling irritated again, though

this time he was more annoyed with himself than with Obi-Wan. He *had* forgotten, just for a second, that winning the battle wasn't important — not if the command ship got away with Supreme Chancellor Palpatine.

Two droid tri-fighters appeared straight in front of them, firing missiles. Anakin called a warning to Obi-Wan as he sent his own ship sharply to the right. Two missiles pursued him. *Let's see them follow this*, Anakin thought, and went into a tight loop. The missiles collided and exploded. Anakin looked for Obi-Wan, just as Obi-Wan's voice came over his comm: "I'm hit!"

Anakin's heart lurched. Frantically, he hunted for Obi-Wan's ship. It looked intact — and then he saw the buzz droids crawling like spiders over its surface, ripping holes in the skin and tearing out wiring. At that rate, they'd destroy the fighter in a matter of minutes.

An unnatural calm descended on Anakin. "Buzz droids," he told Obi-Wan. "I see them."

There was an instant of silence as Obi-Wan absorbed the information. Then his voice came again, cool and almost resigned. "Get out of here, Anakin. There's nothing you can do."

I'll make up something. "I'm not leaving you, Master," Anakin said.

"The mission, Anakin," Obi-Wan reminded him

gently, as if he were teaching a particularly hard lesson to a reluctant Padawan. "Get to the command ship. Get the Chancellor."

Anakin hesitated. Chancellor Palpatine was not just the leader of the Republic; he was a friend and advisor. His gentle wisdom had helped Anakin many times. Only Padmé knew more about Anakin's secret feelings. But Obi-Wan had been Anakin's teacher and companion since he was nine years old. He was the father Anakin never had, the brother Anakin had imagined, the working partner who'd saved Anakin's life and been saved by him more times than either could count. Anakin set his jaw. "Not without you."

"They're shutting down the controls," Obi-Wan said.

Anakin swallowed hard. The buzz droids had already ripped Obi-Wan's astrodroid apart, so that it couldn't fix anything. Without controls, Obi-Wan would spin away into space. Even if his life support wasn't damaged, it would be hard to find him before his air ran out. And the buzz droids wouldn't stop with the controls. They'd go for the life support next.

No! Anakin came toward Obi-Wan's ship at an angle and fired. The shot vaporized several buzz droids . . . and part of Obi-Wan's left wing.

"That's not helping," Obi-Wan said.

"I agree, bad idea," Anakin admitted. *But I have to do something! What else?* "Swing right.

Steady . . ." He moved his ship closer to Obi-Wan's. Closer still . . .

"Wait!" Obi-Wan protested. "You're going to get us both killed!" He sounded as if he was more worried about what Anakin was doing than about the buzz droids.

Anakin ignored him. Obi-Wan always argued whenever Anakin wanted to try something tricky. As long as he held his ship steady, giving Anakin a stable target, he could complain all he wanted. Cautiously, Anakin dipped closer. His wing scraped away almost all of the buzz droids, but despite his care, the maneuver dented both ships — and the last remaining buzz droid ran up his wing. *Better not try that again.*

Behind him, R2-D2 beeped angrily. *Artoo can handle it,* Anakin thought. "Get him, Artoo!" he said.

"Go for the eyes," Obi-Wan advised. Anakin heard a zap, and an instant later the buzz droid slid down his wing and dropped off into space.

"Blast it!" Obi-Wan said. "My controls are gone."

He can still steer, Anakin thought. But without the rest of his controls, Obi-Wan's ship was nothing but target practice for the vulture droids. Desperately, Anakin looked for a place to hide — and saw the Trade Federation's command ship looming ahead of them.

Oh, great, just what we need . . . wait, no, it

really is *just what we need!* "Stay on my wing," he told Obi-Wan. "The general's command ship is dead ahead."

The smoke in front of Obi-Wan's fighter began to clear. A moment later, Obi-Wan's voice complained in Anakin's ears. "Whoa! Anakin, we're going to collide!"

Anakin smiled. Sometimes his Master was so predictable. "That's the plan. Head for the hangar."

The command ship loomed large in front of them. "Have you noticed the shields are up?" Obi-Wan said.

Ooooops. "Sorry, Master." Anakin zipped ahead to blast the shield generator before Obi-Wan's rapidly disintegrating fighter could hit. A moment later, the two Jedi Interceptors flew through the doors of the command ship hangar. Blast doors slammed shut behind them. Obi-Wan's ship crashed at the far end of the hangar as Federation battle droids rushed in from all directions.

CHAPTER 2

As his starfighter crashed to the hangar floor, Obi-Wan ignited his lightsaber. In one quick movement, he cut a hole in the roof of the cockpit and leaped out. Seconds later, the crippled ship exploded.

Battle droids fired as Obi-Wan landed, but he sent their laser bolts singing back at them. He sensed, more than saw, Anakin land and run to join him. Together, they cleared the battle droids from the hangar floor.

As the last battle droid fell, Obi-Wan deactivated his lightsaber and looked at his former apprentice. He knew that he ought to rebuke Anakin for taking such chances during the battle with the buzz droids. He'd risked their entire mission — and the Chancellor's life — to satisfy his personal feelings. But if Anakin hadn't taken those risks, he, Obi-Wan, would very likely be dead. Obi-Wan frowned. *He still has much to learn*, he thought, *but then, so do I.*

R2-D2 rolled forward. "Tap into the ship's computers," Anakin told the droid. R2-D2 beeped and rolled to a wall socket. Soon they had the Chancellor's location — in the sumptuous quarters at the top of the ship's spire.

Anakin frowned. "I sense Count Dooku."

That's no surprise, Obi-Wan thought. The renegade Jedi had beaten them both on Geonosis. Thanks to him, Anakin's right hand was now a mechanical skeleton instead of flesh and blood. Only the timely arrival of Master Yoda had saved their lives. Who else but Count Dooku would the Separatists send on such a crucial mission? And this time, Master Yoda was busy elsewhere. "I sense a trap."

"Next move?" Anakin asked, looking at Obi-Wan.

Obi-Wan smiled. "Spring the trap."

Anakin grinned and nodded. They left R2-D2 in the hangar and made their way through the ship. Several times, battle droids found them, but they were no match for the Jedi. Soon, they reached the elevator to the general's quarters. When the doors opened, Obi-Wan looked around carefully, but saw no sign of droids. Still, it felt wrong. And there was that other presence — "He's close," Obi-Wan told Anakin.

"The Chancellor?"

"Count Dooku."

Cautiously, the two Jedi descended the steps from the elevator into the general's quarters. The main room was enormous, but empty, except for a chair at the far end. Strapped in the chair was Supreme Chancellor Palpatine.

He doesn't look hurt, Obi-Wan thought as they walked forward. *But he's not happy. Well, who would be, under these circumstances?*

"Are you all right?" Anakin demanded as they reached the Chancellor.

"Anakin," the Chancellor said quietly, "droids." He made a small gesture with his fingers, all he could manage with the energy bonds restraining him.

As one, Obi-Wan and Anakin turned. Four super battle droids had come in behind them. Anakin smiled. "Don't worry, Chancellor. Droids are not a problem."

Don't get cocky, my young Padawan, Obi-Wan almost said, but he couldn't scold Anakin in front of the Chancellor. Especially since it would probably make Anakin even more reckless once the fight started. And there was still —

Before he could even finish the thought, Obi-Wan felt his eyes drawn upward. Tall, elegant, and graceful, Count Dooku strode onto the balcony. His face wore the same faintly amused smile Obi-Wan remembered so vividly from their last encounter.

"This time, we do it together," Obi-Wan said quietly

to Anakin. He hoped his former apprentice wasn't going to be difficult. They couldn't afford to lose.

To his surprise, Anakin gave a small nod. "I was about to say that."

Maybe he's learned more than I thought. Obi-Wan shifted his balance, waiting for the next move.

"Get help!" Palpatine said urgently from behind them. "You're no match for him. He's a Sith Lord."

And where do you think we can get help from, Chancellor? Obi-Wan gave Palpatine a reassuring smile. "Our specialty is Sith Lords, Chancellor."

As Obi-Wan and Anakin ignited their lightsabers, Count Dooku jumped down from the balcony. He landed lightly, and Obi-Wan felt the dark side of the Force surging around him. "Your swords, please, Master Jedi. Let's not make a mess of this in front of the Chancellor."

Obi-Wan and Anakin ignored him. Lightsabers ready, they closed in. As Dooku reached for his own lightsaber, they charged. Dooku met them with a mocking smile. "Don't assume that because there are two of you, you have the advantage," he said.

Count Dooku deserved his reputation as a master of the old style of lightsaber fencing. Even with both Anakin and Obi-Wan pressing him, he seemed at ease. The Jedi used every trick they knew, leaping and striking from unexpected directions. Dooku blocked them all. *At least he's not having any more luck hitting us than we are hitting him,* Obi-Wan thought. *That's a big improvement over last time.*

Anakin seemed to be thinking along the same lines. In a lull between fierce exchanges, he gave Dooku a frightening smile and said, "My powers have doubled since we last met, Count."

No, Anakin, Obi-Wan thought. *Don't taunt him.* Anger fed the dark side; they didn't need Dooku's power to be any greater than it already was.

"Good," the Count said calmly. "Twice the pride, double the fall. I have looked forward to this, Skywalker."

Despite the Count's confidence, the two Jedi forced him slowly backward. When the super droids got in the way, they cut them down. At last they reached the first set of stairs to the balcony. As the Count started up, Obi-Wan disengaged and ran to the second set of stairs to attack him from behind. Climbing the stairs, it cut down two of the super battle droids.

He can't fight in two directions at once, Obi-Wan thought as he came up behind the Count. *If we can —*

Count Dooku half-turned and raised a hand. A rush of dark power lifted Obi-Wan off his feet and choked the air from his lungs. He reached for the Force to counter Dooku, but the attack had been too sudden. He saw Dooku twist, kicking out at Anakin with all his weight behind it. Anakin fell backward, and Dooku hurled Obi-Wan over the edge of the balcony.

Obi-Wan dropped to the floor below and lay half-stunned. Distantly, he felt a surge in the dark side, and then a large chunk of the balcony hurtled down at him. His last thought before he lost consciousness was, *It's up to Anakin now.*

As the balcony collapsed atop Obi-Wan, Anakin rushed at the Count and kicked him over the edge, then followed him down. He wanted to rush to the pile of rubble burying Obi-Wan, but he knew he couldn't. *It's up to me now. I can't give Dooku even the smallest opening.* He tried to concentrate on Dooku, but his fear for Obi-Wan was hard to ignore.

Dooku smiled, and echoed Anakin's thoughts. "I sense great fear in you, Skywalker." He shook his head, as if Anakin were a particularly slow student. "You have power, you have anger — but you don't use them."

And I'm not going to, Anakin told himself. *That's the way to the dark side.* Pushing his fear aside, he tried to forget the balcony crushing Obi-Wan and the intent expression on the Chancellor's face as he watched the battle that would decide his fate. Anakin made himself focus on the fight, and only the fight.

All of the super battle droids had been cut down;

only Anakin and Dooku were left. Down the long length of the room they fought, neither one able to gain an advantage. *He's old,* Anakin thought. *Maybe I can just outlast him.* But the power of the dark side flowed around him, denying that possibility. The dark side would keep Dooku going as long as he needed. *What am I going to do? I have to beat him, or the Chancellor and Obi-Wan are dead. Not to mention me. . . .*

Behind him, he heard Chancellor Palpatine calling something, trying to be heard over the crackle and hum of the lightsabers. "Use your aggressive feelings, Anakin! Call on your rage. Focus it, or you don't stand a chance against him."

Anakin hesitated. The Chancellor was no Jedi; he couldn't know about the dangers of the dark side. He only cared about getting out of there alive. *And there's only me to do it.* Surely he could risk the dark side just this once, in order to save the Chancellor and Obi-Wan. He looked at Dooku and let himself feel the emotions that he had been keeping so tightly controlled.

Rage poured through him. This was the man who had belittled him, who had kidnapped Palpatine and nearly killed Obi-Wan, who had cut off Anakin's hand and tried to have Padmé put to death. Anakin used his anger the way he normally used the Force, letting it guide his lightsaber. Faster and faster he moved, and then his lightsaber came down and severed Count Dooku's hands.

Leaning forward, Anakin caught the Count's lightsaber as it fell. The anger still sang in his veins. He set the two lightsabers against the Count's neck and stood panting with the effort of trying to control himself.

"Good, Anakin, *good*," Palpatine said. He was smiling in relief. "I knew you could do it." Anakin felt himself begin to relax at the sound of that gentle, familiar voice. Then Palpatine said, "Kill him. Kill him now!"

Anakin stared at the Chancellor in shock. Dooku seemed just as stunned.

"Finish him, Anakin," Palpatine repeated.

Anakin swallowed hard, fighting the anger that still burned inside him. "I shouldn't — "

"Do it!" the Chancellor snapped.

Dooku tried to speak, but Anakin's hands were already moving. The lightsabers cut through the Count's neck effortlessly. Anakin stared down at the headless body, shaken. *I couldn't stop myself. I couldn't . . .* He deactivated the lightsabers, wondering what Dooku had wanted to say.

"You did well, Anakin," Palpatine said. "He was too dangerous to be kept alive."

"He was a defenseless prisoner," Anakin said bitterly. He looked at Palpatine reproachfully, and realized that the Chancellor was still strapped in the general's chair. He reached for the Force and disengaged the energy restraints. *Of course the Chancellor doesn't understand*, he told himself. Palpatine wasn't a Jedi. Furthermore, he had been trapped, and it must have seemed to him that the only way he would get free was if Anakin killed Dooku. Still, Anakin tried to explain. "I shouldn't have done that, Chancellor. It's not the Jedi way."

Palpatine stood up, rubbing his wrists. "It's only natural. He cut off your arm, and you wanted revenge. It's not the first time, Anakin."

Anakin shook his head. He knew what Palpatine meant. When the Sand People killed his mother, he had massacred them all — men, women, and children. He still dreamed, sometimes, about the children. Palpatine and Padmé were the only ones who knew about the revenge he had taken. Padmé had been horrified as much by Anakin's grief as by what he had done; Palpatine called the killings "regrettable." Neither truly understood how a Jedi would feel about it. And he *couldn't* tell another Jedi, not even Obi-Wan. Especially not Obi-Wan.

The Chancellor nodded, as if he understood what Anakin was thinking, but all he said was, "Now we must leave."

As if to underline the Chancellor's words, the floor began to tilt as the gravity generators shifted. Anakin ran to the fallen balcony that buried Obi-Wan. Using the Force, he lifted the tangled mass away, then knelt to check on his friend. *No bones broken, breathing's all right.* Anakin heaved a sigh of relief.

"There is no time!" Palpatine called urgently as he mounted the steps to the elevator. "Leave him, or we'll never make it."

"His fate will be the same as ours," Anakin said quietly. Never again would he lose someone he loved, the way he had lost his mother. Bending over, he slung Obi-Wan's unconscious body across his shoulders. He staggered under the weight, then caught his balance and headed determinedly toward the elevators.

CHAPTER 3

Slowly, Obi-Wan came back to consciousness. He felt as if he had been pounded all over — in fact, his head was still pounding. And something was digging into his stomach. Carefully, he opened his eyes. He saw a distorted Chancellor Palpatine, reaching down toward him past some sort of screen; beyond was only blackness.

Obi-Wan blinked. The Chancellor wasn't reaching down toward him; he was *below* Obi-Wan, hanging onto something. The blackness was some sort of darkened shaft. "Have I missed something?"

"Hang on," Anakin's muffled voice came from behind him. "We're in a bit of a situation."

Ah. The thing digging into his stomach was Anakin's shoulder, then, and the Chancellor was hanging on to Anakin's ankle. Obi-Wan nodded pleasantly at Palpatine. "Hello, Chancellor. Are you well?"

Palpatine glanced down at the emptiness beneath them. "I hope so."

Obi-Wan's head began to clear. "Where's Count Dooku?"

"Dead," Anakin said shortly, in the tone that meant he did not want to discuss it.

"Pity," Obi-Wan said. "Alive, he could have been a help to us."

"The ship's breaking up," Anakin snapped. "Could we discuss this later?"

Touchy, touchy. But Anakin had saved his life again, *and* he had gotten the Chancellor out unaided. He was allowed to be a little touchy. Obi-Wan stared down at the seemingly bottomless pit.

Gravity shifted, and suddenly they were hanging over a steep slope instead of a bottomless pit. Obi-Wan heard a *chunk-thump* from overhead, and looked up to see something coming toward them. The ceiling? "What's that?"

"Artoo," Anakin said. "I asked him to activate the elevator."

"Oh." So they were in an elevator shaft. Had Anakin gotten tired of waiting? *I don't think I want to know exactly how we got into this,* Obi-Wan decided. *I'll be happy if we can just get out of it.*

Anakin was shouting into the comlink, telling R2-D2 to shut down the elevator. "Too late!" Obi-Wan said. "Jump!"

They jumped. Several floors below, they hit the side of the shaft, sliding along its length ahead of the rapidly moving elevator. Gravity continued to shift until the shaft was horizontal. Their speed slowed as the "slope" they were sliding down leveled off. Unfortunately, the elevator didn't pause.

"Stop the elevator, Artoo!" Anakin yelled at the comlink as they scrambled to their feet.

The elevator stopped. Then, with a horrible grinding noise, it started up again. The three men ran down the shaft, barely staying ahead of it. *The control wires must be damaged,* Obi-Wan thought.

The elevator sped up. Anakin was yelling into the comlink again, but Obi-Wan couldn't make out the words. Then Palpatine stumbled. Obi-Wan caught his arm and urged him forward. *He can't keep this up,* Obi-Wan thought. *Come on, Anakin, come up with something!*

Suddenly, all the doors in the elevator shaft flew open. Barely ahead of the rogue elevator, Obi-Wan, Anakin, and Palpatine fell through into the hallway below.

They leaned against the wall, fighting to catch their breath. *Nothing like a brisk run to clear the cobwebs out of your thinking.* Finally, Obi-Wan straightened. "Let's see if we can find something in the hangar that's still flyable. Come on."

Gravity seemed to be working normally in this part of the ship — the halls were all nice and horizontal, just the way they were supposed to be. As they ran along one, a curtain of blue light sprang up in front of them. Obi-Wan stopped short, holding out his arms to keep Palpatine from running into it. More ray shields appeared behind them and on either side, trapping them.

"How did *this* happen?" Obi-Wan grumbled. "We're smarter than this."

"Apparently not, Master," Anakin said. "This is the oldest trap in the book." Obi-Wan glared at him, and Anakin shrugged. "Well, you're the leader. I was distracted."

"Oh, so all of a sudden it's my fault?"

"You're the Master," Anakin repeated. "I'm just a hero."

Obi-Wan snorted. "I'm open to suggestions here."

Behind the two Jedi, Chancellor Palpatine cleared his throat. "Why don't we let them take us to General Grievous? Perhaps with Count Dooku's demise, we can negotiate our release."

Obi-Wan looked at Anakin, and saw a look of utter disbelief that he knew was mirrored on his own face. *General Grievous, negotiate? When it snows on Tatooine . . .*

"I say . . . patience," Anakin said after a moment.

"Patience?" Obi-Wan stared at his former apprentice. "That's the plan?"

"A couple of droids will be along in a few moments and release the ray shield," Anakin explained. "And then we'll wipe them out. Security patrols are always those skinny useless battle droids."

As if to prove Anakin's words, a pair of battle

droids appeared. "Hand over your weapons," one of them said in a mechanical monotone.

"See?" Anakin said smugly. "No problem."

Behind the battle droids, a large doorway opened, revealing a line of destroyer droids. Obi-Wan glanced around; there were more on the other side of the hallway. Super battle droids appeared behind the destroyers, completely surrounding the Jedi. Obi-Wan shook his head. He and Anakin *might* cut heir way past such overwhelming force, but they couldn't do it and protect the Chancellor at the same time.

At that moment, R2-D2 entered the corridor from an adjoining hallway, screeching to a halt.

"Well," Obi-Wan said to Anakin, "What's plan B?"

Anakin looked from the droids to Chancellor Palpatine and back. "I think Chancellor Palpatine's suggestion sounds pretty good to me."

This is not a good day, Obi-Wan thought as he let the droids take his lightsaber.

Beings all over the galaxy swore that the great General Grievous had no more emotion than the droids who served him. He had been born on Kalee, and even before he became a half-Kaleesh, half-droid cyborg, he had been ruthless. Now, they said, he felt nothing at all.

But those beings were wrong, Grievous thought. There was one emotion common to man and machine, the emotion he felt watching Obi-Wan Kenobi and Anakin Skywalker as they were marched onto his bridge in electrobonds. Satisfaction. If the smooth metal mask that served as his face had been capable of it, he would have smiled.

The guards had brought along the Chancellor, of course, and a little blue astrodroid. Well, he had told them to bring *all* the intruders to the bridge when they were captured, and droids took their instructions literally. The astrodroid was unimportant. It could be reprogrammed easily, once the ship was safely back in Separatist territory.

One of his bodyguards came forward with the Jedi lightsabers. Grievous took them in his metal claw, weighing them. Every Jedi made his or her own lightsaber to be a weapon and a work of art, suited to the builder alone. A close examination of the lightsaber could tell one much about the Jedi who had created it. But there would be time for that later.

Grievous turned to his prisoners, rising to his full height. He deliberately had his leg mechanics lengthened the last time his metal limbs had been overhauled, so that when he straightened up, he towered over most beings. He enjoyed looking down on them. He liked the terror in their eyes when they wondered what terrible weapons hid behind his long cloak, and the fear when they looked up and up at his expressionless metal face.

These Jedi, however, seemed unimpressed. That would change. "That wasn't much of a rescue," Grievous told them. They didn't react. Well, he had a way to get at Jedi. It never failed. He swept back his cape, revealing the lightsabers hanging in its lining. "I look forward to adding your lightsabers to my collection," he said. "Rare trophies, they are."

Obi-Wan smiled. "I think you've forgotten, Grievous. I'm the one in control here."

Had the man gone mad? He was surrounded by enemy droids, hands bound, with no one to come to his rescue. In control? Grievous stared. "So sure of yourself, Kenobi," he purred. "But it's all over for you now.

"Artoo, now!" said Skywalker, and suddenly smoke poured from the astrodroid. Startled, Grievous turned, and an invisible hand yanked one of the lightsabers away from him. The lightsaber flew toward Obi-Wan; he grabbed it behind his back and ignited it, cutting neatly through his electro-bonds. A second later, he freed Anakin.

Another invisible hand tore the second lightsaber from his grasp with a screech of metal on metal. Unbelievably, the two Jedi were free, standing back-to-back and deflecting laser fire from the droids. Even the useless little astrodroid had brought down one of his super droids with some kind of cable attachment.

Grievous backed up, leaving his droid magnaguards between him and the flying laser fire. That was what bodyguards were *for*. Some of his Neimoidian bridge crew had already been hit by reflected bolts, and he wasn't about to let that happen to him. Let the droids tire the Jedi out.

One of the pilots shouted at him over the chaos. "Sir! We are falling out of orbit. All aft control cells are dead."

"Stay on course," Grievous said automatically. He stepped back another pace, calculating furiously. Without aft controls, could they still make the jump to hyperspace? No, and as fast as the repair droids fixed something, the Republic's starfighters would blow it up again. They couldn't —

The gravity grids shifted. Suddenly, the ceiling was "down." "Magnetize!" one of the pilots shouted into the intercom.

A few of the battle droids reacted in time to stick to the floor, but most of them fell to the ceiling along with the Jedi. The Jedi, Grievous noticed with dislike, seemed to take the change in stride. They'd even used the gravity shift to cut down a few more of the droids, who hadn't adjusted quickly enough.

"The ship is breaking up!" the Neimoidian pilot cried.

Just like a Neimoidian to panic, Grievous thought. *Useless beings.* But plainly, they'd run out of time. No point, now, in staying to win this fight. Let the Jedi burn up when the crippled ship crashed.

Without warning, gravity returned to normal. The Jedi dropped to the floor and ran forward. Nearly all the droids were gone; they were coming after him, now. *Too late.* Grievous turned and threw his electro-staff upward. It hit the viewport an instant later, cracking the tough, transparent material. As the Jedi closed in, Grievous jumped with all the force his mechanical legs could provide.

The weakened viewport burst, and air rushed out of the sudden breach. Grievous let himself be sucked away from the bridge along with all the pieces of droids, bits of machinery, and dead crew. He caught a glimpse of the two Jedi and the Republic's Chancellor, clinging to a control console, and then he was outside.

As he was swept away from the ship, he pointed at the hull and triggered the built-in cable in his arm. The anchor struck solidly, attaching to the hull. He let the cable pay out until the automatic blast shield snapped shut over the broken viewport, cutting off the storm of air rushing out of the ship. Then he swung himself onto the ship's hull, his clawed metal feet digging in.

It really was convenient to have a mostly droid

body, Grievous thought as he crawled along the surface of the battleship. An ordinary being would need to breathe, would be damaged by the vacuum of space, would need special equipment to cling to the ship. For Grievous, none of that was a problem.

He reached a hatch and opened it. His calculations were correct; he was in one of the escape-pod bays. He started for the pods, then hesitated. Why not make things a little harder for those annoying Jedi? He crossed to the control panel and began flipping switches, jettisoning all the escape pods, row by row.

Finally, only one pod remained. *There,* Grievous thought. *Let's see them get out of this!* He climbed into the last escape pod and blasted away from the remains of his command ship. There were Federation ships close enough to pick him up, and the clone fighters were too busy with his droids to worry about an unarmed escape pod. He had gotten away.

And with any luck, he could lay the blame for this fiasco on Count Dooku, who wouldn't be coming back to offer his own explanations. Yes, that would do nicely. Planning rapidly, the droid general steered for the nearest battleship.

CHAPTER 4

Anakin felt the ship shudder as he and Obi-Wan cut down the last of the magnaguards. Alarms sounded. "The hull is burning up!" Palpatine shouted.

Looking up at the remaining viewport, Anakin saw sparks flying off the front of the ship. He still saw the blackness of space and the stars, so they weren't in the atmosphere yet. But if the ship was that hot already. . . . He moved toward the navigator's chair to study the readouts.

"All the escape pods have been launched," Anakin said as Obi-Wan joined him. *That has to be General Grievous's work. If we'd only been a little faster, we'd have had him!*

Obi-Wan glanced at the readouts, then at the controls. "You're the hotshot pilot, Anakin," he said, keeping his tone light. "Do you know how to fly this type of cruiser?"

Obi-wan is asking me *to pilot? He must really be worried!* Not that they had any other choices. Anakin matched his tone to Obi-Wan's, acknowledging and confirming the danger. "You mean, do I know how to *land* what's left of this cruiser."

Obi-Wan nodded. Anakin took the pilot's chair — at least the layout of the bridge was more or less the same on any starship, whether Trade Federation or Republic — and looked at the screens. He was just in time to watch a large piece of the ship break away.

"Well?" Obi-Wan said as the ship bucked and shuddered.

"Under the circumstances, I'd say the ability to pilot this ship is irrelevant," Anakin told him. "Strap yourself in."

Distantly, he was aware of Obi-Wan and Palpatine following his instructions, of R2-D2 taking up a position at the auxiliary controls, but his fingers were already busy with the unfamiliar controls. *First, stop the shooting. This switch? No . . . There.* Quickly, he tapped out a message to the Republic's clone fighters: *General Kenobi and I have taken the ship. The Chancellor is safe. Stop firing.* He signed it with his name and the code that would mark it as an authentic message, and sent it off.

Dismissing the fighters outside from his mind, he set himself to fly the ship. It was a lot like trying to fly a large rock. The cruiser had no wings or landing gear. The engines had broken off with the back half of the ship. The few steering thrusters were mostly dead, and the ones that weren't dead were so damaged that anything might happen if he fired them.

And there was no time to experiment. The ship had reached the outer atmosphere, and the friction was heating up the remains of the hull. The room shook and shivered as more pieces broke away.

From the navigator's chair, Obi-Wan calmly called out information on their hull temperature, altitude, speed. Anakin's attention was focused on the controls, not Obi-Wan, but some part of him absorbed the numbers, integrated them, used them. By luck, by instinct, by feel, Anakin flew.

They were well within the atmosphere now, and still moving far too fast. Anakin opened all the hatches and extended every drag fin that still worked, trading the growing heat from the increased friction for a decrease in speed.

For a moment, it seemed to be working. Then there was an enormous jolt, and the speed readout picked up again. "We lost something," Anakin said.

"Everything from the hangar back just fell off," Obi-Wan reported. "Not to worry — we're still flying half the ship."

Anakin spared a glance for the Chancellor, who was clinging grimly to his seat. *He's an administrator; he's not used to this.* But he didn't have time to explain things to the Chancellor, not if they were going to survive this. "I'm going to shift a few degrees and see if I can slow us down," Anakin told Obi-Wan.

"We're heating up," Obi-Wan warned, and began calling out numbers.

I know, I know. Anakin played the controls, opening and closing hatches, using steering thrusters to brake, anything to slow their fall.

Obi-Wan's steady chant broke off. "Fire ships are on the left and right."

Anakin flicked a switch, and the voice of one of the fire ship pilots filled the bridge. "Follow us. We'll put out what fire we can."

Follow you? How? But there were numbers reading out on the comm; coordinates. They'd cleared a heavy-duty landing strip in the industrial section. *Strong enough to stop what's left of this bucket of bolts, and well away from the residential areas so that if we miss, we won't set fire to a lot of apartment buildings. Somebody's thinking.*

"What's our speed?" Anakin demanded, and Obi-Wan started reciting numbers again.

Through the smoking viewport, Anakin caught glimpses of the towering buildings of Coruscant streaking past below them. *Too close. We're too low, too soon.* R2-D2 beeped madly, and Anakin gestured at one of the controls. "Keep us level," he told the droid, and went back to work to slow them down.

"Steady," Obi-Wan said. "Five thousand."

"Hang on," Anakin said. "This may get a little rough. We lost our heat shields."

"Landing strip's straight ahead," Obi-Wan said a moment later.

Too low, too fast, too hot . . . too late. This isn't a landing, it's a controlled crash. And not all that controlled. Someone had been paying attention, though; the landing platform was surrounded by emergency fire speeders. *Now if we can just hit it . . .*

The ship rocked. Anakin saw a fire speeder dodge out of the way just before they plowed into the landing platform, and then the view vanished under a thick coating of fire-suppressing foam. For an instant, he was sickeningly afraid that he hadn't cut their speed enough, and they would slide off the far side of the landing platform. Then the ship shuddered to a stop.

"Come on; let's get out of here," Anakin said, unstrapping himself from the seat. Obi-Wan and the Chancellor followed his example, and soon they ducked out an escape hatch into the open air. A shuttle waited among the emergency ships to whisk them back to the Senate.

While the medical personnel aboard the shuttle looked over the shaken Chancellor, Anakin and Obi-Wan argued about the final step of the mission.

"This whole operation was your idea," Anakin

said to Obi-Wan. "You planned it. You have to be the one to take the bows this time."

"Sorry, old friend," Obi-Wan said. "You killed Count Dooku." Anakin winced, but Obi-Wan didn't notice. He went on, "You rescued the Chancellor, and you managed to land that bucket of bolts safely. You —"

"Only because of your training, Master," Anakin said earnestly. "You deserve all those speeches." *And I certainly don't want praise for the way I killed Dooku.*

"Those endless speeches." Obi-Wan shook his head. "Anakin, let's face it — you are the hero this time. It's your turn to spend a glorious day with the politicians."

The shuttle had reached the Senate landing platform. Anakin could see Master Windu and a dozen Senators waiting to welcome the Chancellor — and to assure themselves of the Chancellor's safety. There was no time for more argument.

"Then you owe me," Anakin told Obi-Wan. "And not just for saving your skin for the tenth time."

"Ninth time," Obi-Wan corrected. "That incident on Cato Neimoidia doesn't count." Anakin rolled his eyes, and Obi-Wan smiled. "See you at the briefing."

Anakin couldn't help smiling back, but his smile faded as he followed the Chancellor out the door of the shuttle. He was no hero this time, no matter what

Obi-Wan said. *A hero wouldn't have done what I did.*

Mace Windu stepped forward to greet Chancellor Palpatine. They exchanged a few stiff words, and then the attending Senators surrounded the Chancellor, congratulating him on his safe return.

Anakin watched for a moment, feeling lost. Behind him, he heard a sudden string of beeping, and then a fussy voice said sternly, "It couldn't have been that bad. Don't exaggerate."

C-3PO! If the protocol droid was there, surely Padmé had come, too. Forgetting his depression, Anakin studied the mob of Senators, searching for his wife.

He didn't see her. He took a step forward, and the Senators began moving away from the landing platform, into the Senate Office Building.

Senator Bail Organa of Alderaan saw him and left the crowd around Palpatine to join Anakin. Together, they followed the rest.

"The Senate cannot thank you enough," Bail told Anakin. "The end of Count Dooku will surely bring an end to this war and an end to the Chancellor's draconian security measures."

Anakin winced, but the Senator's words made him feel a little better. He knew it had been wrong to kill Dooku when he was helpless, but perhaps it wasn't as awful as he thought. Chancellor Palpatine seemed to think it had been necessary, and if Bail was right and Dooku's death ended the war, billions of beings would live instead of being killed in the endless battles. Surely that made a difference? *And I'll never break the Jedi Code again*, he promised himself. Just thinking that made him happier.

Bail was waiting patiently for Anakin's response. Hastily, Anakin reviewed the Senator's last comment in his mind. "The fighting is going to continue until General Grievous is spare parts," he told Bail. "The Chancellor is very clear about that."

Bail frowned and started to say something else, but Anakin was no longer listening. He sensed something, someone, nearby, following them. He sensed — "Excuse me," he said to Bail, and started for the row of giant columns that lined the hallway.

"Certainly," the Senator said to his back.

As Senator Organa hurried after Palpatine and the other Senators, Anakin slipped into the shadows behind the pillar. He was sure — yes! He turned, and Padmé slid into his arms.

Anakin forgot about Dooku, Palpatine, and everything else. Holding Padmé, kissing her, he felt complete again. Centered. Happy.

When they broke the kiss at last, Padmé echoed his thoughts. "Thank goodness you're back. I'm whole again."

Whole. "I missed you, Padmé. I've missed you so."

She shivered in the circle of his arms. "There were whispers that you'd been killed. I've been living with unbearable dread." She clung to him, as if to assure herself that he was real.

Anakin took hold of her shoulders and gave her a little shake. "I'm back. I'm *all right.*"

Padmé smiled, and he pulled her back into his arms, wanting her close. "It seems as if we've been apart for a lifetime," he went on. "And it might have been — if the Chancellor hadn't been kidnapped, I don't think they would *ever* have brought us back from the Outer Rim sieges." He started to kiss her again, but she pulled away.

"Wait," she said. "Not here."

"No, here!" Anakin said, reaching for her again. She didn't know how much he needed her right now — her calm acceptance, her love. She didn't know about Dooku. "I'm tired of this deception. I don't care if they know we're married."

"Anakin, don't say things like that," Padmé chided. "You're important to the Republic, to ending this war." She smiled reassuringly, as if she sensed his distress. "I love you more than anything," she said softly, "but I won't let you give up your life as a Jedi for me."

"I've given my life to the Jedi Order," Anakin said slowly, meaning every word. "But I'd only *give up* my life for you."

"I wouldn't like that," Padmé said thoughtfully, and grinned at him. "I wouldn't like that at all." Anakin reached for her again, but she slipped away. "Patience, my handsome Jedi. Come to me later."

She sidestepped again, but not quickly enough to avoid Anakin's Jedi reflexes. He held her close — and this time, with the pleasant shock of their meeting fading, he felt her trembling. "Are you all right?"

"I'm just excited to see you," Padmé said, but her voice was too high and she avoided his eyes.

"That's not it." Disturbed, Anakin extended his Jedi senses. "I sense more. What is it? Tell me what's going on!"

To his distress, Padmé began to cry. "You've been gone five months," she said through her tears. "It's been very hard for me. I've never felt so alone. There's —"

Anakin could stand it no longer. There was only one thing he could think of that Padmé would be so reluctant to tell him. "Is there someone else?"

To his surprise — and relief — Padmé stopped crying. "No!" she said, with an angry sincerity that was impossible to mistake. "You still don't trust me, but nothing has changed."

But there *was* a change; he could sense it even more clearly now. "It's . . . just that I've never seen you like this."

"Nothing's wrong." Padmé turned away for a

moment, then looked back at him. "Something wonderful has happened." She hesitated, and Anakin thought *Wonderful? Then why are you so frightened? Why were you crying?* And then she took a deep breath and went on. "I'm . . . Annie, I'm pregnant."

Anakin felt his mouth drop open. Of all the things it could have been, he hadn't expected *this. A baby? We're going to have a baby?*

Padmé was looking anxiously at him, waiting for his reaction. *We're going to have a baby,* Anakin thought. "That's . . . wonderful."

Padmé closed her eyes and leaned against him. "What are we going to *do?*"

A host of unwelcome thoughts poured through Anakin's mind. They could never keep *this* a secret. *You're important to the Republic, to ending this war,* Padmé had said, but when the Jedi found out he'd married Padmé, he would have to leave the Order. How could he help the Republic then? What would Obi-Wan say when he discovered how his friend and apprentice had lied to him for so long? And what would it mean for Padmé?

Firmly, Anakin set all those thoughts aside. "It's going to be all right," he told Padmé. "We're not going to worry about anything right now." He paused, and then he started to grin. *We're going to have a baby!* "This is a happy moment. The happiest moment of my life."

As the Neimoidian shuttle came down to Utapau, Grievous studied the area through a viewport. The planet's surface was ridged and drab, dotted with huge sinkholes where the inhabitants built their cities. The shuttle descended into one of the largest and deepest of the sinkhole-cities. A landing platform, surrounded by battle droids and super battle droids, stuck out of the sinkhole wall, and the shuttle came neatly to rest on it.

As Grievous strode out of the ship, one of the droids approached. "The planet is secure, sir," it told him. "The population is under control."

Of course, they're under control, Grievous thought. *Stupid maggots.* He didn't care about the locals. He was supposed to meet the Separatist Council here.

One of his bodyguards approached. "There is a message on the special communication channel," it whispered.

All thought of the Council vanished. Grievous

hurried to the hologram area. Blue light flickered above the hologram display disc, then formed into the image of a hooded figure. Grievous bowed deeply. This was the *real* leader of the Separatists, the *real* power behind the war. "Yes, Lord Sidious," Grievous said.

"I suggest you move the Separatist Council to Mustafar," said the soft, cold voice.

"Yes, Master," Grievous replied.

"Good. The Jedi will exhaust their resources looking for you. I do not wish them to know of your whereabouts until we are ready."

That probably means it will be a long time before the fighting begins again, Grievous thought. He hid his disappointment, and instead said, "With all due respect, Master, why did you not let me kill the Chancellor when I had the chance?"

"It was not the time," Darth Sidious replied. "You must have patience. The end of the war is near, General, and I promise you, victory is assured."

Grievous nodded. But for all his power and confidence, Darth Sidious was not a fighter. *Does he understand how much that useless raid on Coruscant cost us?* A little tentatively, Grievous pressed. "But the loss of Count Dooku?"

Darth Sidious' smile was only just visible below his hood. "The death of Lord Tyranus was a necessary loss," he said. "I will soon have a new apprentice —

one far younger and more powerful than Lord Tyranus."

Somewhat reassured, Grievous nodded. But when the transmission faded, he sat studying the empty air where Darth Sidious' image had been projected. Sith Lords were tricky and treacherous. He would share more of Darth Sidious' confidence, Grievous thought, if he had a clearer understanding of Darth Sidious' plans.

Padmé woke suddenly, alone in the large bed. She lay still for a moment, gathering her thoughts. She had not slept well for months, not since she discovered her pregnancy, but this time something felt wrong. Then she realized what it was. She was *alone*.

"Anakin?"

No response. Frowning, Padmé slid out of bed to look for her husband.

She found him on the veranda, looking out at the lights of Coruscant. Tonight, the glowing strings of amber were patchy. Black, empty spaces betrayed the spots where the battle with the Separatist forces had blown up buildings. In some places, smoke from still-smoldering rubble blurred the running lights of the emergency vehicles still working to rescue beings trapped in the wreckage.

Padmé joined Anakin. He did not look at her,

even when she took his hand, but she could see light reflecting from the shine on his cheeks. He had been weeping.

"What's bothering you?" she asked, though she thought she knew.

"Nothing." Anakin's voice was low.

"Anakin," Padmé said, very gently, "how long is it going to take for us to be honest with each other?"

For a moment, she thought he would remain silent. "It was a dream," he said at last. He spoke heavily, as if saying the words made something real, something that he would prefer to disbelieve.

A dream? That was not what she had been expecting. "Bad?" she asked cautiously.

"Like the ones I used to have about my mother, just before she died."

Padmé caught her breath. Anakin had dreamed about his mother's suffering and torment for weeks. The dreams had finally driven him to go to her, against the advice and orders of the Jedi . . . and he had arrived too late. He had never forgiven himself. Sometimes Padmé thought he had never forgiven the Jedi Order, either. She looked at him. She didn't think it was the memory of his failure that was upsetting him now. "And?" she prodded.

Anakin swallowed hard. "It was about you."

Me? Padmé felt a cold chill, and her hand crept up to the necklace she always wore — the carved bit of japor that Anakin had given her "to bring you good fortune" when he was nine and she fourteen. If Anakin was having those dreams again, about her, she would need all the good fortune she could get. "Tell me."

"It was only a dream," Anakin said, and looked away.

If it was only a dream, why are you so unhappy? But saying that would only upset him more. Padmé waited.

After a moment, Anakin took a deep breath. "You die in childbirth," he said flatly.

"And the baby?" Padmé spoke automatically, almost before she thought.

"I don't know."

"It was only a dream," Padmé said, but she didn't really believe that, any more than Anakin did. His premonitions had been right too often. *Maybe I should have checked with a medical droid earlier,* she thought. But she hadn't dared, for fear the secret would get out.

Anakin moved closer and put his arms around her. "I won't let this one become real, Padmé." She leaned into him, feeling safe and reassured, but she knew it was only an illusion. Anakin had saved her from war, from assassins, from battle droids, and from monsters, but this wasn't something he could cut down with a lightsaber.

Looking up at Anakin, Padmé tried for the first time

to speak aloud all the fears she had kept bottled up inside for the past five months. "Anakin, this baby will change our lives," she said slowly. "I doubt the Queen will continue to allow me to serve in the Senate." Anakin looked stricken, and she hurried on. "And if the Council discovers that you are the father, you will be expelled from the Jedi Order."

"I know." Anakin spoke the words soberly, and she knew that he'd had some of the same thoughts. But Anakin had only been thinking for a few hours; she'd had months. Months to study every angle of the box they were trapped in.

She had accepted the fact that she would have to give up her position in the Senate. It still hurt, but there were many ways for a former Senator to continue to serve. With her experience, she was sure that she could find a position on the staff of one of the other Senators. And she would have the baby to take care of and teach. But Anakin . . .

In the past thousand years, only twenty beings had left the Jedi Order. Anakin had spoken of them once, when they were talking of Count Dooku, the latest and last of the Lost Twenty. And Anakin had always wanted to be a Jedi. He had given his life to the Order — and no matter what he said, Padmé was sure that he *would* give up his life in the service of the Jedi. He had become a hero by taking on dangerous and deadly missions, several of which had nearly killed him. What would he do, if he had to give that up? What would giving it up do to him?

Hesitantly, Padmé spoke the thought that had come to her more and more often lately. "Anakin, do you think Obi-Wan might be able to help us?"

Anakin stiffened. "Have you told him anything?"

"No," Padmé said soothingly. "But he's your mentor, your best friend — he must suspect *something*."

"He's been a father to me, but he's still on the Council. Don't tell him anything!"

Padmé sighed. "I won't, Anakin." *Not until you see for yourself that we have to do this.*

"We don't need his help," Anakin said a little too firmly, as if he were trying to convince himself as much as Padmé. "Our baby is a blessing, not a problem."

It's both, Padmé thought, but she was tired of chasing the same thoughts around and around in her head. She leaned against Anakin, letting his confidence wash over her. They didn't have to settle everything tonight. For now, it was enough to think of the joy the future would bring, instead of focusing on the problems. For now.

To be invited to visit Master Yoda in his living quarters was usually a privilege and an honor, but today it was a privilege Obi-Wan would have preferred to do without. *Meeting in secret, without the full Council . . . I don't like it.* Judging from their expressions, neither did Master Yoda or Master Windu. The dark side enveloped everything in a stifling cloud, making the future unclear. Between that and the war, fear was creeping into the Jedi sanctuary. *Fear is the path to the dark side. What is happening to us?*

And now, this latest news. Master Yoda said, "Moving to take control of the Jedi, the Chancellor is."

"All on the pretext of greater security," Obi-Wan said. In the years since the start of the war, Palpatine had gathered more and more of the Senate's powers to himself. It had only been a matter of time until he came to the Jedi Order. But anticipating something did not lessen the shock when it actually happened.

"I sense a plot to destroy the Jedi," Mace Windu put in. Yoda looked at him with mild disapproval. Master Windu was a powerful warrior, but sometimes he was too quick to see plots and threats. *And after eight hundred years of training Jedi, sometimes Yoda is too patient.* But that the Chancellor wanted to *destroy* the Jedi seemed incredible. As if he sensed Obi-Wan's reservations, Mace went on, "The dark side of the Force surrounds the Chancellor."

"As it surrounds the Separatists," Obi-Wan said thoughtfully. "There is a shifting of the Force — all of us feel it. If the Chancellor is being influenced by the dark side, then this war may be a plot by the Sith to take over the Republic."

"Speculation!" Yoda said with feeling. "On theories such as these, we cannot act." He glared at Mace and Obi-Wan impartially. "*Proof* we need, before taking this to the Council."

Yes, but how are we going to get proof? Obi-Wan thought. Then he answered his own question: "The proof will come once Grievous is gone."

Mace Windu and Yoda exchanged glances. Mace's lips tightened. Then he put into words the thing all of them had avoided saying. "If the Chancellor does not end this war with the destruction of General Grievous, he must be removed from office."

"Arrested?" Obi-Wan felt cold. They were coming perilously close to treason in even discussing such a possibility.

"To a dark place, this line of thought will take us," Yoda said, echoing his thoughts. "Great care, we must take."

Great care, indeed. But if the Chancellor continued the war, what choice would they have?

CHAPTER 6

Master Yoda sat studying Anakin Skywalker. The young Jedi did not consult him often, and it was rarer still for him to request an urgent private meeting. And this trouble, at this time — *Of great importance to us all, this must be. But why?*

"Premonitions," he said aloud. Premonitions were a rare talent for a Jedi, but not unknown. Yoda had searched the paths of the future himself on occasion. No one had done so deliberately in years, however; not since the dark side began to grow, making such foresight dangerous and unreliable. But Anakin was strong in the Force, stronger than any Jedi Yoda had known in all his hundreds of years. And he had not sought the visions, that much was clear, though he was reluctant to speak too plainly of whatever he had seen. Yoda nodded encouragingly. "These visions you have . . ."

Anakin looked down. "They are of pain, suffering," he said in a low voice. "Death."

And make you afraid, they do. But afraid of what? For whom? Cautious, he must be, or he would learn no more, and without knowledge, help he could not. "Yourself you speak of, or someone you know?"

"Someone . . ." Anakin's voice trailed off, and his hands closed into fists, as if he were trying to hold on to something.

"Close to you?" Yoda prodded after a moment.

Anakin's voice, when he spoke at last, was barely a whisper. "Yes."

"Careful you must be when sensing the future, Anakin," Yoda said. "The fear of loss is a path to the dark side." *And with the dark side grown so strong, a close and easy path it is.*

To Yoda's dismay, Anakin did not seem to hear his words. His jaw clenched, and he stared at empty air, as if he were seeing his visions as they spoke, though Yoda sensed none of the changes in the Force that would normally accompany such seeing. *Remembering, he is,* Yoda decided.

At last, Anakin spoke again. "I won't let my visions come true, Master Yoda," he said in a voice of grim determination.

Ah, young one. Strong are you with the Force, but to hold back death — that strong, no Jedi is. Out of his centuries of experience, out of his memories of the thousands of shorter-lived beings he had taught and worked with and cared for, Yoda said gently, "Rejoice for those around you who transform into the

Force. Mourn them, do not. Miss them, do not. Attachment leads to jealousy. The shadow of greed, that is."

Slowly, Anakin nodded, though Yoda sensed resistance in him still. "What must I do, Master?"

"Train yourself to let go of everything you fear to lose," Yoda told him. *A hard lesson it is, but necessary.* And it was a lesson that had to be learned again and again, Yoda thought sadly, remembering the hundreds of Jedi who had already died in the Clone Wars.

The meeting with Master Windu and Master Yoda continued to worry Obi-Wan for the next several hours. He thought about it as he reviewed the latest messages from the Senate, as he prepared for the briefing he was giving, and even as he pointed out the latest battle zones for the crowd of Jedi and answered their questions in the briefing room. But he was not thinking about the Chancellor or the Jedi Council. He was thinking about Anakin.

Master Yoda and Master Windu looked at the big picture — the way that the Chancellor, the Senate, and the Jedi dealt with one another and the different powers and authority and responsibilities that belonged to each. They considered the shifting proposals, orders, and demands like beings studying moves in a game of dejarik on a holoboard.

Anakin didn't look at the big picture. Anakin saw most things on a personal level. That hadn't been a problem while he and Obi-Wan were out battling the Trade Federation in the Outer Rim — after all, a battle droid shooting at you *was* fairly personal, whatever the reason behind it. Now that they were back on Coruscant, though, Anakin would need to consider the political implications of his actions — and everyone else's. Obi-Wan worried about Anakin's reaction to the most recent developments. *Someone* should warn him about what might be coming. Obi-Wan sighed. In this case, he was the only "someone" who could give Anakin a hint. If only Anakin would listen . . .

The door of the briefing room opened. Obi-Wan looked up from the holograms and charts he was shutting down and saw Anakin hurrying toward him. "You missed the report on the Outer Rim sieges," Obi-Wan said.

"I was held up," Anakin said. He sounded tense, and more than a little preoccupied. Then he shook his head. "I'm sorry. I have no excuse."

Obi-Wan turned to shut down the last few electronic star charts. "In short, they are going very well," he said. Perhaps he could ease into politics by starting from the briefing that Anakin had missed. "Saleucami has fallen, and Master Vos has moved his troops to Boz Pity."

Anakin frowned. "What's wrong, then?" he asked bluntly.

So much for easing into the subject. "The Senate is expected to vote *more* executive powers to the Chancellor today."

"That can only mean less deliberating and more action," Anakin said with some satisfaction. Then he saw Obi-Wan's face, and his expression became puzzled. "Is that bad? It will make it easier for us to end this war."

It's not that simple! Obi-Wan bit back the words. Anakin was no diplomat; to him, it *was* simple. "Anakin, be careful of your friend, the Chancellor."

"Be careful of what?" Anakin looked more puzzled than ever.

"He has requested your presence."

"What for?"

"He wouldn't say."

That got a frown, at last. "The Chancellor didn't inform the Jedi Council?" Anakin said. "That's unusual, isn't it?"

"*All* of this is unusual," Obi-Wan told him. "It's making me feel uneasy." At least now Anakin was paying close attention. "Relations between the Council and the Chancellor are stressed."

Anakin's frown deepened. "I know the Council has grown wary of the Chancellor's power," he said. "But aren't we all working together to save the Republic? Why all this distrust?"

Because people can do more than one thing at a

time, Obi-Wan thought. *The Chancellor can work to save the Republic and work to increase his own power, both at once. And if we don't pay attention, he'll have too much power by the time the war is over.* But that would be dangerous to say aloud, even in the Jedi Temple. "The Force grows dark, Anakin," Obi-Wan said instead. "We are all affected by it. Be wary of your feelings."

Anakin nodded, but as they left the conference room together, Obi-Wan could only hope that he had said enough.

The office of the Supreme Chancellor of the Senate boasted one of the best views of Coruscant on the planet. Most windows opened only onto the shadowy gray canyons between the enormous buildings that blanketed the planet's surface. The huge skyscrapers were like manufacutred mountains, making it impossible to see very far.

But the Chancellor's office was above most of the other buildings. From its windows, the skyscrapers looked less like mountains than like a forest of petrified evergreens. Today, though, a smoky brown haze hung over the forest. Gaps in the rows of spikes marked places where buildings had been destroyed in the battle. *The Separatists have a lot to answer for,* Anakin thought.

Chancellor Palpatine broke the silence at last. "Anakin, this afternoon the Senate is going to call on me to take direct control of the Jedi Council."

Anakin's eyes widened. Obi-Wan had said that the Chancellor would be given new powers, but Anakin hadn't expected anything like *this*. "The Jedi will no longer report to the Senate?" he asked, not entirely believing it.

"They will report to me, personally," Palpatine said. "The Senate is too unfocused to conduct a war."

"I agree," Anakin said quickly. Remembering Obi-Wan's words, he added, "But the Jedi Council may not see it that way. With all due respect, sir, the Council is in no mood for more constitutional amendments."

"In this case, I have no choice," Palpatine said almost sadly. "This war must be won."

"Everyone will agree on that," Anakin said. *Though sometimes I think the Jedi Council is so worried about politics that they've forgotten what the real problem is.* As soon as he thought it, Anakin felt guilty. The Council had sent its own members into battle — and lost some of them, too. *It's being back on Coruscant instead of out in the field; it makes me feel hemmed in,* Anakin thought. *And . . . and other things.* He didn't want to think about the dreams right now.

Palpatine had been talking; Anakin brought his

attention back to the conversation in time to hear the Chancellor ask, "Don't you wonder why you've been kept off the Council?"

"My time will come," Anakin said automatically. "When I am older, and, I suppose, wiser." *But my time won't come,* he thought. *Not anymore. As soon as they find out about Padmé and the baby, I'm going to have to leave the Jedi.* Suddenly he felt empty, the way he'd felt when he was nine and the Jedi Council had said he was too old for training. *What will happen to me now?* he had asked Master Qui-Gon Jinn. He had become Qui-Gon's ward, but that hadn't seemed enough, even when he was nine. The Council had relented after Qui-Gon's death, but they'd never countenance this.

"I hope you trust me, Anakin," the Chancellor said.

"Of course," Anakin replied, feeling guilty. He didn't trust the Chancellor enough to tell him about Padmé, or the baby. But he didn't trust *anyone* enough to tell them that. Not yet.

"I need your help, son, " Palpatine said.

Did I miss something? "What do you mean?"

"I fear the Jedi. The Council keeps pushing for more control. They're shrouded in secrecy and obsessed with maintaining their autonomy — ideals I find simply incomprehensible in a democracy."

Anakin barely kept from rolling his eyes in

exasperation. Obi-Wan had said almost the same things about the Chancellor. Why couldn't they all just *stop*, and get on with fighting the war? "I can assure you that the Jedi are dedicated to the values of the Republic, sir," he said to Palpatine.

"Their actions will speak more loudly than their words," Palpatine replied. "I'm depending on you."

"For what?" Anakin asked, puzzled. "I don't understand."

"To be the eyes, ears, and voice of the Republic," Palpatine told him.

What does that *mean?* The Chancellor was the voice of the Senate, and the Senate was the voice of the Republic. Did Palpatine need a Jedi assistant? That didn't make any sense.

"Anakin," Palpatine said after a moment, "I'm appointing you to be my personal representative on the Jedi Council."

Well, *that* was clear enough. Then the words sank in. "Me? A Master?" *The youngest member of the Jedi Council ever! And maybe then they'll let me stay, even if they find out —* He wouldn't finish that thought; the hope was too great and too fragile. Besides . . . "I am overwhelmed, sir, but the Council elects its own members. They will never accept this."

"I think they will," the Chancellor said with a quiet firmness that was utterly convincing. "They need you more than you know."

It took all of Anakin's self-control to keep from pacing up and down the hallway outside the Jedi Council chamber. His head was whirling. It had only been a few hours since Chancellor Palpatine had told him he wanted Anakin on the Jedi Council; it seemed like minutes since the Senate had given the Chancellor the powers that made Anakin's appointment official. So why did it feel as if he'd been standing out here for days?

The door opened at last, and Anakin went in. The Council chamber seemed larger than Anakin remembered. He had been there many times since the beginning of the Clone Wars, to report on the missions he and Obi-Wan had conducted, but he didn't remember it ever taking so long to cross to the center of the circle. The waiting Masters sat, expressionless, in their places — Mace Windu, Eeth Koth, Yoda, the holograms of Plo Koon and Ki-Adi-Mundi. Even

Master Obi-Wan's face gave no hint of the Council's decision.

Finally, he reached the center of the floor, stopped, and bowed to the Council.

Mace Windu spoke at last, formally, as head of the Jedi Council. "Anakin Skywalker, we have approved your appointment to the Council as the Chancellor's personal representative."

"I will do my best to uphold the principles of the Jedi Order," Anakin said with equal formality, but it was hard to contain his joy. He wanted to jump around and shout, or at least grin.

Master Yoda must have sensed some of Anakin's feelings, for he gave him a stern look. "Allow this appointment lightly, the Council does not. Disturbing is this move by Chancellor Palpatine."

"I understand," Anakin said.

"You are on this Council," Mace went on, "but we do not grant you the rank of Master."

What?! Anger swept over Anakin, and with it all his formal control abandoned him. "How can you do this? I'm more powerful than any of you! How can I be on the Council and not be a Master?"

"Take your seat, young Skywalker," Mace said, biting off the words with icy disapproval.

Anakin swallowed hard. Inside, he was still seething, but he forced out the words, "Forgive me, Master," and went to one of the empty chairs. *The*

Chancellor is depending on me; they'll never trust either of us if they think I can't control myself. But nobody has ever been on the Council who wasn't a Master! And I'm good enough. Everybody knows it.

Ki-Adi-Mundi cleared his throat, and the meeting got down to business. "We have surveyed all systems in the Republic, and have found no sign of General Grievous."

"Hiding in the Outer Rim, he is," Yoda suggested. "The outlying systems, you must sweep."

"It may take some time," Obi-Wan said. "We do not have many ships to spare."

"We cannot take ships from the front line," Mace said.

Despite his anger, Anakin found himself nodding in agreement. The Republic was spread too thinly already.

"And yet, it would be fatal for us to allow the droid armies to regroup," Obi-Wan said.

Anakin agreed with that, too.

"Master Kenobi, our spies contact, you must," Yoda said. "Then wait."

Anakin frowned. *Wait? That will give General Grievous time to regroup. But if we don't have enough fighters to send right away, what else can we do?*

The blue hologram of Ki-Adi-Mundi raised a hand. "What of the droid landing on Kashyyyk?"

Everyone agreed that they couldn't afford to lose Kashyyyk, the planet of the Wookiees. It was on the main navigation route for the whole southwestern quadrant. Anakin volunteered to lead an attack group at once; he knew that system well, so he figured it wouldn't take long. But Mace Windu shook his head. "Your assignment is here with the Chancellor," Mace told him.

Anakin swallowed his disappointment. He hadn't realized that being the Chancellor's representative would keep him away from the front lines. *They won't let me do the job I'm good at,* he thought, *and they won't make me a Master so I can be good at this job. It isn't fair!*

It didn't help to hear Yoda say, "Good relations with the Wookiees I have. Go, I will." Or to hear Mace Windu's instant agreement. All through the rest of the meeting, while the Council gave out assignments and planned the strategy of the war, Anakin's anger simmered. He held on to his temper until the Council was over. But when he and Obi-Wan started down the hall toward the briefing rooms, he couldn't resist venting his feelings.

"What kind of nonsense is this?" he grumbled. "Put me on the Council and not make me a Master? That's never been done in the history of the Jedi! It's insulting."

"Calm down," Obi-Wan said. "You've been given

a great honor. To be on the Council at your age has never happened before."

Anakin snorted. *There's never been a Jedi as strong as I am, either.*

"Listen to me, Anakin," Obi-Wan said, and the seriousness of his tone caught Anakin's attention. "The fact is, you're too close to the Chancellor, and the Council doesn't like him interfering in Jedi affairs."

Too close to the Chancellor? Does he think — "I swear to you, I didn't ask to be put on the Council," Anakin said. If that was what the other Jedi thought, no wonder they were making difficulties!

"But it's what you wanted," Obi-Wan said. "And regardless of how it happened, you find yourself in a delicate situation."

"You mean divided loyalties." *But we're all on the same side. Aren't we?*

Obi-Wan shook his head. "I *warned* you that there was tension between the Council and the Chancellor. I was very clear. Why didn't you *listen*? You walked right into it."

That was Obi-Wan, always looking for obscure motives and hidden meanings. But this time, Anakin thought, he was missing what was right in front of him. "The Council is upset because I'm the youngest ever to serve," Anakin told him.

"No, it is not," Obi-Wan said in exasperation. He

hesitated, then said more quietly, "Anakin, I worry when you speak of jealousy and pride. Those are not Jedi thoughts. They're dangerous, dark thoughts."

"Master, you of all people should have confidence in my abilities," Anakin said. Obi-Wan gave a small nod. Reassured, Anakin went on, "I know where my loyalties lie."

Obi-Wan looked at Anakin, then turned away. "I hope so."

Disturbed, Anakin waited for his former mentor to continue. When Obi-Wan said nothing, Anakin decided to push. "I sense there's more to this talk than you're saying."

"Anakin, the only reason the Council has approved your appointment is because the Chancellor trusts you," Obi-Wan said, and stopped again.

"And?" Anakin was getting tired of all these hints. *Just for once, can't you just come right out and say whatever it is?*

"Anakin, look, I'm on your side," Obi-Wan said unhappily. "I didn't want to see you put in this situation."

"*What* situation?" He couldn't mean the appointment to the Council! Obi-Wan was his friend. He knew how much Anakin wanted a seat on the Council.

Obi-Wan stopped walking and turned to face Anakin. He hesitated, as if he was searching for the right words. Then he took a deep breath. "The Council wants you to report on all of the Chancellor's dealings. They want to know what he's up to."

Anakin stared at Obi-Wan, stunned. A tiny part of his mind whispered, *Don't ever ask Obi-Wan to come right out and say something, ever again,* but most of him was trying to absorb what Obi-Wan had just said. "They want me to spy on the Chancellor?"

Obi-Wan nodded.

"That's treason!"

"We are at war, Anakin," Obi-Wan said sadly. "And the Jedi Council is sworn to uphold the principles of the Republic, even if the Chancellor does not."

Something is very wrong here. "Why didn't the Council give me this assignment when we were in session?" Anakin demanded.

Obi-Wan looked even more unhappy than before. "This is not an assignment for the record. The Council asked me to approach you on this personally."

They knew. They knew they shouldn't be asking this. Anakin's head was spinning. "The Chancellor is not a bad man, Obi-Wan," he said desperately. "He befriended me. He's watched out for me ever since I arrived here." Surely, Obi-Wan would understand. *We're on the same side! Why can't anyone else see that? We should be spying on . . . on General Grievous and the Separatists, not on a good man who's working for the same things we are!*

But Obi-Wan was shaking his head. "That is why you must help us, Anakin." But he couldn't face Anakin as he continued, "We owe our allegiance to the Senate, not to its leader . . . who has managed to stay in office long after his term expired."

Anakin stared in disbelief. *They can't blame the Chancellor for that!* "Master, the Senate *demanded* that he stay longer."

"Use your feelings, Anakin," Obi-Wan urged. "Something is out of place here."

"You're asking me to do something against the Jedi Code," Anakin pointed out bitterly. "Against the Republic. Against a mentor . . . and a friend. *That's* what's out of place here. Why are you asking this of me?"

"The Council is asking you," Obi-Wan said.

Anakin stared at his friend, feeling ill. *I promised myself, I promised, just yesterday, that I would never break the Jedi Code again.* And now the Jedi Council itself was telling him that the Code wasn't important if it got in the way of what they wanted. *Obi-Wan* was asking him to do this. "I know where my loyalties lie," Anakin repeated, feeling the hollowness of the words that, only moments ago, he had meant with all his heart.

Obi-Wan took that as an answer, and nodded in evident relief. But as he followed his former Master down the long hall, Anakin wondered how much of an answer it really was.

CHAPTER 8

The sun was setting when Padmé finally returned from the Senate. Outwardly, the entire Senate supported Chancellor Palpatine without reservation, but there was enormous tension below the surface. Most of her days now were spent discussing whether something should be done about the Chancellor, and if so, what that something should be. Padmé herself had grown more and more uneasy with Palpatine's steadily increasing power.

She had worked with Palpatine and trusted him for years, ever since her term as the elected Queen of Naboo, when he had been Naboo's representative in the Senate. She herself had challenged former Senate Chancellor Valorum, opening the way for Palpatine to take control. *Would I have done the same things,* she wondered, *if I had known what Palpatine was going to do with that control, once he had it?*

She didn't know the answer to that; but she *was* sure

that she had to do something about what was happening now. She was aware that the talks bordered on treason. After all, Chancellor Palpatine had done nothing illegal. Padmé often found herself wondering what her Jedi friends would think if they knew what she was doing. Most of all, she wondered what Anakin would think.

The airspeeder pulled up at the landing platform, and Padmé gave herself a shake. *Enough work for one day.* Her back ached and her feet hurt; the robes that hid her pregnancy were heavy and hot; and she was almost too tired to think. She had earned a rest. And she couldn't help hoping that Anakin would slip away from the Jedi Temple again. He couldn't come every night, she knew that, but he'd been away so *long.* . . .

She dismissed Captain Typho and her two handmaidens almost as soon as she was out of the speeder. "I'll be up in a while," she told them. C-3PO hovered uncertainly as they left, until she sent him to check the security droids.

When she was alone at last, Padmé sighed in relief and went out to the veranda to watch the sunset. She leaned against the railing, glad that for once she didn't have to think about what to say and whether it would provoke some thin-skinned fellow Senator.

She wasn't sure how long she'd been standing

there when she sensed someone else on the veranda. Uneasy, she turned and found Anakin standing close behind her. "You startled me!" she complained, even as she held out her arms for a quick hug.

"How are you feeling?" Anakin asked when they broke apart at last.

Padmé laughed. "He keeps kicking."

"He?" Anakin's eyes widened. "Why do you think it's a boy?"

"My motherly intuition," Padmé teased. Even if she'd consulted a medical droid, she wouldn't have asked. Wondering whether she carried a boy or a girl had been one of the few, secret pleasures she had during the long months Anakin had been away. She took her husband's hand and set it against her stomach, so that he could feel the tiny, unseen foot beating against the walls that enclosed its owner.

Anakin's eyes widened. "Whoa!" He looked at her and grinned. "With a kick that strong, it's got to be a girl."

She laughed, acknowledging the way he'd turned her teasing back on her, and he laughed with her. *This is how it should be, always,* she thought, leaning into his arms. And there was more good news to share, that would prolong the happy moment. "I heard about your appointment, Anakin," she said. "I'm so proud of you."

To her surprise, his expression darkened. "I may

be on the Council," he said angrily, "but they refused to accept me as a Jedi Master."

The fragile moment of happiness evaporated. "Patience," she told him. "In time, they will recognize your skills."

"They still treat me as if I were a Padawan learner," Anakin said, as if he hadn't heard her. He clenched his fists. "They fear my power; that's the problem."

"Anakin!" She didn't like it when he got this way, angry and resentful and eager to place the blame on someone else. *But there isn't always someone to blame — it can just be the way things are. You have to deal with it and move on.*

"Sometimes, I wonder what's happening to the Jedi Order," Anakin went on, and now he sounded sad, almost hurt, instead of angry. "I think this war is destroying the principles of the Republic."

Anakin? Padmé stared at him. In the years she had known him, she had never once heard him speak like this. Usually, Anakin refused to talk about anything remotely political. It was the one thing they had never agreed on. But now, at last, he seemed to be looking beyond the straightforward questions of which assignment he would be given and how best to complete it. It gave her the courage to say something she had been thinking for months while she watched Chancellor Palpatine grow ever stronger and more powerful: "Have you ever considered that we may be on the wrong side?"

Anakin stiffened and looked at her suspiciously. "What do you mean?"

"What if the democracy we thought we were serving no longer exists?" Padmé said, voicing her most secret fear. "What if the Republic has become the very evil we have been fighting to destroy?"

"I don't believe that, Padmé," Anakin said, a little too vehemently. "You sound like a Separatist!"

"Anakin, this war represents a failure to listen," Padmé persisted. "You're closer to the Chancellor than anyone. Please, please — ask him to stop the fighting and let diplomacy resume."

She reached out to him as she spoke, but he pulled back. "Don't ask me to do that, Padmé," he said furiously. "Make a motion in the Senate, where that kind of request belongs!" He turned away. "I'm not your errand boy. I'm not anyone's errand boy!"

Something's wrong. Padmé set her own worries aside, and gently touched his arm. "What is it?"

"Nothing." But there were worlds of anger and hurt in his tone.

She waited, hoping he would relent and explain, but he stayed stubbornly silent. "Don't do this," Padmé said. "Don't shut me out. Let me help you."

"You can't help me," Anakin told her sadly. He

tried to smile. "I'm trying to help *you*. I sense there are things you are not telling me."

Has he heard something about the talk in the Senate? Padmé stared at him. *I can't ask. If he hasn't, I'd betray people who trust me. And it isn't fair to ask Anakin to keep the secret if he doesn't fully agree with our position.* "I sense there are things *you* are not telling *me*," she said, hoping that he would open up to her at last.

Anakin's eyes widened, and he looked away. *I was right; there is something.* But he didn't say anything. *Perhaps he can't. Perhaps he's been sworn to secrecy, the same way I've been.*

She shook her head, trying to banish an image of the two of them standing close together, longing for each other but unable to pass through the invisible wall that separated them. "Hold me," she said. She reached for Anakin, trying to deny the wall, or at least make some breach in it that would bring back the hope and happiness she had felt only moments earlier. "Hold me like you did by the lake on Naboo, so long ago, when there was nothing but our love. No politics, no plotting —"

Anakin's face twisted, as if he, too, would like to recapture that magical, lost time. *Not lost, please, not lost forever.* As he took her in his arms, she finished in a whisper, "— no war," and his grip tightened. But in spite of his warm presence, she could not help feeling that they were farther apart than they had been a few days before, when he was in the Outer Rim and she was here on Coruscant.

I don't like all these good-byes, Obi-Wan thought, looking across the Jedi gunship at Mace Windu and Master Yoda. He wondered where the thought had come from. Jedi were always departing on missions; it never used to bother him, whether he was the one leaving or the one staying behind. *It's the war*, he decided. *Too many Jedi are leaving and not coming back.*

"Anakin did not take to his assignment with much enthusiasm," Obi-Wan said, breaking the silence.

"Too much under the sway of the Chancellor, he is," Yoda said, shaking his head.

"This is a dangerous move, putting them together," Mace warned. "I'm not sure the boy can handle it."

"He'll be all right," Obi-Wan said, trying to feel as confident as he sounded. "I trust him with my life."

"I don't," Mace replied.

Startled, Obi-Wan looked at Mace. Surely there was no longer any question of *trusting* Anakin! He might not be the perfect ideal of a Jedi Knight, but he had proven his abilities again and again. And besides — "With all due respect, Master, is he not the Chosen One? The One who will destroy the Sith and bring balance to the Force?"

"So the prophecy says." Mace's tone was skeptical.

"A prophecy misread that could have been," Yoda pointed out.

"Anakin will not let me down," Obi-Wan insisted. "He never has."

"I hope that right you are," Yoda said heavily as the gunship landed. The doors swung open, and the little Jedi Master rose. "And now, destroy the droid armies on Kashyyyk, I will. May the Force be with you."

Mace and Obi-Wan echoed the formal farewell as Yoda stumped down the ramp to meet the clone assault troops preparing for departure. As the gunship rose and headed for the Jedi Temple, Obi-Wan frowned. Never before had he heard the other Jedi Masters state their opinion of Anakin so plainly. And he couldn't keep from wondering . . .

How can Anakin trust us, if we don't trust him?

Even in the middle of a war, elegance and ease filled the Galaxies opera house. The most important and cultured members of the government went there to watch the best performers in the Republic. For a few hours, they could pretend there was no war.

But even here, Anakin thought, the war had changed things. Fewer of the Senators and administrators came to the opera house; the seats were crowded with less important, less busy beings. Red-robed guards stood outside the Chancellor's private box, observing the hallway instead of the performance. The infamous Baron Papanoida loitered nearby. *I wonder what he's doing here?* But no one else looked twice at Anakin, though his plain Jedi robes made him feel a little out of place amid all the magnificence.

The guards let him into the Chancellor's box. Anakin stood for a moment, letting his eyes adjust to the dimmer light. Chancellor Palpatine was seated near the front, where he had the best view of the stage; Mas Amedda and Sly Moore sat behind him. As Anakin saw him, Palpatine raised a hand and gestured him over.

"I have good news," Palpatine said softly, as Anakin bent to hear him. "Our Clone Intelligence Units have discovered the location of General Grievous. He is hiding in the Utapau System."

"At last!" Anakin said. Mas Amedda frowned at him; feeling sheepish, he lowered his voice and went on, "He won't escape us this time."

Palpatine smiled and nodded, but Anakin wasn't sure whether the gesture was meant for him or for the Mon Calamari dancers in the liquid globe before him. "You are the best choice for this assignment," Palpatine said after a moment. "But the Council can't always be trusted to do the right thing."

"They try," Anakin said. Then he remembered the request Obi-Wan had made. *Do they?* he wondered.

"Sit down," Palpatine said. He dismissed Amedda and Sly Moore, then leaned toward Anakin. "You know I'm not able to rely on the Jedi Council. If they haven't included you in their plot, they soon will."

Anakin hesitated. "I'm not sure I understand." Spying on the Chancellor was wrong, but it wasn't a *plot*, he told himself. The Council just wanted more information.

"The Jedi Council wants control of the Republic," Palpatine said flatly. "They're planning to betray me."

No. But Anakin wasn't as certain as he'd been a few days ago. "I don't think —"

"Anakin, search your feelings," Palpatine said gently. "You do know, don't you?"

"I know they don't trust you." Even saying that much felt like a betrayal. But surely Palpatine knew it already.

Palpatine smiled sadly. "Or the Senate, or the Republic. Or democracy, for that matter."

"I have to admit, my trust in them has been shaken," Anakin said.

"How?"

Anakin couldn't think of a thing to say. He couldn't lie to the Chancellor, but telling him the truth would only make matters worse. *We're on the same side! We should be working together.*

But Palpatine nodded, as if Anakin had spoken aloud. "They asked you to spy on me, didn't they?" he asked.

He knows! Anakin looked down. "I don't know what to say." He couldn't quite bring himself to confirm the Chancellor's suspicions. "I'm confused."

"Remember back to your early teachings, Anakin," the Chancellor said. "'All those who gain power are afraid to lose it.'" He paused. "Even the Jedi."

"The Jedi use their power for good!" *The way I*

did, when I killed Count Dooku? Anakin shook off the thought. *I didn't intend to kill him. It just . . . happened. I knew it was wrong. I knew it was not the way a Jedi is supposed to use his power.* But a small voice in the back of his head whispered, *Still, you killed him.*

"Good is a point of view, Anakin. And the Jedi point of view is not the only valid one." Palpatine settled back more comfortably in his chair. "The Dark Lords of the Sith believe in security and justice also, yet they are considered —"

"— evil." Anakin was glad Palpatine had finally picked something he was sure of.

Palpatine smiled. "Evil . . . from a Jedi's point of view. Yet the Sith and the Jedi are similar in almost every way, including their quest for greater power. The difference between the two is the Sith are not afraid of the dark side of the Force. That is why they are more powerful."

"The Sith rely on their passion for their strength," Anakin said. "They think inward, only about themselves."

"And the Jedi don't?" Palpatine said, lifting his eyebrows skeptically.

"The Jedi are selfless. They only care about others."

Palpatine's smile grew. "Or so you've been trained to believe. Why is it, then, that they have asked you to do something you feel is wrong?"

"I'm not sure it's wrong." The Council must have

reasons he didn't know about for asking him to spy on the Chancellor. *But they wouldn't tell me what they were.* A cold, hard feeling grew inside him. *What if we really aren't all on the same side?*

"Have they asked you to betray the Jedi Code?" Palpatine asked. "The Constitution? A friendship? Your own values?"

Anakin swallowed hard and said nothing.

"Think," Palpatine urged him. "Consider their motives. Keep your mind clear of assumptions. The fear of losing power is a weakness of *both* the Jedi and the Sith."

Anakin hardly heard him. He was a Jedi; it was the only thing he'd ever wanted to be, the only dream he'd ever had. *I wanted to be the best Jedi ever!* He'd had trouble, sometimes, living up to the Code. *Like killing Dooku.* He'd always thought it was harder for him than for other Jedi because he'd started the training late, but what if that wasn't it at all? What if *nobody* else was really following the Code? He found himself wishing, with a strength that surprised him, for one of Obi-Wan's stern lectures on the importance of the Code. *I'll talk to Obi-Wan about this later,* he decided. Perhaps Obi-Wan could make sense of all this. Somehow.

The Chancellor had turned back to watch the performance. After another moment, he asked, "Have you heard the legend of Darth Plagueis the Wise?"

"No." The change of subject was a relief. Anakin

didn't want to talk about the Jedi anymore. His feelings were too confused.

"I thought not," Palpatine said. He leaned back, studying Anakin in the dim light. "It's not a story the Jedi would tell you. It's a Sith legend. Darth Plagueis was a Dark Lord of the Sith. He had such a knowledge of the dark side that he could even keep the ones he cared about from dying."

Padmé! Instantly, Anakin forgot about the Jedi Council, about spying, about Obi-Wan and the Code. "He could actually keep someone safe from death?" he asked.

"The dark side is the pathway to many abilities that some consider unnatural," Palpatine answered in a soft voice.

Remembering where they were, Anakin lowered his voice. "What happened to him?"

"Unfortunately, he taught his apprentice everything he knew — and then the apprentice killed him in his sleep." Palpatine smiled slightly. "It's ironic that he could save others from death, but not himself."

Anakin remembered bending over his dying mother, *knowing* that there was some way to save her but unable to sense what it was. *I knew the Force could keep someone from dying! I knew it! If I can find out what this Darth Plagueis learned, I can save Padmé.* Trying to keep the eagerness from his voice, he asked, "Is it possible to learn this power?"

"Not from a Jedi," Palpatine said with finality.

The ballet was ending. Palpatine joined briefly in the applause, then gestured to Anakin to precede him out the door. Anakin nodded, but he was still preoccupied with what Palpatine had told him. The Jedi archives contained considerable information about the Sith, Anakin knew, but access to that information was restricted to Jedi Masters. *And I'm not a Master.* His lips tightened in a combination of anger and determination. *I don't care. Somehow, I am going to find out how to do what Darth Plagueis did. I am going to save Padmé. I will do anything to save her.*

Anything.

Yoda's long ears drooped as he watched the hologram of Mace Windu. The senior Jedi's arguments were unchanged — if the Chancellor did not end the war once General Grievous was destroyed, he must be arrested. That was as close to proof of the Chancellor's intentions as they would ever come.

"Troubled by this, I am," Yoda told the image.

"Master Yoda, I need your vote." Mace's voice was exasperated. "We cannot wait any longer. The Chancellor is already suspicious."

Yoda scowled. "Several Jedi you will need to execute the arrest."

"I have chosen three of our best, Master." Mace

sounded as if he was trying to be patient. Yoda suppressed a snort. Master Windu was not known for his patience.

"Cunning, Palpatine is," Yoda warned. "Caught by surprise, he will not be."

"Then you support my plan?"

Yoda hesitated. *Listen, he does not. Yet move we must, or too late it will be.* "My vote you have. May the Force be with you."

"Thank you, Master."

As the hologram faded, Yoda heard a commotion behind him. He turned to find two Wookiees confronting one of the clone commanders. "Let him pass, Chewie," Yoda said.

The clone commander entered and saluted. "The clones are in position," he informed them.

Time it is to think of the present. Yoda nodded and stumped out onto the balcony where he and the commander could observe and direct the coming battle. Long practice let him focus on the needs of now, but the problem of the Chancellor lay like a bruise at the back of his mind. What would happen when General Grievous was found and defeated at last?

CHAPTER 10

*A*nakin is having trouble adjusting to his new position, Obi-Wan thought as the two men walked toward the docking bay. His former apprentice had brought the Chancellor's news straight to the Jedi Council — General Grievous was on Utapau. But Anakin hadn't been happy when the Council assigned Obi-Wan to lead the attack alone. *He needs time, that's all. Joining the Council is a big adjustment.*

It didn't help that Chancellor Palpatine had recommended Anakin for the job. *Doesn't the Chancellor realize how awkward it is for Anakin to come into the Council and say, "The Chancellor wants me to lead the attack?" It makes him sound arrogant, when he's just passing on Palpatine's requests.* But the Chancellor wasn't likely to listen to Obi-Wan's advice on how to handle Anakin Skywalker.

As they came out onto the platform above the docking bay, Anakin broke the silence at last. "You're going to need me on this one, Master," he said.

"I agree," Obi-Wan replied. When they'd rescued the Chancellor, Grievous had been too fast for both of them together; how would Obi-Wan beat the droid general alone? He forced a smile. "It may be nothing more than a wild bantha chase," he said, as much to reassure himself as Anakin.

Anakin started to say something, then stopped. Obi-Wan waited a moment. When Anakin remained silent, he turned to leave. The thousands of clone troopers didn't really need his supervision to load themselves into the transports, but it never hurt to be sure.

"Master!"

Obi-Wan stopped and looked back. Anakin walked toward him and bent his head in apology.

"Master," Anakin said again, "I've disappointed you. I have been arrogant. I have not been very appreciative of your training. I apologize. I'm just so frustrated with the Council. But your friendship means everything to me."

All Obi-Wan's love for this difficult, talented, head-strong apprentice rushed forward. Anakin had his faults, but he was a good man. He always came through. Smiling, Obi-Wan put a hand on Anakin's shoulder. "You are wise and strong, Anakin. I am very proud of you." A little embarrassed by the depth of his own feelings, he tried for a more light-hearted note. "This is the first time we've worked separately. Hopefully, it will be the last."

Anakin nodded. Feeling much happier, Obi-Wan started down the ramp toward the clone troops. Then the full force of his own words hit him, and he realized that Anakin might be as worried about him as he was about Anakin. He turned.

"Don't worry," he told Anakin. "I have enough clones with me to take three systems the size of Utapau." He waved at the ranks of white-armored clones below, and smiled. "I think I'll be able to handle the situation — even without your help."

"Well, there's always a first time," Anakin replied. His grin seemed a little strained, but the teasing tone was pure mischief.

Obi-Wan laughed. "Good-bye, old friend. May the Force be with you."

"May the Force be with you," Anakin echoed. His voice was serious — almost somber.

As Obi-Wan walked toward the waiting starcruiser, uneasiness struck him. *This is just an ordinary mission,* he told himself. *I'll be back in a week or two. If something's bothering Anakin, we can talk about it then.*

But for some reason, he felt as if he'd said good-bye to his best friend and former apprentice for the last time.

Anakin stood watching until the last clone trooper boarded the starcruiser. Only when the ship took off did he leave the landing area. He felt empty and adrift, as if he'd lost an anchor. *And I never did get to talk to Obi-Wan about the Jedi Council.*

Without thinking about it, Anakin headed for Padmé's apartment. Though she had lived mainly on Coruscant for nearly ten years, her rooms held the peace and comfort of her home planet, Naboo. He needed that peace and comfort right now.

She still keeps the temperature too low, though, Anakin thought as he entered. He smiled. It was an old argument between them. His own home, Tatooine, was a desert planet, and although he had adjusted to the varying climates of planets all over the Republic, he still felt most comfortable when the air was warmer than most beings preferred.

Something in him relaxed as he called a greeting to Padmé and sat down to work on his report for the Council. This was what mattered: this place where he was always welcomed and loved. Where he could be himself, just Anakin Skywalker, eating and sleeping and kissing his wife like other, ordinary people. Home.

He heard Padmé enter the room behind him. With her came the faint traces of a familiar presence. Anakin lowered his datascanner. "Obi-Wan's been here, hasn't he?" he asked.

"He came by this morning," Padmé confirmed.

That must have been right before the Council meeting, Anakin thought. *Why didn't he say anything to me?* "What did he want?" he asked.

"He's worried about you."

Why would Obi-Wan come to Padmé if he was worried about Anakin? Unless — "You told him about us, didn't you?" Anakin couldn't keep the anger out of his voice.

Padmé glanced at him and walked on, into the bedroom. Anakin followed, waiting. Finally, she said, "He's your best friend, Anakin. He says you're under a lot of stress."

"And he's not?"

"You have been moody lately."

"I'm not moody!" He flung the words at her, wishing he could shout at Obi-Wan, too. *They're acting like I'm a child.*

"Anakin!" Padmé looked at him with a tired sadness that cut at his heart. "Don't do this again."

Anakin turned away, wondering how he could explain. *I killed a defenseless prisoner, against the Code. The Jedi Council asked me to spy on the Chancellor, also against the Jedi Code. The Chancellor says the Council wants to take over the Republic. The Council says the Chancellor has too much power. I don't know anymore who to believe or what to believe in. And I'm so afraid of losing you that I can't think straight and none of the rest of it matters.* "I don't know," he told her at last. "I feel . . . lost."

"Lost?" Padmé gazed at him in surprised concern. "You're always so sure of yourself. I don't understand."

"Obi-Wan and the Council don't trust me." *And I'm not sure I can trust them.*

Padmé shook her head. "They trust you with their lives. Obi-Wan loves you as a son."

Maybe Obi-Wan does. But he's gone, hunting General Grievous. He tried again. "Something's happening. I'm not the Jedi I should be." Padmé shook her head again, and he held up a hand to stop her. "I am one of the most powerful Jedi, but I'm not satisfied. I want more, but I know I shouldn't."

"You're only human, Anakin," Padmé told him gently. "No one expects any more."

Yes, they do. And I do. That was why Obi-Wan kept lecturing him about pride and ambition and jealousy — and that was why he hated those lectures so much. Because he knew Obi-Wan was right. A Jedi Knight shouldn't have those thoughts. Anakin closed his eyes. He should have known Padmé wouldn't understand. She wasn't a Jedi.

But she would be the mother of his child. Anakin felt a tingle of fear and excitement at the thought. "I have found a way to save you," he said.

"Save me?"

"From my nightmares." *Surely she hasn't forgotten!*

Padmé smiled slightly. "Is *that* what's bothering you?"

"I won't lose you, Padmé."

"I'm not going to die in childbirth, Anakin," she said quietly. "I promise you."

"No, I promise you!" Recklessly, he made the vow, though he did not yet have the power to fulfill it. Chancellor Palpatine might think that the story of Darth Plagueis was only a legend, but Anakin knew it was true. He could *feel* it. And if Darth Plagueis could discover the secret, so could he. There was time. "I will become powerful enough to keep you from dying."

Padmé caught his eyes and held them. "You don't need more power, Anakin," she said slowly and seriously. "I believe you can protect me against anything, just as you are."

And I will, Anakin thought as he gathered her into his arms. *I will protect you.* No matter what it takes.

All the way to Utapau, Obi-Wan considered how best to find and destroy General Grievous. If they blasted their way in, Grievous would only run away again — the droid general was always careful to have an escape ship stashed somewhere close to his command center. He might not even be with his armies. His command center might be hidden in one part of the Utapau system, while his droids massed for an attack somewhere else.

So Obi-Wan decided to keep his clone troops in space aboard the Jedi cruiser and search the system himself, quietly. That way, he could be sure that when he told his forces to attack, they would be attacking the right place.

Commander Cody accepted the order without question, as he always did. The clones had been genetically engineered to take orders; that was why each major offensive needed a Jedi Knight as general. Though he had worked and fought with the clones for years, their willingness to follow any order, no matter how unreasonable, still made Obi-Wan uneasy. Free beings shouldn't be so . . . obedient.

Obi-Wan snorted. How many times had he complained about Anakin's independence and headstrong ways? And here he was, worried because his clone troops were *too* compliant. Anakin would laugh himself sick if he knew what his Master was thinking.

The planet of Utapau looked peaceful enough as Obi-Wan flew over it in his starfighter. He saw no sign of the droid armies. The huge sinkhole cities looked quiet. Well, he hadn't expected General Grievous to be out in plain sight, and Utapau *was* officially neutral. He'd have to refuel and search the rest of the system.

Arranging a landing was no problem. A worried-looking local administrator even came out to the ship to greet him. Obi-Wan bowed politely to him. "With your kind permission, I would like some fuel, and to use your city as a base to search nearby systems."

The administrator gestured, and a ground crew rushed out to service the fighter. "What are you searching for?" he asked as if it were of no particular interest.

"A droid army," Obi-Wan replied. "Led by General Grievous."

The Utapauan held very still for a moment. Then he leaned sideways, as if he were inspecting the underside of Obi-Wan's fighter. The movement brought his head close to Obi-Wan and hid his face from the windows above. Very quietly, he said, "Grievous is here! We are being held hostage. They are watching us."

"I understand," Obi-Wan replied just as softly. If he made the wrong move, the droids would slaughter thousands of civilians. No wonder the administrator was worried!

"The tenth level," the Utapauan whispered before he straightened up. Obi-Wan nodded and walked back to the starfighter. He made a show of ducking underneath it, to make it seem as if he were studying something the Utapaun had pointed out. Then he climbed back into the fighter.

As the ground crew finished its work, Obi-Wan set up a secure communication channel to his clone troops. "I have located General Grievous," he told the commander. "Report to the Jedi Council at once. I'm staying here."

He cut the signal, then gave a few quick instructions to his R4 unit and slipped out of the starfighter on the far side of the cockpit. By the time the fighter took off, he was hidden in the shadows at the entrance to the sinkhole city. *Now all I have to do is get to the tenth level and defeat Grievous.*

Getting there was actually much easier than he expected. The stairs were blocked and the elevators had been shut down, but no one had bothered to put a guard on the open walls of the sinkhole itself. All Obi-Wan had to do was find one of the giant lizards that the Utapauans used as riding beasts. The lizard climbed the sinkhole wall easily, and soon Obi-Wan was riding across the edge of the tenth level, searching for the control center.

He found it a quarter of the way around the sinkhole — the hordes of battle droids made it unmistakable, even if General Grievous himself hadn't been standing at the far end along with the members of the Separatist Council. That was an unexpected complication. He couldn't take on all of them — and all their formidable bodyguards — at once, not alone. Besides, if he could get close enough to hear what they were saying, he might find out some of their plans. He climbed down from the lizard and slipped along a high, narrow walkway, hoping the sound of their voices would carry once he got near enough.

General Grievous surveyed the Separatist Council with disgust — the Neimoidians, Nute Gunray and Rune Haako, who represented the Trade Federation; archduke Poggle the Lesser, who was oddly fierce-looking for a banker; Shu Mai, San Hill, Wat Tambor, and the rest. Not for the first time, Grievous was glad that his smooth metal face could show no emotion. It would be unfortunate if these beings realized how much contempt he had for them.

The Council stirred. If he let them start talking again, they'd be here all day. They'd already wasted too much time asking questions and solemnly discussing pointless alternatives. It was time to *make* them move. "It won't be long before the armies of the Republic track us here," Grievous told them bluntly. "Make your way to the Mustafar system in the Outer Rim. You will be safe there."

Nute Gunray goggled at Grievous. His large bulging eyes made him look vaguely froglike. "Safe?" he sputtered. "Chancellor Palpatine managed to escape your grip, General. I have doubts about your ability to keep us *safe*."

There was a murmur of agreement from the other councilors. Grievous drew himself up to his full height and thrust his head toward the indignant Neimoidian. "Be thankful, Viceroy, that you have not found *yourself* in my grip," he said in a low, menacing voice. Gunray shrank away, and the murmuring died abruptly. Grievous waited to be sure the lesson had sunk in. "Your ship is waiting," he told the group.

The Separatist Council could hardly wait to leave.

Grievous stood motionless and silently threatening as the Councilors hurried out, casting nervous backward glances in his direction. *It takes so little to frighten ordinary beings,* he thought. *And fear is so useful . . .* Now all he had to do was stay on Utapau until that annoying Jedi fell into the trap. With luck, it wouldn't be a long wait.

When the Separatist Council filed out, Obi-Wan stayed motionless, hoping that some of the hundreds of battle droids would leave, too. None of them moved. *This is it, then.* Obi-Wan took just a moment longer, to center himself in the living Force. Then he took off his cloak and leaped down, landing lightly right in front of General Grievous.

The droid general's smooth metal face was impossible to read, but his tone was puzzled as he said, "I find your behavior bewildering. Surely you realize you're doomed."

"I've brought two full legions with me," Obi-Wan said. "And this time, you won't escape."

Grievous signaled, and his four bodyguards stepped forward, whirling their electro-staffs.

Obi-Wan ducked and ignited his lightsaber. He feinted, to keep the droids' attention on his weapon while he used the Force to drop a huge rectagular slab of durasteel down from the ceiling.

The tactic worked even better than he'd hoped. Three of the guards were crushed outright; the fourth was partially pinned, and was struggling to get at his electro-staff. Obi-Wan's lightsaber cut him neatly apart as he went past, heading for General Grievous.

More droids poured into the room, but General Grievous waved them off. He threw back his cloak, revealing the belt hung with the stolen lightsabers of the Jedi he'd killed. Reaching down, he took two in each hand. *What does he think he's doing?* Obi-Wan wondered, and then the general's metal arms split lengthwise, and Obi-Wan was facing a four-armed enemy with a lightsaber in each hand.

"Count Dooku trained me in the Jedi arts," Grievous said, and attacked. He spun two of the lightsabers like deadly buzzsaws, while he stabbed with the other two whenever he saw an opening.

It was almost like fighting four different people at once. Obi-Wan's lightsaber blurred as he blocked and parried, but he knew he couldn't keep that up for long. *Time for a different approach.* He leaped, flipping high over Grievous to land behind him.

Grievous didn't have to turn; he just rotated his mechanical body until he faced the other way. But even doing that took time and threw off his attack, just enough to let Obi-Wan's lightsaber swirl past his guard. Two of his four arms dropped to the floor, still gripping their stolen lightsabers.

Before Grievous could adjust, and attack with his

two remaining lightsabers, Obi-Wan reached for the Force. He lifted Grievous into the air, throwing him against one of the beams that supported the upper level. The impact shook the lightsabers out of his grasp. They landed on the floor of the control center, while Grievous slid past the edge of the floor and fell to the level below.

The room was filling up with blaster fire; the clone troopers had arrived and were keeping the battle droids busy. Obi-Wan rushed to the edge in time to see Grievous scuttle toward a one-man wheel scooter. *I knew it! He has an escape ship somewhere, and he thinks he's going to get to it while these droids keep me busy! Well, not this time.*

In a fury of light, Obi-Wan sent a volley of shots back at the battle droids and whistled for his riding lizard, just as the general kicked his scooter into motion and roared away. The lizard jumped down, landing on a battle droid. Obi-Wan leaped onto the lizard's back, and took off after Grievous.

Anakin frowned as he hurried through the halls of the Senate Office building. It should be good news that he was bringing to Chancellor Palpatine, but the way Master Windu talked during the Jedi Council meeting had made him uneasy. *The clone commander said that Obi-Wan has found General Grievous.* The hologram transmission had, for once, been perfectly clear, with none of the wavering and static caused by jammers or other interference. Anakin had even seen the clone troopers in the background, preparing for the assault.

He'd expected the other Council members to be elated. Instead, they'd looked grave and made ambiguous remarks about watching the Chancellor's reaction to the news. *The war is going to be over soon. Of course he'll be happy! What else are they expecting?*

But Chancellor Palpatine received the news with the same serious expression as the Council members had. "Finding this droid general is not the same as defeating him," Palpatine murmured. "We can only hope that Master Kenobi is up for the challenge."

"I should be there with him," Anakin said.

"It upsets me that the Council doesn't fully appreciate your talents," the Chancellor went on. "Don't you wonder why they wouldn't make you a Jedi Master?"

"I wish I knew." Anakin shook his head. "I know there are things about the Force that they are not telling me."

"They don't trust you, Anakin." Palpatine paused. "They want to take control of the Senate."

"That's not true," Anakin said automatically. Jedi didn't want power. *But if the Jedi Council doesn't care about power, why are they so worried about the Chancellor?*

"Are you sure? What if I am right, and they are plotting to take over the Republic?" Chancellor Palpatine shook his head in mild exasperation. "Anakin! Break through the fog of lies the Jedi have created. I am your friend. Let me help you to learn the true ways of the Force."

Anakin felt a cold chill. Palpatine wasn't a Jedi. "How do you know the ways of the Force?"

"My mentor taught me everything," Palpatine replied calmly. "Even the nature of the dark side."

"You know the dark side?" Anakin stopped short as the sense of the words crashed down onto him. "You're a Sith Lord!" he said, and ignited his lightsaber.

CHAPTER 12

Chancellor Palpatine, whose Sith name was Darth Sidious, looked calmly at the angry young Jedi with the glowing lightsaber. This was the point toward which all his plots and plans had been heading for many years. "Yes, I am a Sith Lord," he told Anakin. As Anakin raised his lightsaber, Palpatine added gently, "And I am also the one who has held this Republic together during these troubled times. I am not your enemy, Anakin."

He could sense Anakin's growing confusion, and suppressed a smile. These Jedi expected all Sith Lords to be like those apprentices of his, Darth Maul and Darth Tyranus — ready to whip out a lightsaber the moment they were discovered. But a lightsaber was such an *obvious* weapon. Words were better. All you could do with a lightsaber was kill the man you faced. With words, you could change his mind, so that he would help you instead of fighting you. That was *true* power.

And Anakin was listening to him. Time, now, to begin the final stage that would turn Anakin to the dark side at last. Palpatine let his tone fall into lecturing. "Anakin, if one is to understand a great mystery, one must study all aspects of it, not just the dogmatic, narrow view of the Jedi. If you wish to become a complete and wise leader, you must embrace a larger view of the Force."

He paused, to give his words time to sink in. Then, in a deliberately different tone, he went on. "Be careful of the Jedi, Anakin. They fear you. In time, they will destroy you." He put pleading into his voice, like the kindly uncle he had pretended to be for so long. "Let me train you, Anakin. I will show you the true nature of the Force."

Palpatine could see Anakin considering it, but then Anakin shook his head. "I won't be a pawn in your political game, Chancellor. The Jedi are my family."

There *had* to be a way to shake that confidence of his — ah, yes. "Only through me can you achieve a power greater than any Jedi. Learn to control the dark side of the Force, Anakin, and you will be able to save Padmé from certain death."

"W-what are you talking about?"

"I know what has been troubling you," Palpatine said gently. "Listen to me. Use my knowledge, I beg you!"

"I won't become a Sith!" But Anakin's denial was

too passionate, as if he was trying to convince himself as much as Palpatine. "I should kill you!"

But you haven't killed me, have you, my fine young Jedi? You were already wondering about the truth of those overly simple Jedi teachings, and now I'm not acting the way you think a Sith Lord should. A little more, and you'll join me — perhaps not this minute, but soon. When you've had time to calm down and think.

But I must move slowly, Palpatine reminded himself. A misstep could still spoil all his careful work. "Of course you should," Palpatine agreed. "Except for the fact that we are both working for the same goal — a more perfect future for the Republic."

"You have deceived everyone!"

"A painful necessity." What had the boy expected him to do — begin by announcing to the entire galaxy that he was one of the feared and hated Sith Lords, and *then* try to get elected Chancellor? "The Republic was rotting from within. The system had to be shaken to its core. Yet no one, not the Senate, not the courts, not even the Jedi Council, could do anything. I was the only one who dared to clean up the mess." The old anger and conviction shook him as he spoke, and he felt Anakin's reaction to the truth of his words.

He paused. *Time to let him think.* Palpatine made a show of studying Anakin's lightsaber. "Are you going to kill me?" he asked calmly, as though it were a minor matter of curiosity.

"I would certainly like to," Anakin growled.

"I know you would." Palpatine allowed himself a smile as he turned away. "I can *feel* your anger. It gives you *focus*, makes you *stronger*. The question is, will you kill me if it means plunging the galaxy into eternal chaos and strife?"

Anakin lifted his lightsaber. Palpatine kept his expression relaxed and disinterested. *If I've pushed him too far, too fast . . .* But Anakin did not complete the movement. At last, he lowered the lightsaber and said, "I am going to turn you over to the Jedi Council."

"But you're not sure of their intentions, are you?" Palpatine almost smiled again as Anakin's eyes slid away from his. He would win this contest, after all. "I want you to meditate on my proposal," he said coolly. "Know the power of the dark side. The power to save Padmé."

Anakin stared at him for a long moment, then finally turned off his lightsaber. As if nothing unusual had happened, Palpatine walked to his desk and sat down. Seeing the surprise in Anakin's eyes, he said, "I am not going anywhere. You have time to decide my fate." *And to think about my offer.*

As Anakin turned and all but ran from the room, Palpatine added softly, "Perhaps you'll reconsider, and help me rule the galaxy. For the good of all."

Anakin's Jedi senses would hear that final whisper. His ambition would bring him back to Palpatine, if his fear for Padmé didn't.

And then, once more, there would be two Sith Lords, Master and apprentice.

Ruling the galaxy, for a thousand years.

General Grievous is an even more reckless driver than Anakin, Obi-Wan observed as his lizard raced through the tunnel city after the general's wheel scooter. Blaster fire from clone troops and battle droids filled the air, and there were explosions everywhere — not to mention armored transports full of droids and clones. The scooter hurtled through them as if they weren't there, narrowly avoiding crash after crash and crushing those in its way. Obi-Wan's lizard was having a hard time keeping up.

A stray laser blast whizzed past Obi-Wan's ear, and he reached for his lightsaber. It wasn't there. *It must have been knocked loose right after I jumped on the lizard*, Obi-Wan thought. *I hope Anakin never hears about this.* But now he had to guide the lizard so that they avoided the shots, instead of just deflecting them. They lost ground.

As they moved farther into the city, the tunnels became more crowded. Obi-Wan lost more ground as he wove through the battling droids and vehicles. The crowd was slowing Grievous down, too; Obi-Wan saw Grievous' scooter roll up onto the curving walls to get around a mob of battle droids running up the tunnel toward them.

Obi-Wan smiled suddenly. His lizard could do things the general's scooter couldn't. He urged the lizard up onto the wall, and then to the ceiling. The lizard used its natural abilities to cling upside down, and Obi-Wan used the Force to cling to the lizard. Nobody else was using the ceiling as a highway, so they didn't lose any more time dodging traffic. They gained on Grievous rapidly.

Ahead, Obi-Wan could see the tunnel opening out into a small landing platform. He dug his heels into the lizard, which leaped forward. He was next to Grievous now, close enough to strike at him, if he'd only had his lightsaber. Unfortunately, Grievous hadn't dropped his electro-staff, and he was close enough to strike at Obi-Wan.

As the staff swung at him, Obi-Wan grabbed it and yanked hard, throwing Grievous off balance. Calling on the Force, he leaped from his lizard to tackle the general. The tactic worked; Obi-Wan and Grievous fell to the floor of the landing platform together, and the electro-staff went flying.

General Grievous did not spare a glance for the missing staff. He pulled out a blaster. Obi-Wan grabbed for it, and it, too, went flying out of reach. Obi-Wan rolled and grabbed the electro-staff. It wasn't as good as a lightsaber, but it would do.

His first blow caught General Grievous squarely in his midsection. Obi-Wan swung again and connected with one of the general's arms. The metal arm bent, but did not break. An instant later, too fast for even Jedi reflexes to avoid, Grievous' other arm struck Obi-Wan.

It was like being hit with a metal construction bar. Obi-Wan's shoulder and half his side went numb, then flared into pain. The electro-staff went flying once more, and he barely dodged the next blow. *That was brutal! I'd better not let him catch me with any more of those.*

Using the Force, Obi-Wan leaped, putting all his weight and momentum behind his kick. Grievous hardly seemed to notice it. His metal limbs and the durasteel shell that encased his body were tougher than those of any droid Obi-Wan had ever faced.

There must be some way to get at him! Obi-Wan dodged another swing, and saw a corner of Grievous' stomach plate shift as the droid general moved. *It must have been loosened when I hit him with the electro-staff. Maybe I can get some of that armor off of him . . .*

As the general swung again, Obi-Wan ducked and closed in. He grabbed the loose corner and pulled. The plate came free — and the general's metal arms closed around Obi-Wan and lifted him high. Then he was flying through the air, to land heavily on the far side of the platform. Half-stunned, he slid across the surface and almost over the edge. At the last minute, he grabbed hold, stopping with his legs dangling above the long, long drop to the bottom of the sinkhole.

Dimly, Obi-Wan saw General Grievous pick up the electro-staff and start toward him. He struggled back to full consciousness, thinking, *I need a weapon!*

Then he saw the general's abandoned blaster, lying a few yards away.

Barely in time, he called the blaster to him, and fired. General Grievous stopped moving forward. Obi-Wan poured shot after shot into the general's open stomach area. The half-droid made a sound that was part choking noise, part metallic screech, and then there was a small explosion inside his metal body.

Holding the laser pistol ready, Obi-Wan watched as more explosions shook the cyborg general's metal casing. Finally, flames burst from his eye slits, and General Grievous collapsed in a smoking heap. Obi-Wan reached out with the Force, to sense any flicker of remaining life.

He found none. Heaving a sigh of relief, he started back toward the tunnel to recapture his lizard, and realized he was still holding the laser pistol. He looked at it with distaste. *So uncivilized!*

Tossing it over the edge of the landing platform, Obi-Wan went to see how the battle was going. He didn't really have any doubts. Clone Commander Cody was competent, and he had more than enough troops to handle the battle droids. General Grievous had been the real problem, and that was taken care of.

All that's left is to notify the Council — and the Chancellor. And then . . . then we'll find out the Chancellor's real intentions.

When Anakin finally found Master Windu in the Jedi Temple hangar, his head was still spinning. Master Windu and three other Jedi were preparing to board a gunship, and at first, he was not at all pleased by Anakin's interruption.

"What is it, Skywalker?" Master Windu snapped. "We are in a hurry. We've just received word that Obi-Wan has destroyed General Grievous. We are on our way to make sure the Chancellor gives his emergency powers back to the Senate."

"He won't give up his power," Anakin said heavily. He felt Master Windu's attention focus on him, and swallowed hard. "Chancellor Palpatine is a Sith Lord."

"A Sith Lord?" Master Windu sounded as horrified as Anakin had been. "How do you know this?"

He told me himself. "He knows the ways of the Force. He has been trained to use the dark side."

Master Windu stared at him for a long moment. At last he nodded. "Then our worst fears have been realized. We must move fast if the Jedi are to remain in control."

As Master Windu signaled the other Jedi to board the gunship, Anakin said, "Master, the Chancellor is very powerful." He hesitated. "You will need my help if you are going to arrest him."

Mace Windu's eyes narrowed. "For your own good, you stay out of this conflict," he commanded sternly. "I sense much confusion in you, young Skywalker. Your fear clouds your judgment."

"That's not true, Master," Anakin protested.

"We'll see," Mace responded. "If what you say is true, you will have earned my trust. For now, you *stay here*. Wait for us in the Council Chamber until we return."

He still doesn't trust me. He never has. But Mace Windu was a senior Council member, a Master. As long as Anakin was a Jedi, he had to follow Master Windu's orders. "Yes, Master," he said, trying to keep the resentment out of his voice.

Mace nodded once, and entered the gunship. Anakin stayed where he was until the gunship took off, hoping until the last minute that Mace would change his mind. When the ship finally vanished into the endless stream of traffic, he turned and went back into the Jedi Temple.

The Council Chamber was dim and empty. Anakin sat in one of the chairs and tried to meditate, but his mind and heart were in too much turmoil. Now that he was alone, his mission accomplished, the Chancellor's words kept replaying in his mind. *Learn to control the dark side of the Force, and you will be able to save Padmé from certain death.* Anakin felt cold, remembering the screams that echoed through his dreams. Again, he heard Padmé's dying cry: "Anakin! I love you."

The Chancellor's voice spoke in his mind, words he had *not* said before: "You do know that if the Jedi destroy me, any chance of saving Padmé will be lost."

No! Anakin reached out blindly, not to the Chancellor, but to the one he loved. To Padmé. And then he sensed her presence, as if she were there, not just in the Jedi Council Chamber, but in his own mind and heart — a true joining through the Force.

Padmé was alone in the central room of her apartment, when she felt Anakin's presence in the room with her. *What is he doing here at this hour?* she thought, and looked up. She blinked and shook her head. The room was empty, but just for an instant she thought she had seen the Jedi Council Chamber.

And then the connection took hold fully, and she knew. Anakin was there, alone in the Council

Chamber — and he was here, too, with her. She felt his love, and his fear for her — the terrible fear that was eating at his heart. The fear that she would die. She hadn't known how terrible his fear was.

I am not afraid to die. She'd told him that once, when they were being led into the arena on Geonosis for execution, and it was still true. She was only afraid that he would not know how much she loved him. As the Force connection began to fade, she spoke again the words she had said then, when she first declared her love for him. Anakin wouldn't hear them, of course, but perhaps he would feel the love behind them, the love that was stronger and deeper now than it had ever been.

"*I truly, deeply love you,*" Padmé's voice said in Anakin's mind. "*Before I die, I want you to know.*"

The last of the Force connection faded, but her words echoed: *Before I die, before I die, before I die.* Anakin shuddered. *Padmé, no!* But the link was gone, she was gone, and he was alone in the Council Chamber. As he would be alone, always and everywhere, once Padmé was dead.

"No!" The word tore from his lips. He was on his feet, panting as if he had been running. *I can't do this! I can't let her die!* And then he *was* running, out of the Council Chamber toward the platform where his airspeeder was parked.

The trip to the Senate Office building seemed to take forever. Anakin was vaguely aware of other traffic dodging and beeping at him, and of the gauges on his control panel all pushing into the red zone. Then he was running through the halls toward the hum of a lightsaber in the Chancellor's office.

He stopped in the doorway, shocked motionless. Wind whistled past him from the gaping hole that had been the huge window overlooking Coruscant. Shards of glass littered the floor and dusted across three crumpled figures in Jedi robes. Only one Jedi still stood — Mace Windu, his purple lightsaber menacing Chancellor Palpatine. "You're under arrest, my lord," he told the Chancellor, motioning to Anakin to stay back.

But Palpatine was not looking at Mace Windu. "Anakin!" he cried. "I told you it would come to this. I was right. The Jedi are taking over."

But . . . but . . . That's not right. They came here because I told them you were a Sith Lord, not in order to take over. But they'd already been on their way to arrest Palpatine when he arrived with the news, a different part of Anakin thought.

"Your plot to regain control of the Republic is over," Master Windu said. "You have *lost.*"

"No!" Palpatine raised his hands. "*You* will die!" Blue Force lightning shot from his fingers toward Mace.

Anakin took an involuntary step forward. "He is a

traitor, Anakin!" Palpatine cried as more lightning poured from his hands.

"He's the traitor!" Mace said. He grimaced with the effort of repelling the lightning. "Stop him!"

Anakin's head swiveled from one man to the other. The Force lightning was hurting Master Windu now, hurting him badly. But the Chancellor was aging before Anakin's eyes. His hair thinned and his skin shriveled. Deep furrows appeared in his forehead. His hands twisted and turned gray-white. "Help me!" he cried. "I can't hold on any longer."

But Anakin stayed frozen. At last Palpatine collapsed, exhausted. "I give up," he said in the whispery voice of an old, old man. "I am . . . I am too weak. Don't kill me. I give up."

Mace Windu pointed his lightsaber at the cringing Chancellor. "You Sith disease," he snarled. "I am going to end this right now."

"You can't kill him, Master," Anakin protested. "He must stand trial."

"He has too much control over the Senate and the Courts," Mace replied. "He is too dangerous to be kept alive."

"It's not the Jedi way." But the Chancellor had said the same thing about Count Dooku. If Jedi Master and Sith Lord made the same argument, were they really so different? *And I need him to save Padmé.*

But Master Windu wasn't listening. He raised his

commander after clone commander, on world after world. With every message, his faint smile grew.

The clone troops followed orders. That was, supposedly, why each battalion was led by a Jedi. What the Jedi had forgotten was that the clones served the Republic, not the Jedi Temple . . . and he, Darth Sidious, was the Supreme Chancellor of the Republic. The clones would follow the Chancellor's orders unquestioningly. Even if they were ordered to kill their Jedi leaders.

Order Sixty-six commanded the clones to do just that.

Still smiling, Darth Sidious leaned back, picturing the scenes all over the galaxy. Jedi on jungle planets, crystal worlds, water worlds, in the heat of battle and safe in their command centers, all dying at the hands of their own clone troops. He could sense it happening, though not in detail — but he could feel the dark side growing stronger with every Jedi death.

His only regret was that he couldn't be there in person to watch each one of them die.

CHAPTER 14

The trouble with droids is that they can't think, Obi-Wan told himself as he hacked his way through the battle droids that still clogged the sinkhole tunnel city on Utapau. An army made up of living beings would have seen how badly outnumbered they were, and given up. The droids just kept on fighting.

At least he had his lightsaber back. One of the clones had found it and returned it. *I'd hate to have to fight battle droids with nothing but a laser pistol,* Obi-Wan thought. He guided his lizard up the wall of the sinkhole, to get a better angle. *These droids —*

Suddenly, Obi-Wan felt a peculiar tremor in the Force, and started to turn his lizard. The lizard shifted just enough that the sudden intense blast of laser fire didn't destroy both it and Obi-Wan, but only knocked them off the wall of the sinkhole. As he made the long fall to the bottom of the sinkhole, Obi-Wan saw that the laser fire had come from *his own troops.* The clones were trying to kill him! *I have a bad feeling about this,* he thought, and hit the stagnant water below.

More laser blasts hit the surface of the water. Obi-Wan let the momentum of his fall carry him deep down, far below the level the blasts could reach. He fumbled at his belt pack for a moment before he found his breath mask and put it on. Now he could stay underwater until the clones gave up.

It took them a long time. No one could say clones weren't persistent but at last they must have assumed the great fall had killed him.

Fortunately the clones didn't know about General Grievous' little escape ship. Obi-Wan had only told them that Grievous was dead; there hadn't been time to go into details. *If I can get to that ship, I can get away. It's a Trade Federation model — even if the cruisers in orbit spot it, they'll think I'm a Separatist running away from the battle.* Of course, he'd still have to sneak past thousands of clone troops to get to the secret landing platform, but at least the clones wouldn't be waiting for him when he got there.

And once he was away from Utapau, he could find out what was going on. The clones weren't supposed to be *able* to betray the Republic. Something was very, very wrong.

The battle for Kashyyyk was over. Outside, the clones and Wookiees were picking up bits of smashed battle droids and repairing their own equipment. Yoda had left them to it. The clones did not need a commander to show them how to clean up debris, and the Wookiee meeting hall was quiet — a fine place to meditate. Chewbacca and Tarfful, the two Wookiee commanders, stayed to one side, and the clone officers kept near the entrance where they could keep an eye on the troops outside, and where any incoming messages would not disturb their commander.

Centuries of practice had made it easy for Yoda to slip his mind nearly free from his body, to rest in the living Force. Lately, he had taken the opportunity to do so whenever it arose. For as the dark side grew stronger over the years, so had his belief that someone was trying to reach him through the increasing gloom.

Eyes closed, Yoda gave himself up to the Force. Yes, there it was — the sense of someone reaching for him. Almost, he succeeded. Something brushed close to Yoda . . . no, someone, someone who felt familiar. And then, suddenly, shock waves ripped through the Force. *Jedi are dying.*

Yoda's eyes popped open. Two clone officers were coming up behind him. *To consult me, they pretend they are coming.* But Yoda could sense the faint aura of the dark side clinging to them. Something was very wrong, indeed.

So he was not surprised when the two clones

reached for their weapons. His lightsaber hummed in his hands, and an instant later two white-helmeted heads fell one way, and two bodies the other.

More, there will be. The clone officers would not have acted without orders, and a thousand more clones waited outside. Help, he must seek.

Fortunately, help was close at hand. The two Wookiees had seen the whole thing, and they recovered quickly from their surprise. Yoda explained what he needed, and the Wookiees nodded and exchanged comments in their barking language. Then Chewbacca picked Yoda up, and he and Tarfful retreated. They took Yoda out a back way, not a moment too soon. Seconds after they left it, a clone tank fired from a low hill nearby, and the meeting hall disappeared in a ball of fire.

It took the clones a little time to discover that Yoda had not been inside the hall when it blew up, but as soon as they did, they spread out in a search pattern, hunting for him. By then, the Wookiees had hidden him on one of the small boats. But he couldn't stay in hiding here. Too dangerous, it was, both for him and for the Wookiees. Besides, he had to get off the planet to find out what was happening.

When he told them the problem, the Wookiees nodded and barked at each other so fast that it was difficult even for him to follow the conversation. Then they turned and offered him one of their escape pods. Yoda accepted at once. The only problem left was how to get past the clone troops to the pod.

Senator Bail Organa was in an uneasy frame of mind as he flew his sleek airspeeder through the dawn light. Rumors had been flying around the Senate since early the previous evening. At first, the rumors were good — the Separatists had given up, the war was over, the Jedi had killed General Grievous. But before any of the rumors could be confirmed, new and frightening ones took their place — stories of rebellion, treason, murder, and betrayal. Bail didn't believe any of them, but they had grown and spread throughout the night. Finally, he had decided to see for himself just what was going on.

The first thing he saw was a cloud of black smoke billowing upward from the Jedi Temple. As he drew nearer, he saw white-clad clone troopers everywhere. *Where are the Jedi? Did the Separatists attack the Temple?*

No one seemed to be actually shooting, so Bail decided to land. Perhaps he could find out more. He picked a landing platform near the Temple entrance. Four clones stood guard in the doorway, but they lowered their weapons when they saw his Senatorial robes. "Don't worry, sir," one of them said. "The situation is under control."

"What's going on?" Bail asked, trying to sound casual instead of desperately anxious to know.

"There has been a rebellion, sir."

A rebellion? The smoke and the clone guards suddenly took on a new, sinister meaning. *The Jedi rebelled? Or . . . the clones? This doesn't make sense!* "That's impossible!"

"Don't worry, sir," the clone said again. "The situation is under control."

Bail frowned and started toward the Temple doors. As long as it was safe, he'd just go in and see for himself. But the clones blocked his path. "I'm sorry sir. No one is allowed entry." The clone paused, and to Bail's surprise and dismay, raised his blaster rifle. "It's time for you to leave, sir," he said pointedly.

Reluctantly, Bail turned back toward his speeder. It wouldn't do any good to get himself killed — and he didn't want to find out whether the clone troops really would fire on a Senator.

Just as he reached the speeder, he heard shots. Turning, he saw a boy, no more than ten years old, wearing Jedi robes and a desperate expression. He held a lightsaber, and the clone troops were shooting at him!

As Bail stared in horror, one of the clones looked up from the fight and pointed straight at him. "Take care of him," the clone told the four who had been guarding the door, and then he went back to the fight.

Bail leaped over his speeder an instant before the laser bolts started crashing around him. But the speeder wasn't armored; the clones would destroy it — and Bail — in a few moments, once they concentrated their fire. His only hope was to get away.

More clones were pouring out of the Jedi Temple; the Jedi boy must have been cut down. Angrily, Bail set the speeder in motion. A few stray shots followed him, but then the clones turned and went back inside the Temple. *Why should they bother with me? I'm not a Jedi.*

On the flight back to his office, Bail had a little time to think. Clone troops didn't act without orders, and there was only one person who could have ordered them to attack the Jedi Temple. Chancellor Palpatine. And Palpatine didn't leave loose ends. He must have some plan for disposing of the other Jedi who were off-planet. Also, Bail himself would become a loose end, if Palpatine heard about his visit to the Temple. Of course, Bail hadn't told the clones his name; if they hadn't recognized him, the Chancellor would never know. But Bail wasn't foolish enough to depend on that.

Bail flipped his communicator on and snapped orders. By the time he got back to his office, his two aides had packed up his most vital papers and were ready to go. There was one bad moment when two of the Chancellor's red-robed guards stopped them and demanded identification, but they were satisfied with his Senatorial ID card. Still, Bail's shoulders sagged in relief when he and his aides boarded the Alderaan starcruiser.

Captain Antilles, his pilot, was already on board with the rest of the crew. Bail wasted no time on pleasantries. "Were you able to get hold of a Jedi homing beacon?" he demanded.

"Yes, sir," Captain Antilles replied. "We've encountered no opposition. The clones are still a bit confused."

That's not surprising, if they've killed off all their Jedi commanders. Bail shuddered at the thought. He knew the confusion wouldn't last long — but at least it had lasted long enough for them to get away from Coruscant.

Bail gave the signal for the starcruiser to take off. They had the homing beacon; there was no more reason to stay. *Hopefully, we can intercept a few Jedi before they walk into this . . . catastrophe,* he thought as the ship left the atmosphere. He refused to think about just how few Jedi might be left to answer his bootleg beacon.

Padmé heard the sound of a vehicle outside and hurried onto the veranda. A stab of relief made her head swim when she saw that it was a Jedi starfighter — and Anakin was climbing out of the cockpit onto the veranda stairs. "Are you all right?" she demanded, needing to hear it even though she could see that he was well. "I heard there was an attack on the Jedi Temple. You can see the smoke from here."

"I'm fine," Anakin said. His deep voice was tired; there was an edge to it, and to the way he moved. "I came to see if you and the baby are safe."

"Captain Typho's here," Padmé assured him. "We're safe. What's happening?" Behind them, she heard C-3PO asking R2-D2 the same question.

"The situation is not good," Anakin said heavily. "The Jedi Council has tried to overthrow the Republic."

Padmé stared at him in utter shock. He wasn't

joking; she could see that he wasn't joking. "I can't believe that!" she said at last.

"I couldn't either, at first," Anakin told her. "But it's true. I saw Master Windu attempt to assassinate the Chancellor myself."

How? How can this be? Padmé found a chair and sat down, stunned. "What are *you* going to do?" she asked at last.

"I will not betray the Republic," Anakin said. He swallowed. "My loyalties lie with the Chancellor and with the Senate. And with you."

With me, yes; I believe that. Padmé could hear the sincerity in his voice when he said that, and she had never doubted his loyalty to her. But there had been something odd in his tone when he spoke of the Chancellor and the Senate. Anakin had never cared much for politics. He cared about people, about Padmé and — "What about Obi-Wan?"

Anakin turned away so that she couldn't see his face. "I don't know," he said. "Many of the Jedi have been killed."

Not Obi-Wan! But . . . "Is he part of the rebellion?" Padmé asked hesitantly, though she wasn't sure she really wanted to know the answer.

"We may never know," Anakin said.

"How could this have happened?" Padmé asked. She looked up, and saw Anakin against the cityscape. The dawn sky was red and smoky — smoky from the burning Jedi Temple, as it had been smoky for days after the Separatist attack. Everyone kept saying that the war was almost over, yet the violence kept growing. "I want to leave," she said suddenly. "Go someplace far from here."

"Why?" Anakin sounded genuinely puzzled. "Things are different now. There is a new order."

Things are too different. War and death and betrayal are everywhere. My friends in the Senate are near to treason, and I'm not sure they're wrong. And I can't talk to you about it because it would be your job to arrest them. And maybe me. "I want to bring up our child somewhere safe," she said, and realized in some surprise that she had summed up everything she felt in one sentence.

"I want that, too," Anakin said. "But that place is here."

No, it isn't. Can't you see how dangerous Coruscant has become? But Anakin was a fighter; he'd been away at war for months. Coruscant probably did seem calm and peaceful to him, after all that.

"I'm gaining new knowledge of the Force," Anakin went on. Soon I will be able to protect you from *anything!*"

Padmé reached out to him. "Oh, Anakin, I'm afraid." *Afraid for our child. Afraid for the Republic. Afraid for myself. Afraid for you.*

"Have faith, my love," Anakin said, taking her into his arms. "Everything will soon be set right. The

Separatists have gathered in the Mustafar system. I'm going there to end this war."

Padmé shook her head wordlessly. How many times had they heard that doing this, winning that, killing the other, would end the war? And the war went on. She couldn't believe in the end of the war anymore.

"Wait until I return," Anakin begged. "Things will be different, I promise." He kissed her, long and lingering. "Please, wait for me."

She couldn't believe in the end of the war, but she could still believe in Anakin. "I will," Padmé said, and hugged him.

Anakin smiled in relief, and gave her a careful hug in return. Then, reluctantly, his arms dropped and he looked over at his fighter. With equal reluctance, Padmé let him go. As he climbed into the fighter, she felt tears sting her eyes, but she refused to let them fall. Anakin still had a job to do, and she wouldn't keep him from it, though she wanted so much to have more time with him.

C-3PO backed away, waving to R2-D2. The fighter took off. As it flew into the blood-red dawn, Padmé let the tears come. She felt more alone than she ever had in her life, and she didn't understand why. After all, she still had Anakin.

Sneaking through the Utapauan tunnels to General Grievous' hidden starfighter was not just a matter of dodging the clone troops that crowded the stairs and tunnels. Obi-Wan had commanded these clones; he knew the search patterns they would use and which areas they were most likely to inspect first. But the tunnels were home to a number of unfriendly Utapaun creatures, some of which were large and hungry as well as unfriendly. Several times Obi-Wan had to fight his way past them.

When he finally reached the tiny landing platform, he was relieved to see that the clones had not yet discovered the ship. The whole area was as deserted as it had been when he had chased General Grievous into it. Hardly daring to believe his luck, he slipped into the fighter. No laser blasts flared. He studied the controls briefly, then set the ship in motion.

Obi-Wan flew low, hugging the surface of Utapau, until he was well away from the sinkhole city and the masses of clone troops and transports. The clones wouldn't expect to find Obi-Wan in a Trade Federation fighter, but they might shoot it down all the same. The Separatists were still the enemy — at least, the few times Obi-Wan had seen clone troops in the Utapau tunnels, they had still been fighting Separatist battle droids. There was no reason to take extra chances.

On the far side of Utapau, Obi-Wan headed into space. As soon as he was out of scanning range, he activated the fighter's comm and punched in the main Jedi communication frequency. To his surprise, all he got was static.

Frowning, he tried another frequency, with the same result. And another. Finally, he set the comm to scan. After a minute, it began beeping steadily. *A Jedi homing beacon! But there aren't supposed to be any other Jedi out here.* He picked up his comlink.

"Emergency Code Nine Thirteen," Obi-Wan said. "I have no contact on any frequency. Are there any Jedi out there? Anywhere?"

A wavering hologram image appeared above the comm. Quickly, Obi-Wan locked on to the signal, and the image steadied. To his surprise, it was Senator Bail Organa of Alderaan. *What's he doing with a Jedi homing beacon?*

"Master Kenobi?" The Senator sounded pleased to see him, at least.

"Senator Organa," Obi-Wan said. "My clone troops turned on me. I need help."

Bail Organa did not look surprised, and his next words explained why. "We have just rescued Master Yoda," he said. "It appears this ambush has happened everywhere. Lock onto my coordinates."

Darth Sidious looked at the incoming message coordinates and frowned slightly. Mustafar? He hadn't been expecting a transmission from that planet yet. Had something gone wrong? He pressed the response button, and a blue hologram appeared. It was a Neimoidian — the Trade Federation viceroy, Nute

Gunray. *My apprentice has not yet reached Mustafar, then.*

Gunray bowed deeply. Behind him, Darth Sidious could see the rest of the Separatist Council. "The plan has gone as you had promised, my lord," the Neimoidian told him.

"You have done well, Viceroy," Darth Sidious responded automatically. "Have you shut down your droid armies?"

"We have, my lord."

He smiled. "Excellent! Has my new apprentice, Darth Vader, arrived?"

"He landed a few moments ago," Gunray replied.

"Good, good. He will take care of you." The ambiguity of the words pleased him. He reached for the controls, to end the transmission, and paused.

The transparent blue faces all turned to look at something outside the range of the hologram pickup. Their expressions changed from surprise to bewilderment, and then to fear. Darth Sidious leaned forward in anticipation.

A glowing lightsaber slashed across the pickup field. A head fell one way — Poggle the Lesser, Sidious noted — and the body the other. The rest of the Separatist Council shook off their stupor and fled, screaming, as the transmission cut off at the other end.

"I see my apprentice has arrived," Darth Sidious said softly. "Yes, he will take care of you."

Bail Organa's coordinates were closer than Obi-Wan had expected. It didn't take long for him to reach the Alderaan starcruiser. The first thing he saw when he entered the ship was Master Yoda, standing placidly next to the worried-looking Senator.

"You made it!" Senator Organa said.

"Master Kenobi, dark times are these." Yoda's gravelly voice sounded refreshingly ordinary after everything that had happened. "Good to see you, it is."

"You were attacked by your clones, also?" Obi-Wan asked.

Yoda nodded. "With the help of the Wookiees, barely escape, I did."

If Master Yoda says he barely escaped, it must have been a hair-raising trip! It's a pity he'll never say anything more about it. "How many other Jedi managed to survive?"

Yoda bowed his head. "We've heard from . . . none."

None? Obi-Wan stared, speechless.

Bail Organa nodded in confirmation. "I saw thousands of troops attack the Jedi Temple. That's why I went looking for Yoda."

"Have you had any contact with the Temple?" Surely *someone* must be left. Master Windu . . . Kit Fisto . . . Anakin! Anakin was on Coruscant — had he been at the Temple?

"Received the coded retreat signal, we have," Yoda said.

The one that requests all Jedi to return to Coruscant! But if the clones were in control of the Temple . . .

"The war is over," Bail Organa said, his voice was bitter.

One of the pilots appeared in the doorway. "We are receiving a message from the Chancellor's office."

"Send it through," Bail told him.

A moment later, the oily voice of Mas Amedda, Chancellor Palpatine's chief aide, filled the room. "Senator Organa, the Supreme Chancellor of the Republic requests your presence at a special session of the Senate."

"Tell the Chancellor I will be there," Bail said.

"Very well," Mas Amedda replied, and the transmission ended.

Bail looked at Yoda and Obi-Wan. "Do you think it's a trap?"

"I don't think so," Obi-Wan replied after a moment's consideration. "The Chancellor won't be able to control thousands of star systems without keeping the Senate intact." Bail looked with concern at the two Jedi, and Obi-Wan replied to his unasked question about returning to the Jedi Temple. "We *have* to go back. If there are other stragglers, they will fall into the trap and be killed."

Yoda looked at him and nodded. He didn't have to say anything. They would go to the Jedi Temple and destroy the signal beacon that was calling other Jedi home to die. And perhaps — just perhaps — they would also learn how all of this had happened.

Bail parted from Obi-Wan and Yoda at the Senate landing platform. The two Jedi used their mind-clouding abilities to pass the red guards, then raised their hoods and slipped off. Bail watched them go with considerable misgiving. They were undoubtedly two of the best and most powerful Jedi in the galaxy, and they were warned and ready — but there were thousands of clone troops and security guards. If they were discovered, and it came to a battle . . .

But there was nothing he could do about that. He told Captain Antilles to keep the starcruiser ready to leave at any moment. Then, signaling his aides, he started for the Senate.

It was a shock to see the Senate building looking so . . . normal. The endless lines of traffic flowed around it at all levels, as if nothing unusual were happening. It was even more of a shock to see the sinister, hooded figure in the central pod, flanked by Mas Amedda and Sly Moore. The voice *sounded* like Chancellor Palpatine, but —

Then Bail heard the words the Chancellor was speaking: "The attempt on my life has left me scarred and deformed, but I assure you, my resolve has never been stronger."

Well, that explains the hood. Bail missed the next few sentences as he looked for the Naboo pod. Senator Padmé Amidala would tell him what he'd missed. He hurried over. "I was held up," he said in a low voice. "What happened?"

Padmé looked at him with shadowed eyes. "The Chancellor has been elaborating on a plot by the Jedi to overthrow the Senate."

"That's not true!"

But Padmé only looked at him hopelessly and said, "He's been presenting evidence all afternoon."

And the Senate will go along with it, just as they always do. But why would the Chancellor want to destroy the Jedi? With the war over —

As if he could hear what Bail was thinking, the

voice from the central podium announced, "The war is over! The Separatists have been defeated, and the Jedi rebellion has been foiled. We stand on the threshold of a new beginning."

The Senate burst into applause. As the noise went on and on, Bail stared at the hooded figure of the Chancellor in bewilderment. Now was the time for the Chancellor to give up his emergency powers, to return the Republic to its full democratic status. But the Jedi . . .

The applause began to die. The Chancellor held up his hand for quiet. When the arena was silent at last, he said, "In order to ensure our security and continuing stability, the Republic will now be reorganized into the First Galactic Empire, which I assure you will last for ten thousand years!"

Empire? Bail stared, stunned. He saw the same look on Padmé Amidala's face. Of all the possibilities, they had never anticipated anything like *this*! And the Senate was applauding! Palpatine went on, describing his new Empire in glowing terms, and with each sentence, the applause grew louder. Padmé looked away, and Bail saw tears in her eyes.

"So this is how liberty dies," she said softly. "With thunderous applause . . ."

Bail's mind began to move at last. He was a Senator; he could speak out against this . . . abomination. He started to stand, and Padmé put a restraining hand on his arm. He stared at her. "We cannot let this happen!" he said. Surely she agreed with him!

But Padmé shook her head. "Not now!" she said urgently. She glanced toward the podium, and then toward the entrances, and for the first time Bail noticed the red-clad guards and clone troopers standing at attention. They had always been there, it seemed; first, as part of the ceremony and respect due the Senate, and later, during the war, as a security measure to protect the Senators. But just who would they be protecting now?

Feeling cold, Bail relaxed back into his seat. Padmé nodded sadly. "There will be a time," she said, but she sounded as if it was more of a hope or a dream than a certainty.

Yes. There will be a time, Bail thought. He stared at the figure on the podium, and felt his face harden. He had been devoted to democracy all his life. He would spend the rest of it trying to restore what the Chancellor — no, Emperor, now — had taken away.

It hurt Obi-Wan to see black smoke billowing from the Jedi Temple. It hurt more to enter and find clones dressed in Jedi robes, waiting to ambush any real Jedi who came in. But what hurt the most was seeing the bodies of beings he had known and worked with, lying everywhere, and the Padawans and younglings. No one had survived.

Most disturbing of all were the bodies that had been killed, not by laser blasts, but by a lightsaber. *The Sith Lord!* Obi-Wan thought. Who else would use a lightsaber against Jedi? Obi-Wan swallowed hard. It had to be the Sith. Nobody else would . . . it *had* to be him.

Obi-Wan and Yoda had no trouble disposing of the first few clones they encountered. Once they were inside, they had even less trouble avoiding the others. The Jedi Temple was an enormous warren of passages and rooms; it took new Padawans years to learn their way around all of the sections. The clones had been there for less than a day.

Still, avoiding the clones took time. It was full night by the time they reached the main control center. Yoda stood guard while Obi-Wan reset the beacon and then added a few twists to hide what he had done. When Yoda gave him an impatient look, Obi-Wan explained, "I've recalibrated the code to warn any surviving Jedi away." That was much better than simply disabling the beacon.

"Good." Yoda nodded his approval. "To discover the recalibration, a long time it will take. To change it back, longer still." He gestured toward the door. "Hurry."

But Obi-Wan shook his head and crossed to the

hologram area. As he reached for the switch that would replay the recordings, Yoda said gently, "Master Obi-Wan, the truth you already know. To face it will only cause you anger and pain."

No. He had to watch the killings. He needed to see the face of the Sith Lord who had helped butcher all the Jedi in the Temple. "I must know, Master." His finger hit the button.

A hologram sprang up, showing the carnage in grim detail. Clone troopers fired on unsuspecting Jedi, cutting them down. And then a lightsaber flashed, held by a cloaked figure who cut down Jedi after Jedi, and Obi-Wan leaned forward. The figure turned. It was Anakin.

"It can't be," Obi-Wan whispered, heartbroken. "It can't be!"

But the holographic recording was pitiless. It played back the fight, exactly as it had occurred, and Obi-Wan had to watch Anakin kill and kill again. And then another figure entered the pickup, hidden beneath a hood. To Obi-Wan's horror, Anakin turned and knelt before it.

"The traitors have been destroyed, Lord Sidious," Anakin said.

"Good, good." The voice — that was Chancellor Palpatine! He was Darth Sidious, the Sith Lord? "You have done well, my new apprentice. Do you feel your power growing?"

"Yes, my Master," Anakin said, and Obi-Wan shuddered.

"Lord Vader, your skills are unmatched by any Sith before you," the cloaked figure said. "Now go, and bring peace to the Empire."

Empire?! Obi-Wan's fingers flew over the hologram keys, shutting off the scene that was far too painful to continue watching. Instead, he searched the holovid network for recent news. In seconds, the two Jedi learned what had been happening in the Senate while they had been slipping through the silent halls of the Jedi Temple. Chancellor Palpatine — the Sith Lord Darth Sidious — had declared an Empire instead of the Republic. The Sith ruled the galaxy once more.

Obi-Wan switched off the hologram completely, and the two Jedi stood in silence. How long had Darth Sidious been planning this? He had used the war, obviously — Count Dooku had been a Sith. Then Obi-Wan remembered: the first Sith he had encountered, back when he was still a Padawan. The Sith with the double-sided lightsaber, who had killed his Master, Qui-Gon Jinn. Did this plot go back that far?

Yes, it had to. He saw it, now, the whole clever, subtle plan. The Jedi knew that Darth Sidious had urged the Trade Federation to start the long-ago war on Naboo. Now Obi-Wan could see the true purpose of that war: to provide the opportunity for Senator Palpatine to become Supreme Chancellor

Palpatine. And then Palpatine must have seduced Count Dooku to the dark side, so that by the time his term as Chancellor was running out, the Separatists would be ready to start a larger war. Because of the Separatist threat, the Senate had begged Palpatine to stay on as Chancellor, and granted him more and more "emergency powers" in an effort to win a war that always *seemed* about to finish, but never was quite won.

Even the clone troops — the Jedi had accepted without question that Master Sifo-Dyas had arranged for their creation. But Sifo-Dyas was long dead. And that bounty hunter, the one who had provided the original genetic material for the clones . . . he'd told Obi-Wan that a man named Tyranus had recruited him. Obi-Wan had thought it was another lie; they'd found no man named Tyranus. *But I'll bet there was a Darth Tyranus! Why didn't I see it then?*

The war had thinned the ranks of the Jedi, and spread those who remained out over many worlds, so they would be easy prey when the time came for the final attack. And now — now only the two of them were left here. Obi-Wan could still hope that others had survived elsewhere, but the devastation he had seen in the last few hours had convinced him that no other Jedi remained alive on Coruscant.

Yoda broke the silence at last, saying what they both knew. "Destroy the Sith, we must."

Not just Emperor Palpatine; the Sith. There are

always two, a Master and an apprentice. Two of them, and two of us. And one of them is — "Send me to kill the Emperor," Obi-Wan said. He bowed his head. "I will not kill Anakin."

Yoda gave him a stern look. "To destroy this Lord Sidious, strong enough, you are not."

I know, but — "Anakin's like my brother," Obi-Wan said in anguish. "I cannot do this."

"Twisted by the dark side, young Skywalker has become," Yoda said firmly. "The boy you trained, gone is. Consumed by Darth Vader."

Obi-Wan flinched. "How could it have come to this?"

"To question, no time there is." Yoda started toward the door of the control room.

"I don't know where the Emperor sent him," Obi-Wan said, in a last, desperate attempt to avoid the duty he knew he must face. "I have no idea where to look."

"Use your feelings, Obi-Wan, and find him, you will," Yoda said, as if he were instructing a reluctant Padawan. "Visit the new Emperor, my task is." He looked at Obi-Wan with sympathy and understanding, but no pity. "May the Force be with you."

"May the Force be with you, Master Yoda," Obi-Wan replied. Yoda was right, as usual. He *did* know where to start looking for Anakin.

CHAPTER 17

Padmé was still awake when the alarm went off. She reached for the laser pistol she kept hidden by her bed, but the noise stopped almost at once. A false signal? She checked the readouts and saw that C-3PO had shut off the alarm. Swiftly, she pulled on a robe and went downstairs. C-3PO wouldn't deliberately let in an enemy, but he didn't always have the best judgment. And these days, it wasn't always clear who was an enemy, and who wasn't.

She heard voices as she came down the stairs. C-3PO was talking to — "Master Kenobi!" Padmé hurried down the last few steps as the protocol droid discreetly withdrew. "Oh, Obi-Wan, thank goodness you're alive!"

"The Republic has fallen, Padmé," Obi-Wan said gravely. "The Jedi Order is no more."

"I know." Padmé gazed at him, seeing the new lines in his face. "It's hard to believe." She took a deep breath. "But the Senate is still intact. There is some hope."

"No, Padmé," Obi-Wan said sadly. "It's over. The Sith now rule the galaxy, as they did before the Republic."

Padmé stared. "The *Sith*?" It was Palpatine who was in charge of the Repub — of the Empire. Surely Obi-Wan didn't mean that *Palpatine* was a Sith Lord!

"I'm looking for Anakin," Obi-Wan went on. "When was the last time you saw him?"

"Yesterday," Padmé said cautiously. Her head was spinning. Anakin had told her that his loyalties lay with the Republic, and with the Chancellor . . . but if the Chancellor was a Sith and the Republic no longer existed, what did that mean? And if there really *had* been a Jedi plot — no, no, she couldn't believe that, but still . . . she couldn't tell Obi-Wan too much until she understood.

"Do you know where he is now?"

She couldn't look at Obi-Wan's tired, worried face and lie to him. Her eyes fell. "No."

"Padmé, I need your help," Obi-Wan said. "He's in grave danger."

"From the Sith?" Padmé felt a moment's relief. Anakin was a Jedi; if the Sith were, somehow, behind everything that had happened, it made sense that he was in danger. But Obi-Wan was shaking his head, and her heart went cold even before she heard his words.

"Anakin has turned to the dark side."

"You're wrong!" Padmé cried. "How can you say that?"

"I've seen a security hologram of him killing . . . younglings."

"Not Anakin!" Padmé protested. "He couldn't!" But he had, once before — when he murdered the Sand People who'd killed his mother. *He was angry then. He lost control. He wouldn't just . . . He* wouldn't!

Obi-Wan was still talking, saying more horrible things — that Palpatine was a Sith Lord and Anakin his new apprentice. "I don't believe you!" Padmé burst out. "I can't."

The tired, sad voice stopped. "I must find him," Obi-Wan said after a moment.

But if he's — if you think he's a Sith . . . "You're going to kill him, aren't you?" she said, half accusing, half begging him to deny it.

Obi-Wan did not deny it. His head bent, and he said softly, "He has become a very great threat."

Overcome with horror, Padmé sank onto the nearest chair. She saw Obi-Wan's face change, and realized that she had let her robe twist close around her, so that he could see the unmistakable outline of her pregnancy. Too late, she pulled the robe away. "I can't —"

"Anakin's the father, isn't he?" Obi-Wan said gently. When she did not answer, he shook his head. "I'm so sorry." He pulled up his hood and walked toward the veranda. Padmé saw an air-speeder there; that must have been what set off the alarm. She felt torn. If Obi-Wan was right, she should call him back and tell him where Anakin had gone. But she *couldn't* betray Anakin. But —

The airspeeder took off. Obi-Wan was gone. Padmé's head bowed, and she found herself staring at the japor necklace. *Anakin.* She needed him here, now, to explain away all this horror. But Anakin was on Mustafar.

A long time later, Padmé looked up. With decision, she crossed to a comlink. "Captain Typho, prepare an interstellar skiff," she said, then turned back to her bedroom to dress. If Anakin was on Mustafar, she would go to him.

Obi-Wan slipped through the darkness at the edge of the landing platform. Trailing Padmé hadn't been difficult. Though she had been in danger many times, she had never learned to watch the shadows around her for possible threats, and her security guards had no reason to suspect that she might be followed. *She always believes the best of everyone, until she's forced to see the worst,* he thought sadly. Such faith should be a strength, not a weakness.

Judging from Captain Typho's tone, her security officer was very unhappy with the Senator at the moment. "My lady," the captain was saying, "let me come with you."

"There is no danger," Padmé told him. "The fighting is over, and . . . this is personal."

They've probably been arguing ever since they left the Senator's apartment, Obi-Wan thought.

Captain Typho paused at the foot of the landing ramp and bowed. "As you wish, my lady," he said formally. "But I strongly disagree."

"I'll be all right, Captain," Padmé said softly. "This is something I must do myself." She waited until the captain returned to the speeder and took off. Then she and her protocol droid climbed the ramp into the skiff. The skiff's engines started and the ramp began to retract.

Now! Obi-Wan thought, and leaped. He landed lightly on the end of the ramp and dove into the skiff just before the outside door closed. Padmé and her droid were in the cockpit. They didn't see him enter, and by the time the ship was safely in space, Obi-Wan had found a place to hide. All he had to do now was wait.

Outside the underground door of the office at the base of the Senate, Yoda paused. This was the domain of Mas Amedda, once the Vice-Chair of the Senate and now Chancellor — *Emperor* Palpatine's majordomo. Here, Mas Amedda prepared to run the Senate meetings; it was from this chamber that the Chancellor's podium rose into the center of the Senate. And tonight, the Force told him, it was here that Palpatine had come to see the finish of his evil plan.

Softly, Yoda approached the chamber. All four of the beings in the room — the two red guards, Mas Amedda, and the hooded figure of Darth Sidious — were too focused on the hologram in the center of the room to notice him. Darth Vader, who had been the Jedi Anakin Skywalker, had apparently been reporting.

"— taken care of, my Master," Vader said.

"Good, good," Sidious said. "Send a message to all ships of the Trade Federation. Tell them the Separatist leaders have been wiped out.

"Very good, my lord."

"You have done well, Lord Vader."

"Thank you, my Master."

As the hologram faded, Yoda stumped into the room. Before the guards could react, he used the Force to fling them against the walls. They collapsed in motionless heaps as Yoda said to the Sith Lord, "A new apprentice, you have, Chancellor. Or should I call you 'Emperor'?"

"Master Yoda." The Emperor inclined his head. "You survived."

"Surprised?"

"Your arrogance blinds you, Master Yoda," Darth Sidious hissed. "Now you will experience the full power of the dark side." He raised his arms, and the Force pulsed as blue lightning blasted Yoda across the room.

Mas Amedda looked from the Chancellor to Yoda, his eyes narrowed maliciously. He turned and left the room. Another wave of dark power lifted Yoda and flung him hard against the wall. Yoda used the Force to cushion the impact, but he pretended to be knocked unconscious. *A surprise, I will give him.*

"I have waited a long time for this moment, my little green friend," Darth Sidious sneered. He stepped forward, and Yoda pushed off, propelling himself straight at the Sith Lord. He knocked Darth Sidious over the desk and stared down at him.

"At an end your rule is," Yoda told the Emperor. "And not short enough it was, I must say." He ignited his lightsaber and brought it down, to be met by the Emperor's blood-red Sith blade.

Even from space, Mustafar glowed like a hot ember; as her ship neared the surface, Padmé saw rivers of lava and oceans of molten rock. Fissures leaked fire from the heart of the planet, and smoke rose from cracks and vents on the blackened surface. It was hard to control the skiff in the shifting air currents, but eventually C-3PO fought it to a safe landing.

Through the cockpit window, she saw Anakin running eagerly toward the landing platform. Hastily, she unstrapped and ran out to meet him. His embrace reassured her; his arms made her feel secure once more. "It's all right," he murmured. "You're safe now." She looked up gratefully, and he said, "What are you doing out here?"

All the things she had been pushing out of her mind since leaving Coruscant came flooding back, and she looked down. "Obi-Wan told me terrible things."

She felt Anakin stiffen. "What things?"

"He said you have turned to the dark side," Padmé blurted. "That you killed younglings." Her voice sounded accusing, even to her own ears. This wasn't the way she'd meant to ask him for the truth.

"Obi-Wan is trying to turn you against me," Anakin said, and she heard the stirring of a terrible anger in his voice.

"He cares about us," Padmé told him. "He wants to help you."

"Don't lie to me, Padmé," Anakin said. His arms dropped. "I have become more powerful than any Jedi dreamed of. And I've done it for you. To protect *you*."

What has that to do with Obi-Wan? With what he said? But she knew. It was Anakin's excuse for whatever fearful things he had done. As if saying "I did it for love; I did it for you" would make it right. Padmé drew back. "I don't want your *power*." She swallowed. "I don't want your protection." She reached for him, pleading, wanting him to be the man she loved. "Anakin, all I want is your love."

"Love won't save you," Anakin said, and it sounded like a threat. "Only my new powers can do that."

"At what cost?" Padmé asked. "You are a good person. Don't do this."

"I won't lose you the way I lost my mother!"

"Come away with me." She put a hand on her swelling stomach. "Help me raise our child. Leave everything else behind while we still can."

"Don't you see?" Anakin leaned forward eagerly. "We don't have to run away anymore. I have brought peace to the Republic. I am more powerful than the Chancellor. I can overthrow him, and together you and I can rule the galaxy. We can make things the way we want them to be."

Padmé recoiled. "I don't believe what I'm hearing! Obi-Wan was right. You've changed."

"I don't want to hear any more about Obi-Wan!" Anakin's temper burst loose. Her fear must have shown on her face, because he made a visible effort to control himself. "The Jedi turned against me," he said more softly. "The Republic turned against me. Don't you turn against me, too."

I'm not against you. I'm against what you've done, and what you're planning to do. "I don't know you anymore," she told him. Couldn't he see what he was doing? Couldn't he feel her heart breaking? "I'll never stop loving you, but you are going down a path I cannot follow." In despair, she reached for the connection they had had through the Force, for that one moment when she had known him completely even though they hadn't been together.

But even a Jedi couldn't create a Force connection just by trying, and Padmé was no Jedi. Desperate as she was, she could find only a faint thread of what they had shared, thinner than a strand of spider silk. It still joined her with a familiar trace of . . . goodness? Sensing that, she felt a stirring of hope. She spoke to that part of him, trying to call back the Anakin who was her husband, her lover, the father of their child. "Stop now," she begged. "Come back! I love you."

For a moment — for the barest instant — she thought she would succeed. Then Anakin's expression changed. "Liar!" he cried.

He was staring at something behind her. Padmé turned, and saw Obi-Wan standing in the door of the skiff. *He tricked me!* "No!" she said, knowing that this new Anakin would never listen to her now.

"You've betrayed me!" Rage made Anakin's face unrecognizable. He lifted his hand and curled his fingers into a fist. Padmé felt herself choking, unable to breathe.

Don't! Don't kill our child! But she had no breath to cry out with, and even the ghost of the Force connection was gone. The world darkened, and she felt herself falling. Her last conscious thought was a feeling of relief. She would rather die here, now, than live and have to watch what her Anakin had become.

Obi-Wan ran forward as Padmé collapsed. He flung his cloak aside, and bent to check on her. She was still alive, and not, he sensed, in immediate danger. But Anakin was already there, his face an angry mask. "You turned her against me!" he cried, flinging the accusation against Obi-Wan.

"You have done that yourself," Obi-Wan told him. Here, in Anakin's presence, he could feel what the hologram couldn't show him: the roiling cloud of the dark side that surrounded his former apprentice. It made the coming duty a little — a very little — easier. "You've let the dark side twist your point of view until now . . . now you are the very thing you swore to destroy."

"Don't make me kill you," Anakin said.

The words struck straight to Obi-Wan's heart. Surely something of his friend and student was still left, for him to say that? But even if there was, no Jedi had ever returned from the dark side. Yoda had warned them all, over and over, throughout their training: *If once you start down the dark path, forever will it dominate your destiny.* Anakin had turned to the dark side. It was too late for him. Sadly, Obi-Wan said, "My allegiance is to the Republic, Anakin. To democracy."

"You are with me, or you are against me," Anakin replied.

"Only a Sith Lord deals in absolutes, Anakin," Obi-Wan told him, and ignited his lightsaber. *Now I will do what I must.*

Anakin's face twisted as he ignited his own weapon, and the battle began.

Strong, this Sith Lord is, Yoda thought as their lightsabers whirled and clashed and whirled again.

It should not have been a surprise. With the strength of the dark side growing, the Sith must, logically, have grown stronger, too. But always before, his own years of study and practice and his own strength with the Force had been more than enough to prevail. This time, he wasn't sure.

But Palpatine didn't seem entirely sure, either. Suddenly, he launched himself into the air, heading for the door. Yoda did a back flip, bounced off the wall, and reached the entrance before him. "If so powerful you are, why leave?"

"You will not stop me," the new Emperor croaked. "Darth Vader will become more powerful than either of us."

"Faith in your new apprentice, misplaced may be," Yoda replied. *As is your faith in the dark side of the Force.* Even if Palpatine killed him here, today, the dark side would not truly win. For the dark side was anger, hatred, despair — all the forces of ruin and decay. Powerful, they were, to tear down and destroy, but they could not build anything lasting. Palpatine's ten-thousand-year Galactic Empire would be lucky to outlast his lifetime.

That thought gave Yoda new energy, and he pressed his attack. He drove Palpatine back across the room, into the Chancellor's podium. Palpatine hit the controls, and the podium began to rise, carrying him up into the Senate. But the podium moved slowly; Yoda had plenty of time to flip himself into the air and land beside the Emperor, to continue the fight.

As the podium rose into the Senate arena, the fight intensified. Twice, Yoda came near to pushing Palpatine over the edge. They were high enough now that a fall could be fatal, even to a Sith Lord. *Or a Jedi Master.* The cramped space within the pod left little room for maneuvering.

An end, I must make. Yoda redoubled the speed of his blows. Palpatine parried one, then another — and then the red lightsaber spun out of his hands and over the edge. Yoda raised his weapon for the final blow.

Force lightning spat from the Emperor's gray fingers, surrounding Yoda in a blue nimbus. But Yoda had faced Force lightning before. To deflect the first bolts, he had to stop his intended strike at the Emperor. Once his initial surprise was over, he reached out to the living Force. The lightning bent, arcing back toward the Emperor.

"Destroy you, I will," Yoda said grimly. "Just as Master Kenobi, your apprentice will destroy."

The Sith Lord only redoubled his attack. Hurling Force lightning, the Emperor backed away, to the very edge of the platform. Following him was like walking against hurricane winds. Never had Yoda faced one so strong in the dark side. Before he came within reach, a particularly strong blast knocked Yoda out of the pod.

As he plunged over the edge, Yoda realized that Palpatine was right about one thing. He, Yoda, had indeed been arrogant. *It is a flaw more and more common among Jedi*, he had told Obi-Wan once. *Too sure of themselves, they are.* And he had fallen into the same trap himself.

He landed much sooner than he had expected, in an empty Senate pod floating below the Chancellor's. As he climbed to his feet, the pod jerked, throwing him sideways and knocking him down once more. Palpatine was using the dark side to rip more pods free, crashing them into Yoda's pod to keep him off-balance.

This game, two can play. Yoda reached out with the Force and caught one of the hurtling pods. He threw it back at Palpatine, who barely dodged in time. Then Yoda leaped, using the flying pods to get back up to the Chancellor's level.

As he reached Palpatine's pod, the Sith Lord hit him with another blast of blue lightning that knocked Yoda's lightsaber out of his hand. Palpatine's lips curled in anticipated triumph, and the dark side pulsed as he drew even more Force lightning to his bidding.

Yoda caught it. The blue energy built into a glowing ball in his hand, ready to throw back at the Sith

Lord the moment his attack stopped. But Palpatine didn't stop; the Force lightning came in a steady crackle, building more and more, until neither of them could hold it any longer, and the blast knocked them both out of the pod.

Palpatine was larger and heavier; he managed to catch hold of the edge of the pod as he fell. But Yoda was small and light. The explosion threw him high into the air, with nothing to grab to break his fall. Half-stunned, he began the long fall to the Senate floor.

As Anakin's lightsaber hummed toward him, a calm certainty filled Obi-Wan. Anakin was going to kill him. Oh, he'd make Anakin work for it. He'd fight with everything he had. But he was positive, with the sureness that came from any Force-driven insight, that he would die at Anakin's hands.

His lightsaber came up in an instinctive parry. They had sparred together so often that they knew each other's favorite moves. Obi-Wan hardly had to think to counter Anakin's attack. Lightsabers humming, they battled their way down the hall and into the control center. It felt . . . familiar, like another practice session, except for the exploding equipment.

He saw the same emotions reflected on Anakin's face. "Don't make me destroy you," his former apprentice said again. Then his expression changed to a sneer. "You're no match for the dark side."

"I've heard that before, Anakin," Obi-Wan said. "But I never thought I'd hear it from you."

They were in the conference room now. There were headless and limbless bodies on the floor; Obi-Wan recognized several of the Separatist leaders. *Anakin has been here before*, he thought. But still his arms moved, weaving light into a deadly shield against all of Anakin's blows.

Anakin did a back flip onto the table to gain the high ground. But Obi-Wan had been expecting something like that, and did not follow. Instead, he threw himself into a long slide, bowling Anakin over.

As he fell, Anakin lost his grip on his lightsaber. Obi-Wan caught it and stared at it in surprise. *How can Anakin kill me, if he doesn't have a lightsaber?* Then Anakin charged him. Before Obi-Wan could swing his own weapon, Anakin was on him. His left hand gripped Obi-Wan's right wrist, holding off the deadly lightsaber; the mechanical right hand fought to repossess his own weapon.

Durasteel and servomotors proved stronger than flesh and bone. Anakin wrenched his lightsaber away, and attacked once more.

Out into the hall, they fought, then onto a balcony above a river of lava. A slender pipe led from the control center to a collection plant on the far side of the river. As Anakin's attack intensified, Obi-Wan was forced onto the pipe, where a single misstep would send him plunging into the fire.

*   *   *

As Yoda fell, he reached out to slow his fall with all the mastery of the Force he had learned in his long years. It was enough, barely. He landed hard, but not too hard.

Bruised and battered, but alive, he crawled into a service chute. There would be no second chance to kill the Emperor; he would summon his clone troops immediately for protection. All Yoda could do now was escape.

Activating his comlink, he called to the one person on Coruscant he knew he could still trust — Bail Organa. The Senator did not waste time demanding explanations, and he followed Yoda's instructions as carefully as any Jedi would have. Sooner than he would have believed, Yoda dropped from an access hatch into Bail's speeder and was carried away into the night.

Away from the Senate, Bail gave Yoda a questioning look. Yoda told him the only thing that mattered. "Failed, I have."

Bail nodded somberly, and turned his speeder toward the spaceport. *Obi-Wan, we will look for,* Yoda thought. *Better fortune, he may have had.*

From the damaged podium, Darth Sidious watched his clone troopers search the shadows. Mas Amedda had brought them, too late to help do anything but clean up.

Sidious knew he should have been pleased with the outcome of the fight. He had won, though it had been a near thing. But an uneasiness was growing within him, a sense of some threat not yet resolved.

Below, the clone commander boarded a Senate pod and rose to the level of the podium. "There is no sign of his body, sir," he reported, saluting.

"Then he is not dead," Mas Amedda replied.

Sidious nodded and reached out with the dark side, trying to sense where his enemy was hiding. As he did, the feeling of risk grew stronger, and he understood. Not a threat to him, but to his apprentice. He must see to this personally. "Double your search," he told the clone commander, though he doubted they would find anything. He turned to Mas Amedda. "Tell Captain Kagi to prepare my shuttle for immediate takeoff. I sense Lord Vader is in danger."

Mas Amedda bowed. "Yes, my Master."

Crossing the collection pipe was difficult, even for a Jedi. At one point, Obi-Wan slipped and nearly fell into the lava, but his Jedi reflexes and agility let him recover. On the far side, Anakin rushed him again, driving him back onto the collection plates.

But the collection plant had never been designed to take the weight of two men, and in the heat of the battle in the control room, they had smashed the shield controls that protected the plant from fiery lava, weakening the structure. A spray of lava from the river that melted one of the supports provided the final straw. A huge section of a collection arm broke away and fell into the lava, carrying the two Jedi with it.

Still the fight continued, even as the collection tower sank slowly into the lava. And still, neither man could gain an advantage.

But that's not really true, Obi-Wan thought as he ducked and wove and parried. Both he and Anakin felt the anguish of their need to kill the other. But Anakin had turned to the dark side, and despair and pain strengthened the dark side. It gave him an advantage Obi-Wan could not match. Unless he let go of his own despair and let the living Force move him — the Force that bound all living things together, even Obi-Wan and this new, deadly, evil Anakin.

It was hard. It was, perhaps, the hardest thing he had ever tried to do. For in letting go of his anguish, his despair, and his pain, he would have to let go of the Anakin who was his student, his brother, and his dearest friend. He'd have to admit that this time, he could not save the man who had saved his life so many times, whose life he had saved at least as often.

Obi-Wan couldn't do it. As the collection tower sank farther into the lava, he looked for a way to escape. A droid platform floated on air near the tower. Obi-Wan took another swipe at Anakin, then grabbed a hanging cable and swung out toward the platform. At the height of his swing, he flipped himself into the air, landing precisely.

The platform wobbled, but it held his weight. He leaned to one side, steering it away from the collection tower. Perhaps the sinking tower and the lava would do what he had been unable to finish.

But when he looked back, Anakin was standing on a worker droid, coming up fast. "Your combat skills have always been poor," he taunted. "You're called the Negotiator because you can't fight!"

"I have failed you, Anakin," Obi-Wan told him. "I was never able to teach you to think."

Anakin nodded. "I should have known the Jedi were plotting to take over."

"From the Sith!" Obi-Wan cried, shocked. "Anakin, Chancellor Palpatine is evil."

"From the Jedi point of view!" Anakin retorted. "From my point of view, the Jedi are evil."

The words stabbed at Obi-Wan, even though he knew that Anakin was speaking out of his own pain. He felt the dark side grow stronger, feeding on his despair. And then, as Anakin came close enough to swing his lightsaber once more, the Jedi in Obi-Wan rose up and at last he did the thing he hadn't thought he could do.

He let go. Calm, centered, free — for the

moment — of sorrow and despair, resting in the living Force as he had been trained to do, Obi-Wan Kenobi looked at his former friend and student, and did the unexpected. He made a soaring leap into the air and landed on the high bank of the lava river.

"It's over, Anakin," he said, looking down. "I have the high ground. Don't try it."

"You underestimate the power of the dark side!" Anakin shot back, and with the last word, he jumped.

And Obi-Wan's lightsaber moved, slicing through Anakin's knees and then coming up to take his remaining hand. Anakin's lightsaber fell at Obi-Wan's feet. What was left of Anakin fell on the burning black sand almost at the edge of the lava.

Anakin — no, Obi-Wan reminded himself, not Anakin. Darth Vader. Darth Vader scrabbled at the sand with his metal arm, trying to pull himself away from the lava river. Obi-Wan looked down at the maimed body, and at last felt tears sting his eyes. "You were the Chosen One," he said, not to Darth Vader, but to his dead friend Anakin, the man whose spirit Darth Vader had murdered. "You were supposed to destroy the Sith, not join them. You were to bring balance to the Force, not leave it in darkness." He swallowed hard. He couldn't see the body through his tears; he could barely make out the shine of Anakin's lightsaber on the ground at his feet.

"I hate you!" Vader screamed.

As Obi-Wan bent and picked up Anakin's fallen lightsaber, Darth Vader slipped too close to the lava, and his clothes caught fire. In an instant, the flames engulfed him, and he screamed. Obi-Wan stared in horror, unable to make himself move. But as the flames began to die, he murmured his response to Darth Vader's final cry of anger and hate: "You were my brother, Anakin. I loved you."

The screams died, and the flames. Dashing tears from his eyes, Obi-Wan turned away — and saw a shuttle coming in to land. Whoever it was, Obi-Wan didn't want to meet him. He ran back to Padmé's skiff. C-3PO and R2-D2 had already taken Padmé on board, and he was glad. All he wanted now was to get away from this place. Later . . . later he might be able to think about what would come next.

CHAPTER **20**

As the Imperial shuttle closed its wings and settled on the topmost landing platform, Darth Sidious saw a small starship fleeing from Mustafar. But he could not order the shuttle into pursuit — the uneasy urgency was stronger than ever, and it was tied to the planet, not the ship.

The clone troopers disembarked first, fanning out through the quiet building to make sure nothing would endanger their Emperor. They found only bodies. Then, as Darth Sidious inspected the control room, one of the troopers came in through an exterior door.

"There's something out here," he reported.

That's it. As quickly as he could, Darth Sidious followed the troopers outside, onto the black sand banks of a lava river. A charred heap lay on one side. *No; it can't be!*

But it was. His promising new apprentice, who was to be the greatest Sith who'd ever lived — maimed and burned, perhaps dead. Darth Sidious ground his teeth in frustrated anger. Part of him wanted to turn on his heel and leave what was left of Darth Vader to burn to ashes in the rising lava. Even if he was alive, even if he could be saved, Vader would be crippled.

And not just with his mechanical limbs. The Force — dark side as well as light — was generated by living beings, and it took living flesh to manipulate it. Darth Vader would never be able to cast blue Force lightning; that required living hands, not metal ones. And with so much of his body replaced by machinery, he would never come close to the potential he'd had.

It was a great pity, Darth Sidious thought, controlling his anger, but perhaps not irreparable. Even diminished, Darth Vader would still be very strong, and there were no Jedi left to challenge him. Darth Sidious had seen to that himself. So he kept walking until he could bend over the body. And to his surprise, his apprentice *was* still alive.

Relief swept his doubts away. "Get a medical capsule immediately," Darth Sidious commanded, and clones ran off to do his bidding. Leaning down, he placed a hand on Darth Vader's forehead, using the dark side to keep him alive.

When they fled from Coruscant, Yoda left their destination to Bail Organa. The Senator chose an obscure archaeological project on the asteroid Polis Massa. There they set up a homing beacon, and waited hopefully for Obi-Wan.

With nothing to do but wait, Yoda automatically found a quiet room and sat down to meditate. The being who had been trying to contact him surely could not reach through the newly strengthened fog of the dark side, but the habit had become strong. And to his surprise, this time the contact succeeded.

Qui-Gon Jinn! No wonder the presence had felt familiar. *Still much to learn, there is.*

Patience, Qui-Gon responded. *You will have the time I did not. With my help, you will be able to merge with the Force at will, and still retain your individual consciousness.*

Eternal life, Yoda marveled.

The story of Darth Plagueis was true, in a way. The ability to defy death can be achieved, but only for oneself. It was never accomplished by Darth Plagueis, only by a Shaman of the Whills, and it will never be achieved by a Sith Lord. It is a state acquired through compassion, not greed.

To become one with the Force, and influence still have. The thought was stunning. *A power greater than all, it is.* Yoda bowed his head. *A great Jedi Master, you have become, Qui-Gon Jinn. Your apprentice, I gratefully become.*

He felt the former Jedi's approval, just before Bail

Organa entered to tell him that Obi-Wan was landing. The contact was broken, but Yoda knew that Qui-Gon would have no future difficulty in reaching him, now that he had done it once. At least some good news, there was to tell Obi-Wan.

When the skiff landed, Obi-Wan jumped from the pilot's chair and gently lifted the still-unconscious Padmé. Yoda and Bail were waiting at the bottom of the ramp. Bail took one shocked look at Padmé and said, "Take her to the medical center, quickly."

They have a medical center; good. Obi-Wan had been half afraid that the medical facilities on an isolated asteroid would be too primitive to deal with whatever ailed Padmé. She *should* have come around once Darth Vader stopped choking her, but she hadn't — but Obi-Wan didn't know much about pregnant women. Maybe something else was wrong.

With relief, he handed Padmé over to the medical droids and went to sit in the observation room with Bail and Yoda. Moments later, one of the droids came up to the window. "Medically, she is completely healthy," the droid said. "For reasons we can't explain, we are losing her."

"She's *dying*?" Obi-Wan said, horrified. *No, no!* He couldn't take another loss like this.

But the medical droid bobbed its head. "We don't know why. She has lost the will to live."

I know why, Obi-Wan thought. *Anakin has broken her heart.*

"We need to operate quickly if we are to save the babies," the droid continued. "She's carrying twins."

"Save them, we must," Yoda commanded. "They are our last hope."

The medical droids went to work. They insisted that Obi-Wan join them, though he wasn't sure what he could do. But the droids felt that human contact would help, and — these were Anakin's children, and this was the last thing Obi-Wan could do for his dead friend. He stood by, holding Padmé's hand and feeling helpless.

As the droids delivered the first of the babies, Padmé stirred. She looked at Obi-Wan in puzzlement; then she saw the medical droids and seemed to realize what was happening. "Is it a girl?" she whispered.

"We don't know," Obi-Wan said, feeling harried. "In a minute."

"It's a boy," the medical droid said, holding him up. The baby was wrinkled and red-faced, his eyes squeezed tightly shut against the light, but Padmé smiled and reached for him. "Luke," she said, her fingers just brushing his forehead.

"And a girl," the second droid said. Unlike her

brother, this baby's eyes were wide, and she stared in Padmé's direction as if she wanted to see and memorize her face.

"Leia," Padmé said.

"You have twins, Padmé," Obi-Wan told her. "They need you. Hang on!"

Padmé's head rolled back and forth on the bed in a gesture of negation. "I can't," she whispered. Wincing, she reached for Obi-Wan's hand. She was holding something — a carved piece of wood on a long cord.

"Save your energy," Obi-Wan told her, but she held up the carving as if it were something precious.

"Obi-Wan," Padmé gasped. "There *is* good in him." She paused, panting. "I know there . . . is . . . still . . ." Her voice faded, and her hand dropped away. Obi-Wan felt the life leave her.

She believed in Anakin until the end, he thought, and bowed his head. He didn't know whether his tears were for Padmé or for his lost friend, or both.

The medical capsule kept Darth Vader alive during the trip to Coruscant. Medical droids from the Imperial Rehabilitation Center on Coruscant, the best in the galaxy, were ready and waiting, thanks to the Emperor's urgent message. They examined their patient at once. Much work was necessary, they reported. The amputations alone would have been a simple matter of replacement; it was the burns that made matters so difficult. Special connections would be required to overcome the scarring. Worse, Darth Vader's lungs had been seared by the fire. He would need a permanent ventilator system in order to breathe. And —

"Do it," the Emperor snapped.

The droids bobbed their consent and went to work. Darth Sidious paced. Even an Emperor, even the Dark Lord of the Sith, with all the resources and technology of the new Galactic Empire behind him, can do little to hurry the healing process.

Much later, a medical droid appeared. "My lord, the construction is finished," the droid informed him. "He lives."

"Good," Darth Sidious said with something very like relief. "*Good.*"

The droid brought him to the operating room. A black figure lay on the operating table. Black gloves and boots covered the new mechanical limbs; a mirror shiny black mask hid the scarred face. The table began to tilt, moving the figure to an upright position. There was the sound of breathing.

Yes, Darth Sidious thought. *He will terrify them. And even if he is not as powerful as I had once hoped, he will still be far more powerful than anyone else.*

"Lord Vader," Darth Sidious said. "You may rise."

A deep voice, distorted by the speakers inside the mask, responded. "Yes, my Master." The helmet turned, as if the burned and weakened eyes within were scanning the room, adjusting to the screens in the helmet that magnified and intensified everything so that they could pretend to see. "Where is Padmé? Is she all right?"

And now, the final touch, Darth Sidious thought. *The words that will bind him forever to the dark side. And they won't even be a lie, not really.* "I'm afraid she died," he said, putting a hint of gentle sorrow and reproach into his voice. "It seems that in your anger, you killed her."

Vader groaned in protest. And then he screamed. Leaning forward, he broke the straps that had held him to the table, and screamed again. Things imploded and flew around the room — spare parts, droids, anything that wasn't tied down — as Darth Vader gave expression to his pain and despair.

And while Darth Vader screamed, Darth Sidious smiled. His apprentice was his, now. Forever.

The conference room on Bail Organa's starcruiser looked exactly like every other conference room Obi-Wan had ever sat in. He didn't want to be there. He didn't feel up to making decisions about the future, and he certainly didn't want to think about the past. But he and Yoda and Bail were the only ones left to decide. So there he sat, trying to make his tired brain think about what to do with the body of his best friend's wife, and with the two infants who were, perhaps, the last hope of the galaxy.

"To Naboo, send her body," Yoda said. "Pregnant, she must still appear. Hidden, safe, the children must be kept."

"Someplace where the Sith will not sense their presence," Obi-Wan said.

"Split up, they should be."

Bail Organa raised his head. "My wife and I will take the girl. We've always talked of adopting a baby girl. She will be loved with us."

Hidden in plain sight, Obi-Wan thought, and nodded. "What about the boy?"

"To Tatooine. To his family, send him."

Remembering that harsh, dry planet, Obi-Wan winced. But there was nowhere else, and Tatooine was a world on the margins — the Hutt crime lords who ruled it had never been part of the Galactic Republic, and they would keep their distance from the Empire as well. "I will take the child there, and watch over him," Obi-Wan said. He looked at Yoda, wanting reassurance he knew Yoda could not give him. "Master Yoda, do you think Anakin's twins will be able to defeat Darth Sidious?"

"Strong the Force runs, in the Skywalker line,"

Yoda replied. "Only hope, we can." He looked at Bail. "Done then, it is. Until the time is right, disappear we will."

Bail nodded and left to give orders to his pilot. Obi-Wan rose to leave as well.

"Wait a moment, Master Kenobi," Yoda said.

Obi-Wan turned, thinking *What now?*

"In your solitude on Tatooine, training I have for you."

"Training?" He had never heard of any Jedi training for Masters.

Yoda smiled. "An old friend has learned the path to immortality — your old Master, Qui-Gon Jinn."

"Qui-Gon?" Obi-Wan stared. "But . . . how?"

"The secrets of the Ancient Order of the Whills, he studied," Master Yoda said. "How to commune with him, I will teach you."

"I will be able to talk with him?"

Yoda nodded, and some of the old, old grief that had lived with Obi-Wan since his Master's death lifted. "How to join the Force, he will train you. Your consciousness you will retain, when one with the Force. Even your physical self, perhaps."

How ironic that we should discover this power now, when the Jedi are no more, Obi-Wan thought. Then he looked at Yoda. The Jedi were not gone. Not yet. He heard the thin, high wail of an infant echoing down the hall, and almost smiled. There was still hope for the future.

EPILOGUE

Senator Padmé Amidala was given a state funeral. Huge crowds lined the streets to pay their respects to their former Queen as the flower-draped open coffin rolled past. She was wearing the carved japor snippet her beloved Anakin had given her so long ago, when he was nine and she fourteen and war was unthinkable, and the Sith Lords a bad dream.

Obi-Wan and Yoda watched the funeral from Bail Organa's starcruiser. It was as close as they dared come. The Emperor's attention would surely be fixed on the funeral, and they would not take the risk of being found.

Shortly after, the Emperor took his new apprentice off to a remote area of the galaxy where construction of a new superweapon was just beginning — a gigantic space station with the power to destroy whole planets with a single laser blast.

Once the funeral was over, Bail Organa set his

cruiser on a carefully planned course to Alderaan. Shortly after the ship left Naboo, it flung two small escape pods in opposite directions along the Outer Rim. One carried Jedi Master Yoda toward the uninviting and uninhabited swamp planet of Dagobah; the other carried Jedi Master Obi-Wan Kenobi and a wailing infant boy in the direction of Tatooine. The girl, as planned, went on to Alderaan, to be raised as a princess by Bail Organa and his wife, the queen of Alderaan. She was joined by the droids R2-D2 and C-3PO.

When he reached Tatooine, Obi-Wan sold the escape pod for spare parts. In the crime-ridden city of Mos Eisley, the pod would be untraceable within hours. With the credits from the sale, Obi-Wan bought an eopie riding beast for the trek out to the small moisture farm where Anakin's stepbrother, Owen Lars, still lived. Owen and his wife Beru agreed to raise their nephew. Obi-Wan told them only that the boy's parents were both dead; he did not give any details of how Anakin and Padmé had died.

As the twin suns began to set, Obi-Wan rode into the Tatooine desert. In his pack, he carried Anakin's lightsaber. He would keep it, through the long, lonely exile, as a memento and a reminder — until the future day when he could give it to Anakin's son, Luke Skywalker.